When the prince of her dreams comes riding into Celia Healey's life, it is like the happy ending of a 19th-century Irish romance. But Celia's happy ending is really only the beginning....

ALL THEIR KINGDOMS

Madeleine A. Polland

Celia is a country girl, daughter of a well-born but impoverished Galway family. In Ireland's post-famine years, her education as a lady is no more than her ambitious father's investment in her future; Celia has been raised to marry well—but not for love.

Then Matt O'Connor comes riding out from Dublin: the knight on a white horse, the golden boy rich enough to satisfy Tom Healey's greed and the one man for Celia's heart from the moment they meet. But the love story of Celia Healey and Matt O'Connor, unashamedly and irresistibly romantic, is only the beginning of a richly textured novel about three generations of an Irish family—a brilliantly plotted story of love, loss, betrayal and ironic triumph.

Celia's wedding sweeps her into all Matt's kingdoms: the grand house on Dublin's

(continued on back flap)

Books by Madeleine A. Polland

THICKER THAN WATER
THE LITTLE SPOT OF BOTHER
SHATTERED SUMMER
PACKAGE TO SPAIN
CHILDREN OF THE RED KING
DEIDRE
TO TELL MY PEOPLE
SABRINA

ALL THEIR KINGDOMS

Madeleine A. Polland

DELACORTE PRESS/NEW YORK

For my family

AUTHOR'S NOTE

For this book, like others I have written, I got the idea from the past of my own family. Both story and characters, however, have taken on such a life of their own that it has become a work of pure fiction, characters and events bearing no resemblance to actual facts.

Published by
Delacorte Press
1 Dag Hammarskjold Plaza
New York, N.Y. 10017

Manufactured in the United States of America

Second Printing—1981

Designed by Giorgetta Bell McRee

LIBRARY OF CONGRESS CATALOGING IN PUBLICATION DATA

Polland, Madeleine A
All their kingdoms.

I. Title.
PZ4.P7735Al 1980 [PR6066.O38] 823' .914 80–19132

ISBN 0–440–00019–X

Chapter 1

THE house was cold. In spite of pools of golden sun across the threadbare carpet, it held the dank chill of one set in trees, and never properly warmed. Celia shivered as much with irritation as with cold, and moved into the sun, feeling it at least upon her feet. Aimless and frustrated, she looked round the big square salon, where delicate furniture of a bygone age stood cloudy with the bloom of damp. The Lord himself might know, but no one else, when anything new had been purchased in this house, and age had thrust the stuffing through the fabric of the sofas, and peeled the velvet from the chair arms. It was all the more pathetic for the hopeless efforts to hide the worst of it with shawls and cushions, and to keep the bigger furniture against patches where the pale pink fluted flowers, trailing the dark-green walls, were brown with mold.

Restlessly the girl moved over to the long sash window, into the full sun. She was heart weary of being cold. It had always been cold in the convent too, clammy in the summer and icy in the winter, storing the chill breath of the sea; covering her thin hands with chilblains. She had longed to come home, forgetting that it would be no better. And now there was this—this nonsense from her mother that she must not sit in the kitchen, the only warm place in the house, since it was unbecoming to a lady. A lady! Saints in heaven but what chance had she of being a lady in this barren place; except in all the theory the nuns had pumped into her in the long years over in Kinvarra.

Dark brows drew down over deep-blue eyes, and her round face took on the look of severity her mother was always telling her to avoid. It was discouraging to gentlemen and put wrinkles on the face. The only wrinkles Celia felt herself likely to get were those from screwing up her eyes, searching for the gentlemen of whom her mother spoke so much.

Smiling a little, she looked up the gentle slope of vivid grass to the windblown thorns toppling on the bluff above the river. On the right a deep belt of elms and hollies hid the stables and the farm, and down to the left, like a tiny painting in the corner of some massive canvas, was a small view of the river itself, and the green deserted fields beyond. Monstrous strange, but not a gentleman in sight! She could do as she liked with her face, for the moment anyway.

Humor was never far below the surface, and her eyes were still soft as she turned from the window. A tall girl, and now at eighteen certified as the lady so carefully manufactured by her mother and the nuns. But still showing an unelegant tendency to grow out of her dresses every time they took their eyes off her. In the long unusual hall, running the full length of the front of the house, the door through to the kitchen was open, and she could hear her mother clattering about in the dairy at the back. Her mouth tightened, and exasperation touched her face as she went swiftly through the large dim kitchen, past the turf roaring in the range, tempting her to stop in the warm glow. With one longing glance, she went on.

Her mother was churning butter in the dairy, leaning with all her weight on the heavy handle, as she felt the butter "come" and the churn grow heavy. She was as tall as Celia, still with the same loose-limbed look, and the face she turned to her daughter had once been gentle, large eyed. Now it was lined past her age by sorrow and disaster, and the long hopeless grind of poverty. In the cold colorless place she looked a hundred.

"Mother!" The girl was torn with fury and pity, feeling her young strength. "Mother, let me do that! You'll hurt yourself!"

For a moment the mother's face softened, and she even smiled.

"No, child," she said. "I am long past that." Her expression closed again and she went on churning, fearful, at the vital moment, of losing the butter. Celia watched her and noticed with fresh irritation that the brass bands binding the churn shone and glittered in the gloom. For pity sake, surely even a lady could be allowed to polish a strip of brass. She did not venture to say so to her mother's exasperated face.

"Go do as you are bid, child," she said, snatching a hand to thrust back a strand of gray thin hair under her cap. "Do as you are bid, and don't trouble me further than I am already troubled."

The girl stood mutinous, angered by the situation, touched to the heart by her mother's weary face, and savaged by a feeling of guilt she had done nothing to deserve. She wanted to tear the handle of the churn from her mother's hands, shouting at her that it was not her wish to be so idle. Shout away her anger and frustration.

"Not my fault," she wanted to shout at her. "Not my fault you wanted to make me a lady. I didn't ask for it."

Once she had said this, unable to hold back. She would forever remember her mother laying down the piece of patching in her lap, and looking at her, appalled, across the thin lamplight.

"*Make* you a lady?" she had said, and her voice was heavy with shock. "That was in God's hands," she said then. "You were that by birth. All we have struggled to do is see you know how to live as you were born."

Celia had got up quickly and gone from the shadows beyond the lamp. A lady. In this bleak shell of stone and mortar set in its barren land. Why could they not have kept their money, and sold the burden to whoever would have it. Live in some comfort somewhere in a small house. To say this would have been unforgivable, she knew, and in time she came back and settled again beside her mother in silence, relieved that patching, at least, was something a lady might be allowed to do.

It had all seemed all right while it was happening. Even as a small girl she had understood that in spite of the big house and the acres of the green land, and the river and the farm and all the beauty she took for granted, they were very, very poor. Very poor. All to do with something called the Famine. It was now 1873, so it had happened about twenty-five years ago. Before she was even born. Years of bad crops, and then the dreadful years when the potatoes had rotted and blackened in the fields and clamps, and the poor people in the country had died by the thousands of starvation. The big houses that had tried to help their people were not yet recovered, even after all these years; their barns emptied, their livestock and, in the end, their very horses killed, in a desperate attempt to feed the starving on the blackened barren acres. These were the houses and the families, like hers, to be scarred for generations. And it grew worse. When Celia was small, there had been an old couple in the house and some help on the farm. Now there was no one to help but a simpleminded child, working in a slapdash fashion for her meals.

Against this lay her mother's grim determination that neither Celia nor her brother should suffer in the end. They should, by sheer determination, be wrenched back to the life that she remembered now like some distant and impossible dream. Before the day when the people had run screaming from the withering fields, clawing and tearing at the potato clamps that were their winter food; only to find inside them the same black slimy devastation.

A career for Hugh Charles. And for Celia, the training for a good marriage. For them, life would begin again.

The father had listened to her urgent plans, eyeing her in silence, and to her astonishment had agreed with her, keeping his own reasons to himself. In the big decaying house they had lived on as less than peasants; less than the people from the fields whom they had struggled to save, so that for Celia and Hugh Charles, there would be a road back. Firmly the mother thrust from her mind the unpalatable fact that for Hugh Charles, the road back did not yet seem paved with gold. He had been to St. Jarlath's College, over the fields in Tuam, but as a boarder, in order to meet the right kind of friends, who would now be of use to him in his legal practice in the same small market town. She would not acknowledge the creeping certainty that they had as little money as Hugh Charles himself. And that his progress to riches was severely hampered by the grim fact that none of his clients seemed to have the wherewithal to pay his fees. On the subject of Hugh Charles silence lay heavy between the parents, and both of them let their eyes now rest on Celia.

Limp and helpless, the girl stood watching her mother. Turned from the sun so that it would be cold even in the height of summer, the stone-walled dairy was full of icy shadows, yet sweat stood clear on the older woman's face. She let go the handle and took the bung from the churn. Inside the butter lay thick and pale, salt smelling, ready for the market in Tuam tomorrow.

She stood up, and looked with weary patience at her daughter, her hands on her aching back.

"Child," she said then, "tell me how it would help anything to have you doing this?"

"It would save you," Celia answered rebelliously, knotting irritably at the fringes of her shawl.

She was taken aback by the expression of total resignation on her mother's face; a smile as if at some gentle hopeless joke.

"Save me for what, Daughter dear?" she said. "I am done."

"Mother!"

"Done long since," she repeated flatly. "But you marry

well, and get away." She paused as if for a moment shamed by what she had implied of her own life. "Who knows then what you may do to help us."

"I am an investment," said Celia bitterly.

"In your own happiness, and so in ours."

Celia didn't answer her, trying without conviction to relate the word *happiness* to her dour and uncommunicative father. Once her mother may have known of it. It still lay lurking, easily summoned for some fleeting moment, in the back of her faded eyes.

The mother's mind was also on her husband, Thomas. All they had put into Celia's education and training was to her some bright, secret hope for a new life for the child. A safe content she had once thought to be her own. Now little more than memory. But her husband, Thomas, she knew, regarded Celia exactly as the girl herself had said. An investment. Money had been spent so that his daughter could attract money. And he would want his share of it for the derelict farmland.

Celia put her next thought into words, and couldn't hide the bitterness, her fine eyes cold as she looked down at her mother.

"And where, Mother, am I to find myself a rich husband? Is he to come search for me on a beautiful white horse, like a prince in the fairy tales you tell to children? We must tell them in the village where he can find me. He might not recognize me as his princess. We have no carriage. I can go nowhere. Or are we perchance to have a ball at Holly House?"

She stopped, shamed by the dead misery of her mother's face, blanched by one thin shaft of sunlight from the high window; gray as her hair and lined with troubles beyond enduring; forced by a harsh, unloving husband to endure without murmur. Celia knew herself bitterly unkind. She longed to move over quickly and kiss her poor sad mother; to embrace her thin shoulders with love and comfort and smooth the sorrow from her face. But years of almost total separation had left them too much strangers. Although her throat closed with tears of pity, the gesture was beyond her.

"But I am sorry, Mother," she managed to say. "Truly sorry. I do forget myself and lose my gratitude for all you've done for me."

After a brief smile in which forgiveness lay almost shy, her mother moved back to the churn and the cold shadows as if her life belonged there.

"Go now, child," she said. "I have to put this in the pats for the morning. Take a turn along the water in the good air. You look a little pale."

Bitterness surged again. My looks, thought Celia, are as important in this marriage market as my bit of Latin and my watercolors and three ways of making pigeon pie. The mother was reaching down the big-ridged butter pats and for a moment the girl paused in spite of herself to watch her, touched with memory. She scalded them in the bowl of boiling water waiting on the slate bench, scrubbing them with salt so the butter wouldn't stick. Celia sighed. Once, long ago, she had been allowed to help, but it was a woman from the village who made the butter then, whirling it between the pats into splendid unexpected shapes that fell so easily from the wood. When she herself tried, the butter slid to the stone floor and guiltily she would scrape it up and try again, her ill-shaped pat a murky gray. She smiled. She had loved the dairy then, cool and dark, with the salt sharp smell of the buttermilk in pans along the benches. Huge slabs of butter and stacks of neat pats, each one stamped by a wooden stamp with an uplifted hand. The same thing was on the cover of the family records, and on an ancient flag her father still had somewhere. Part of some long-forgotten family crest. In those days her mother had still been hopeful, and they laughed together when her father couldn't hear. She sighed now, wondering if, as the long lean years closed in after the Famine, all the money from that butter had gone to pay for her schooling in Kinvarra. And Hugh Charles's down in Tuam.

She turned away. All she could do for her mother now was try and please her. Keep her hands white and her cheeks pink, and her manners on the tip of her tongue and remember all the nuns had taught her. Until the day came, and her face creased in wry amusement, that some fine young man up to his ears in gold came riding by and scooped her up behind him onto his horse. She was too bored and desperate to find it really funny. The only things that would come to Holly House were the birds and the rabbits burrowing in the soft brown earth around the cliff. Not even Hugh Charles would bring his friends here, and came himself as rarely as decency allowed.

The mother slapped the butter with a vigor that did a little to unloose the knot of pity that twined with anger in her heart. The girl had grown well. Not a regular beauty, and a little tall for the taste of most men, but intelligent and lively, with these fine eyes that smiled so easily. As if, she reflected, that would be of value in this house, or in the one that would be Celia's if Thomas had his way. Poor innocent, thinking she could bide her time and please herself. A bitter image crept into her mind of her husband scrubbing the pigs that he was going to send to market. The same return was wanted from his daughter. The butter got a fresh lash of despairing sorrow. Who would have to tell the girl, and wipe the smile from her face forever?

Old Joseph Hession. Three wives in the grave already. True he was rich, and the girl might be comforted by journeys to Dublin and to England, for the man spent as little time as he could in the gaunt house across the lake from Bunanaire. Even that was reputed to be full of all the kinds of things that Holly House had long ago sold, for food. One of the hard ones, Mr. Hession, who had come from nowhere when the Famine was at its end, buying the big houses from their starving owners, and setting themselves up as the new Quality. God help them. Absentee landlords now, the most of them, and their agents rack-renting and evicting; the poor deprived people starving in the ditches through the green country. Thanks be to God, it was not so bad round here, but further over in the Joycelands and in the cold rocks of Connemara, they said there were more dead than living. And people like Joseph Hession wanting all the land for trees and sheep and anything else would make them money, hated by everyone who knew them, and the Brotherhoods after them now, and the new Home Rule League, and ricks being burned and cattle maimed and crops fired. What a life for Celia. The girl would have been better off to stay as she was, and take her chance with some young farmer. She shook herself from her muddled and useless thoughts, and reached down for the stamp from the shelf. The uplifted hand put her in mind of the one house where it seemed life flowed smooth and untroubled, under the same crest, they being second cousins of her father's. Only over the hill, but it might as well have been the far Americas for all they saw of it, since some foolish quarrel between her husband and the man O'Connor. Dead now, poor man, and the whole lot gone to his rich nephew with a Dublin business, and a taste for traveling foreign so they said. Everyone spoke well of him, but that was all she knew; though she vaguely remembered him staying with the uncle as a child. Only houses like that, she thought hopelessly, with businesses behind them, could manage to live when the land was dead.

While her mother brooded away, Celia, unnoticed, slipped out. Bored and mutinous, she rambled on the riverbank, grateful for the warm breeze after the numbing chill inside the house. It was sweet, too, with the spring scents off the land, and the sedgy grass along the river was adrift with yellow kingcups. Beyond the river lay her father's pastures, untended, and springing with the growth of thistles, his stringy cattle moving through them feeling for the grass. Away over the green gentle country, clear in the pale distance, Croagh Patrick reared its perfect cone against the sky.

Celia sighed. She loved her home, and always had. She'd have been glad to be the dairymaid and live in it untroubled. Behind her, road and river ran on side by side toward the house, dividing just before it where the small bluff rose above the water. The road ran on along the front of the house, set in the shelter of the bluff. Only two stories, a big farm, no more, but gaining strange grace from its length, and the row of windows tall along its front; all belonging to the curious hall. Beyond the house the road narrowed to a track, turning round to the stables and the farm buildings, banked and darkened by the immense and ancient stand of hollies from which the house had got its name.

None of the political miseries and tensions in the green land touched Celia, although she couldn't but know of them; the only restriction being that she must never go alone beyond the rusting iron fences of her father's land. There were houses like theirs scattered all over the west of Galway, and the stony fields of Clare, but poor though they were, reduced since the Famine almost below the level of survival, the families still stayed; most of them related one way or another to her parents. Not for them the rack-rent freedom of months in Dublin or England. Her blue eyes gleamed, part compassion, part anger. A day at Galway Fair would be a monstrous pleasure.

She felt deep pity for her mother, and after a few weeks at home was beginning to feel pity for herself, and to find herself a poor kind of fool, asked to dangle her talents before the men of this struggling land. Even in the big houses and the old families, they didn't want the harp or a girl who could paint on silk. They wanted food. And money. And a strong worker for the land.

Celia's father was growing restive, watching her in hostility with his small washed-out eyes. He was a heavy man, tall, pale faced with sandy crinkled hair like wire. Colorless. Even his deep-set eyes were a pale, pale blue, darting round him always as though he expected, probably with justification, that everything in his world was there to do him harm. Cold-bloodedly he had gone into the business of starving himself to educate his children. Not with any dreams of restoring the old decencies, like his poor fool of a wife, but estimating his daughter particularly as an investment and an ultimate asset, with as little interest or affection as he would calculate the value of the cattle in his almost roofless barn.

He thought it was time for the returns.

"Mrs. Healey, ma'am," he said coldly after a month of

watching Celia apparently forgetting all she knew. He stared down at the plate of mashed swedes and gravy that made his dinner, flanked by a tankard of buttermilk. B'God after all he'd spent, couldn't the girl be used to get money to lay in a bit of meat! "Mrs. Healey, ma'am, it's time that girl was handfasted. I'll speak to the matchmaker."

Beside him his wife, Rose, stood humbly, anticipating his every want, although, God knew, there was little enough to give. And there would be less for herself and Celia afterwards, when he had stamped off again in his habitual surly silence to the fields. Now she looked at him as directly as she dared, but could find no answer. Nor would he have listened had she found one.

Joseph Hession. She had heard after the Mass down in Tuam last Sunday that there were terrible doings on his land. What a place to put the girl, where even her own would be turned against her, and she'd be hated like the man himself. Faint stupid hope crept into her mind that when he came back from Dublin, and saw Celia, he wouldn't take to her. She'd be well taller than himself, the scrawny little bantling. Wryly she shook her head as she lifted the lid of the wooden bin for the meal to feed the chickens. What man, and he neither blind nor mad, would not want Celia.

Celia herself, with a protective instinct to be out of the house whenever her father might be in it, had taken her box of watercolors on the bright clear day, and her small stool, and drifted off to the wilder stretches of the river, where he was never likely to be found at any time. Boredom had been replaced by chill shrinking fear since he had let drop some broad determined hints about her future, his lightless eyes hard with satisfaction. Her mother would tell her nothing, but when the girl searched for it, there was no comfort in her face. The most Celia felt she could hope for was one of Hugh Charles's scapegrace friends, but even that she knew was wrong. They wouldn't have the money to please her father, who, she realized now, wanted return on every guinea spent. To get it he would, if necessary, wed her to a dancing bear.

Bending above the lively little stream, she filled her water jar from the peat-brown water, and, still agitated and resentful, spread her stool and settled herself with her drawing block on her lap. Not many sheets left in that, and would she ever get another, if she wasn't bringing what she should, she thought bitterly. Involuntarily she calmed and let it all slip from her mind, as she looked at the scene she had chosen for her picture. The river turned here in a small arc, widening and growing smooth between the fields, its placid surface reflecting the soft May sun. Along its edges purple flags reared among the spiky sedge, and the thornbushes were adrift with sweet white blossom. She sniffed at it and smiled a little ruefully. It was well she was easily pleased, or the whole thing would be driving her to madness.

Her talent with the watercolors was not as great as her mother thought it, nor as small as she did herself. A lack of patience with details was overcome on the paper, as in other things, with a gift for catching an impression. Rapt in what she was doing, she forgot everything else, lost in real pleasure that even with modest ability, she was able to put the gentle scene on paper. Dabbling her brush to clear it in the water jar, she stared in frowning concentration at the grass and sedge below the gnarled trunk of a leaning thorn. Not vivid green, for the tree deprived it of the light. Not exactly brown. Not withered; and yet not fresh. Thoughtfully she withdrew her brush, and against all the solemn warnings of her teacher and her mother, sucked it to a fine point between her lips and dipped it in the yellow paint.

"M-m-mm." The voice spoke behind her just as she laid the brush to the paper. On a falling cadence, full of disappointment, but warm and deep. "Indeed, Miss Celia," it said, "it's impertinent of me to interfere, but were that painting mine, I would have chosen umber there."

Chapter 2

HER startled hand slid sideways, and a streak of yellow blurred across the pale sunlit blue she had worked so hard on for the river. As she whirled abruptly round, the water jar went flying from its small bracket on the side of the easel.

"Well, damn me for a meddling eejit," said the voice. Its owner looked down remorsefully at the ruined watercolor and the scattered blotches of paint water darkening the front of Celia's dress. "I'd have done less damage to have done it all like anyone else, and pulled your doorbell for an introduction."

"It doesn't work," Celia said, stupidly and automatically. "The wire is broken this ten years past." She stared at him as if he had dropped from the high white clouds themselves, her brush dripping yellow in her hand, and her eyes wide.

"Then that comforts me. I might have missed you, did no one hear me."

"But what would you be doing looking for me?"

"What better could I find to do, on a fine good day like this?"

She realized the deep-set green-brown eyes were laughing at her; enjoying her confusion; her natural friendliness and humor at war with the foolish impropriety of exchanging senseless conversation with a young man she had never met, and who would appear to be trespassing on her father's land. His amusement was challenging her to set aside the doubt and shock that had her answering so stupidly; glancing anxiously up along the river to the house. A smile creased a strong-boned face of rich warm coloring, with a long determined chin below a generous mouth. Shameless, her mother would say, to be inspecting him, but she had realized he stood at least half a head taller than herself; and she was no small-boned miss to level with the top of a pint pot. As her astonished survey reached his head, she found it crowned with thick straight dark-brown hair, the sun getting red lights from it. Like rust.

By the saints, it seemed to be the one they were all waiting for. Tall. Handsome, charming without a doubt, and before God, my dearest mother, she said to herself, you would never believe it, but he has in his hand the reins of a snow-white horse. Where are you with a length of rope before he gets away? Helpless laughter welled in her, making her forget what was proper and what was not.

"I thought you would never come," she said, and it was his turn to look confused, and somehow pleased to be matched at his own game, even if he didn't understand.

"Is the—the horse yours?" she said then, desperately, to stop herself laughing. Just for anything to say. And gestured grandly with the paintbrush hand, flinging spatters of bright yellow ochre down the immaculate fawn facecloth of his riding coat. Even a little for good measure on the white gleaming flanks of the horse.

"Oh—ah!" That'll put paid to the laughing, she thought. "I do beg your pardon." She bit her lip to hold herself against a wild sense of the ridiculous, unable to apologize more. In all the romances they had passed secretly from hand to hand back in the convent, she never knew one where the fellow finally came riding on his fine white horse, and the girl threw paint at the both of them. Anyway he was at fault himself. He should have been dressed in shining armor, and the paint would wipe easily off that.

But it seemed she really had offended him. The laughing indeed was at an end. Unreasonable dismay filled her, for she had only spoken to him for the minute, when he turned away from her in silence, leading the white horse off across the field. It was on the tip of her tongue to shout to him to come back, it wasn't as bad as it seemed, and the nuns had taught her, like the two kinds of pigeon pie and all the strings of the harp, how to take paint stains from the clothes of gentlemen. But she knew from the romances that when a man like that came on his white horse, it would be a princess he was looking for, and all the gentle manners that went with her. Not Celia Healey yelling like a hoyden after him the length of a field. In sad silence she watched him go, and the great brown shaggy wolfhound came loping to him from the trees across the road. Her mother would turn her from the door, did she ever come to hear she had let one of these rare creatures slip through her fingers within minutes of meeting him. Nor would it be the first time in her life she had come to grief for laughing in the wrong place.

But he was only going to one of the windbent thorns along the road to tie the white horse to its branches and she watched him walking all the way back, still unsmiling, the big dog at his heels. The dog was long in the leg and with a sort of controlled impetuosity, as though at any moment he might give up the effort and leap into the air, or run in circles like her father's terrier. Her scrutiny did nothing to perturb the man, planting his shining brown boots firmly in the ragged grass and springing clover.

"B'God," she said when he reached her, still too astonished to remember her pretty manners and all the things she shouldn't say. "The way you came across the field there, I thought you'd like to throw me in the river."

"Nothing, Miss Celia, would be further from my thoughts."

Both of them smiled now, touched by some sudden mutual pleasure.

Celia dropped her eyes, and for all her height, and her old skirt and her outburst of hilarity, looked touchingly like the kind of girl her mother prayed she was.

"You have the advantage of me, sir," she said then. "In that someone has told you my name. Who would do that, now?"

Not her mother, for certain. Had she caught sight of him she'd have him freezing up in the salon eating stale cake and making all the proper conversation while she tried to hide her apron underneath a cushion. Nor her father, who would do no more than order any stranger from his land. Especially for letting his horse crop at his thistle-strangled grass.

"Half the countryside, Miss Celia," he said. "And they told me something else. They said you were the most beautiful girl in Galway. And I'd not argue with that," he added with a small bow, and a strange formality that left her unembarrassed. He smiled gently to look at her, standing there with the dirty water drying on her dress, staring at him with bright curiosity, her fair hair ruffled by the scented wind.

"Matthew O'Connor," he said then, "Miss Celia." He gave another correct small bow, "and I'll ask you to believe me I was on my way up to present myself to your parents."

Her hands flew to her mouth.

"Oh, don't do that. That wouldn't do at all."

She blushed, the warm tide rising up her fair face. But it wouldn't be fair to her poor mother to allow her to be caught with the churn or the hens or sweating at the flour stone. Then her mind came to rest on what he had actually said, and her brows lifted.

"Matthew O'Connor. From Owenscourt? Across the hill?"

"The very one. Your second cousin, I believe, or tenth, or thirty-third. I would never know. Near enough, anyway, to present myself as one of the family. What's the matter? Is there something wrong? Has your father told you Matt O'Connor is someone no nice girl should know?"

She laughed then and pushed back the fair hair.

"No, Mr. O'Connor. No one has told me that."

But they had told her, her mother and Hugh Charles, that

he was a sort of legend in the country, although he didn't live there. The heir to all the Owenscourt acres. The rich one they all envied. And with all the gifts. The golden boy. The knight on the white horse. Memory edged back.

"I recall your uncle," she said then, "that had the house. I believe my father quarreled with him. Some old story." And not only with him, she thought bitterly. How many other decent people had her father sent packing. "Indeed." She blinked at him, and he regarded her gravely, a small smile on his wide mouth. "Indeed, now I think of it, I recall you too. A long time ago."

He grinned then.

"And I you. Long little bag of bones. You went off somewhere."

"To school. But you were always away."

"I live in Dublin. Came to my uncle for the holidays."

Long recollection. Some voice saying, "The O'Connor lad is down again." And an extra face in the crowd of boys that sat along the river bridge at evening when they would be walking home from saying the Rosary in the old gray church; or a distant figure pelting bareback on a pony through the fields. His parents sometimes, remote in their fine carriage. Rich. She remembered the word. Rich. For all he ran like any other, with the village lads.

"You are here now on holiday?" she asked politely, trying to piece it all together.

"No, Miss Celia, I am not. My uncle died over a year back. Owenscourt is mine. He had no living son, you see."

"Yours?"

He seemed too young for it. That huge flat-fronted house. The big park leading down the long slope to the lake. Acres and acres of well-tended farmland. Money. Holy Jesus, did her mother get wind of this one she'd have him caught and bound before he knew what was happening. He was so much all her mother longed for, that hostility rose in her, and he was puzzled by the sudden hardening of her face; the light dying in the blue eyes; the sudden defensive tilt of the chin.

"Well, Mr. O'Connor, I've no doubt in such a large place you have much to do. I'll not be keeping you. And I'll have to try and settle my picture."

It was on the tip of his tongue to tell her he had nothing to do at all. That he still had the same excellent agent as his uncle had, although he preferred to refer to him as his manager since "agent" was so malodorous a word round here. The only important thing he must do was come down every couple of months to ride his lands and listen to his tenants, and settle all their problems and discuss all plans for the land with the agent. Proving to them all that he was no absentee, rack-renting landlord. His real life lay in Dublin. In the long bright workshops along Baggot Street, full of the smells of fresh wood and sawdust and paint and glue and varnish and bright gold-leaf. The huge wheel mounted in the middle of the floor, that his father had allowed him turn as soon as he was high enough to reach it. He had helped the wheelwright when his father made the fine state coach for Queen Victoria of England.

Nevertheless he loved Owenscourt; had always been happy here, and still knew a deep excited pleasure that it was all his own.

He brought his mind back to Celia, quelling an impulse to tell her all about it. Somehow he had antagonized her, and it had happened with the mention of the house. Surely to God, she hadn't been trained to carry old scores that never even mattered at the time. He realized her father would probably turn him from the house. But why should she care for ancient quarrels?

"I have the manners of a heathen, Miss Celia," he said quickly. "All your work destroyed, and never a glance for it. Here! I'll get you another pot of water. We as near as know each other now. Cousins are cousins after all, and I knew your brother Hugh Charles very well."

And a foxy bundle of double-dealing he always was, he might have added. How did the parents of such a mean and colorless youth come to beget the sister?

Celia watched the neat control of his movements; stepping

beyond the wet ooze and the kingcups, to balance expertly on a stone as he bent to the water with her jar, rinsing it with meticulousness. He came back straight up the bank and set it again beside the easel, taking the yellow paintbrush from her hand. He didn't even look at her, all his attention now concentrating on the ruined painting.

"I'll throw it away," she said. "Do another." Without thinking she drew close to him, and together they stood in the soft sun staring at the hopeless smear of yellow across the smooth river. Celia felt a sudden unreasonable desire to snatch it. Take it away and hide it somewhere. Keep it forever.

Matt had other ideas.

"Have you ever heard," he said, and the pollen from the trampled kingcups lay in golden dust all up his boots. He looked thoughtfully at the watercolor. Not bad at all. A real nuns' pretty piece. The very smell of the convent was on it in its niceness. She'd do better someday. "Have you ever heard, there's a river away over in China called the Yangtze?"

Celia stared at him, puzzled by the question. What was that to her?

"They call it the Yellow River," Matt went on, his eyes intent on the block, the paintbrush dabbling again in the yellow ochre. "What you can't cure you have to live with. So we'll have to have a Chinese picture."

Now she couldn't follow him. A few quick sweeps of the brush. He looked and grinned and went back to it, and a few more sweeps and dabs and her poor destroyed river had become a deep and sullen brown.

"That's not yellow!"

"Ah, no. They only call it that. Sure everything in China's yellow, no matter what color it is. Did you not know that?"

"Have you been there?"

"Yes," he said, and she didn't know if it were true.

Quickly and skillfully his brush was moving along the riverbank, removing the soft long grass she had taken such pains with, replacing it with dank yellow mud. A few dabs of brown and black and there were stones, big boulders half sunk in the water's edge. Mesmerized, she drew closer until she stood against his shoulder, her eyes on the dancing brush. Her mind was aware of her picture changing as she watched, but her senses were alive too to his closeness and his height; the feeling of compact strength so much at variance with the long fine hand that moved so quickly and correctly. Her eyes strayed, taking in the thickness of the rusty hair, the neat flat-set ear with a vigorous sidewhisker growing to just below it. The strong chin was clean shaven.

He turned suddenly and caught her staring and she couldn't hide her anguished blush. Nor would he pretend he hadn't seen it, looking at her from the deep-set eyes with a sort of hilarious satisfaction.

"How about a few houses?" he said then, and Celia would have agreed to anything that would take his attention from her; struggling to regain her poise and dignity. All the lessons in deportment she thought she had long mastered, brought to nothing by this arrogant— Honesty stopped her. There was nothing arrogant about Matt O'Connor. He just had this quality of being more absolutely himself than anyone she had ever met, although God knew they were few enough. But it seemed as if Matt O'Connor found it wonderful to be himself. Without doubts or questions as to what anyone might think of him.

"Put in an elephant," she cried suddenly and began to laugh. "If you want to. Or why not Dublin Castle?"

She got a quick sidelong grin as her reward, bright eyed, delighted to welcome her into his fantasy.

"They have no elephants in China," he said repressively. "But you're completely right to put in Dublin Castle. You never know when they might take it out there."

A dabble in the water, and a few quick flicks of gray and black, and Dublin Castle stood strong and square and imposing on the banks of the Yellow River.

"The flag. Put the flag on top."

They were both laughing helplessly now, and she was holding to his arm, all propriety forgotten, only the ridiculous picture real. The big dog padded round them with soft frustrated growls, as if to ask who was she, daring to share some moment with his master that had not been shared with him.

"Ah, now," he said as he painted in the tiny Union Jack, "that's too fantastic altogether. We'd better make the rest of it more real or no one will believe it."

So Dublin Castle was surrounded with little Chinese houses with their crescent roofs, blue tiny figures moving in between them. He paused.

"We'll give the cows a bit more beef, and turn them into buffaloes."

The soft blur of the hawthorns was darkened, and with tall twisted trunks, they were ancient pines, towering over the little houses.

She had stopped laughing, fascinated by his quick skill.

"Enough," he said then sadly. "Enough. We wouldn't want to spoil it. I'll leave Croagh Patrick exactly as it is. We might have borrowed it from China yesterday."

"In exchange for Dublin Castle," Celia said, and he gave her another quick appreciative grin. Then he sobered, and they looked at each other, a little confused, as if they had shared some experience far more important than the picture. As if they had indeed been together on the long impossible journey to the land of China.

And had to come back.

"When shall I see you again, Celia," he said then, and she didn't even notice that he had dropped the "Miss." "Can I escort you home?"

Reality came rushing back and sick embarrassment, nor words possible to explain the cold inhospitable house, the grim father and the mother so desperate to catch a rich husband for her daughter; she would stop at nothing, but it must all be so correct.

"They'd kill me," she said, and Matt frowned to see all the laughter leave her face; replaced by nervous fear and some strange exasperation.

"Who would?"

She tried to explain, lamely, but who could tell even him, and even as a joke, about finding her knight on a white horse in her father's fields instead of in her mother's parlor.

"You'd need," she said, and the anxiety in her eyes roused Matt to anger, "you'd need to get to know me properly."

"Properly?"

He wanted to see her laugh again. "What was improper about Dublin Castle?"

For one quick moment she did smile, the blue eyes gleaming.

"You'd need," she said then again, not revealing how impossible she thought it, "to call. You know?"

"Ah, yes," he answered gravely. "I know. And when is your mother At Home?"

Celia did not know if she should laugh or cry. This was the sort of thing they had taught her at Kinvarra. And what did it mean now. Her mother laboring at the churn or on her knees in a sacking apron, stoning the cold slabs of the kitchen floor; or struggling in her pattens through the pigsty mud. At Home. To receive the calling cards of all the county ladies on a silver tray laid out in the hall, or sit making sweet mindless conversation over tea and chocolate.

Then like a door opened in darkness, she remembered Galway Fair.

"Wednesday," she said bravely, and fiercely, wondering at the same time how before heaven she was going to get her mother to put on her one good dress and sit in the salon on Wednesday afternoon. She felt Matt's eyes on her, puzzled, aware of some deep distress.

"Wednesday," he said. "After all I am your cousin. I would have called this morning, but I did not expect to go round by way of China."

She smiled then, and seemed easier, but he did not press to see her home, where there was clearly something wrong, and he was aware he must go easy.

"I must be away now," he said. "I have to take dinner with my cousin in Tuam, and I have it to ride yet. Good-bye, Miss Celia. I shall call on your mother on Wednesday."

His grave and courteous good-bye touched her more than any smile, and even as he walked up the field she was beginning to disbelieve in him. He would leap onto the white horse and vanish, just like the ancient heroes of Tir-na-n'Og. But like any human he unhitched his horse from the thorn, and rode away through the long grass, followed by the big slavish dog. As he reached the road he turned and raised his hand, and even at that distance she was furious to be caught still watching him, almost as impossible a fantasy as Dublin Castle on the banks of the Yellow River, among the buffaloes and Chinese pines.

"And what did you paint today, Celia child?" her mother asked her, indulgent and conciliatory, never mentioning that the girl was late for the meager meal. Guilt tore her at the future she could not hold off much longer. Her husband was adamant that the betrothal should take place before the end of the month, and the marriage quickly after.

"Nothing today, Mother. I couldn't find the mood for painting. But the day was good."

Guilt filled her in turn, who had never lied to her mother, nor indeed to anybody else, and she felt the ridiculous picture must show through, luminous, from the bottom of her block where she had it hidden. The mother noticed nothing, save, with a pang, some extra light of beauty in her daughter. She put it down to the sun and the good fresh air.

Proudly she laid down a few small pieces of meat, swimming on the platter in thin gravy. She had hoped to give the child more, but Thomas had come famished from the fields. Celia knew better than to ask what the mother would eat herself. As she chewed at the stringy beef, she ransacked her brains to know what she was to do on Wednesday. At Home her mother would surely be, but not as she was wanted.

By Wednesday morning she had still managed nothing and her young face was desperate. The clouds hung low above the sodden pastures, and the gray straight Irish rain was sluicing down. No matter what she managed, no one but an eejit would come calling on a day like this. A small smile touched her lips. He was an eejit, of course, and God alone would know what he might do. Her father, as she had remembered, had gone to Galway in the starlight dark before the dawn, set, as he always did, to spend the night after the Fair with his brother in Oranmore. He was well out of the way, and there must be some way she could lead her poor mother by the nose.

"Mother," she said to her firmly, catching her spending a few guilty minutes drying herself at the kitchen range after coming in from feeding the hens. "Mother, I am forgetting all I ever learnt at Kinvarra. I wouldn't like not to be able to handle my home when I get one."

She didn't understand the look of panic with which her mother answered. The despairing glance and the quick sign of the Cross.

"Against what, in the name of God," Celia thought, but went on pressing her.

" 'Tis no day to go out, Mother dear, and Father is well away. Come let me show you, for the afternoon, how they taught me in Kinvarra we should live. It would be good for me to practice."

The almost childish and excited ease with which her mother acquiesced shamed her. Poor soul, she should do more to please her; for herself. It was a long time before her mother stopped cocking an anxious listening ear for the sound of cartwheels, lest something had driven her husband to change his mind and come back home.

"I tell you, Celia," she protested, half laughing. "You have me mad to do this. And who do you think would come, other than the poor squatters in the ditches, did they get to know. At Home indeed. Amn't I always so?"

But Celia persisted. The frail exquisite cups and plates were unearthed from a dark cupboard where they had lain untouched for most of her life. Some of the lovely things she had never seen before. Anger rose in her to see her mother's anxious face as she took them out.

"Don't tell your father," she begged. "They were my own. He thinks there is no more to sell."

"As if I would."

No need to tell her that only one cup would be used, and that unlikely in this fearful day, and in the end they sat shivering together, before a shovelful of glowing turf from the kitchen range, over which they had piled new sods, and the sluicing rain fell down the chimney on them, filling the room with gray acrid smoke. In the kitchen, tea was laid for six, and Celia looked at the charade with sinking heart, almost praying that he wouldn't come. Better to be left with Dublin Castle and the buffaloes, than be made a fool of now.

But she sat encouragingly, stitching away correctly, at a piece of embroidery left over from the convent, and her mother lay back in her unaccustomed idleness and watched her, and neither of them knew each was pitying the other, and each hoping the other was getting pleasure from it all.

Her mother was fast asleep when Celia heard a dull thumping on the front door. They had been able to do nothing about the broken bell. With immense control she managed not to run all down the length of the long hall, filled with the gray light of the streaming day. Part of her mind noticed the holes in the rugs, waiting to trip him, and the delicious smell of baking from the kitchen that must be got rid of by the morning. Over all was her conviction that he could not possibly come, and she stared at him unbelievingly as she heaved back the screeching door, swollen with the rain and lack of use. Water streamed from his sodden cloak, and blackened the fine leather of his boots, and the fur was plastered flat on his beaver hat.

"Your horse?" was all she managed to say, peering round him as if he might be hiding it. Pretending he was not a prince.

"I walked over the hill," he said. " 'Twas no day to take an animal out."

"But you came."

"Didn't I say so?" The deep eyes gleamed. "And I'd be grateful now if you would let me in, for I'm mortal wet."

Embarrassed, she flurried to let him past her, taking his soaking cloak and hat to hang them in the kitchen beside the range. He followed her closely in a manner unsuitable to a formal guest, and his bright observant eyes roamed the beautiful bare hall with the worn rugs, the dark farmer's kitchen with the tea laid down for six, and finally the clammy moldering salon, adrift with gusts of smoke. The poor mother was fast asleep, snoring a little, in the gloom beside the hissing fire, her red work-worn hands tangled in the leaking stuffing on the arms of her chair.

In the dead dreadful silence Celia saw it all as he must see it, and writhed to know both his eyes and mind too sharp to miss one bit of it. Or what it meant. Oh, why, before God, had she been so foolish. Hands locked together, staring straight ahead to try and crush the tears of rage and mortification blinding her, she didn't see the shadow of compassion cross his face, wiped away at once by the twitch of irrepressible laughter.

"Well now, Miss Celia," he said, and his voice was not quite steady. "I'm glad to find your mother At Home. Will we give the poor lady a little longer now, and make tea for her there in the kitchen?"

Chapter 3

MATTHEW O'Connor! Celia! Do you really understand who the gentleman was? What art of wind in this world brought him here?"

Her voice was amazed and reverent, staring at Celia across the glowing fire where they were reveling in an island of peace and luxury, their supper between them made up of all the good things cooked for tea that must be eaten to the last crumb before the morning.

Matthew had long gone, leaving Celia's mother repeating herself over and over again, bemused by his charms and kindness bursting into her arid life. And so much so good, Celia had thought, watching him tramp out cheerfully before he left, to close in the hens, rather than have her mother leave her chair.

"And why don't you do it?" he had asked the girl bluntly, when he realized there was no one else.

The mother half rose anxiously from her chair.

"Oh, no, it wouldn't be fitting," she protested urgently.

"To what?" Matt said, looking from one to the other, the girl clearly furious, and suited by it, b'God, he thought. The mother looked anxious and embarrassed, knowing she had said too much.

"To being a lady," she mumbled, knowing it should not be discussed; such things were taken for granted. Matt merely made wide speculative eyes at Celia, not in criticism, but rather as one who slots in one more piece of some confusing puzzle.

"Well, I find it more fitting to me than you, ma'am," he said to her. "Can Miss Celia venture to the yard to show me the run?"

Celia went mutely, her head high and her cheeks scarlet, bitterly angry at being trapped in the whole charade that was none of her making. But she had the sense not to try and say so, standing in the windy yard, watching Matt moving like a shadow through the purple dusk of the clearing evening, cheerfully cursing the unwilling hens, shooing them in to roost as if he had done it all his life. He came back to her when he had carefully latched the sagging door, looking ruefully at his boots.

"There's a right and wrong time to do everything," he said to her, "and it seems to me this is the right time for leaving an At Home." In the lamplit kitchen she shot him a quick defensive glance to see if he was laughing at her, her temper rising, and with it flat despair. Had they ruined everything between them, herself and her mother? Would he ever come again, and indeed could they ever let him? No one would blame the man if he made the tale the talk of Galway or wherever else he lived. As for her father, he would bring the house down round their heads, did he ever find the waste of food and turf.

While he said good-bye to her entranced mother, she waited in silence and then led him to the front door, deserted by all the fine bright confidence with which she had prepared the afternoon.

On the portico he turned and against the greening sunset sky she couldn't see his face.

"Thank you, Miss Celia," he said, and his voice seemed muffled. Bored, she thought, with having to produce his manners to a scheming fool. "I'll know now about the Wednesdays. But might you be painting again before the next one? I'll promise not to lay a finger on it."

"I would be likely," she answered, a little short suddenly of breath, unable to say anything else; and knew the nuns and her mother both would say she was being brazen.

When she got back into the salon, her mother was bolt upright in her bursting chair, eyes bright with excitement and a charm about her the girl barely remembered, and that pulled sadly at her heart.

"Well, tell me about him," Celia said then, when his name had been repeated like a litany. "Tell me about him. I know he comes from Owenscourt but that is all."

It had been chill outside and she held her hands out to the glowing fire, half her mind wondering how in the world they were to get rid of the turf smell by the morning. Her mother needed no encouragement.

"Comes from Owenscourt!" she cried. "Owns it, Daughter. Owns it." Celia had to remember to listen as if she knew nothing at all. "The old uncle died there some time back and left the whole place to him, and it only a few years back he got the coachbuilding business in Dublin from his father, the poor man, killed in a railway accident there at Athlone, and his wife with him and the pair of them, God rest them, no age at all. That young man falls on riches everywhere he lays his hand, but I was told he was done with Owenscourt for he has a grand house in the middle of Dublin; and you know Owenscourt's not like this place. The uncle always kept it up, and what would he want with the two, a young fellow like him."

Celia brooded on the whole excited tale, staring into the red heart of the fire. Truly the prince on the white horse. No fairy tale.

"Since the house is only over the hill, and they're related to us," she said, "why don't we know them?" Her mother gave an exclamation of impatience and exasperation, all barriers released.

"We did once," she said. "We did once, and why not? But

your father—" For one moment she hesitated, dragged back by all the years of frightened loyalty. "He'd quarrel with Almighty God Himself," she burst out then, discretion gone with the turf smoke and the sugar cakes. "He had a quarrel with this lad's uncle, over some boundary, you'd have been no more than a baby, no matter that I felt the boy a good friend for Hugh Charles, we were never let to speak again."

Educating us, thought Celia bitterly, for a wider world, and then closing all the doors to it.

"He's very handsome," she said almost absently.

"Oh, and brilliant." Her mother was alight with the most stimulating afternoon that she remembered. "Brilliant they tell me. 'Twas his father made the coach for the Queen of England when she came to Dublin, and they say this lad can paint or turn a poem; and does all the designing for the coaches."

Paint, certainly, thought Celia. She was amazed. She had found a legend in the fields. Nor had her mother even mentioned the rusty hair and the fine deep-set eyes; the strong jaw and the mouth that found it hard to keep from smiling. The feeling for splendid foolishness that had set Dublin Castle down beside the Yellow River, its small brave flag stiff in the Chinese wind.

Abruptly she jumped up. These were the only things that mattered. She was swept with anger to hear her mother speak with such excited respect for someone merely of her own family. Someone no more than she had been herself, before her husband stripped her not only of money but of confidence and self-respect. Destroyed her and closed her away from all the life she knew. It annoyed her too, to realize that she herself had capitulated immediately to the legend; annoyed her to find herself sick with fear that he might never come again. Firmly she began to gather up the pretty china, and told herself the man was nothing special. There would be others like him. Then she began to laugh, as he would laugh himself, at such a hopeless falsity.

"And imagine," said her mother, who had come up to the table after her, scraping carefully at the crumbs so that not one might be left to betray them. "Imagine. All that, Celia, and he knew how to close in the hens."

Three days later Celia was smiling as she rambled back into the house from a walk along the river. Apart from a certain conspiratorial light in her mother's eyes, nothing had been changed, and there seemed no lesson in the fact that Mr. Matthew O'Connor, of Owenscourt, knew how to shut in the hens. She was still firmly banned from all the menial tasks and sent to gather color in her cheeks along the river. He had not come today. Nor yesterday. But the possibility invested every day with a secret warm excitement. There was a new lightness in her step and color in her cheeks beyond what the riverbanks could do. She had brushed her hair until it shone and her old blue skirt until she had to stop lest it should fall apart. She was not disappointed as she came back into the house, barely knowing yet what she looked forward to. He would come tomorrow. Or the next day. Between her fingers she twirled a small bunch of pink-tipped daisies and the first buttercups that every year spelt beauty and disaster in her father's fields. An old swaybacked horse stood with drooping head and shrunken flanks, tied to one of the rings at the hall door, but she gave it no more than a glance. Such were the horses of most men who came to do business with her father.

The sight of her brother sitting at the kitchen table did no more than widen her contented smile, although in truth she hardly knew him now. The years of school had separated them, and now Hugh Charles kept his life among his cronies of the town, and came little up the winding road to Holly House.

"Hugh Charles," she said, in surprise, her face affectionate, for she had never found reason to be otherwise. "We find you well? It's good to see you."

Hugh Charles only nodded his head of pale wiry hair so like his father's, and his round light eyes looked evasive and embarrassed. She noticed then a sheaf of papers before him on the table, and that her father was in from the fields; unheard of at that time of day, sitting in his armed chair by the fire, his own heavy face moved by some unusual excitement. In the dark corner by the chimney breast her mother effaced herself as was her custom in the presence of her husband, but the look she gave to Celia was one of desperate apology and sorrow. The girl realized that all their varying expressions were directed toward her and that as she came in, some talk had ceased and silence fallen on the room.

She looked at the one person she didn't know, as if he might provide her with some answer. A small man sitting beside Hugh Charles, with a long face and hair like seaweed plastered flat from the middle of his head. He too was looking at her, but a shaft of sun falling through the window to light the dust on his greening suit, fell also in the oval lenses of his rimless glasses; so his gaze was sightless and opaque. Her father had set before him a glass of the ceremonial whisky produced only for the important mark of some occasion.

What occasion? With some chill unhappy premonition that it was to do with her, she looked from one face to the other. Only the small stranger spoke, clearing his throat portentously, and making every word a pronouncement. He moved, and the sun left his glasses, clearing eyes of a soft depthless amber like calf's-foot jelly. She took a wild immediate dislike to him, overwhelmed by a sense of threat. And he the core of it.

"Is this the girl?" he asked.

Nervously she looked across towards her mother as the one most likely to tell her something. Her eyes widened. Had her father found out about the poor happy afternoon? But what would that be to Hugh Charles and the horrible small man with jelly eyes?

"What is it?" she said. "What is wrong?" No one dead, or sick, since all of them stood here. "What is it?" she said again.

Her father answered, the strange look of satisfaction bright in his eyes.

"Sit down, girl," he said. "Sit down. There is something to tell you."

Obediently she sat, as far as she could get away from all of them, laying her small posy on the table in front of her.

The small ugly man grew restive.

" 'Tis not the custom," he said querulously, "to have one of the parties—one of the parties present."

Her father brushed him aside like an insect.

"Ye need have little to say," he said, "since you have nothing to do, and you only here for the formality. 'Tis all long agreed, and were it needed my son Hugh Charles here could put it all down on the papers."

All what?

Filled with senseless fear, for no one had yet threatened her, she looked from her father to the stranger, who asserted himself by taking a pinch of cheap ill-smelling snuff and savoring it noisily through each nostril. The father's hand gestured at him.

" 'Tis Jimsie Gregg," he said. "The matchmaker."

The matchmaker. She could only repeat it. The go-between. Scurrying from family to family to agree all the claims and bargains of an arranged marriage. The girl to bring a cow, did the man have in hand a winter's turf, or a patch of land to graze it, or even when times had been good a few hoarded guineas buried in the earth before the hearth. And after it all, great drinking and celebrations and never a word to ask if they wanted it, to the two poor young souls concerned.

What was it all to do with her? She felt the hairs along her arms go stiff and her head was cold, as if death had laid a hand on her. It was difficult to breathe.

Jimsie moved restlessly and cleared his throat. It was not the custom at all, though they would never listen to him, and there was little enough of custom about this match, with both sides long ago agreed to all of it, and not a guest nor a relative for a hooley after; like at a decent matchmaking there'd be a score or more and a barrel of black porter and food for all. He had the whisky and God knew it was probably all he'd get unless a bit of the bacon he could smell simmering on the range, with barely enough turf to keep the thing going at all. The man was in need of selling his daughter, for that was all it came to. And he having nothing to offer on his side of the bargain at all, for who'd want his half-starved cattle.

He drew himself up.

"I've said it all," he said portentously, trying to get back his position. All this talking should have been his, and it was damaging to his importance to have one of the parties sitting across from him staring at him as if he were the hangman himself. "I've said it all. And the man is willing."

And what of the girl, thought Celia, as if it was someone else. To still her shaking hands she began to rearrange her posy.

"Sold," she realized. "Sold." Like many a poor girl with no more to offer than her strength and her red hands around a patch of land, and the ability to give the man a child a year. She could offer a little Latin and hang her own pictures on his walls. All except one.

". . . someone," her father was saying and she hadn't heard the rest, "who can give you the life you were educated for, and be agreeable too, to put a bit of money into the land here, for with your looks and the abilities we have provided for you, you'll be an asset to any man who gets you."

She had not heard him say so much in all her life. Sold. It must be someone terrible when even her father had to summon all these words to explain him away. Numbly she picked up another buttercup. The tall flowers always at the back, Sister Sacristan used to say.

"Who?" she asked, and she could hear her mother crying. The sun had gone in and the room was gray, the neglected fire sunk to ash.

"Joseph Hession. From Cahermore House."

There was a long dreadful silence and the flowers fell to the table. She saw her own sick panic echoed in her mother's helpless eyes. Hugh Charles watched her slyly as he might watch a coursed hare being savaged by the dogs, and in that second she became aware of a lifetime of unacknowledged bitter jealousy. There would be no help from Hugh Charles.

A strange sound of wordless protest burst from her throat. Then her still, appalled face came to life and she whirled on her father.

"No," she shouted at him. "And NO! No. I have seen him. With Aunt Honor at Bunanaire. He is older—older than you —my father! No—no—teeth!" She could hardly speak. "And that fearful house across the lake, 'tis like a prison. Without a tree— No," she shouted at him again. "No."

Even her father was daunted by her vehemence, and in the moment of shocked silence, the matchmaker clicked his china teeth and shook his plastered head in pompous disapproval.

"Didn't I tell you," he said in pained reproach, "it wouldn't do at all to have one of the parties present. Not the right procedure at all."

The father wheeled on him.

"Isn't it done," he shouted, disturbed in spite of himself by his daughter's shattered face. "Your work is over, and do you want to, you can get out. Amn't I only telling her."

Jimsie looked down his nose and held his peace. Get out indeed. Before the meal and drink that was his right, though it would hardly be worth waiting for in this starving house. The drop of whisky must have cost them half they had.

Thomas Healey turned back to his daughter, and tried to search for the best thing he could offer her, even his callousness touched by an unfamiliar shame.

"You'd be able to do as you like with the house," he said, placatingly. "Joe would have no objection."

"Joe!" she cried. "Joe! You sold me to your friend for money, as you would sell a heifer in the market. All arranged. And by this little—little—"

She gestured wildly and now the tears were coming, and she could find no word for Jimsie Gregg.

All pity left her father. He rose thundering from his chair.

"It is indeed, miss, all arranged! Your brother has all the papers here." His pale face was suffused with an ugly red. As if the chit of a girl thought she could change it. No, indeed. "You'll do as you're told, miss."

In desperation she looked at her brother.

"Is that what the papers are all about?"

He ruffled them, his face expressionless.

"It is."

"How could you help them? How could you do it to me?"

Beside the range the mother wept helplessly in the shadows, and Hugh Charles sat with a waiting stillness, as though, like God Himself, his time had not yet come. And didn't answer. There was bread set to rising on the side of the range and the soft smell of the yeast was homely gentle background. Outside in the hollies a thrush fluted to the fitful sun. Celia looked at her brother who would not meet her eyes, looking down at his papers, and with sick fearful certainty she knew that, like her father, he was in it for the money. A share for him.

"Did you think," her father said then, and he had calmed himself, "did you think, miss, that all that money was spent for you?"

She stared at them, not knowing what she had thought. Nothing much at all until that day a while back on the riverbank. Many things she had half feared but not one of them had touched the horror of the reality. Somewhere at some far distance she heard a long thin stuttering cry that was neither words nor sobs; a wail of hopeless shock and disillusion. Vaguely she knew it for herself and saw her mother start toward her. Before any of them could reach her, she seized her shawl and bolted from the room. Hugh Charles half rose from his chair and Jimsie Gregg rolled his eyes up at the smoky ceiling and drained his jar of malt. 'Twas the most irregular and disorderly matchmaking he had ever been called upon to attend. Couldn't they have waited until his meal was done, and he gone, before they started on the girl.

The father laid a hand on his son's arm.

"Let her go," he said dourly. "She has no choice but to come back."

Into the middle of their anger walked Matt, who had found the front door open, and although well aware it wasn't

Wednesday, was determined to seek out the reality of Holly House.

By the time Celia came slowly home with sick reluctance through the sunset, because, as her father said, she had nowhere else to go, her mother was waiting, twittering, on the doorstep in the rose-red light, fretting incoherently as to where she would find the money to buy the brideclothes.

Even looking back afterward, down years of almost magical content, Celia felt the wind of the storm that had blown around the house that day. And felt always too a faint resentment that she had been in her absence bought, even though it was in the end by Matt; instead of coming to him dowered and dressed as his bride deserved.

"You should have asked me first," she said when it was all over, knowing even as she spoke that it was unfair. No more than the last nagging remnants of her fairy tale. The prince on the white horse should surely have come to kneel before her, a knot of ribboned rosebuds in his hand, instead of shouting and bargaining for her across the kitchen table, although Jimsie Gregg had been given short shrift from the affair.

She didn't feel ready for it all, felt she had been hurled into a position she had barely thought of, forgetting they were going to hurl her into the same place with Joseph Hession. When Matt O'Connor came back the following day she told him before God he should have asked her first, looking at him as bewildered as if she had never set eyes on him before.

All her deep astonished heart told her it was the warp and woof of golden dreams come true, but for the moment the half-known prince of the fairy tale had turned too sharply into Matt O'Connor, hammering out settlements that did not please her father nor Hugh Charles either, and demanding an almost immediate marriage to get her from their house.

He was standing beside the white horse, ready to go, most of his mind still full of all the practicalities and the besting of those two rogues inside, but when she said that he turned, dropping the reins. His brown eyes were full of surprised and shamed remorse. In his determination to get her, he had moved too fast.

"Have I spoilt it all for you?" he said. "Have I been a fool? But Celia, there was no other way to do it. Any minute they'd have signed you off to that old rake across the lake there." His voice was so humble, and his handsome face so full of self-reproach, she almost shouted at him that no, everything was perfect. Dear God, what if he should change his mind and ride away? Why couldn't she hold her foolish tongue?

Matt had no intention of riding away, realizing with his native sensitivity that in all the turmoil the girl had felt forgotten, and the whole thing was brutally uncivilized. Useless at this point yet to offer her a lifetime of setting it all right.

"I put the cart before the horse," he said ruefully, and smiled at her, and she knew that bought or not, all her objections meant nothing, and she'd have run at his stirrup like his dog Boru all the way to Owenscourt, were she in danger of losing him.

He kissed her hand then, gravely and quietly, like a seal on the good promise.

"Go see your mother," he said. "I think she is a little overwhelmed, poor lady, and your papa," he grinned, "is in no mood to be good company."

He was gone then, along the riverbank where the water held the pale light of the hazy sun, and Boru rose like a shadow from the bushes to lope at his side.

"Me and the dog," she thought, and could not steady the wild swing of her feelings from passionate delight to sharp resentment. "I would imagine he bought him too."

It was Matt who settled everything, and Celia was touched to see how even in a few brief days, her mother's face had changed and softened under his kindness and good manners. Curiously, now that she was going to marry one of the richest men in the county, it no longer mattered about being a lady and they sat companionably in the warm kitchen, hearing the strong young woman Matt had sent over from Owenscourt, against all protests, banging the churn around the dairy; and talking of the bridal dress that was being made in Galway.

Matt had ended all the anxiety about clothes.

"Mrs. Healey, Mother, ma'am," he said, "all she'll need is a bit of something to be married in. We can go shopping when we get to Dublin."

Celia saw the faint blush of pleasure on her mother's cheeks at what he had called her, and in his glance at her was the gleeful pleasure of the spree that they would have among the Dublin shops. Slowly it was beginning to dawn on her what it would mean to be Mrs. Matt O'Connor.

The promise of money had done nothing to soften her father's attitudes; indeed, something close to an unaccustomed shame kept him even more than normal from the house. He was only there to quench the happy atmosphere when they laid his meals on the table, and in all honesty waited then for him to go away, so that they might get on with all the urgent and delicate sewing, in a house that seemed inexplicably warmer and brighter.

So rapidly the month passed by that Celia was still faintly disbelieving and confused when she found herself walking up the ancient sun-striped aisle of Tuam cathedral on her father's arm. He too had the promise of a new life, but he was damned if even that would make him smile; or even buy himself a new suit, tramping grim and wordless beside her drift of pale blue silk in the ancient greening fustian in which he had waited for her mother in the little church at Letterturk some twenty-seven years before, the shafts of sun between the arches catching the dust on his worn boots.

Up in the cold shadows where the real knights and princes in their day had brought their swords for blessing, Matt stood below the altar, impeccable in his black suit, Hugh Charles all sycophantic smiles beside him as his man.

Would she have felt more, she wondered in the strange swimming emptiness that held her, had he come indeed with his bunch of roses, and were she being married in a drift of white and flowers; and had the beautiful old church been full of rich and splendid guests? The tall man waiting for her seemed now a stranger, come too suddenly, before she had time to understand what she was doing; overtaken by the day. Yet there was no instinct to withdraw; no threat of tears or vapors; drawn up the aisle with a sense of inevitability, oblivious of her sullen father, stepping from sun to bitter shadow and then back again to sun, until she stood beside him, feeling she had walked a thousand miles to get there. He smiled at her, and took her hand, nor did she remember again that anybody else was there until it was all over. Astonished, she received her mother's kisses, and realized that she was married.

Matt had thought of everything. His own lawyer had come down from Dublin, a calm dark-bearded gentleman with watchful eyes and the beautiful name of James Cornelius O'Duffy. Across Matt's gleaming table her father and Hugh Charles had glared at him with a suspicion and hostility that was entirely justified, since they were correct in thinking he was there especially to see they could never lift one penny more than was agreed upon. Hugh Charles was particularly bitter, despite his smooth and courteous manner, having come to various small agreements with Jimsie Gregg over the matter of Joe Hession's money, and what might be slipped from it in the passage from one hand to another.

"It is not," Matt had said courteously to Celia and her mother, "that I do not trust Hugh Charles to see to the legal business."

Privately he would trust him as much as he would trust Boru, asked to lie down with the kitchen cat. "But you, my love, and all our children must be safe if anything should happen to me."

The quick surge of embarrassment at the impropriety of mentioning their children was quickly overwhelmed for Celia by the ridiculous idea that anything could happen to Matt. People like Matt were surely the immortals; protected from everything, even from death, by some splendid special grace that was their own.

There had been a wedding breakfast laid at Owenscourt in

a splendor of cutlery and crystal that drew tears from Mrs. Healey's eyes, and the brilliant early sunshine of a perfect wedding day flooded the dark-green stuccoed walls of the dining room, bringing translucence to the delicate medallions of the marble mantel. Even Celia had heard of Robert Adam in Kinvarra, and still looked with astonished pride at all the splendor that had so suddenly become hers. Or would it be like that? Never for one day had her mother been allowed to feel her life was shared. But Matt was not her father. Longing tore at her to get away from them all and understand what she had done. Get to know this handsome stranger, who was flattering her mother and bringing down to gales of laughter his cousin, the small plump Canon of the cathedral who had married them; being smoothly polite to Hugh Charles, and ignoring the boorish father, even as he ignored him. Thomas Healey had refused with such surly determination to have anybody else there, that even though it was his own house, Matt had given in, for the sake of peace and for the sake of Celia's mother. Wild with excitement and delight, she would nevertheless have to bear the husband's temper when they were gone.

"We'll come back," Matt had said to her disappointed face. "We'll come back and have a ball. We'll ask the whole county, Mother dear, and drink the house dry, and have bands playing in the bedrooms do we wish it. And we'll forget to ask Thomas."

The agreeable Canon, far from simple behind his round bright glasses, beamed from one of them to the other, delighted to the core of his warm heart to see the match between Matt and the girl, and knowing well the shifty-eyed men had not come from it with empty hands. Mentally he noted that they would take watching, even while he spread his bright good nature over the small gathering and gave it with Matt all the true festivity it had.

Celia saw it all as through a window, clear and brilliant, marked with sharp impressions she would carry all her life, and yet unreal; removed to some distance from which she knew that some time she must bring it back.

She set it all aside, and smiled and ate and sipped at the heady excitement of champagne, and waited only for the moment outside the front door when they climbed into the gleaming carriage below the feathered elms and the family stood with all the servants to wave them good-bye; Boru raging at the top of his great voice, where he had been chained in the yard. The agent, Bonnington, whom she had grasped as no more than a kind, intelligent face, threw his hat into the air and called for cheers for them as they drove out the white gates, and suddenly she smiled at Matt and knew with delight that it was her wedding, and would like to have gone back and done it all again, understanding and savoring each second.

But they were off down the curving avenue beneath the trees, and at the grand gates the lodgekeeper's tribe of ragged children raced out to wave and shout to them and one of them threw a bunch of wildflowers into the carriage. Matt waved back at the children, and gathered the flowers carefully from the soft rug, putting the poor draggled things together into a bunch and giving them to her.

"There now, my love," he said, "we can leave all the hullabaloo and take a bit of time to get to know each other. Isn't that what you want? Were we even introduced? Except by a few Chinamen?"

Under the blue forget-me-nots that wreathed her bonnet, she nodded, touched that he should read her every thought, yet aware of the hint of indulgence in his eyes for the idea that he and she had ever need of such foolish formalities. He was right, of course. In between the bursts of simple panic to find herself riding away with a man she hardly knew, lay the calm certainty that she had known him all her life. He took her hand, enchanted with her diffident beauty, knowing himself guilty of rushing her, yet he had need to be back in Dublin and he was damned if he was leaving her unprotected with that thwarted villain of a father. And the brother no better.

Across the country road the trees arched in a green tunnel, the young leaves bordered with the gold light of the sun. The fresh lush grass filling the ditches under the mossy walls was starred with marguerites, and the tall pale spikes of foxglove; no sound save the larks shrilling from the fields beyond the walls and the steady gentle clop of the two horses. She had just begun to relax against Matt, believing it all at last; driving away with her prince to a new world; new as if it had been made but yesterday; for her and Matt. Their own. Where nothing else could reach them. Radiance had begun to touch her, and the bemused ecstatic beauty that was the privilege of every bride.

Matt turned to speak to her, and she could see in his own face the whole tender promise of the future they had as yet no time to talk of.

"Dearest," he said, and then suddenly, "Jesus Christ almighty!" Her hand was dropped and the poor small flowers went flying once again in the folds of the rug, thrown aside as he leapt to his feet in the swaying carriage.

"Peter! Stop! Stop the carriage!"

She had no idea what he had seen, ready to be furious at his peremptoriness; smashing the first gentle moment they had known together. The horses slithered to a halt, hooves rasping on the small stones of the road, and with immense and angry unwillingness she turned round in her seat to see what it was Matt stared at with such a mixture of pity and astonishment on his face.

The sight of wandering, starving people was not new to her. It was far more common farther west where the stony land gave little cultivation at the best, and in these barren years, the bare inhospitable country was full of such pathetic people; no more than skeletons, dispossessed by ravening landlords of what little they had ever held; roaming the starving land, struggling to eke out their dreadful lives by roofing the ditches with whatever they could get; sad silent children and old people dying round them almost unnoticed in the damp and cold. Why, oh, why, although her heart bled for all of them, did they have to touch this morning with their helpless fearful sorrow. Could not God, she thought resentfully, have given her today.

But there was something not quite usual about this pair. They looked by no means starving, and the man had leapt immediately from the ditch; no gaunt slow-moving skeleton. They were still even fairly clean, only damp and rumpled from the long grass. The girl had managed to burnish her strange tendrilly fair hair. She hung back as the man rushed forward, and he stopped and turned back to give her his hand. His dark face was alight with the same eagerness and pleasure that marked Matt's and he would clearly have run to the carriage had he been alone. But the girl, no older than Celia herself, was far gone with child, and he slowed his pace to hers, leading her awkwardness along the sun-patched road as if she were a queen. He had laid down the knotted bundle that was clearly all they owned, and came empty handed to the carriage, not quite the height of Matt, but thicker set, with a shock of jet-black hair falling over eyes as dark and steady blue as Owenscourt lake on one of God's best days. She came barely to his shoulder, a little pale slip of a girl with eyes like pools, and this light hair curling round her face and down her shoulders, seemingly impossibly frail for the swollen burden of her child. In her free hand she carried, incredibly, a linnet, limp and songless on his perch in a cage of reeds, and with a start of shock Celia found sudden identification with herself, wondering what it was she might be carrying, were it she wandering homeless on the roads. Her mind flew at once to the painting they had dubbed the Chinese Masterpiece, rolled carefully in one of her brand-new valises, talisman of happiness that didn't seem to get a chance to start. She sighed, touched with understanding and pity.

Yet she could not find herself drawn to the girl. They made a strange exotic pair, as they came closer, something about both of them totally unsuited to such disaster; only the man's eyes still showing the monstrous shadow of what had overtaken them. His glance flicked for one moment over the girl in the bonnet of blue flowers and then came back to Matt, lighting with a grin of pleasure that showed all his fine strong teeth, and dispersed the look of catastrophe from his face.

"John Julius Cannon," Matt said then, and although his delight was as clear as the other's, he couldn't hide his look of shock.

"What brings you here?"

"Like this," he almost added, but managed to stop, and below him, in the dust of the road, the young man knew it, and used the words for him, grimly and softly.

"Like this," he said. His accent was the soft flat tongue of the west, but no peasant's voice, and his face more furious than shamed, defiant, placing himself grimly beyond anybody's pity. " 'Tis a bad tale, Mr. O'Connor! Like many more these days in Ireland."

"Mr. O'Connor be damned." Matt was out of the carriage and down into the road to take his hand, and from the way that old Peter had turned on the box, his face benevolent, the young man was no stranger to him either. "It was never more than Matt before," Matt went on, his face warm with real affection. "It's years, John Julius, years. They told me you'd gone to America."

"I did, a while. But I was always hoping to get the mill going again, and the father could never do it on his own. You're right, Matt, it's years."

The pure pleasure of seeing his friend had thawed his defensive pride, and they stood a long moment in the sun, eyes bright with memory, searching each other's faces for some message of the years between.

" 'Tis John Julius Cannon, Celia," Matt cried up to her then, as if she should know all about it, but before she could decide what to do or say, or had got more than a blue flash from the man's eyes, Matt was off again, and she watched in silence the bright gladness of his face.

"Do you mind, John Julius, the day you split my head in a faction fight over beyond Maam Cross and damn you for a fool but we were on the same side anyway!"

"And no right to be in it at all," John Julius cried, "and it a bitter affair between a mess of Joyces and their half cousins!"

For a few moments they laughed, belonging only to the shared past of their boyhood; then Matt's face sobered.

"But before God, John Julius, what has you in this state?"

John Julius also lost his smile, and his blue eyes darkened almost to black. He breathed heavily with an anger he could still scarcely control, walking away a few paces and back again before he could quiet himself to speak.

"You'll remember the father had a bit of land rented from Lord Bunaffrey."

"I do. I do." A small farm, but a spotlessly white house better than most, and much of the furniture would have done credit to his own. A tall gentle mother with the same astonishing blue eyes. "I do," Matt said again, held by the memory.

"He died of typhus, poor man, soon after I was back from America, and I got the farm. It was doing well. Well. A good, decent piece of land."

"I know. I was there with you."

"You were indeed."

He didn't look at Matt now, but Matt never took his eyes off him, living through it.

John Julius breathed deeply again and went on.

"We were just up to a good bit of profit, and things looking better than for years; a couple of good harvests. Then three months ago my mother died, God rest her, and we had to bury her. Peg fell sick then with the child and I had to spend more money for her in the dispensary. 'Twas enough just to put us behind with the rent, so didn't the devil-spawned Englishman choose that moment to raise it. When we couldn't pay, he had the machines in before we could turn round and the house pulled down about our heads. He wanted the land for trees."

"Bunaffrey?"

"Ah, no. He's always in London or somesuch. He just wants the money. No. Porter, the agent. An Englishman, God rot his soul."

"And his trees," said Matt, but almost absently, turning then to the fair-haired girl who had listened to the whole story with a vague abstracted look, as though it was no concern of hers.

"And this," Matt asked, "is your lady?" He chose his word carefully, having some immediate instinct that she was not his wife, and watching, Celia knew that in that moment he had turned John Julius from his friend into his slave. She sat uncomfortably turned round in the carriage, and looked down at the couple in the road, and at Matt, completely absorbed in both of them. All her irritation was drowned in some deep and anxious certainty that they had walked along the sunlit road on this her wedding morning to take some permanent place within her life. And the certainty that it would not always be for good. She half stood up, a hand out as if to ward off danger.

"Matt," she cried, and would have begged him to come away, reminded him what day it was, but Matt barely glanced at her, absorbed in something in his own mind. In that moment she understood that it was not holding hands and being alone at last that would make her marriage real. It was real now, her husband about to embark, she felt instinctively, on some course that would not please her. In this moment the white horse was in the stable and the prince was about his own affairs.

"This is Peg," John Julius said then, and put his arm round her, and Celia saw the great pools of eyes upturned to Matt and the childish lips parted in a smile that with her careful upbringing she could not even recognize for its blatant seductiveness, but which filled her nevertheless with a sort of blind fury she recognized no better for the jealousy it was. Not once did the girl even look at her, only at Matt, but he saw nothing wrong, only the poor fragile creature, heavy with the weight of her child, her little linnet in her hand, and her great eyes turned up trustingly to his face, waiting for some help as if it was her right.

"Dear Jesus God," said Matt, apparently to nobody at all and seemed almost white with rage. He turned back sharply to his friend as if come to some decision.

"Well, John Julius," he said, his hand on his arm. "And

ma'am. God has been good to both of us today. My wedding day," he added as if he had just remembered, and for a moment both men smiled up at Celia in the carriage, and she softened a little at the warmth of John Julius's blue eyes. The girl chose the moment to concern herself about the bird. "I have," said Matt, "both work and a cottage to give you." He held up a hand at John Julius's exclamations. "Had I not crossed you today, Bonnington would have had them at the hiring on Sunday at Tuam, and got us no doubt some misbegotten idler."

The girl looked as if their own farm or the ditch or Matt's cottage would be all the same to her, but John Julius was almost incoherent.

"Where were you going?" Matt asked him, to brush aside the thanks. "What were you going to do had we not met?"

Between them lay the known specter of starvation, the overcrowded workhouses, where the people died as freely as in the muddy ditches.

"To the mill. It would have been a roof. After that, God knows. There's little work. But we need shelter now."

"You do." Matt's eyes flicked over the pregnant girl.

"Matt." The other young man's teeth were compressed. "D'you realize that were the child born, it would be dead now, and probably Peg with it. It would have made no difference to Porter. He'd still have put us out."

"I know," said Matt. "Now listen, Johnju." He used the old name of childhood. "Lest one place be no better than the other. It's no palace nor a fortune, and we'll have to get Bonnington give you all you need to clean it and burn sulfur in it before you go in. There was typhus there and that angers me—a feckless couple had it, and paid. Anyway, I'll tell Bonnington myself."

Celia stared at him, anger coiling inside her like a spring.

How could he tell Bonnington, when they were on their way to Galway, and then on in Matt's own coach to Dublin. He had told her so much about the coach, which his father had built for his mother. Just as comfortable as the Queen's own. Matt seemed to have lost count of that.

"Get on up there," he was saying to John Julius. "No, let me go first, for I think your lady would need a little help."

Speechless, Celia sat while Matt took the girl's limp hands, first carefully placing the linnet in his wife's lap, and John Julius pushed her from behind. Between them they heaved her into the seat opposite Celia, from where she took the linnet back as cautiously as if she felt it had been given into bad hands. Celia didn't notice, not knowing where for decency's sake to look, scarlet up to the blue flowers of her wedding bonnet at the embarrassment of being so close to a woman surely just about to give birth. She turned her head and looked fixedly across the sloping fields to the distant sunlit stretches of the bog, averting her eyes fiercely from the shapeless bulging body under the thin brown dress, never to know that one day her own adored elder son would marry the baby that now so angered and embarrassed her.

Her family had left, but the startled servants came running out in a body at the sound of the carriage, sure there had been an accident, and they set down the girl, and the linnet, and the clanking bundle of belongings, and John Julius, in the middle of the ring of their astonished faces before the pillars of the front door. Bonnington lifted his hard brown hat and listened carefully to what his master told him, running his severe and experienced eye up and down John Julius and understanding that once again, for all his odd ways of doing things, and he could read the resentment in the bride's face, his young master was probably right. But as for the filly with the bird, he would stake his life she spelt a deal of trouble for someone. With the help of God it wouldn't be his business.

Once more they were waved from the stableyard, and Celia tried not to notice the covert glances that asked each other how the new young wife had taken to this caper.

Along the avenue the larks still shrilled from the fields beside them, and the sunlight filtered golden through the green leaves. Nothing appeared changed. But when Celia looked back this time, the group below the elms had been increased by two. John Julius waved with even more affection and enthusiasm than all the rest, but at his side the girl stood immobile, one hand holding her little bird and the other laid protectively over her baby, as if it too had begun to flutter in its cage.

Already she was phrasing the words she had held back almost from the moment the carriage had stopped; resentment and a feeling of neglect on what should have been her perfect day. She, and she alone, should have reigned today at Owenscourt. She alone. Tears of anger and disappointment were hot in her eyes, but Matt seemed unaware of wrong.

"There's Ireland for you," he said abstractedly and bitterly before she could get out her first protests.

Curiosity ousted them.

"What do you mean?"

"Would you know Castle Cannon—beyond Maam Cross?"

She shook her head.

"That was the family," he went on, even as she thought with a fresh wave of anger and self-pity that he had never even seemed to notice the new bonnet. "Normans. Built the castle. Over a few hundred years, of course, they turned into Irishmen like all the rest of us. So the next lot of English drove them out, and razed the castle." He gave a short bark of laughter touched by no amusement. "All the young family of that day were off with the Earls of Clanricard, fighting for Queen Grainne from Carrigahowley up there in Clew Bay. Trying to hold Connaught from the English. The rest of them were off later with the Wild Geese, when Ireland could well be doing with such men, God help her."

He had forgotten her, staring off into the green gentle fields that gave no hint of the grim centuries of bloodshed and sorrow in their ravaged history.

"The last of them," he said then, "the last of the Cannons, had the mill at Slaughterford." In the very name he spoke another fearful tale of blood. "But what use a flour mill in a famine? There wasn't enough grain in Ireland to bake a loaf a village. John Julius's father took the farm on rent from Bunaffrey—his wife was some way-out cousin to Bunaffrey, that's the only way he got it at all. Now Bunaffrey's agent has torn the house down round their ears for a few guineas and put them to the roads. Does anyone at all know what they're doing in this poor country."

His face creased then.

"I'm surprised at the wife," he said, and said it firmly. Were John Julius going to live on his land, wife she must be whether it were true or not, or there'd be hell on earth with all the women. "Peggy D'Arcy," he said. "A family of poor hand-me-down gentry, living on the relics of old decency."

Like us, thought Celia bitterly, until he went on.

"Horse copers all of them, and adventurers, and by now little more than tinkers, some of them. I'd not have thought her the wife for John Julius Cannon."

He fell silent and she could find nothing to say, all her petty complaints eclipsed, and she stared as he did through the thinning trees to where the fields were giving way to coarse rushes and bright-green treacherous grass. The narrow road stretched away ahead of them over the brown sun-slashed wilderness. The road ran higher than the bog itself. A few rocks, strung like beads along its edges, gave the only warning or protection for the careless and unwary, who might drive over the edge and sink forever in the harmless-looking grass. Bog cotton fluttered white in the wind away into the brown distance, and one solitary curlew wailed its endless sorrow.

Celia dared not break the silence, swept with deep ashamed relief that she had not begun to speak. There was all life ahead for herself and Matt. All life to learn to understand the kingdom of her prince.

Once again he seemed to read her very thought, taking back the hand he had flung aside to leap down after John Julius. With his other he returned the salutation of an old man heaping turf into the panniers of his ass, below them in the glittering bog.

" 'Tis better, dearest," he said, and shamed her once again by a deep tender look, demanding as much understanding as he had given her, " 'tis better now you spare me half an hour for things like that, than have the Brotherhoods or the new

Home Rule or somebody like that maiming our cattle in the fields and firing the winter feed. As no doubt they'll be doing now, over on Bunaffrey's land. And John Julius," he added, as if she might need the crunch of the explanation, "was my best friend here as a boy. I couldn't leave him on the road."

She didn't need the last part. *Our* cattle, he had said, binding her to him with the instant word from the heart that made responsibility a weight of love. The instinctive word that had already bound her mother, and got more gratitude from John Julius than even the roof over his head and the work that would keep him.

"Oh, Matt," she said, and could tell him none of her thoughts yet.

But Matt was done with sorrow and responsibility.

"Get on up there, Peter," he shouted suddenly. "Is it you or the horses dropping dead, or the both of you. Come on with it."

Peter flicked his long whip above the horses' ears, and Matt took off his elegant gray hat and threw it on the other seat, stretching his legs to let his feet rest up beside it, putting an arm around her, comfort, apology, and warm promise of his love. They spanked along the ribbon of bog road in the sun, down to eat their dinner in the hotel at Oughterard with all the fishermen, beside the island-studded beauty of Lough Corrib; into the old city of Galway as evening came green down over the dark hills of Clare, spiked with the first stars; and warm lamplight waited for them in their suite in the Great Southern Hotel.

Chapter 4

No fairy tale ever told further than the coming of the prince on his white horse, and the splendid marriage in the castle of the king. Sometimes in the years of conscious, almost superstitious happiness, Celia paused to wonder with a small smile what had befallen all the other fair princesses.

She herself had wakened that first morning in Galway to the pale dawn outside the holland blinds, and the raw fighting scream of gulls across the harbor. The first light laid pale gleams along the knobs of the huge brass bedstead and seared the folds of silk and velvet at the windows; brought the fringed and buttoned chairs out from formless shadows. Matt lay with his head buried in her shoulder, his arm heavy across her body, and for a long time she didn't move, only sliding her eyes round to encompass the rusty tousled hair among her own. Her face was gentle, filled with disbelief, and in the end, softly and uncontrollably she began to laugh.

Matt wakened with cold sadness to her trembling, struck with dismay; knowing brides were apt to wake in tears, but feeling that before God, he had not thought his would be one of them. Carefully he stifled his disappointment, and mustered his apologies and reassurances, unwilling to lift his head from the perfumed tousle of her hair. The wanting of her rising in him like a tide, even with the tears. Then he realized with amazement that she was laughing.

Pleasure and warm love swept him that he had been right. What good God, in these straitlaced days, had managed to find him such a girl; who had matched him last night with an astonished and delighted passion, touched with all the diffidence and impulses of her innocence; bringing him to a tenderness that was almost tears itself.

Now in the morning she woke beside him laughing.

In the end he lifted his head, squinting round at her smiling face in the gold light.

"And what is on you, Mrs. O'Connor," he said severely, "at this hour of the morning when all decent people are still asleep?"

"Oh, Matt," she said, and put her hand through the thick hair, running it like water through her fingers. "Matt! My poor mother told me I must pray to God to ask Him help me endure it as best I could."

Matt's eyes were very bright. He looked at her a long moment, then drew her to him again in the sinking depths of the feather bed.

"I don't think, dearest," he said, "we'll have to trouble Him much on that score."

The Dublin house stood opposite a church, in a small quiet road leading from a garden square. All the tall narrow houses were elegant and spruce, well painted; small shrubs in boxes on the steps outside fanlighted doors. As they stepped at last from the traveling coach, Celia looked up at the number, thirty-one, that was to last her all her life, bright glittering brass on the dark-green door. Two children walked sedately with a bonneted nursemaid from the square, carrying their colored hoops, and a victoria whispered past, open to the mild air. Matt raised his hat to the two ladies riding in it, well aware of their bright determined scrutiny.

"You're away now," he said to Celia, as he led her across the narrow pavement to the front door that was just opening. "Give those two half an hour over the teacups and all Dublin will have it that Matt O'Connor has gone to the West for a wife."

"And isn't it the truth," she asked serenely, quite unperturbed about the ladies and the teacups, full of confidence and longing to come to grips with them and all the other aspects of Matt's Dublin life. As he was longing to show her off. Already she could not recognize herself as the diffident and discontented girl who had fretted and grieved round Holly House. Quickly before they went in, she glanced up and down the little street, empty now in the quiet of the afternoon. Her first glimpse of Matt's world. She remembered Owenscourt, almost like a dream. Matt's Dublin world. The world of Mrs. Matthew O'Connor.

The housekeeper was waiting for them in the narrow hall. A thin gentle soul called Mrs. Bradley, full of respectful pleasure, her narrow face flushed with eagerness to please, trying to hold to the severity she thought becoming to her position. Matt told Celia she had been with his mother since before he himself was born, and her welcome was as warm as if it were her own son brought home his bride.

"Did I marry the devil himself," he whispered, "the kind heart of that one would set itself to love him. She'll be good to you."

They followed her up through the house, and Celia was aware of her pride in it. Two rooms and the narrow marble stairs only on each floor, the drawing room across the front of it, looking out tall sash windows to the gray stone of the church. At the door Celia halted with the weight of almost unbearable content, aware of all her nervous terrors that she might hate Matt's house and upset him in the changing of it. Late sun flooded through the long windows on furniture old and new; the delicate pieces of Matt's childhood mixed in peaceful elegance with stuffed and braided chairs and a long curly sofa with mahogany arms, piled with velvet cushions. There was the gleam of rosewood from a spinet and beside the window a harp, catching light in its golden frame. Dark-green walls were covered in pictures; over the marble fireplace a portrait of a woman, obviously Matt's mother, his father on the far wall.

She stood and looked at them and he came and put an arm around her. She sensed in him an uncharacteristic anxiety. All she felt was a sense of welcome and benediction, from the two unsmiling but serene faces. Nor as long as she lived did she ever try to alter the house from what these two benign presences had made it. Which was, she knew, what Matt had silently asked her, that first day she set foot in it.

As she fell in love with the house, so she fell in love with Dublin, having never been in a city more than Galway now and again on a Fair day, or to ride through it in the hired sidecar to Kinvarra. The bustle of the wide streets enchanted her; the gracious length of Sackville Street thronged with cabs and carriages and the smart rigs of the city bloods; curtained elegant shops in Grafton Street, and between them the broad quiet river, sliding from the green pastures down to the sea.

The residential streets were charming; houses laid in exquisite Georgian squares and crescents, delicate with wrought iron and shining glass, fine rigs and carriages of their owners drawn up before their doors. It gave her a proud thrill when Matt would point to one and tell her it was from his Shops.

"And little care he's taking of it," he would usually add darkly, although to her it seemed to gleam as if he had just let it go.

"I do love it, Matt," she said. "It's a lovely city. I know I'm going to be happy here."

He smiled at her and had not the heart to tell her of the other Dublin. Of the Coombe and the fearful middens that passed for homes down Henry and Moore Street, the powder kegs already of many an explosion, and God knew there would be more to come; the whole lovely city raw and bitter with political dissent. But what was it to her, and she as good as on her honeymoon; it was in the nature of dreams to be destroyed, but not for him to lift a finger against any one of hers. And was she not really in the right? Set in the blue circle of the mountains and the sea, Dublin was a jewel and he had loved it all his life.

True to his word Matt put his head together with Mrs. Bradley the moment they arrived in Gardiner Street.

As if by magic a tiny smiling seamstress with a club foot had come limping in through the back door, followed soon by the arrival, at the front, of a small obsequious gentleman, driven by a glittering groom in a highly polished van, drawn by a well-kept bay. When the double doors at the back of the van were thrown open, Celia at the hall window could see inside stacks of more bolts of material than she had seen in all the shops of Galway when they had gone shopping for the wedding gown. Left to herself she would have run into the street to look, as they ran to the ribbon man who came on Fair days into Tuam, but gently Mrs. Bradley restrained her.

" 'Tis his job, ma'am," she said, "and 'twould shame him not to be allowed to do it."

And shame you too, ma'am, Mrs. Bradley thought privately, for the pompous little gossip would have it in the very Coombe before morning, about the new Mrs. O'Connor not being able to conduct herself.

With the discreet advice of Mrs. Bradley and the leaping eagerness of the plump draper, and the occasional talented interference from Matt, Celia equipped herself in the next few weeks with what seemed the trousseau of a princess. Finally choosing, with a determination that puzzled the housekeeper, a peignoir of fine yellow silk, printed with small delicate colored birds.

"And why that, ma'am?" Mrs. Bradley asked her. "Is it not a trifle on the bright side?" Privately she felt she should do all she could to protect Mr. O'Connor from such a spectacle. At the delicate moments of either early day or late at night.

"Mr. Morrissey," Celia said firmly, "told me that it came from China." And looked at the old lady with such serene and tranquil radiance that there was no more she could say on the subject.

"Did it now," she said, indulgently, and summoned the dressmaker forward with the tape. The new young mistress, and God keep her, for it was clear Mr. Matthew doted on the ground she walked on, had such good taste that it could be overlooked if she faced her husband in the bedroom with all the unfortunate brilliance of a bird in a golden cage.

Nor did Mrs. Bradley ever understand why they set such store over some daub of a picture, and the good God knew Mr. Matt himself could do better any day. And the house full of what they called old masters, and some of them only bought a year or two, but on some scale old and valuable it seemed already. This one was in her experience a strange poor mess of a picture of some foreign part, and somehow Dublin Castle sticking up like a sore thumb in the middle of the fields. She gathered the young lady had painted it someplace, and that was odd again and she having told her she'd never been farther than Galway City and her school at Kinvarra. But there they were the pair of them, and the young madam squeezing her hoops along the narrow landings that they might walk arm in arm the length and breadth of the house, deciding where they'd hang it. As though they had paid a fortune for it to Mr. Mac Combridge himself up there in Grafton Street.

Matt had taken it down to the Shops and had it framed, the frame laid with fine gold leaf as splendid as the Queen's coach.

"Where'll we put it, love?" he asked her as he placed it gravely into her hands, and helpless laughter engulfed them both at the ridiculousness of it in its proud gold frame.

"It's not very good, Matt, is it?" she said ruefully.

"It's the best either of us will ever do," he answered, and she knew that to be true. "And," he added with a wicked gleam, "it'll be a terrible confusion to our friends." She knew that to be true too.

They hung it in the end at the foot of the stairs where no one could fail to see it; and where the morning sunlight lit it through the fanlight over the hall door, falling brave and bright on the small, stiff Union Jack. It was to cause great discussion between their sons in years to come, standing on the last step of the stairs to look at it; familiar now from a suitable distance with Dublin Castle as it really was, glowering over slums too terrible for their mother to be allowed to know. Their schoolbooks too had taught them where to look for little crescent houses under towering pines and water buffaloes beside a muddy river, and they were well aware that they did not belong together. They accepted it as some obscure joke between their parents; and one of them, more perceptively, as some odd expression of their love which held his own life in such warm content.

She had not yet been taken to the Shops in Baggott Street, although she realized very quickly that here lay the center of Matt's mind and heart and all the focus of his brilliant talent.

"Get to know the house, pet," he said to her. "And Bradley; and the other servants. And see to your clothes. And have Bradley drive you round the town. She's Dublin born and knows it inside out."

And can be trusted, he thought, not to take you where it would shock you, or even run you into trouble in the troubled city. "Then you shall come and see me where I belong." He laid back a wandering strand of hair from her face. "I don't want it to be just another of a thousand confused impressions."

She knew he was right and kissed him every day and let him go, setting herself to pass the hours until he came back in the ways she thought would please him best.

"As soon as summer is over," was the next plan, when he had looked with passionate pleasure at her in all the new clothes, "we'll invite the town to meet you. There's not a tinker's cat here from July to September."

His eyes blazed his pride, and she knew that not one detail of the new clothes had escaped his artist's eye, nor had the piles of cards that had appeared, as soon as she arrived, on the silver salver down in the hall.

He stood up one day from where they were sitting talking of all this in the two green velvet armchairs beside the long window in their room. Matt lounged in his shirt-sleeves in the warm misty evening, and Celia wore one of the new dresses, a pale blue ruffled muslin exactly the color of her eyes; immensely smart with the new smaller, lighter hoops.

From the mahogany press Matt took down an inlaid box, the lid delicate with tracery of ivory and lapis and fine colors in enamel. Laying it on the table he unfastened a thin gold key from his watch chain. Smiling at his small mystery, he laid it down beside her.

"Open it," he said.

"What is it, Matt?"

"Open it."

It opened as if the keyhole and the hinges had been lined with silk. For a long moment she touched nothing, her eyes filled with sudden tears for the loss and happiness mingled in this moment.

At last she picked up a collar of glowing pearls and thought of them as they lay round the neck of his mother in the portrait. Reverently she drew them through her fingers.

"Oh, Matt. For me?"

"And who else should have them?" he asked her, and she knew that for him too the moment was almost beyond bearing, and had taken long approaching; she regarded it as final and binding as her wedding ring. With one hand she held to his, and with the other lifted out the lovely things, with a small secret prayer of relief and gratitude, for had they been brilliant and glittering she would have found it hard to wear them. They might have been made for her.

"Oh, Matt," she said again, softly.

Amethysts and aquamarines, and soft opals; brooches of heavy gold and looped gold chains; and a little watch with a face of mother of pearl and the hands moving from a center flower of turquoise. Deep bracelets that snapped like handcuffs round her wrists; handcuffs of an enchanted prisoner. Others of ivory banded with fine gold. A locket edged with pearls and when she opened it two strands of hair, one brown, one fair.

"Mine," said Matt, "God help me, and my brother's."

"Oh, my love? Your brother?" She looked at him with sad questioning eyes.

Matt smiled and touched her face.

"There's not much of it, you'll see," he said. "He only lived a week. But whatever the little spalpheen did to my mother, then that was all of us. When we have our children, we'll need about six lockets, please God."

He spoke of some time away into the future, and now that the effort was made was clipping on bracelets and hanging necklaces one on top of the other round her neck, delving into the coffer like a child at Christmas. A creeping certainty of her own struck her into embarrassed silence.

He took out a deep gold ring, chased with flowers, and his face grew sad again.

"Her wedding ring," he said. "Myself I would have left it on her but these things were all over by the time I got there."

With this he set aside the carnage and the horror of the railway accident, the loved handsome parents so mutilated that he was never allowed to see them again outside their shrouds.

Celia didn't even know what to say for such loss, but Matt sat down again in his own armchair.

"You're forever complaining," he said, "being a very complaining woman, that I've never asked you to marry me." He looked around him and seized a stem of pampas as tall as himself from a vase beside them, dropping before her on his knees.

"Mrs. O'Connor, ma'am," he said portentously, "I venture to bring you this small token of my regard." He shook his tall tribute and the dust floated down from it all over both of them.

" 'Tis rice for the wedding," said Matt. "Madam, I have long admired you from afar, and gather my courage now to ask you for your hand. In marriage, I mean," he added. "I'm not a great fist at this sort of thing. Long, madam, from afar."

Celia rose in a flutter of her muslin skirts, her eyes downcast, trembling suitably, jingling with all her jewels.

"Oh, Mr. O'Connor, you take me by surprise. I hardly feel I know you."

"Well it's about time you did," he said bluntly. "But we'll make it legal first."

Carefully he slipped the gold ring on the finger of her right hand. "They always wear it on the right hand in China," he said, "and have I asked you now at last?" In his face was all the tenderness and passion of even their few months. "Have I asked you now?"

She was crying, and Matt kissed the tears.

"B'God they always told me brides wept," he said against her cheek, "but it's the first time for you."

"Matt," she said when she could. "Matt. The window. Imagine if one of the priests were to see us."

" 'Twould be an education for him," Matt said. But nevertheless led her gently back into the shadows of the evening room.

It was the talk about the honeymoon that drove Celia in the end. Greece, Matt had decided, when they had enough of Dublin, and the great heat was gone. October, he said, and she was torn with longing to be there with him among all the beauty he described.

"We should have gone at once. At once, in May. And then we'd have had the flowers. Poppies. Like blood. Sheets of them. And dark-blue daisies."

The artist in him was talking, and she had not the heart to stop him.

It was after dinner in the cool of a heavy summer day, and they walked sedately in the little garden square in between the laurels and the laurestinias and the bright neat flowers. Pale lilac dusk was creeping over the city from the sea, and the sweet smell of turf was heavy on the air. The roses were luminous in the last light, endowing the small square with some transient beauty of neither day nor night. To Celia, so often, it seemed the sun had never ceased to shine since that bemused day in Tuam cathedral. As if some golden tide had taken her and was sweeping her inexorably through a life so new and wonderful that she was sometimes taken still with loneliness; touched by a bewilderment that clamored even for the reassurance of the bleak familiarity of Holly House. Then she would hear Matt's gig rattle round the corner, or hear the sound of his voice through the house, or his soft whistling as he bent above his drawing board, or stood before his easel.

And she would know more deeply with every passing day that she would follow him to the farthest corner of this gold-edged world.

But not Greece in October.

"Matt," she said, and should have realized that his exuberance did not make a public square a good place to tell him devastating news. That he was going to have a son. She knew it was a son.

"Matt. We can't go to Greece in October."

"Why not?" She could see his mind running to Holly House, her only tie. Nothing wrong there. Got that varmint well under control. No trouble there. "Why not?"

"Because." She groped for words, blushing scarlet as his puzzled eyes raked her face, struggling to have the courage to use the actual words.

"Because," she blurted out in the end, "you can't take three people on a honeymoon. And there's one I can't leave behind. The heir to Owenscourt."

One expression chased another across his face, finishing with a blazing pleasure that was touched with awe. He took her and held her at arm's length, searching for any change, or any sign of sorrow, oblivious of all the other people in the square, driving two tutting ladies into the flower beds.

"I've done it again, haven't I?" he said ruefully. "Done it again. Put the cart before the horse."

She began to laugh, putting her hands over his on her shoulders, her face echoing his delight.

"Oh, no, dearest Matt," she said. "Oh, no. The horse came first. I particularly noticed it."

When he had calmed down and was walking her home

with an exaggerated care, he stopped under the arch of clipped yew leading from the gardens, his hand on the iron gate.

"Well, I'll tell you what we'll do," he said. "If we can't go to Greece we'll go the next best place on earth."

"China?"

He grinned.

"No, we'll spend the last of the summer down in the West. At Owenscourt."

Chapter 5

CELIA was grieved and confused to find herself approaching Owenscourt with some inescapable sense of foreboding; telling herself it was only the shadows of Holly House that still hung over her; reminding herself constantly of the situation as it actually was. A young bride, already enraptured with her husband and a coming child, returning to their beautiful country home. Owenscourt. She looked at Matt's intent and eager face; marking every familiar post; his eyes raking with critical pleasure over his golden fields. It was no more, she told herself, than one of the tricks of the child within her. Mrs. Bradley had told her with gloomy gusto that from now until he was born she could expect to be the victim of endless notions as mad as the devil himself.

The corncrakes rasped hoarse counterpoint against the summer whirring of the reapers, and now the grass grew dry along the ditches she had last seen tall and green. Soft flowers of early summer had given way to tangles of purple vetch and the tall strong spikes of yellow loosestrife, and the rustle of the wind in the arching leaves was stronger, harsher, as if it whispered a warning that in the end it was their enemy; and would bring them all, brown and yellow, to the ground.

"We need rain," Matt said, thumping back on to the seat beside her, having stood up in the carriage to see better the quality of the wheat beyond the wall. "The land is as dry as a desert. Still, there was rain early on. The grain's well full. If it holds off now until it's in, it should be a grand harvest, thanks be to God. Say a novena or one of these things women say, to keep it dry till then."

She smiled at his satisfaction in finding the grand gates open, the plump woman smiling and bobbing outside the tiny lodge where the washing for six children hung like a stream of welcoming flags flapping in the warm wind. The crop-headed brood themselves were dancing round screaming like they were let loose from the nearest madhouse, showing just the same delight as when the couple went away, and Matt reached out and threw a handful of coins skillfully into the middle of them.

"Heaven protect me," he said, "if there's not one for each. I never remember how many of them there are, only how much they eat. The father walked into the lake one night a year ago with drink on him, and I have them there since, eating and drinking me into Queer Street."

Celia took his hand, her own feelings forgotten. This was why the Land League and the Brotherhood and the anti-Boycotts had no holds over Matt. He looked after his own. Now he looked down at her, certain that her touch meant her shared pleasure in his return to this beloved house.

"Better smarten up," he said, pulling his cravat tighter. "They'll all be lined up on the doorstep there to welcome us."

"How will they know?"

"How will they know? Haven't they the eldest of that brood there with the fear of God in him standing at the back gate, to shoot up to the house like a bullet the minute he saw us passing."

Already through the trees of the avenue they could see the small neat group of servants assembled on the portico, Bonnington and his wife out in the front as was their privilege. But as they came past the white gate to the stables, ready with their smiles and pleasure, Boru shot round the house like a thunderbolt, hurdling the whitewashed well, to bark and slaver and howl, circling the carriage with his wild pleas to his master, until the horses had to be stopped for very danger. Then he began to leap in toward Matt, beside himself with excitement and delight.

The welcome had become a shambles. None of the assembled servants dared go to help, terrified of the half-mad dog, and all semblance of welcome was lost in the monstrous uproar of his barking. Celia cried to Matt for God's sake get out and get him, lest he leap into the carriage and all over her, but it was Bonnington in the end who raced up and dragged him back, followed quickly by Matt, his face taut with rage, getting down to give him the only welcome that would calm him.

"That's my boy," he said, and took him from Bonnington. "That's my wild Irishman! Though you seem to have forgotten your manners." He signed to old Peter to carry on and walked with his hand on the dog's collar the rest of the way to the front door, Boru silent and slavish, his nose to Matt's legs.

"Jesus Christ," cried Matt, and he was too angry now to attend to any speeches of welcome. "Jesus Christ, who let him out?"

"I'm sorry, sir." Bonnington was as furious as Matt. "We all know it's the rule! Boru stays tethered in the barn until you go and let him out yourself. I don't know, sir."

His expression boded ill for when he found out, but with his thin, sweet smile, freed of the task of holding Boru, he came to open the carriage door and hand Celia down, his eyes still dark with annoyance.

"Ah, ma'am," he said, " 'tis a terrible disorderly welcome. The devil roast the fool that let the animal out," he added with uncharacteristic asperity. With an effort he cleared his face. "Are you well, Mrs. Matt. You're welcome back to Owenscourt."

She accepted his hand and the apology, and the warm kindness of his faded eyes, but there was no time to think of it, her mother's arms around her the moment she placed a foot on the ground.

"Mother! Oh, Mother! I've missed you."

She hadn't known how much, and kissed her again, and had a quick impression that her mother had grown bigger. She held her at arm's length, and realized with warm amusement and affection that she was right. Her rail-thin mother had gained weight. Her hair was shining and well coiffed, and her gown, though plain and suitable, was well made of good material. With raised eyebrows and a small conspiratorial wink, she acknowledged whatever parlor revolution had taken place in Holly House.

"And my father?" she asked, offering the convention for the servants listening at her side.

"Harvest. It's a busy time. The land," her mother answered vaguely for the same ears. "He bids you welcome."

The whole scene had become more orderly, Boru calmed and glued to his master's heels, Matt's manservant coming out to help old Peter with their bags, and Bonnington's wife poised for the second time to make her formal speech of welcome home.

Before she could open her mouth it was all brought to a halt again by the start of a great rhythmic roaring and thumping from somewhere in the direction of the stableyard beyond the house. Matt's mouth fell open, and after a moment of astonished silence, he gave a great shout and clapped Bonnington on the shoulder. He looked as excited as Boru, who began, from sheer contagion, to bark again.

"Bonnington," Matt yelled. "It's here. Bonnington man, it's working!"

Bonnington forbore to tell him the number of sleepless nights it had cost to get it so. Not one of them was used to the yoke, and the man sent from Dublin as the expert, drunk as a fiddler's bitch in the barn the whole day through; but not a man but was determined the machine would be working for Mr. Matthew when he came.

He nodded his beaming pleasure, his wrinkled face alight, as if he had given a child a long-awaited toy.

"It is that, Mr. Matt, sir. It is that."

"Celia!"

The baby was forgotten and her delicate condition, and all the exaggerated care. He grabbed her hand and so let go Boru, who raced ahead as if he knew where they were going, letting out great deep roaring barks, beside himself again, knowing no one would say no, since his master was in the same state.

"The thresher," Matt yelled. "The thresher. Come on."

He was off around the house, towing Celia, the great dog leaping round them in a frenzy, and by the time they reached the farmyard, Celia's smart arrival bonnet was hanging down her back and some of her hair with it, and her face was bright damp pink. A long pain jagged down her left side.

"Only," she told herself fiercely, "what Mother always called a stitch."

Matt was oblivious, standing in the middle of the whitewashed yard, gazing with little short of rapture at a huge red shining machine outside the barns. To Celia, straining for her breath, it seemed no more than yet another roaring leaping monster, a thousand times bigger than Boru, belching steam from a tall thin funnel ridiculously turned at the top like the petals of a flower. Bands and belts whirred and revolved, and she had to admit the whole thing was shining bright and clean. From the back of it, improbably, it vomited a stream of wheat, and the wind caught the great whirl of the chaff.

Celia was country girl enough to sum it all up fairly quickly. The fine handsome monster, being fed sacks of grain at one end of it, belched and rattled away and threshed it in as many minutes as it would take hours with a patient ass around a threshing floor. Or even for the poorest people a flail, in the manner that was old for threshing grain when Christ was born. She began to feel the touch of Matt's own excitement, able to understand the enthusiasm with which he threw aside his coat and leapt onto the cart with the two hands feeding in the grain.

Another Matt she did not know. Quickly and carelessly wet with sweat in his hot city clothes; reveling in his own strength as he heaved the heavy stooks, effortlessly as his own farm hands, who stood back to let him do it, affection and indulgence on their weathered faces; for hadn't they been at it all the day before, and mastered what Bonnington was saying, that it was no more than an engine like would pull a train. Only it put all its strength to the shucking of the corn.

Matt beamed down at his wife, pausing a moment to wipe the sweat from his forehead with his shirt-sleeves, and she found it hard to recognize the fine-dressed Dublin dandy, driving the neat streets in his shining gig.

"The first! A rare sight for sore eyes," he cried, and the men extended their indulgent looks, finding it good to have the woman of the house among them in the farmyard. "The first in Ireland!"

Celia's mother came out through the kitchens, fighting her way through the bedlam of farm dogs and cats, and the irrepressible Boru, who were racing mad to catch the rats and mice and small bewildered rabbits bolting from the tall stooks, all driven to some collective frenzy by the thumping of the great engine, and the heat and the wind and the whirling chaff.

"Celia Daughter!" she hissed against the noise. "The child."

Celia smiled at her, forbearing to remind her it was in far worse conditions she had managed to rear her and Hugh Charles. She put an arm round her.

"Truth to tell, Mama," she said, "I had forgotten him."

Some echo of concern seemed to reach Matt up on the ruck lifter, for he grinned suddenly and sighed, and then reluctantly handed back his fork.

"Ye did well, sir," they cried to him, and, "It's a rare yoke, sir!"

He waved a hand to them with one last lingering look at the stream of golden grain pouring from the thresher into the sacks, and then jumped down to rejoin his wife. As he looked at her, she knew his mind still concerned entirely with his fine machine, even though he said contritely, "Did I do him any harm? Racing you like that? I wanted to see the thresher. 'Tis the first in Ireland. It should mean a lot of money saved for many people. Help them all a bit, please God."

Celia smiled.

"He didn't mind," she said. "We must be rearing a farmer. Or he knows that he's the heir."

Her mother clucked reprovingly that they should mention the child between them where Bonnington might have overheard, and Matt put an arm through hers and one through Celia's and began to lead them from the farmyard.

"It will have cost you a fine few guineas," Mrs. Healey said, still held in her heart by the terrible cautions of poverty her daughter was only just beginning to shake off.

"But they'll not burn my ricks," answered Matt obscurely, and then turned sharply, halted suddenly by the realization of a gap in the pleasure of his homecoming.

"Bonnington!"

"Sir." The lifted hat.

"John Julius! John Julius Cannon. Where is he?"

"Away to Galway with some cattle. He'll be back the night."

Matt turned, satisfied, and went a little farther before he wheeled again. The thread of depression that had touched Celia deepened. She thrust away her understanding of it.

"Bonnington!"

Again the lifted hat. "Sir."

"Anyone! Anyone who has enough grain may come and use the thresher when we are done. Anyone! See to it. Put the word round."

Celia was touched by the pleased smile on the older face. Bonnington was as aware as Matt, where hope lay for the starving people of the land.

Matt turned again, and at last, their hair full of chaff, in the comparative silence of the thumping machine, trailed by a satiated and exhausted Boru, they were able to go back round their house again to their front door, Matt's coat across his shoulder. Through the first creeping fingers of the evening, under the darting swifts, through the heavy shadows of the windbreak elms, and between the tall white pillars, into the dusky house. In the inner hall the last sun fell through the glass dome as a gentle glow across the polished floor, and at the foot of the stairs Celia paused in a moment of pure weariness.

A girl stood immobile at the top, in a haze of soft sun, the sedateness and formality of her black dress highlighted by the frosting of white lace at neck and wrists. Tendrils of pale hair that escaped her cap, curled round the perfect face. Expressionless pools of eyes watched her mistress make her slow way up, overcome now by the long journey and the wild noise and excitement of the homecoming, and instinctive as a recoil, Celia paused again, her hand on the polished rail. Acknowledging what she so senselessly feared in Owenscourt; and who had loosed Boru to destroy the dignity of her arrival.

Matt smiled with pleasure, and gave Celia his hand to lead her on up.

"You will remember Peggy?" he said. "Wife to my friend John Julius? Didn't Mrs. Bonnington write to me to say she thought she'd make you an excellent maid! I told her get her trained for you."

"And didn't ask me," some cold resentful corner of his wife's mind observed, and she took her hand from his. "Or tell me."

Matt saw nothing wrong.

"And how are you, Peggy?" he asked her warmly as he reached the top of the stairs. "And John Julius?"

"Well, thank you, sir," she said. She dropped a neat curtsy, but not before the huge eyes had slid blankly over Celia and flickered up to rest on Matt's face.

"And the baby," Matt went on, oblivious.

"A great comfort, sir," she said respectfully. "In the best of health."

Their daughter Antonia had been born the night after they arrived in Owenscourt, in the hayloft up above the stables; all Bonnington could give them while their cottage was being readied. Celia crushed always the tart involuntary comment that only Peggy Cannon would have chosen so outlandish a name for her child.

She had to admit that Peggy never did a single incorrect thing. She was neat and expert and knowledgeable in the unpacking and arranging of all her clothes, and when she was at last alone, Celia stood and stared into the old cloudy mirror over her dressing stand; wondering if it was she who was at fault, persnickety and hostile; thrown from her usual good-natured tolerance by one of these whims of the baby Mrs. Bradley talked so much of.

She picked up the heavy silver brush and smoothed back her newly brushed hair, as if removing from it the traces of Peggy Cannon's hands. She was not wrong. Through all the respect and care had come clearly the subtle note of disparagement and contempt; everything taken from the valises looked at just too long, and then set aside with an expressionless deliberation saying plainly that no better should have been expected. With mounting anger Celia thought of her little maid Rosie, left behind in Dublin, and the ecstatic admiration and pleasure with which all these lovely things had been packed for her.

Blankly, Peggy even managed to convey that in her eyes, Celia's long, beautiful fair hair had no particular quality, and might have offered her all the problems of a bunch of seaweed, were she given it to brush.

"That will do, Peggy," Celia had said abruptly, and could have bitten her tongue out, seeing in the girl's face the satisfaction of bringing her to irritation. "I'll do all the rest myself."

Peggy withdrew as formally and respectfully as she had come in, and shortly Matt came back from his first race round the land, touched already with the glow of the sun. Glancing round the immaculate room, he spoke again of how fortunate she was to have Peggy for a maid.

She said nothing, calming herself.

"All I have," he said, "is part time from one of the stableboys. I have to share him with a horse, and he wouldn't know a bridle from a collar stud. He'll have to learn it takes more than a livery to make a valet, the poor eejit. I could do with Peggy myself."

Over my grave, thought Celia.

"I don't think she'd know as much about your clothes," she managed to say, and as he kissed the top of her head she felt off him the sweet warm breath of the fields. He went off into the other room, where she could hear him slamming his valises and cursing the absent stableboy, who seemed to know even less than his grand green waistcoat would imply.

After their supper, with a fine trout from the lake, and the candles still in the windless evening, he pushed back his chair and said he would take a run down to the cottages to see John Julius.

"Go you to bed, my darling," he said, "for he and I have years of talking, and you must be sleeping for the boy."

It was bright day when Matt came back, lining the dark curtains with an edge of gold, and the birds were singing in the elms. As he tumbled into bed, she could smell the whisky on his breath and he realized he had disturbed her.

"Sorry, my love," he mumbled into her hair. "Sorry I woke you." He chuckled thickly. "A great night," he said. "A great night."

"And was Peggy there?" she asked him, unable not to.

"Peggy?" A long pause, and she thought he was already asleep. With faint surprise he dredged up the words. "Why wouldn't she be?"

Celia pretended to be asleep when the girl brought in the cans of water later on but even behind her closed lids, she could sense the lingering; and the soft smile of contempt, and oh, God, the waste of it, that a man like Matthew O'Connor should be in the bed with *her*.

For two hot weeks the thump of the threshing machine was the heartbeat of the house, and up the long back boreen to the farmyard poured Matt's doubtful invitees. They came, in the warm hazy light that was not quite sun, from as far as word had reached, even from the starving country to the west, from where they could carry their poor stooks in the compass of their hands. Cautiously in the iron gate, and up the rutted lane between the loose stone walls; giving each other no more than a brief good day, lest anyone betray to the others his ignorance of what the whole matter was about. They had heard of the great machine only as legend of a monster might sweep across the country.

"Bring your stooks to Owenscourt," they had been told, "and the gentleman there has an engine will have the grain out and clean before you can bless yourself, and all the chaff too to take away with you."

Little but codology to men who had all their lives walked behind the patient ass around the threshing floor, while the women snatched the gleanings and prayed to the Sacred Heart to keep the rain till it was done. Yet they came, reaching fearfully for any handhold in their perilous lives; with their asscarts or their panniered asses or dragging the stooks on sleds; or even carrying over their shoulders the meager harvest of some handkerchief of land from which they had picked the stones to make its walls. Breathless, they stood and watched and waited for their turn, looking at each other now in their common amazement at the clean stripped grain pouring into the mouths of the sacks, before, even as they had been told, they could have blessed themselves. Their starveling children, with shaven heads and spindled legs, ran screaming among the whirling chaff, and Bonnington gave it all to them, saving their fragile pride by saying it would be bedding for the ass, or for themselves, knowing well that in the coming winter there would be few that wouldn't eat it.

Only Celia's father didn't bring his grain, plodding with sour determined obstinacy behind the ass, round the threshing floor beyond the yard of Holly House.

The dry, hazy weather held until the fields both large and small were stripped. Food. For one winter anyway, along with the sound potatoes in the clamps. Over the stony country in the heat lay a hushed, astonished and grateful air, such as the faithful might feel in the turn of Christmas night. By God's mercy a good harvest and dry weather for the taking of it. Starvation held at bay, and even maybe a little over to sell, or for the purchase of a pig, or to offer with some daughter into marriage.

Matt had told Bonnington bid them all come back, and their families with them, for a hooley in the coach house to celebrate the harvest, and by the bidden night the wind had cleared away the haze. As if denied their rights too long, the purple clouds were shouldering in above the lake, heavy with the threat of rain.

Long strangers to festivity, they came diffidently again up the long boreen in the heavy dark-blue dusk, this time with their shy shawled women, trailing crowds of big-eyed barefoot children. The men were the more confident, having been up here before, telling the women how they had used the great engine standing covered in the yard, and wasn't Mr. O'Connor a good decent gentleman who belonged with his people and not some English upstart to take everything from the land and give back nothing but sorrow to those who had once owned it all.

They were still unprepared for the emptied coach house, alive with lanterns on the rafters; trestles laden with more food than the younger ones had ever seen; big barrels of porter waiting in the shadows and the girls from the kitchen already racing through the farmyard with the urns of tea. It took Bonnington and John Julius a long time to get them all away from crowding at the doors; even to coax the leading men to gather round the porter, and the women at the urns of tea. The children lined like starveling birds along the tables, waiting with a terrible submissive patience for somebody to say that they could eat.

It was the first thing Celia saw when she came in on Matt's arm, stricken at once by their poor patient little faces.

"Oh, Matt," she cried, "let them have it!"

"And who's stopping them," Matt said reasonably, but he moved swiftly to a table and picked up a boiled potato and broke it open, putting in a good slice of rich rare beef, giving it to the nearest child. Celia could sense the terrible control of all the others, not leaping to snatch the food out of his hand, and from the shadows all the men and women watched in turn.

Quickly Celia grabbed John Julius's arm. Already she had begun to realize that in any problem whatsoever, people always looked around for Johnju.

"Get them eating," she said urgently. "Get them eating. It's cruel!"

But the children were already at it, and in seconds there was a swift rush also for the porter barrels and the tea.

They moved in terrible silence, clinging to the fragments of their pride, yet thorough and determined as a swarm of locusts, and in no more than minutes the tables were completely stripped. Every loaf of bread and round of cheese, every slice of meat and every wedge of pie; the huge enamel jugs of buttermilk drained to the last drop. Only the children, twittering now like happy sparrows, scrambled for the crumbs, their parents retreating back into the shadows, their eyes on Matt, half shamed, waiting for some retribution they felt sure must come, to have gone in like that like animals at the good man's food.

Celia was holding to his hand so hard, it hurt, and for moments they stood dumbly, torn with pity; unable to begin to measure such deprivation; too stunned to think what to do next.

"For God's sake," Matt said hoarsely, "the fiddler! The music!"

They had thought to bring him in when perhaps an hour was up.

There was nothing to clear from the trestles but the empty platters and Matt's people raced to take them down, as the old fiddler was pushed in wiping his wet mouth. In the back kitchen he had been gathering his own strength from the black bottle of poteen set there at the fireside for the chosen. Tentatively he raised the thin wailing of his tuning fiddle to the rafters, and then the first authentic battering of a jig. The deep breath of the melodian wheezed in and not one person moved. The gaunt faces with their empty eyes stared out from the walls and Matt wondered what in God's name he should do with them, all of them so long half starved out of the energy for happiness. He wondered had he been right in bringing them at all. Food was not enough. Would anyone before God ever be able to manage to teach them how to live again.

Quickly he stamped into the middle of the floor and began footing to the jig, smiling, dancing over until he could hold out his hands to one of the women. For a long moment she stared at him blankly and then suddenly tossed back her shawl and followed. A tall woman who might one time have been beautiful, and no way of knowing the age she was under the fall of tangled, dirty hair.

For a few moments she danced listlessly, and then suddenly drew herself up in her drab gray dress, and her bare feet began to match him, step for polished step, her head up now, and her fine eyes flashing. Smiling her pleasure to be footing it with so handsome a young man.

John Julius raced and pulled out another, a great lump of a protesting woman, whose huge breasts crashed up and down as she began to dance, and she had to hold her stomach lest it fall apart. Yet her slender ankles wove as fast as John Julius could dance, and in the end, shrieking with toothless laughter, she shamed him into stopping. Warmly he kissed her on both cheeks and handed her back among her friends. And now it was like the food and they were all at it and couldn't get enough; yelling at the sweating fiddler for more jigs and reels and pieces and in the end barely hearing if he played or not, the dust rising round them in a haze from the old beaten floor. When Celia saw Matt in the dusty thick of it with Peggy Cannon, she had to look away, telling herself there was no harm, wasn't she his best friend's wife, and what else would he be doing for good manners. It was only a trick of the dim lights made Matt seem flushed with some especial pleasure when he came back to her, hot and tousled as his tenants. Fleetingly she remembered his promise of a ball and the bands playing for her mother even in the bedrooms.

But Matt's guests tired easily, having no strength. And

grew drunk easily; even their great spirits weakened by the years of hunger. The huge room was opaque with heat and with the odor of their sweating dirty bodies, and one by one the men were either sliding to the floor, or rising to the heat of faction fights among the barrels, having to be held back by their friends. The lanterns were growing dim along the rafters and the women and the children began to have the look of giving up, and waiting to be dragged back to the cold nightmare of their lives.

Matt came down to where his household were grouped around the back door to the house.

"Time to be gone," he said tersely. "Mother, by damn, you have a great foot. We'll do it in the house sometime. Come now, get you all out that way into the house. Celia and I must walk the length of them."

He looked almost apprehensive, and gripped her hand tightly as they began the shadowy walk down under the fading lanterns, and for all his firm grip, she felt suddenly a creeping terror of the gaunt scarecrows who lurched to line their path. Deadly silent now, they had lost the impulse of the food and music; all of them looking at herself and Matt, with a dumb emptiness that made her feel ashamed. No better, but for the grace of God and the love of Matt O'Connor, than they were themselves. A strange atmosphere held them, as palpable as the fading light. Not hostility, for who could be hostile to the one man who tried to help them, but as if they all cried aloud together in the silence, looking at the handsome, well-dressed young couple, and asked God if it were fair. It would all have ended on a strange unhappy note or even worse, were it not for John Julius.

"I'll come with you," he said, slipping from the crowd and taking Celia's other arm, and Matt flashed him one comprehending look.

John Julius. She had seen little of him, a laborer after all on her husband's land, with his mud-walled cottage like all the others down by the back gates. Nor could Matt favor him too much for fear of making trouble. Yet every time she saw him, she could know why Matt loved him.

It was an openess. A squareness. A poised good humor, with character strong enough to change the charming dark-blue eyes to flints when it was needed. And of course, she admitted wryly, those very dark blue eyes; enough to charm the heart from any woman.

Now he looked at Matt across her head, both of them estimating the strange unhappy silence in which Matt was beginning to wonder if before God they would rush him. And what would he do with Celia if it did come to trouble; smiling amiably all the time on both sides of him, bidding them good night and a safe journey home.

Suddenly John Julius's face cleared.

"A song, Matt!" he cried. "We can't let you go without a song."

"Will that do it?" Matt's eyes asked John Julius.

"Give us time anyway," John Julius answered.

Celia herself stared at Matt. A song? From Matt? Something else she didn't know! Did Peggy Cannon know that he could sing? John Julius was already beckoning the fiddler, and the hostile eyes were turning.

"Mr. O'Connor will sing!" John Julius shouted.

There was a murmur of something in the silence, and Matt grabbed John Julius.

"What'll I sing, in God's name, Johnju, that won't start the splitting of heads?" Both of them were aware that with their skinful of porter, the guests were as touchy as a keg of powder. "They're ready to boil," he said urgently.

John Julius grunted his assent and grinned.

"You'd be wise to avoid the 'Fenian Boy,' " he said, and Matt gave a quick grin back. Were it not for Celia in between them, he'd take it all more lightly.

He looked once more at all the thin and faintly threatening faces, and then slowly laid a hand on the fiddler's shoulder, even in that one deliberate gesture bringing them some sort of peace, by telling them they were coming back to something that they understood. He smiled once at Celia and then began to sing, with gentle great deliberation. The old fiddler caught him at the end of the first line, and there was a sound among the crowd like the hissing in the rocks at turn of tide.

"She is far from the land," sang Matt, on sad falling cadence, "where her young hero sleeps."

Mr. Thomas Moore's ballad that had brought London down in tears. The story of his friend Robert Emmett and Sarah his poor young love. Robert Emmett, who had tried to fight too soon, and too young, for all the things this crowd of shadowy scarecrows had lost. Celia could feel the resentment seeping away under the spell of the strong emotional voice, and the old, tragic, familiar tale. "Aren't we all in it together?" Matt seemed to be saying to them. "All of us. And Ireland too."

As he drew to the last poignant notes, with the fiddle sobbing at his shoulder, he was able to take her hand again and lead her through a different silence to the open doors. John Julius left him with a wink.

In the yard the night was warm and there was a smell of rain on the wind. Matt blew out a long breath and laid a hand on Boru's head.

"I wasn't at all sure," he said, "that one of them mightn't have taken a puck at me. Then they'd all have been away."

Celia shook her head. At no moment had her fear been of anything so tangible. Rather of their terrible condition and all it signified. Saddened by the way their apathy had so soon come back after their brief outburst of life.

"I don't think they'd have done that. But I do think you made them some sort of promise."

Matt stopped, appalled, looking down at her.

"How?"

"With that particular song."

"Me! No, my love. Don't mistake me. I'm no banner carrier. Nor pikeman, come to that. They must never look to me in that way. I'm a respectable citizen who wants no more than to do the best for his people and his land. You'll never find me there at the rising of the moon."

In the lamplight streaming from the house he grinned at her, but she was serious, and knew that at heart he was also, for all his flippant words.

"I don't think they'd ask that of you," she said gravely, picking up her skirts to go up the front steps. On the portico she turned to him, trying to put into words the wave of feeling she had felt in the ragged crowd as the clear beguiling tenor went through the old ballad of the boy who had died for their very wrongs. "I think you made them feel they are not alone."

He stopped again on the soft rug of the front hall, and in the warm flood of lamplight his face had sobered.

"Well, that's what I said, isn't it? For better or for worse they're mine. Like the land they came from. That's what Owenscourt is all about. Like you, for better or for worse." He smiled and stooped and kissed her. "I have to do the best I can for them."

It had been like a pledge, she thought. His pledge to his land and everything that went with it. Instinctively she laid her hand against her waist. His pledge too when the time came.

At the big window on the back of the house at the first landing, they could see them all streaming off like shadows into the soft night. Soundless. The men carrying their fallen comrades as from a field of battle.

Matt put an arm round her.

"Come to bed, dearest."

She had to admit Peggy was a good maid, waiting for them without a hair out of place after a race up the back stairs. With unaccustomed firmness Celia told her it was late, and she must herself be tired. She could go. Peggy bobbed her way out, lips tight, and Celia caught Matt's surprised look. She went to him.

"I am too tired, dear heart," she said, "for anyone but you."

The next morning when she awoke, Matt was already up and dressed and gone, and she was still having her breakfast when he came racing back through the door. Immediately Celia sensed the heightened awareness in Peggy's body, although she never lifted her eyes from what she did. Matt, thank God, never even seemed to notice her.

"Celia! Are you dressed? I've something to show you. Come on down."

His eyes were excited, and the cool breath of the morning fresh about him, restlessly walking the room while she finished eating.

When she was ready, he took her hand and ran her a little faster than she cared for down the stairs and out the hall door that had been left open between the bay trees. The purple clouds were still hanging with their empty threat above the dusty parkland, and a soft gusting wind skimmed across the surface of the lake, and rustled in the elms.

"There," Matt said proudly, halting at the foot of the steps. " 'Twas sewn in canvas in the coach house there. My father had it made for my mother when she was carrying me. You and your mama can race the country in it!"

Celia blushed scarlet lest the boy at the pony's head had heard, but walked on down, enchanted by the small neat basket trap, low enough to get in and out of when she was heavy, with bright-yellow wheels and cushions. Inevitably the patient pony in the shafts was snow-white. Neither trap nor pony looked the scale for the racing of the country, but they were a charming pair.

She moved to the pony and, choked between tears and laughter, laid her head on his sleek white neck. He rolled a quiet speculative eye at her as if to ask her had they even been introduced before she started crying on him.

"All you all right?" Matt cried, but could only spare a second for anxiety, walking in circles round them all. "Are you all right? His name is Higgins, I'm afraid. The fellow I bought him from thought him like to some friend of his."

Celia lifted her head.

"I knew," she said, "that someday, somehow, there would be one for me!"

"One what?"

Only then she told him at last, halting him on the other side of Higgins's neck, about the dreams and the demands and the joke about the prince on the snow-white horse, and how in the end she actually found him. But down in her father's fields so that she had to scheme and plot and get him where he should be for the catching; in her mother's drawing room.

The first rain pattered down between them and Higgins stirred, but Matt didn't smile. He listened gravely to it all, and then took her hand from Higgins's silky mane and kissed her fingers, his eyes dark with something that might almost have been anger.

"I can only hope," he said, "most humbly, to make you happy in my kingdom."

His kingdom. There was hardly an hour that she didn't realize how little she yet knew of it; or him. Too soon even for her to know that he could sing like Orpheus to quench anger; or for him to know that all his kingdom didn't love her as he did.

She could see Matt waited for an answer, the astonishment already showing on his face that it should take so long.

"Dearest, dearest Matt," she said. "What else could I ever be."

Chapter 6

OWEN was born on a wild night in February, with a gale clashing the bare black branches of the elms, and hurling rain in gusting torrents at the windows. There had never been doubt about his name.

"Why is this house called Owenscourt?" Celia had asked Matt once.

"Because the one of the family that built it was called Owen," Matt had answered. "But oddly enough there's never been an Owen since."

Celia laid a hand over the child.

"There will be one soon," she said.

At the end of September trouble had developed with the baby, and the good worried doctor from Tuam would take no responsibility of letting Celia travel back to Dublin. She spent the long chilly winter resting obediently and staring at her swollen ankles; longing miserably for both Matt and for the child. Her mother, who had come to Owenscourt for a few days to welcome her back, had never gone home again across the hill to Holly House. With little discussion it was agreed that old Thomas was far better suited by the strong-armed dairymaid who had of late become the object of his surly attentions. Hugh Charles moved with his smooth manners and placating smile between both houses, unwilling to alienate either, lest he should lose out somewhere in the heel of the hunt.

Matt, unwilling, had gone back to Dublin to be about his business, and it was one of the consolations of Celia's long dragging winter to watch her mother growing gradually younger; reemerging into an almost mischievous grace she never remembered in her before.

Also into authority and strength that Thomas had sapped along with her good looks. Celia was warmly glad to have the chance in peace, snug in Matt's luxurious small study, buttressed against the wind and cold, to talk to her of her bewildering and wonderful new life, as she had never talked to her before.

It took a long time before she could bring herself to speak of Peggy Cannon, still bound by a sense of impropriety. In the gray days coming up to Christmas she had been advised against even the effort of the stairs, and lay on the velvet sofa in her bedroom before a glowing fire. Outside the window the elms were spectral on a cold sky and all the birds were mute. The lake was vanished in a dank mist. Celia withdrew her eyes from the world where nothing seemed to mark one day from the other in the dying year. Impossible to believe that one day those trees would be green again. And when they were, she would have her son to hold.

She made a great effort to speak of Peggy sensibly, clear of the petulance of her condition and its dragging weariness, and saw with relief the instant narrowing of her mother's mouth. It was not, then, all inside her brooding mind. Mrs. Healey bit off an end of sewing thread as if it might have been one of Peggy Cannon's ash-colored curls.

"That one," she said. "That one's bad, and there's no other word for it. There's not a man on the estate doesn't think she's more innocent than the world before Adam and Eve, and not a woman will pass the time of day with her. But she's too smart to do anything anyone could point a finger at."

Which is why, thought Celia miserably, Matt sees nothing wrong with her.

"I hate," she said aloud, "to have her about me."

Especially in their bedroom, where she could pick up Matt's clothes that the stableboy had forgotten. Touching them with some horrible careful pleasure, knowing well that I am watching. Smoothing them with those long supple fingers, every gesture a caress; making love to him as plainly as if she touched him. And looking at me all the time with those great eyes as innocent as my unborn child.

She was aghast at herself that she should so clearly understand these things about Peggy, full of secret embarrassment that would not allow her to be explicit with her mother; aware that her understanding came from her own passion for Matt, and that the subtle and insolent miming of it was deliberate, and made her more ill than did the child. Even though all the reason and sense she could muster told her that Matt did nothing to encourage it all; was not even aware of it.

Were it not for John Julius he would never notice her. But for how long? How long before awareness was forced on him; insidiously and unobtrusively destructive as the dry rot that ate the floors from under Holly House. Matt was far from unaware of women, and the day must come when he would notice one so willing.

"She'll need watching," her mother said.

Watching? That was exactly what Celia did too much of.

"What shall I do, Mother?"

"Do?" Her mother looked up sharply. "What can you do. Anyway, the Peggy D'Arcys of this world never want the men. They only want the pleasure of upsetting other women. And she's making a good fist of it with you. Aren't you the one with Matt O'Connor's name and his houses and his money and his life, and the child coming? Remember she's only a servant."

"Ah, but she's not," thought Celia, but held her peace, twisting at the purple fringes of her shawl. "She's John Julius Cannon's wife, and for Matt, that's different. And as for me, no money and no houses in the world would compensate were I asked to share Matt."

It was only when at last they came back to Gardiner Street in the big traveling coach, that she felt her marriage had really begun; stepping down with her son in her arms before the green door, savoring it all as if it were for the first time.

I've been waiting for the beginning of my marriage, since the first time we drove out of Owenscourt, she thought wryly when they had settled in; looking from the baby's dormer window over the chimney pots of Dublin. Away beyond Howth a great smear of primrose light ousted the storm clouds for a gentle sunset. Everything had interfered, she thought. Everything. From John Julius Cannon in the middle of the road to the precious child behind her in his crib. What would come to interfere now?

Nothing did. Mrs. Bradley brought in her cousin's niece from beyond Kingstown, a fisherman's child with the salt wind in her cheeks, who proceeded to look after Owen with a passion as careful as if he were the Crown Jewels themselves in London's Tower.

It was a quiet year, cementing all they had hurtled into without time to think. Days of sun and rain and peace and lamplight and the harp beside the winter fires, Matt singing softly beside her, leaning on her chair. And the child upstairs in his bright room growing strong and cheerful and content. Her world closed round her, so small and perfect, and unbelievably happy and secure that sometimes when Matt was out, she would walk round the house, savoring it, laying a hand on all the things that made their life; marking as if for memory the way the light fell through the tall windows and the sound of Owen laughing in the room upstairs. Sometimes she would even weep a moment from very fear, and protest to God she was not greedy and beg him not to take it all away; or she would slip across the road and light a candle in the incense-haunted shadows of the church; as women from the first times had made over their children the sign to protect them from the evil eye. So she made it above her very life. Haunted still by the fearful insecurity of her unbringing.

Matt gave her a year of it; patiently observing her need to learn what she was doing, and to take a grip on the marriage that had taken her by storm. Watching her growing content with all the tolerant pleasure of his own love; wrapped in his own busy and creative life.

On a day of pale February sunlight, with tender shoots breaking the brown winter earth of all the window boxes, Owen had his birthday. Matt came home early from the Shops, racing up the marble stairs to the sounds of jubilation at the top. Owen was proudly astride the gift that had been made for him in the Shops, with as much care as if it were a carriage for the Lord Lieutenant; delivered that morning: a fine rocking horse with scarlet harness all a-jingle with golden bells.

"Snow-white, of course," said Celia, smiling as he came in the door.

"What else?" said Matt. "What else?" and grinned at her across the baby's head. Owen was beside himself with excitement, shouting at the horse, his face flushed and his soft hair already bright with the rusty lights that marked his father's.

Gracie, his nursemaid, hovered, beaming, beside him, hands outstretched like the picture of the guardian angel on his mantelpiece. And by the door Mrs. Bradley stood smiling, her thin face alight with love, unable to stay away. Owen turned to be sure that she was there admiring him, and at once slipped from the saddle. Gracie had him before Celia or Matt could stir.

"There's the man," she cried, forestalling the tears. "There's the man. Get back on now quickly or the horse might run away."

Owen remembered that, baby though he was. Years later he was to tell his mother that he never felt sure he wouldn't wake up some morning and look across the room, to find the loved white horse had run away.

He didn't understand it when his mother laughed and answered with big eyes and a sidelong smile in the direction of his father.

"I'll confess to you, Owen," she said. "For a long time I felt the same myself."

His father only grinned, and he was baffled, but content. One of these endless secret jokes between his parents that made for him a warm security.

Now his mother looked at him ruefully, back in the scarlet saddle, clutching the reins, his small uncertain face turned to Gracie, pillar of his world.

"I swear," Celia said to Matt, "he has no need of us at all."

She never expected the prompt answer.

"I was waiting," said Matt briskly, "for you to find that out. You will never be more right. Could you spare me the time now for a honeymoon, would you think, Mrs. O'Connor? It'll be about three white horses behind the cart, but that's no matter."

She forgot her child, looking up into the deep compulsion in Matt's eyes behind his smile. The promise. She blushed scarlet, certain that Mrs. Bradley at least was well aware of the way he could still turn her limbs to water with a look. For an awkward moment she lifted a hand and brushed a thread from the fine black broadcloth of his coat. There was a mark of charcoal on his shirt.

"You're blushing, Mrs. O'Connor," he said, his eyes wicked now. "You don't have to. A honeymoon's a very proper thing."

"Be quiet, Matt!"

"You haven't said if you'll come."

She moved over and laid a hand on her child's bright head, as if in the slow movement she relinquished him. He turned her his toothless smile but her eyes were on his father, gravely, and his face grew quiet too. They might have been alone, and the two women were careful not to look at them.

"Oh, yes, Mr. O'Connor, I'll come," she said.

They went in early May. To Greece. Finding the ancient truth of the wine-dark seas as they sailed through the islands round the Peloponnese to Athens, where they hired a carriage as old as Greece itself, whose springs caused Matt a deep professional distrust. With it went a hairy villain of a driver, prudently in possession of a shotgun. He stank of goat and soured retsina, and through his tattered whiskers his smile was toothless and disarming as Owen's own, covering a guile and sense of honesty that would have shamed Iscariot. When, after a few battles, he found to his surprise that in the red-haired Kyrie with the quick temper he had met his match, he settled down and served them well.

They wandered with their paintboxes, and Matt painted more than she did, as, depressed by his quick skill, she would leave her easel and wander in the flowers. They took donkeys up the long stony track at Delphi, followed by Stavros and his shotgun and a long whip to keep the donkeys moving, until they came to the brambled gap among the ancient brickwork, where he assured them through his whiskers that the Oracle had sat to give her wisdom to the world. "Interesting," Matt said, staring at the dark hole, and grabbing at his restless donkey. "But we don't have to ask the old girl anything. Not one single thing."

Celia sat, her donkey immobile as if death had overtaken it, now it was allowed to stop, and she could hear the bees humming in the dark-blue daisies, and somewhere above them on the craggy hill, a nightingale was singing deliriously in the high heat of the afternoon. Even if it were different gods, it was surely tempting them to assume too much.

"Nothing?" she said, and her voice was small with all her superstitious fears.

"Nothing," Matt said firmly, and gave her donkey a tug to get it on between the fallen stones. "Nothing. We have everything we want and we are going to live forever."

"Given by the hand of Matt O'Connor." She smiled at him.

"Given by his hand," he said firmly.

And under the dark-blue sky among the blood-red poppies with that same hand warm over hers, she felt at last she could believe him.

As their journey went on it grew slower, through the deep peace of Epidaurus and the new miracles of Troy and Agamemnon's great Mycenae. All the high excited spirit of the early days, and their determination to see all of the ancient world faded away into the heat, and the haunted lethargy of a land enmeshed in its own glowing past.

Slowly they clopped from one small taberna to another, all of them miraculously owned by some distant relatives of their driver. Long days of brilliant heat and breathless beauty hushed by the awe of the ever-present past; lunches with harsh dry wine that sent them singing through the blazing afternoons, sprawled together under Celia's red umbrella, trying to learn Greek songs from Stavros, and teaching him in return the drinking songs of Dublin and a couple of political ballads that should, said Matt contentedly, cause considerable confusion to his English customers.

Slowly they drifted through the oranges and vines across the sun-drenched plain of Arcos, and finally at Navplion they petered to a stop, halted in the end by the exquisite lassitude of their own content.

The red land rolled down roughly to a dark-blue sea, wide and tranquil as the sky itself. Only with the coming of sunset was it possible to discern the edges of the world; the darkening water drawn against skies of gold and amber, trailing long swathes of ragged scarlet to promise their next perfect dawn.

It was almost a week later that she spoke to him, like some drugged sleepwalker from the shores of Lethe. Days had passed of languorous heat beside the timeless shining sea; and nights of star-drenched silence so absolute, it took the awakening mind with fear, lest beyond the tiny casement there should be now a void, the whole known world soaked away into the glittering stars.

But the known world was creeping reluctantly into her mind as she walked barefoot in the pale endless sand, where they strolled before going back to their tiny taberna that Stavros had found for them from yet another cousin, for their lamplit supper underneath the vines. She held two thick skinned oranges that Matt had picked for her, still on the branch of their dark leaves, her white skirts held up from her bare brown legs and her sun-gilt hair pinned haphazard on the top of her head.

"Matt," she said slowly, and stopped and got no further.

"My love?" he said.

His eyes were on the long sweep of the rugged coast, trying to decide what color he should use to paint it, when the time came in some gray winter to implement his sketchbook. Not brown. Not red. Perhaps even purple might be closer and the shadows almost black.

"Matt," she said, the words dragged from her, torn between the two perfections. "Matt, we have a child."

Matt grinned and turned to her, pushing back a blown strand of her hair, his own now bleached almost red by the sun, his face and arms deep brown above his open shirt; his feet bare.

"I was wondering, Mrs. O'Connor, ma'am, when you'd remember. Owen is the name."

She knew he teased her, and yet she was silent, knowing the pain of all her awakenings in these breathless silent nights, in the hard old beds, watching the pale moon ride the sky and begging God not to let anything go wrong with Owen. Never trusting the careful arrangements Matt had made that any wire to Athens was to be brought to them at once, no matter where they were and regardless of all cost.

She did not yet realize that he knew it all, tuned to her every anxiety, watching with infinite gratitude her sweet determination that this time should be for him alone.

"So we must go home now," was all he said, "tomorrow," and she nodded, unable to put such sadness into words, although they both knew the moment was exact.

"Come on, then, for the Last Supper," he said flippantly, for he could hardly bear to look at her, knowing he would never see her so again. Her young beauty against the tranquil beauty of the evening sea; gravity, mischief and some high bright integrity more subtle than pride, that was entirely hers. "Come on, Mama," he said. "Your feet are getting cold."

From then on she was fretting to be home, but she woke in the first blaze of the following dawn, panic touching her as she discovered Matt was missing from her side. When she started up she saw him at the small window, sketching, his pad on his knees in the yellow light.

"What, Matt?" she asked him drowsily. "What is it? What are you drawing?"

"Nothing," said Matt. "Nothing."

And she slept again, but aware now of the day, drifting in cold sadness through the fringes of her sleep.

As they stood at last at the crowded rail of the Channel steamer canting into Kingstown Harbor, she looked over at the sheen of wind along the green flanks of Howth and the soft round clouds stacked above the Sugar Loaf; breathed the haunting turf reek from the white town, and she reached for Matt's gloved hand. Owenscourt was like a dream, and Peggy Cannon no more than a half-forgotten name. Appalled, she realized she could not even bring to mind her son's small face nor the touch of his soft hands. She could only look at Matt, holding to her bonnet in the cold gusty wind, as if with the grinding of the boat against the pier they would both suffer some irreparable loss.

In hours she had slipped back into her place as though she had never been away, in the tall house opposite the priests; with Owen's jubilant voice hooting through the rooms, lurching round on his own two legs; hung with all his gifts from Greece. And in the following days Matt was full of plans. Now was the time at last for her debut into Dublin society.

"Or at least as much of it as I can stand myself, dearest," he said. "For there's much with which I have small patience. But my friends are wondering how long I mean to keep you to myself, or are you some deformed creature that I keep behind locked doors."

His eyes told her the ridiculousness of this.

"Get yourself some grand new clothes," he said, "and we'll be off with the best of them."

Whistling, he let himself into the street, snapping his brown fingers at a wandering cat, delighted now that he was here, to be back in the bustle and pressure of the Shops. Where they were also beginning to ask him, Sir, did he have a wife at all, and would he ever bring her down to see them the way his father did his mother, God rest the pair of them.

"I will," he said cheerfully, "I'll bring her any day now," and turned to his work, tossing aside a thick coroneted letter. You'd think Lord Moran would never be able to leave his house again, the poor man, until he got his new barouche; and his coach house already full to Matt's knowledge, with as many rigs as would furnish a Sunday out in Phoenix Park.

Celia watched him out of sight, along the narrow street and the railings of the tall clean houses. She bit her lip ruefully on her own misgivings, no longer nervous. What must be must be.

She was waiting for him when he came home that evening, standing at the bottom of the stairs in the shadowed hall, touching Dublin Castle with a thoughtful finger.

"Something wrong?" he asked, giving his hat and cane to the housekeeper, who slid out of sight with rapid discretion.

His wife's face was a mixture of hilarity and ruefulness and deep delight. Bright eyed, she kissed Matt, and he raised one thick rusty eyebrow.

"Matt. You know all this about launching me in Dublin society."

They were going arm in arm up the white stairs, her blue skirts crushed against the banister, the sun laying pools of golden light on the wall above their heads from the landing window.

"I do. It's time—" His voice was firm. He thought she was going to object.

"My love," she said, and stopped him. "I am afraid we have put another cart before that particular horse."

Chapter 7

AFTER the birth of Emmett their marriage at last settled down and took on some sort of order, instead of, as Matt remarked, the pair of them living like Arabs between Owenscourt and Dublin, with a rest every so often for a confinement.

"It hasn't been quite as bad as that, Matt!"

He could not ruffle her as easily now, nor tease her into such instant anxiety in her desire to please him. She was beginning to learn security and her true value in her husband's eye. The nervous girl from Holly House giving way to a poised young mother, as calm in the demands of her two houses as she was tranquil and unperturbed in the face of Matt's mischievous exaggerations.

He took her at last to see the Shops, and she was reluctant to leave Owen behind, avid for him now to experience every aspect of his father's life.

Matt wouldn't have it. "I'm as anxious as you are, dearest," he said, "to take him everywhere. Didn't I go down to the Shops first on my own father's shoulders. But Owen's too small yet, and the very devil for fiddling, and there are too many ways of getting his fingers cut off or even his head. I've no mind for bloodstained leather in Lord Kelvin's gig!"

She only smiled.

"Come on. Are you ready?"

It was all so much bigger than she had expected, since it looked no more on the outside than a long wall with high blank windows; at one end of it the huge doors of the coach house with a judas gate where the employees came and went. At the other were the elegant bow windows and fanlighted door of Matt's own rooms, where he received all his customers, pouring them fine port and laying his designs for them across the wide mahogany table.

"But it's a lovely room, Matt," Celia said, and meant it, pausing in the doorway, caught at once by the rich, welcoming and prosperous air of the embossed leather walls, matching the bindings of the shelves of books; the gleaming furniture and the dancing fire reflected in the crystal decanters on the chiffonier. "Did your father do it?"

For once Matt could say no.

"I did it myself," he said, "when I took it over. He had it, I thought, too much like an office. Better, I felt, look rich right from the opening door, and then they'll think you're worth spending money with. Close all these doors now as you follow me, otherwise my hair and my life will be filled with sawdust."

The first of the shops lay at the end of a short passage, carefully sealed off with double doors, and they were all waiting for her there. All work had been stopped, and they were lined up along the benches, from the manager Joseph Lind down to the youngest of the new apprentices. Celia saw that their reaction to her varied with their age. Some of the older men had tears in their eyes, seeing her only as the present representative, and with two sons already, of the family they had come to serve when they were children. Welcoming her from their hearts, she thought, even if she had been cross-eyed and four foot high and twenty stone, simply because she was Matt O'Connor's wife. The younger ones looked at her with admiration for her looks, and even a degree of friendship, because they respected Mr. Matt and were well treated. And would probably come in time to the same possessiveness as the old ones dropping off the twig. There were, to her surprise, two girls, delighted at her amazement.

"Did I never tell you?" Matt said smiling at them, and she shook her head.

"Mary Grace and Annie," he said, and she shook hands with them. "They do all the fine painting on the crests and coats of arms. B'God, we'd be lost without them."

Lastly the young apprentices, and she shook their hands gravely while they scuffed their feet and rolled their eyes and grew scarlet with embarrassment, but nevertheless looked to their manners. Did they not, and every other day as well as this one, they would not last inside O'Connor's.

Matt clapped his hands.

"Away now, the lot of you. Thank you for the welcome. I hope you'll be good enough to show Mrs. O'Connor what you're doing."

"I had thought, Matt, it was what it sounded. A row of shops all separate."

Matt smiled down at her.

"Sheds, not shops. Mind your dress."

There was no division between one shop and another, all combined in a great long shed where the light fell clear through a glass roof like a station, and all the doors opened into the same high-walled yard for storage; the whole place aromatic with the smell of gum and resin and sawdust and new dry wood and the sharp tang of varnish.

"The only one separate," said Matt, "is the paint shop, and we have to keep that dry. And this fellow, for example," he said, "generates a lot of damp."

The man looked up and smiled and touched his fingers to his forehead, going back at once to shaping the first curve of a wheel over a caldron of steam. There were two of them, pale and sweating, yet slow and careful in every touch of the pliant wood between their fingers. Soft-spoken men.

"From Bristol." Matt told her, and they nodded, pleased

that she should know. "There's no man in Britain can turn a wheel like the men of the West Country."

She saw it all, from the first great untouched sheets and planks of timber, shipped from all the world for its special purposes; down through the shops to the vast coach house at the end where in all their shining splendor, a gig and a victoria stood waiting, their shafts at rest, for some owner to collect them. The gig had coronets gilded on the sides, and in the shadows Matt ran a critical hand over them and grunted.

"There," he said, and his pride was strong in his handsome face. "What would you think of all that, now?"

For a moment she found it hard to speak. Another kingdom, and each one more splendid and demanding than the last. With it all his bright good nature and the quick sensitive understanding that came with his gifts; added to that his splendid physical beauty as he stood there with his eyes on her waiting for her all-important praise.

"Matt," she said and kissed him. "What can I say. You know that it is the best in Ireland."

Pleased, he kissed her back.

"In all Britain," he said, and his eyes told her what he would not say. That without her it was nothing. That it crowned all his achievement to have her standing there in her soft pink dress, her eyes alight with admiration.

"Come," he said. "Come on now and drink sherry with old Lind and a few of the others, and then we'll drive out to Kingstown for our dinner by the sea."

When they came back home, he had something else to show her.

"I wasn't idle," he said, "while you were producing that bad-tempered baby."

"Poor Emmett," said Celia. Emmett had indeed cried more in his few months of life than Owen in his two years.

"Poor me," said Matt. "I need my sleep. I have something to show you upstairs."

He led her on up above the drawing room to his workroom, where she had learnt not to go without an invitation, and pulled the chain on the hanging gas lamp above the table. Out of the shadows sprang a picture already framed in gold. Celia herself as she had walked that last evening in Navplion, on the pale endless beach with the oranges in her hand, forever young in her white dress.

She looked at it in silence, suffocated with more emotion and happiness than she could encompass; touched beyond any words.

"I couldn't stand it," said Matt, "that you wouldn't look like that forever."

"So I do now."

"Now you do."

"That's what you were drawing that morning in the dawn."

"Yes. Now you can grow old as fast as you like."

She turned and put her arms about him, laying her head on his shoulder.

"Only when you do, my dearest Matt. Only when you do."

And to both of them it seemed impossible. Their own life was set and perfect as the picture on the easel, even though these were years of fearful turmoil in the country itself. The outraged, victimized poor were beginning to organize their campaigns more forcefully against the absent and tyrannical landlords. All the harsh western lands were adrift with the wandering and homeless and starving people. Hurled without warning from their homes by landlords who set no foot in Ireland save when the fancy took them for the shooting or the hunting; and God protect any poor farmer who might try to interfere with either on his bit of land. Matt's acres were acrawl with refugees from further west, and all his resources strained to care even for his own, should the harvest not be up to standard; able to do no more than instruct Bonnington to give the wanderers something to take them on their way, probably only to the great workhouse above the sea in Clifden, already crammed to its four grim walls with the starving and the dying. In the streets of Dublin, from his shining carriage, he watched the weather with an eye as sharp and critical as if he stood in his own fields, and had Bonnington write to him every evening. Usually it was a sorry tale of hamstrung cattle and burnt fields around the country and a dreadful resentment smoldering towards fire. But there was never trouble on his land, even though it meant he had to leave Celia more often than he cared; to curb his impatience, on the slow noisy train to Galway, and then on the long drive out to Owenscourt through mellow land that gave the lie to all of it. To do no more than ride the land and show them he was there.

Every time he went, no matter how she struggled to control it, the flood of hostility to Peggy Cannon would swamp Celia like a sickness. She did not want to go herself and yet could not bear to admit the thought of the woman, and Matt, in the same house. By now she realized he was aware of it and had no patience with it, watching her with a sort of threatening calm whenever he said he must go into the country. As if he dared her even to change the expression on her face. While he was actually away, jealous imaginings ate her like a cancer, all the more terrible for their secrecy and guilt and the fact that she knew them to be nonsense. Matt did not see Peggy Cannon as she did, but no amount of reasoning in all her lonely battles could convince her.

"You will come back quickly," was all she dare say.

"Of course," he would answer. "As soon as possible."

By the warmth of his kiss she would know whether she had managed in that farewell to keep the image of Peggy Cannon from her eyes.

In 1880, when Owen was six, and Emmett four, they went down for one of what seemed to Owen the endless magic summers belonging alone to Owenscourt. Below the glow of happiness with which the child looked westward, there had been long letters from Bonnington, rather more vague and urgent than usual, his thin hand straying on the pages. There was a new movement in the persecuted land, started against an agent called Boycott, belonging to Lord Erne. He had flung a starving family onto the roads for what amounted to a few pence rent, ripping the roof away above their heads with his machines before they were even out the poor gap of their front door, and the woman in near birth to a child. Celia thought of Peggy Cannon and the linnet. For the first time, it seemed, according to Bonnington, the people themselves had found an answer to such tyranny. Within a day there was not a thing the man could get done for him inside the county. Not a farrier would shoe a horse, nor a laborer carry a bale of hay; no man would look at him across the street nor give him time of day, nor any woman wash his clothes nor sweep his house nor sell him food if he should starve for it.

" 'Tis the fashion now in all quarters," wrote Bonnington primly, "and please God it may be the thing will bring these persecutors to their knees."

Celia's mind was elsewhere, torn with the ambivalence she felt over every one of these summers that brought Owen to such rapture. Before she even thought properly, her mind had seized its chance.

"Is it wise to take the boys down there, Matt?" she said. "If there is all that trouble. Would I not do better to let you go alone, and take them to Kingstown or Sandycove or even to Salthill in Galway and then we'd be near you. Would it not be safer?"

Matt turned and looked at her. He was weary after a long day at the Shops, and his eyes looked a little tired and hot from the hours of close work. That did nothing to dim the long considering look he gave her, as if debating whether he should speak. In the end he merely shifted in his chair, and stared out the window at the shadows creeping over the church roof.

"Isn't Owenscourt where they belong," was all he said, mildly, but she took it for the order that it was. "And isn't it well," he added, "that they see all sides of it. And I'd have thought you'd want to see your mother."

She closed her mouth on the leaping bright suggestion that her mama could come and stay with them in Salthill, and instead went over to give him a contrite and wordless kiss that was apology and promise all in one. He was a little heavier now, giving balance to his height, and all his air of swift enthusiasm tempered with authority. She thought him far more handsome than when she had married him and felt shamed she should so mark the bright happiness of these years with the drab, unquenchable tarnish of her stupid jealousy. Matt put an arm around her acknowledging the apology.

"Owen would perish," she acknowledged. "Simply perish, if he were not allowed there at least once a year."

"Maybe you and your mama can have a week or ten days in Salthill at the end," said Matt generously, and her shame was deeper, knowing she did not deserve it.

At six Owen had the same alert impulsive look as his father, physically quick and excellent at all sports, disarming in his openness; a contempt even as a child for the devious and cheap. With his small copy of Matt's face it would seem he had absorbed Matt's spirit, or set himself out to do so. Every one of his father's interests was faithfully copied by the bright-haired child, begging every Saturday to be taken to the Shops, where he would painstakingly attach himself to one of the men, poking the fire under the steam bath or stirring the pots of glue; carefully cleaning the fine brilliant paintbrushes of the design shop. Matt took little apparent heed of him, only the quick occasional sidelong glance betraying his pride and pleasure. And when a vehicle was finished they would stand together in the shadows of the coach house, their hands behind their backs and the selfsame expression of satisfaction on both their faces.

It was Owen too, knowing he was named for the house, who would always be around the land with Matt at Owenscourt. Across the front of his father's saddle when he was small, and on his own shaggy pony later, jogging at Matt's heels as if he might be Bonnington. As proud of every acre as if it were already his.

Until he began to go about with Antonia.

She was his first thought that year, when Celia went up to tell them they would be going west in the following week. Emmett smiled too, his fair bland face implying that he was clever even to remember the place at all.

"Owncour," he said proudly.

"Darling," said his mother, delighted with him. Her Benjamin, her fair one, who reached to all her quiet moments when Matt and Owen seemed to crowd the biggest room simply by being in it. Emmett was a slightly silent, dreamy child, with an air of being completely contented with the life inside his own head; any excursions outside it were merely by way of pleasing those he loved. He climbed down from the white rocking horse and laid his head against his mother's pale-blue skirt. Gracie looked down at him from her sewing, repressing faint disapproval. Not half the little man that Master Owen was.

Master Owen had leapt up from where he was painting at the big oilcloth-covered table, already showing some measure of his father's talent.

"Hurrah, hurrah, hurrah," he shouted and began a war dance round the table, tousling the rug and dropping his paintbrush with a splodge of scarlet in the middle of his picture. "Oh, hurray, Owenscourt! Mother, I can see Antonia. I can, can't I, and we can finish putting the dam across the stream. We can, can't we? We can."

She shushed his eagerness, and did not see how she could stop them. Even she knew it was carrying too far her foolish fears of Peggy Cannon to suggest that not only was she beyond the pale, but her child was also. Yet she found it difficult to be pleasant to Antonia. A withdrawn and unapproachable child, who appeared to have no feelings towards anyone; except her father, to whom, when she was small, she would cling with all the passion of a little monkey. As if to life itself, staring out from the shelter of his arms at an apparently hostile world. Her father's astonishing dark-blue eyes under a fall of jet-black hair. A peaky introverted little face.

Now she was attached to Owen.

They had begun to draw together in the short days at Christmas, and by Easter they were as thick as thieves; Antonia in her outgrown skirts as nimble as any boy, ready, determined and unsmiling, to prove to Owen there was nothing that she couldn't do. Owen was delighted, bored by the ever placid company of Emmett, and a little apologetic first towards his father lest he think he was being abandoned.

"You see, she is my age, Papa, and it's good to have someone to play with like that."

Matt touched the small anxious face.

"Go on away, Son, and be happy," he said, touched to his warm heart to see his child stumping off on some expedition with John Julius's daughter, a calico bag of food between them lest the boring business of coming back to eat should make the day too short.

"Are they safe, Matt?"

Celia, not so warmly, also watched the small figures dwindling down toward the lake.

"Haven't I beggared myself fencing in the lake?" he asked her. "And they know not to leave the land. And aren't there plenty of people all around to watch out for them. Leave them alone, Mama. Antonia's a year older."

When he found a pony for the girl, Celia failed to hold her tongue.

"Matt! Not even Emmett has a pony!"

"He doesn't want one," Matt answered with his maddening reason. "When the day comes he'll even sit the saddle of my horse I'll get him one. But I'll have no pony eating its head off while Emmett does his traveling in the basket trap with Gracie."

"But Antonia!"

She tried to stop, knowing her anger was not against the child, but against yet another encroachment of the life of Peggy Cannon on her own. Among all the words crowding to her lips she searched for something she could say about the impropriety of giving a pony to the daughter of her lady's maid, deeply and sickly aware that her anger was not because Antonia was the maid's child but that the maid was Peggy Cannon. Why could the canker never leave her even in as trivial a thing as this. It was as though Peggy threatened her always, with some vague and future danger that could only be averted by thrusting her from their lives. And she was wife to John Julius. She was as likely to be thrust out as herself.

"The child's a neat little rider," Matt said. "And her brother is too. They learnt on the asses round the land as Owen did. Be fair, Mama, the nearest Emmett has ever been to a horse is the wooden one up there in the playroom."

Their eyes locked, hers full of a desperate appeal to be rescued from what she could not help. Matt's obdurate, seeing nothing but a petty jealousy she must learn to quell. Both of them aware of what the disagreement was about, both forgetting that the rocking horse was white, symbol of their happy marriage.

It may have been that Matt remembered. He came to her across the porch between the pillars and took her hands in his, kissing her warmly and deeply, feeling all the unhappiness that shook her.

"Let it go, dearest," he said to her. "Let it go," and the request was over far more than the passing annoyance that Antonia should have a pony. "Let it go."

Matt was unaware that even between the children the same divisions couldn't be forgotten.

They were building a dam where the brown tumbling stream fell down a slope of greening stones towards the little bridge before the lake, Antonia with her worn skirt kilted up around her bare legs, her long black hair hanging like a flag about her intent face. As they packed in stones and earth above the little waterfall, Owen slipped and fell, covering his breeches with the sedgy mud.

Antonia peered through her hair.

"You'll be killed for that."

"For what?"

He looked at her in astonishment. He was never killed for anything except things killing was right for, like telling a lie or half murdering Emmett when he got too silly.

"For what?" he asked her again, pushing and packing the mud that still let through a steady trickle of water, falling with firm maddening plonks into the pool below.

Antonia was busy herself, not looking up as she spoke, as if what she said was so self-evident, it was hardly necessary.

"Ah," she said, "the rich always have to take care of their clothes. Isn't my mother always sewing away at your mother's."

Owen barely understood Antonia's mother's function in the house, and was too young and uncomplicated to see the underlying resentment.

"What's rich?" he asked her, standing with a fistful of mud while the breach grew bigger.

Antonia looked at him pityingly, thrusting aside the long strands of black hair, plastering them with muddy water.

"Rich is what you are," she said, almost scathingly. "And the big house and all you want and dressed like a gentleman and we only building mud pies. Aren't all my brother's clothes Emmett's old ones?"

Owen was upset, regarding it as an insult, having on only an old pair of breeches, and one of the gray ganseys Matt had got for them all down in Tuam, the same as the men wore in the fields, and the right thing, he said, for the holidays.

"Well, I don't care," he said boldly, not knowing what else to say, and bent again over his dam, never dreaming that he would hold the same argument with the prickly Antonia when they were both grown up; the girl still trailing all the resentments of her mother.

None of these strains reached life in Dublin, where there was complete content, without the growing edge of their relationship that neither Matt nor Celia seemed to be unable to avoid in Owenscourt. For Celia there was always the effort of endurance. The never-changing faint and barely unexpressed contempt; all the invented messages that brought the girl to the bedroom unnecessarily when Matt was there. The small continuous encounters when, though Matt did no more than speak pleasantly and pass by, the girl had seen to it that even for a moment she was in his mind.

She was always glad to get away from Owenscourt,

haunted beyond the present irritations by some premonition of future trouble.

She alone had to suppress pangs of guilty pleasure when they would all pile into the carriage, her mother weeping on the doorstep and the two boys, particularly Owen, glum and silent, to drive off into Galway City where Matt lodged the traveling coach. Antonia would run beside the carriage all the way down to the grand gates where she got lost in the customary clamoring brood.

"I can't be right," Matt said, "and she a good woman and her husband dead years back, but I swear there's more of them every time." Desperately he turned his pockets inside out for pennies.

"I feel," he said, looking back at the house between the trees, as they left the shrieking mass behind them, "as if I have a leg off every time I leave it."

It was clear from the bags of stones and mosses and poor drying plants with which he hoped to recreate Owenscourt in the window boxes of the city, that the sad-faced Owen felt exactly the same.

Celia herself could not wait for the soft autumn dusks, flooded with lamplight in the squares and crescents; the first fires sweet smelling through the house; the smoke rising from the piles of leaves along the gardens; the sharp exhilarating touch of frost, and with it all the social life that had taken them so long to reach. Their friends were in a circle that edged on the artistic; evenings of music and good food and the bright sharp edge of Dublin conversation. Celia realized what her mother had long ago hinted, that Matt was excessively attractive to women, nor did he conceal his pleasure in their attentions; flocking round him like a swarm of colored birds, begging him to sing for them; with many of them, their pretty manners only a surface on the red claws of nature as they vied to get him entirely to themselves. Yet none of them troubled her as Peggy Cannon did.

He would come back to her sometimes in hot crowded drawing rooms grinning sheepishly, with the air of a man who had been through a storm, and she would greet him unperturbed, and struggle to understand why she felt no threat. Here she understood, without rancor, flirting gently herself with the gentlemen who were far from indifferent to her fair intelligent beauty, that it was Matt's arm on which she would leave at the end of the evening; Matt's carriage that would take her home; and Matt's bed to which she would be taken with undiminishing pleasure.

"Why," she asked herself constantly, "could she not take the same attitude with Peggy Cannon?"

One year, since Matt was too busy with the Shops, they didn't go to Owenscourt for Easter, but to Celia's secret delight took instead a small yellow-painted house in a Georgian crescent running out beyond Kingstown towards the old Martello Tower. From the tall windows they could look out at the high green bulk of Howth and watch the evening sunshine on the Golden Spears; and to the boys' delight, see the white mail boats coming in and out between the long arms of the piers. However late, Matt was able to clop down along the country lanes, with the new railway puffing between him and the shining sea; to be with Celia in time for supper.

Owen and Emmett reveled in the picnics on the lower slopes of Howth, banked with curling fern and budding rhododendron. Celia sat contentedly in the shade among the picnic baskets while they rolled and tumbled down the green hill above the sea, under the indulgent eye of Gracie and the new young groom with the strange French name of Bourdain, and the crisp black hair and bright blue eyes that were obviously captivating Gracie. Watching the beginning of a decorous courtship, Celia hoped that she might keep them both if they should marry.

One soft bright day she came up from the strand with Gracie and the two boys, who had been bowling their hoops along the endless shining sand. Both children were sun flushed, bright eyed, and lively in the clear air, Owen as always a little overexcited; overcome with the splendor of his golden days and more specifically with the fine shell of a sea urchin he had found down at the water's edge.

"Will you look at it, Emm. It's a sea urchin. An animal lived in there, didn't it, Mama. Didn't it!"

Emmett leaned with his obliging smile, and Owen let go his red hoop and leaned the urchin on his leg the better to show off his treasure with two hands. The strand spread glittering in the evening sun, the last bait diggers bent black above the golden pools, and a small wind came whispering from the sea and took the hoop. Out into the middle of the road among the carriage wheels bowling their owners for the evening drive.

"Me hoop," cried Owen and was gone, before either Celia or Gracie could reach out a hand, and it was suddenly a black-clad arm from nowhere that shot out and hauled him back to safety and retrieved the hoop.

It was seconds before Celia could even look up, clutching the child in a reaction of sick terror while Gracie railed at him with fury born of shock. Only the loud and safe reality of Owen's howls brought her round, free to look away and thank the hand that had saved him.

Three grave-looking gentlemen, but the one who had moved so rapidly had a blanched white face above a spade beard and two singularly penetrating eyes. His lifted hat revealed a balding dome. Object of every political picture and cartoon in Ireland.

"How strange," she said, too distraught to be anything but blunt. "Mr. Parnell."

He bowed formally, his clothes as grave and black as an undertaker's.

"I am flattered you recognize me, madam."

"And I have to thank you, sir, for catching my son. He is very impetuous."

"It is in the nature of children."

There was no more to say and after a few stiff sentences during which she found herself quickly restless under the strange deep-set and compelling eye, he bowed again and said good-bye. She moved off after Gracie and the chastened and tearful Owen and all the time she could feel he stood and watched her.

There was no chance to decide whether or not she should tell Matt, for Emmett forestalled her the moment he came swinging into the house, alive with pleasure to have left the city. Emmett poured it all out about the wicked Owen running out into the street and the black-haired man who had run out to catch him.

"Believe it or not, Matt, it was Charles Stuart Parnell. I recognized him from all the pictures."

The last thing she expected was that Matt would break into immediate anger, completely unconcerned about Owen.

"Really, Matt. I did only exchange two words with the man. Would you not have had me thank him? He did save Owen's life even if you don't happen to like him."

"I didn't say I didn't like him. The man will crucify himself for Ireland. In him lies the hope for all of us. He will go down in history. But that is another matter to having my wife speaking to him in the streets of Kingstown."

Even as he spoke, drawing-room gossip flashed through her mind. The savior of Ireland, it seemed, had a fearsome reputation with women and might well lose everything for Ireland over his affair with his agent's wife. All of London was agog and scandalized with it all.

"Was Gracie with you," demanded Matt.

"Of course."

That seemed to make it a little better and she shrugged and let it go. It was unlikely to happen again and it was not worth angering Matt on this lovely evening.

But, she thought—so. So. Sauce for the goose is sauce for the gander. I have to accept his outburst over Charles Parnell for only half a dozen words in the street. Can he not accept that Peggy Cannon affects me in exactly the same way and for the same unreasonable reasons. She stared out from their upper window over the darkening sea to the great dim bulk of Howth, solid as a continent in the dusk. Should she try and speak of it all. From that trivial incident she might make him understand. Bring into the open this only flaw in their perfect marriage. It lay between their eyes and their minds all the time in Owenscourt. Turning, she smiled ruefully and gently at her handsome Matt, reading now in a circle of lamplight. She knew it useless. Matt did not like emotions turned into words. Into pictures—yes, like the one of her forever young with her branch of oranges. That was a protest of feelings he had felt too deep for words. But to ask him to examine his feelings for Peggy Cannon and her non-existent ones for Charles Parnell— She smiled again and laid a hand on his shoulder.

"Will I get a shawl," she said, "and we'll take a turn by the sea before it is quite dark?"

And lost the only moment, never to recur.

Chapter 8

It was during those stretching, settling years that they had all driven over one fine summer day from Owenscourt to Westport, for the wedding of Hugh Charles. In the open victoria on the day before the wedding, they faced off through the mountains with Mrs. Healey beaming opposite, beside the proud small figure of Owen, stiff with self-consciousness in his first real sailor suit.

For two years or more Hugh Charles had been the secret laughingstock of all the county, and the object of all their fascinated speculations. Watching with alarm as his father drifted into senility under the warm affections of the dairymaid, he had with speed and prudence abandoned his meager and unprofitable business in the law and returned to Holly House to run the land. He didn't say what it was that had him starting from his sleep at nights cold with apprehension. He feared the dairymaid could be sharper than she seemed; and alone with his father in the house, might manage God knew what sort of infiltrations into the money they had got from Matt. He was terrified that his father would fall too far under the influence of the plain, hefty middle-aged woman who now so improbably dominated all his life, living with some sense of secrecy and prudence only in two rooms on the upper floor; seldom even sighted except when seen scuttling up the stairs with a laden tray after one of her orgies of cooking for old Thomas. And even these she did late and early to avoid being seen.

Hugh Charles sweated in fear to think what foolish sense of gratitude might be breeding in his father's aging head.

At last he rode determinedly up to Holly House.

"Let's be honest, Father," he said, trying to avoid wrinkling his face against the solid odors of the one room where they lived and slept, composing it instead carefully into an expression of disarming honesty, sitting with little conviction on his natural slyness. "With the rheumatics now you're in no state to run the farm. I tell you they're eating the money from you out there round the land. Who else is there to tell them otherwise?"

The old man looked long out through the clouded window as though he could see them all, crowded down there eating up his money, and his face grew fierce.

"Don't I send the woman out?" he said.

He glowered from his armchair, refusing to admit what he had admitted for months by sending the woman out, with his orders to the men. Hugh Charles kept his careful smile, and tried not to show that it was exactly the woman he was afraid of; being unsure of the exact depth and loyalty of his father's feelings for her.

"Aha, the woman," he said, and spread careful deprecating hands, hunched against the cold of the room. His mother had begun to pull the place together before she finally got up and left, but the improvements hadn't reached this far. He had no thought for her. Everyone knew there was nothing Matt O'Connor wouldn't do for her, and he was only very careful always to be civil and never to cross her for that might be crossing Matt, who was in the end the source of everything for them all.

"The woman, Dada," he said, and did not think how ill the

childish word sat on his thick lips, "can turn a churn with the best of them, but she's no farmer. Are you quite sure she's caring properly for the money?"

Thomas shot him a glance from under tufted snow-white eyebrows, moist eyes filled with a doubt he knew he would never have the strength to resolve. He shifted painfully in his chair, and with quiet satisfaction Hugh Charles watched the thought creeping into his mind that there was one way to keep a check on it all and who should you trust better than your own son. Although in God's name he had always thought Hugh Charles far too like himself for safety. Still and all, he was the right one to do it.

"Would you think that," he asked him. "Would you think she might be cheating me?"

Hugh Charles shrugged, an expression of unwilling sadness on his face. She may, he implied, do everything from washing your feet and paring your corns to combing your wisps of hair, but she is only a woman after all. And hasn't one of them already gone without any reason and left you. He leaned to the poor fire and rubbed his hands, and then looked up and planted that very doubt. His father clasped his knotted hands over his stick and struggled for the shrewdness of judgment he had prided himself on before it was all eaten away in pain.

"She's only a woman after all," said Hugh Charles.

Old Thomas grunted. Wasn't the boy right. His wife had proved a poor sort of a thing, and in the heel of the hunt gone off and left him, and his daughter had as good as sold him down the river into the claws of Matt O'Connor. Frowning and blinking for a long time out at the pale daylight over the fields, he turned at last and gave in, and relegated the dairymaid to her proper position; Hugh Charles came smiling back to Holly House.

But he was younger and wilier than the failing old man. While he managed to keep him content in his room upstairs with long spurious reports about the farm, on the ground floor and in the stables, at the race meetings and meets and bars and coursing meets around the country, he set out to establish himself as a gentleman farmer. And would have them all take note as to the gentleman.

Matt had ridden over one day, ostensibly to welcome him back to Holly House, but in fact to try and discover what he was up to; having no more trust of Hugh Charles than when he had brought his own lawyer down from Dublin for the wedding contract.

He snorted with disgust, yet could not help but be amused.

"You should see the squireen," he said to Celia when he came back. "The breeches, by God, and the cut of them, and the checkered waistcoats and the stock held in with a pin like a horse's head and it having the look of pure gold."

"Ah, come, Matt, he probably got it in the bazaar in Galway!"

"But the height of the talking! And the new hunters in the stables. Will you tell me who is paying for that, and from the sullen look of the men about the fields I'd say they're waiting for their wages. And the fences falling down and the sedge man-high in the ditches. I'll have to keep an eye on him. I can't have them all on my hands in a bad harvest. But tell me too who is paying the Hunt Subscription, and the fellow up to his neck in debt in Tuam! But the grandeur of the laddo! The grandeur. And as a farmer he wouldn't know a bullock from a haycock. Didn't I tell you long ago he'd be no better than his father."

Celia looked at him, sunburnt from riding his own fields; in a loose shirt open to his brown throat and an old pair of nankeen breeches stuffed into soft boots. She recalled his grandeur the first day she had met him, but he was after all then on his way to take dinner with the Canon, and call perhaps on the way on the respectable family in Holly House with the object of meeting their daughter.

She smiled.

"Yes?"

"I was just hoping that when poor Hugh Charles goes riding round his land in all his finery, no stupid girl is going to throw yellow paint all over him."

Matt was off again, grinning, before he changed his face to bellow at Owen, who had come trotting round the house on his pony followed at a discreet distance by Bourdain; yelling at him that if he was going to ride any animal of his then he was not going to look like a sack of meal on it. Poor Bourdain came in for it next for allowing the child to sit badly.

Celia watched a moment and then left them to it, going off to search out her mother and tell her about Hugh Charles and all the new High Style over in Holly House.

On the morning of the wedding they left the Great Southern Hotel, on the high open bluff beyond Mulraney, where they had spent the night; a comfortable small drive into the church at Westport. Beyond them out to sea, Carrigahowley Castle slumbered in the warm sunshine on its island, wrapped in a spurious air of peace belying its bloody history. Across the shining bay the high cone of Croagh Patrick held its crown of cloud, and as they came round the head of the bay towards the town, swans in their hundreds lay like ships asleep among the tiny green islands scattering the shallow water.

"Oh, Mama, the big white birds!"

Owen was enchanted, and Celia smiled at him, proud of her handsome child, enchanting herself in her dress of pale silk, ruffled from neck to hem, and her hat, for bonnets were going out, that was no more than a fistful of roses tied with rich thick ribbons underneath her chin. Matt in his wedding finery looked admiringly at her and she at him, and Mrs. Healey looked at both of them and never forgot neither night nor morning to thank God for the way the whole queer business had turned out. A small wind came up and cleared the cloud from the high summit of Croagh Patrick, a firm promise of a fine day for the wedding as they bowled up to the church. They were pleased with themselves and in fine spirits.

"Oh, dear," thought Celia, in the few brief minutes it had taken them to walk the length of the dark and musty little church up to their places at the front of the congregation. "Oh, dear."

Hugh Charles, true to his present character, had led them to believe he was marrying something in the nature of an heiress. The daughter of an agricultural expert with a grand house, and unlimited money to spend on the marrying of his six lovely daughters. He had met her, apparently, at some county race meeting where only the quality were to be found, crowded on their brakes and carts, laying their rich and easy bets on the finest bloodstock in the land. Her mother, it appeared, was some sort of intellectual.

Matt had been as observant as Celia on their journey up the aisle.

"Agricultural expert," he whispered, nudging her sharply. "This all belongs to no more than a thistle cropper."

After all Hugh Charles had said, they never thought they might be doing wrong. But the short walk between the congregation had revealed no more than heavy boots and shiny country suits, and the bright dowdy finery that was the small-town best of Westport and the country round. All the faces turned in a sort of outrage to survey the Dublin finery being paraded so blatantly and tastelessly up the aisle.

"Will they rush us, do you think, on the way out?" Matt asked her, and she knew from the light in his eye that he was going to make nothing easy, being of such honesty of thought himself that little annoyed him like pretension.

"I can't take my dress off now," she whispered back.

"Why not?" said Matt.

An aged harmonium wheezed uneasily from the shadows behind them and slowly the bride came up the aisle to take her place beside a blanched and shaking Hugh Charles, who had materialized from the vestry a few moments earlier. Behind her trailed five ugly girls in pink bombazine and cheap paper roses, the worn toes of old slippers showing underneath their dresses.

"What did I tell you," Matt hissed, looking at the red outdoor complexion of the burly man who bore the bride on his arm. "Thistles! What's her name?"

"Alicocq. Be quiet!"

"What!"

She was pale. Pale as Hugh Charles himself, but then all brides were pale. Although this one had thick black, heavy hair that already had the air of coming down below its wreath of orange blossoms. Despite that she exuded an air of strong superiority over everybody present, including her bridegroom.

Celia managed to keep Matt in check through the marriage ceremony and the short Low Mass that followed, offering her own prayers of thanks that she had not to handle his boredom through the long responses of a High Mass; slightly startled by the one shrewd sweeping glance the bride threw over all the bridegroom's family as she turned to come down the church when it was over. Like a call to battle.

She felt astonished at such self-possession at such a time. Had Matt offered her the Satan as his first cousin as they came down from the altar on their wedding day, she would have smiled and shaken the proffered hoof, and never noticed there was anything wrong.

Her speculations were cut short by Matt's remarks when he found it was a Temperance wedding, indeed all the company being ardent Pioneers and disciples of Father Matthew. Celia's heart sank for Hugh Charles, and it sank also for Matt, who could not be held for more than ten civil minutes by the wilting lemonade and tasteless sandwiches.

"Let's go home," he said, and Celia could feel his good humor giving way. All the local people were holding away from them in their Dublin clothes as if they were a couple of cases of famine fever.

Before she could answer, the bride swept down on them with a regal air her yellowing bride gown didn't merit, Hugh Charles smirking at her heels.

"You must be Cee-leeah," she said, and bent with kind condescension to be kissed. Under Matt's sardonic eye Celia complied, remembering she was after all her brother's wife, for better or for worse, and would live at Holly House. No need to make an enemy at the very wedding feast.

"Ai'm delaighted to meet you," Alicocq said, and they all fell silent before the devastating refinement.

Hugh Charles looked down at his shining boots and fidgeted, and Celia knew he would give the same boots at a second's notice for a good stiff brandy. How was it going to work out? "Every since Ai met youah brother," the girl was going on, "Ai hev felt sorry for you."

Celia's astonished eyebrows asked her why. At her side she could hear Matt rumbling, and her mother gasped. She reached out a foot and stamped on Matt's toe.

"All alone out theah," Alicocq went on, "the only point of real society, Hugh Charles tells me. It will be so much easier for you when Ai am thea, and can take mai share of the local entertaining. Ai hev plenty of experience heah, where we hev always entertained a great deal."

Matt looked over at the weak lemonade and barren sandwiches, and Celia did not know what to say, caught between pity and embarrassment and the terrible danger of meeting Matt's eye. But she had no need to say anything. Alicocq had taken charge.

"Ai won't wait the customary time," she said, tossing her veil with authority and loosing another coil of heavy hair. "Ai shall hev mai first At Home almost at once."

Matt slid a hand under Mrs. Healey's arm and squeezed it.

"I hope someone comes," he said deferentially, and she flicked him up and down with her opaque eyes, not usually reckoning that men needed much attention. Celia could feel Matt leaning a little heavily on her shoulder, and struggled to keep down the laughter that was choking her. "The At Homes in Celia's mother's day were famous," he went on, "weren't they, dearest. And this," he added, with a sudden sharp edge to his voice, for he did not like to see his loved mother-in-law overlooked, "this is Mrs. Healey. Your bridegroom's mother."

"Ah, yes," said Alicocq, and freed a limp hand again from her fading roses. "Ah, yes." To the reigning queen of Holly House, the dowager meant little. "Ai understand," she added with unconcealed relief, "that you live now with Mr. O'Connor."

"And won't interfere with me," she implied, and Celia saw her mother's mouth crumple with laughter.

"Well," said Mrs. Healey, as the bride continued on her regal way, "I'd have given my son credit for more sense. Well, he's made his bed and now he must lie on it."

"Haven't we done enough now for civility," Matt said then, and this time Celia couldn't hold him.

He edged them firmly towards the looped opening of the airless tent, and before anyone could protest they had made a swift round of farewells and apologies.

"So very sorry. A long drive."

"The child will be too tired."

"Matt has to be off to Dublin in the morning."

They retrieved Owen from where he was happily picking a bouquet to pieces and were gone, followed by the self-righteous glances that said didn't they know all the time that city people had no manners, and to go like that before the bride and groom.

In the carriage they stretched out blissfully, bowling past Croagh Patrick and out towards Carrigahowley suspended like a fairy castle in the mist, back to the splendid cheerfulness of the hotel, where in their sitting room above the shining water, Matt flung himself into an armchair and demanded that Owen pull his boots off.

"Ai do faind," he said loftily, "that mai feet get tired. That's the man, Owen. Will we go back now?" he said to Celia and Mrs. Healey. "Will we go back now, and tell her about the dairymaid?"

They laughed until they held their sides, and Owen, sensing the atmosphere, danced round in Matt's boots and his mother's hat.

"Poor girl," said Celia.

"Not a bit of it," said Mrs. Healey, and Matt nodded.

"Not a bit of it."

He lunged for the long green bellrope and called for champagne for all of them. By the end of the first glass they were helpless again with laughter, Matt mincing up and down the room in his stocking feet being Alicocq, and round them Owen leaping and shrieking with laughter himself, not understanding what was so funny, but knowing that in the present mood no one would stop him.

They piled again into the carriage when they could face it, and drove home, still in their finery, singing along the lonely road around the head of Lough Mask, falling silent only where the long fingers of shadow crept through the vast valleys over to the west, looking up in silence at the small white houses perched in their dreadful isolation on small green patches in the barren land, stalked in their loneliness by the constant specters of famine and of death.

Owen did not know why they fell silent, but lay against his mother and watched the great hills moving past him, rounded on the sky, sleeping at last for most of the way home.

By the time that Owen was eight, and the blond and steady Emmett just turned six, Celia was in a period of immense tranquility, sure of herself, and proud and secure in her children; her husband no longer a bright fragment of some astonishing dream, but a flesh-and-blood man whose love sustained and held her and whose needs and vagaries she must meet with every day. She had even managed to discipline herself to accept Peggy Cannon without apparent reaction, although nothing would ever still the disturbance that seized her should she even look out a window and see the girl picking her way across the yard into the house, knowing that for an hour or more she must bear the condescension and the insolent eyes. In her bedroom and Matt's.

However, all of it now was overlaid by the never diminishing power and certainty of their marriage and their love. She walked her days in a state of positive content, savoring each hour as a precious gift, not as she once had done in fear and superstition that God would come and take it all away; rejoicing now in her world and the power it gave her; deeply aware at last that she had as much to offer Matt as he to her. She was a long way now from the Chinese Masterpiece, and even the girl with the oranges in her hand, looking back at her as she might at a tiny figure through the wrong end of a telescope. Herself. But far far away.

She was quite calm when Matt looked up from a long letter from Bonnington with creases across his forehead. He announced unwillingly that he was afraid he must make a quick visit to Owenscourt.

"Why, Matt? It's dreadful weather."

It was a dark November, and for traveling it must be something serious.

She reached for his cup and poured him more tea. It was one of the changes since the children, that she was now expected to be up early and preside across his breakfast table. She lifted the lid of the silver dish.

"More kedgeree?" He shook his head.

"Bonnington says he must give up work. He's ill."

Celia looked back across the years.

"He's been looking frail for a long time. Hanging like a creaking gate. Will you let him go?"

"I don't want to. He's invaluable. Perhaps we'll see what we can do with a younger man to help him. But I must go down and talk about it."

Tranquilly she saw him off the next morning for the train, secure in the thought that without her presence, there would be little reason for Peggy Cannon to be in the house. And there would be little time for Matt to go and see John Julius with so much to settle.

"Take care, my darling."

He was preoccupied, wrapped in his traveling ulster against the foggy cold, his beaver hat down on his nose.

"Mind the boys," he said.

"I will."

Bourdain whipped up the horses and he was gone, into the chill mist of the Dublin morning.

He came home five days later in much higher fettle, two at a time up the marble stairs, throwing his ulster and his hat on the green sofa in the drawing room, rubbing his hands eagerly before the fire.

She hugged him, delighted to see him back so cheerful.

"The boys?" Always his first and last thought.

"Perfect. Owen has another big back tooth."

"Is Bonnington better, then?" she asked him, settling herself back in her chair.

He didn't even hear her.

"I imagine that this visit, I've done the best thing Owenscourt has seen for many a long day," he said.

He walked over and kissed her again with a smile, as if he had only just seen her. She could feel the cold smoky night on his skin.

"What's that," she said. Found, she thought, some really promising lad to help Bonnington. She picked up her crewel work again. Cushions for the little sitting room at Owenscourt.

"I've made," Matt said beaming, "I've made John Julius Cannon my agent."

She should have known, but it did nothing to soften the blow that was almost physical. She knew her eyes grew dark and the smile left her face. John Julius indeed. Who better. By now he knew every corner and acre of Owenscourt and was that necessary cut above the other laborers of which he had so long been one. And because it was all Matt's he loved it as he would love his own. Oh, there would be no one for the job like John Julius. Matt was right in that.

But.

Matt was taking Peggy Cannon from a subservient position in her bedroom, and bringing her to her dinner table. At least once a month as they had entertained Mr. and Mrs. Bonnington. Giving to her a position of much more equality. She would not need any longer to curtsy when she met him, waiting for him to pass by, unless he himself saw fit to speak. She could stop and chat as old Mrs. Bonnington would do. They would live in the white pleasant house beyond the stables.

"They will move into the house," was all she said, lamely.

"They will. Next week. The Bonningtons are going back to Attymon where her family came from."

He said no more, but the smile had left his face, and his eyes were severe as he settled himself into his chair; letting her know in silence that there would be no nonsense. That if John Julius Cannon was his agent, then she had certain duties to his wife. He was baffled by her, seeing no more in Peggy Cannon than in any other woman on the estate; except that she was the wife of John Julius and for that she had his friendship, and by God, she should have Celia's also.

But for Celia, the man in the middle of the road with the dark-blue eyes, and the girl with the linnet in the cage, had moved out at last as she had known they would do, from the background of her life to take their place in its immediate forefront.

Chapter 9

As it turned out the time was short for the enduring of Peggy Cannon. Matt was feverishly anxious to get down to Owenscourt for Easter, alert to all the pleasures of going round his lands with John Julius, who had sent him concise and excellent reports all through the winter. Easter was only a month and not too hard to handle, except in things like finding Antonia sitting eating apples on her stairs with an inimical look on her thin face that said she knew she was in the right, and rather enjoyed the displeasure she would cause. Owen saw Celia's face and drew her to one side.

"Mama," he whispered. "It's all right, isn't it? Papa said to us that Antonia and James were different now, and we could be much better friends with them."

Papa did, did he. Papa said a bit too much without speaking to her first. Honesty quelled her spurt of anger. Would she have minded were it Bonnington's child, sitting there looking at her with shrewd blue eyes above the apple? Would she have wanted to turn her out? She ruffled Owen's hair and saw the smile come to his doubtful face.

"Of course," she said. "It is exactly as Papa said."

Owen beamed.

"You should see old Bonnington's house now that Antonia's mama has it. It's grand."

"I can imagine," Celia said wryly, and smiled at Antonia, who gave her back an unchanged and speculative stare.

Matt was as happy as a dog with two tails, he and John Julius coming in together in the gray days, flushed with the chilly wind, to close themselves for hours in the agent's office, full of their plans for Owenscourt and the bettering of the farmlands.

Faced with the inevitable evenings, Celia called up her defenses and would have no more of the comfortable little suppers by themselves she had enjoyed with the Bonningtons. As well as her mother there would be Hugh Charles and Alicocq from Holly House. And Canon Walsh, who was always ready to ride the nine miles from Tuam to escape for an evening from his bleak clerical establishment. She brought them all to her table and to her excellent meals in an attempt to lose Peggy Cannon in the number.

Furious, she had to admit the woman was too subtle and she was outclassed. No one was going to crowd out Peggy Cannon. Did they all talk eagerly of something of interest, she would sit in lovely silence, very upright, the fair hair gleaming on her shoulders in the candlelight, until in the end Matt, and it was always Matt, would turn to draw her into the conversation, when she would have the table to herself, never at a loss in her high light voice, all the others spent.

Did the others fall silent, then it would be Peggy who talked, even above the long determined vowels of Alicocq, slender hands gesturing, well-kept fingers never betraying that she had ever done menial work, long dark lashes fluttering for Matt's admiration.

Across the candlelight and the fine food, the Waterford glass and the splendid silver of Matt's family, an undeclared war was waged between the two women. Celia to put Peggy Cannon in the background, that was her place even now; and Peggy Cannon to reduce and undermine.

It was always with obvious pleasure that Matt took up the port decanter and passed it for the prelude of the serious talking of the evening; catching Celia's eye for her to remove her ladies. Up in the drawing room around the coffee cups Peggy never spoke at all, reverting to her air of mute derision, looking at the lovely velvet chair before she sat in it as if it might not be quite clean; silently questioning the quality of the fragile Meissen cups; putting down the coffee barely tasted.

Celia could feel her mother seething just as she was, on the other end of the long sofa, and she would finish up an evening of entertaining Peggy Cannon as exhausted as if it had been a harvest home.

"Mama," she said one night, "that woman dominates this house."

Peggy had gone drifting out on John Julius's arm at the end of a particularly trying evening, carrying proudly, under her warm shawl, the first of the bustles that were only now becoming the rage of Dublin. She was also one of the first to cut a fringe to the front of her hair, maddeningly above crimping it, since the fair tendrils fell perfectly into the fine curls that were whispered as the newest royal fashion in the palaces of England.

"Dominates it." She gathered her own shawl round her and stared after Peggy and John Julius as Peggy's dress became a pale shadow in the chilly spring night. Matt had gone quickly back to his port after his good-byes, and to enveigle the Canon into a game of whist. "I swear to you, Mama, she is better dressed than I am, and it costs me a fortune up there in Dublin."

Mrs. Healey sighed. The thorn in her daughter's marriage grew sharper with the years.

"You must allow her all her talents," she said. "She makes every stitch herself. She's very clever with the needle."

"But, Mama, how does she find out? And who is there to show off to?

"Except Matt," she thought, but her mother answered differently.

"There's you," she said shrewdly. "And she reads *The Ladies' Home Journal* just as you or I do. Hasn't she John Julius in buying it for her every Fair day when he's in Galway. And isn't she in with him too, every time that she can go. In and out of the shops the livelong day."

Celia didn't ask her mother how she knew all this.

"Mama," she said, "how did I let it happen?" and her mother understood her. How had she become the victim, in her own house.

"You're afraid of her." And she thought, privately, have good reason to be. Mind you John Julius would kill the woman did she ever do anything serious to upset the marriage, but then the damage would be done.

Celia voiced her thought.

"Have I not a right to be afraid of her."

Her mother idly picked a dead leaf off a bay tree at her side, and looked out over the dark park, where an owl hooted somewhere, down beside the lake.

"You have," she admitted. Constant dripping would wear away a stone and the handsome Matt O'Connor was no stone. The woman had been put into a better position by what Matt himself had done for the husband. Celia must be as aware as she was of a new light in Matt's eyes as he looked at the fashionable agent's wife, so much more noticeable than Celia's maid. A new response, to open and deliberate seductiveness that was all ostensibly harmless, since it was in public. In Matt's expression now there was admiration and a slight excitement, as if some tree he had transplanted was blossoming beyond all expectation. Transferring to her, almost innocently at the moment, all the deep and lasting affection he had felt so long for his friend John Julius.

John Julius too was aware, silent in Peggy's presence at the supper tables; allowing her to take her stage; embarrassed to the core of his heart that she should so use the privilege Matt had given him. Aware too, as Mrs. Healey was, of the riding lessons she had asked for and was being given; and of the artlessly contrived meetings arrived at by careful watching of Matt's every habit; far more dangerous than the sly sliding glances before others.

Only Matt himself seemed heedless, enjoying it all with blithe pleasure, innocent in his own innocence of intent; happy as if God had been good enough to give him a second sun.

After talking with her mother, Celia knew there was one thing she had to end, too dangerous to be resolved simply by the end of the time in Owenscourt.

She could not control a little flutter of ebbing courage as she lay in wait for Matt in the hall one afternoon. He came down dressed for riding, a little more elegantly than was his custom in the country, and she did not think herself wrong in feeling she had surprised a bright expectant look on his face.

"Matt."

She came out through the archway from the inner hall, and he turned at the front door. Two horses, saddled, stood at the hitching rail below the elms.

"Yes?"

"Matt, I have to ask you for something, my dearest."

She did not realize how lovely she looked, in a soft dress of ruffled muslin the color of the lilacs that would soon fill the avenue with perfume. The curls of her new fashionable hair piled softly on her forehead. His face was gentle as he looked at her.

"Well, that's rare enough," he said, "for a white blackbird. Did you ever before?"

His expression was indulgent and she was distracted.

"I have never needed to ask," she said. "You think of everything I want."

"But this."

"But this," she said and in the silence while the words grew important, the horses moved and clinked beyond the door. Quickly she brought it out while she was still able.

"I want you, Matt, to stop going for these rides alone with Mrs. Cannon. People will be talking."

He made a quick furious gesture of impatience, but she

recognized his anger was against the breaking of a mood, for something he thought trivial.

"And who are people?"

His eyes were cold and his crop tapped on his soft boot. She felt him more handsome than usual in his anger, but would not soften nor look away.

"Your own people on the estate, who respect you."

"She is my agent's wife."

"She is young and beautiful, and no matter whose wife she is, she is not yours, and there will be talk. I imagine John Julius could not stop her since it was you who gave the invitation."

Never had she spoken so to him before and he turned abruptly and stood with his back to her, unsmiling. She knew she would have her victory, but not with good grace, and felt saddened by the first bad moment that had lain openly between them. Furious with Peggy Cannon that she should have caused it.

He turned back.

"Very well," he said curtly. "I'll take Bourdain."

She sent the little kitchen boy racing to tell Bourdain, who removed himself reluctantly from a bale of straw, where he had been enjoying the mild sun, and planning his next moves in his endless campaign against the virtue of the wily and evasive little Gracie.

"Bad cess to it," he said, "to have to go out and play the gooseberry to Mr. Matt and his fancy lady, for that's all I have to do."

He caught the bleak glare of old Peter, who pottered at the bench in the saddle room, and retreated.

"Well now," he said, "you're right. I'd imagine it's more true she'd like to be his fancy lady, but Mr. Matt'd have more sense."

He breathed on the brass buttons of his jacket and rubbed them with his cuff, and ran a duster on the gleam of his black boots.

"Maybe 'tis jealous you are," said old Peter through a toothless grin, "and you having ladies on the mind."

"Jealous!" Bourdain reached down a saddle, looking appalled. "I'd not go near that one with a barge pole, did the devil himself come to me with all the temptations, and the way he did with Jasus himself, and offered me a kingdom. Ye'd be a wise man to keep yer distance from that one."

"Divil the time I did anything else," said the old man. "Get along now and don't be keeping the master waiting."

Celia came back onto the steps to wave to Matt as he rode away, followed by Bourdain leading the spare horse, with his hat tilted down in protest over his handsome young nose. From the bushes beyond the house Boru materialized like a shadow and went loping after them, and Celia gave a small satisfied smile. Matt was well looked after. She stood a moment when they were gone beyond the gate, pleased and a little surprised that her stand had been so easy. Turning from the door, she went upstairs to put on her habit, to ride over herself to Holly House across the hill, where there was now a beaten path between the hollies; to spend the afternoon with Alicocq.

To her astonishment she had developed both respect and much affection for her pale superior sister-in-law with the slipping hair. She and Matt had laughed until they could barely stand at all their imaginings of the bride's arrival at what she thought to be the glories of Holly House; only to be welcomed by the dairymaid. Or even less than that, by the unexplained vision of her broad rump racing up the stairs with her trays, while Hugh Charles settled himself in his splendid tailoring before the port bottle in the dusty shadows.

In actual fact, on discovering the reality of her husband's home, Alicocq had at once, and without a word, locked herself into her bedroom, and Hugh Charles outside it, for two days. When she emerged, her drab clothes were as immaculate as ever, her would-be aristocratic nose just a little higher in the air, and no expression whatsoever in her amber eyes.

Hugh Charles confronted her wanly across the breakfast table like a man awaiting sentence.

He was already astonished and bewildered to find the

breakfast laid in the musty dining room he had not seen opened since he was a child. B'God she must have been up all night preparing it. He looked at her with even greater apprehension.

No mention was made of her absence, and there was nothing to read in her face as she handed him a cup of chocolate. Where in blazes had she found all the clobber. At least she was here. His eye began to brighten, but hesitantly, feeling there would be a price to pay before he could take anything easily.

"Hugh Charles," she said, in the high nasal voice that seemed so deceptively ineffectual, crooking her little finger around her own cup. "There is a good strong fireplace in your father's room. You will have the blacksmith come today and put a grid on it. That will be sufficient for all that woman's cooking. There is a small room next door that can be made into a scullery. She can come down the back stairs and the back stairs only, for going to the well or into Tuam for whatever she may want. You will tell your father I do not wish to see her in my part of the house. Would you care for some hot bread?"

Gaping, Hugh Charles pulled down his yellow waistcoat and nodded his consent, and astonishingly even old Thomas heeded her, his sullen fire dimmed by the long agony of his rheumatics. Slowly, with reference to nobody, she dragged Holly House out of its shadows and began to turn it into the squireen's residence Hugh Charles pretended that it was.

Celia and Matt and Mrs. Healey were bidden to their first formal supper party on the evening of Easter Sunday, and she and her mother stood amazed to see the dining room that had lain so long lost to the cobwebbed shadows. It was warm with a roaring fire that did not dare to smoke, the furniture polished brilliantly above the dark bloom that would never leave it; the table set with many of the dishes that she and her mother had dragged from their hiding places for the famous day they were At Home. In addition to the Canon, Alicocq had asked a vague young couple from the far side of the county whom Matt and Celia had never thought to be worth the distance, despite their noble blood. Alicocq was out diligently twice a week with the pony and trap, carefully collecting suitable friends for the advancement of Hugh Charles, and for the provision of guests for her excruciatingly dull soirées.

"Wouldn't she shame the pair of us," Mrs. Healey said as they drove home, the pony's hooves cracking in the clear silence, the full moon bleaching the green slopes of the hill between them and Owenscourt.

"Ah, I wouldn't think so," Matt said. "Not for me. I would think I'd prefer a plate of turnips in the kitchen and a night full of good talk."

"She's a good woman," answered Celia, "with a strong heart. I can't help but admire her."

The thing she admired and envied most about her was her treatment of Peggy Cannon. On first meeting her, Alicocq had swept her once from head to foot with her pale jelly eyes. Putting up a languid hand to retrieve some falling hair, she had then ignored her. Aware of Peggy's fury, Celia was filled with secret pleasure, but puzzled that she could not summon the same strength.

She went often to see Alicocq, driving over in the little basket trap with her sewing in a bag, to sit by the windows in the long hall that was now used as a room; catching the afternoon sun in the soft gleam on the fine furniture that had been Mrs. Healey's last hopeless contribution to the house. Although she would never admit to it, Celia knew the girl was lonely, and galled by the secret establishment upstairs in the house she tried so hard to make perfect. Nor did Hugh Charles feel that his improved social standing belonged inside his home, constantly loping off in his checkered waistcoat and his hard hat, two greyhounds at his horse's heels, for a horse sale or a coursing or the small secret shebeens where the county bloods would gather to gamble away their guineas and their horses and sometimes the very roofs above their heads.

Before their Easter stay at Owenscourt was over, Celia

was sure that, like Alicocq, she was with child, almost sick with pleasure to be able to tell Matt. Without one word being spoken, she knew he felt he had waited far too long to get his daughter.

"My daughter," he said and kissed Celia tenderly, his satisfaction blazing in his face.

"Our daughter," she corrected him, as anxious as he was to have a girl after the two boys.

"Take great care now," he said, but she dismissed it. The doctor in Galway where she had driven on the excuse of going shopping, had told her she was in perfect health. And indeed she had never felt better, not even bothered by the queasiness that had dogged her with the boys; confirming her certainty that it was a girl. She decided to leave it until after the baby was born to suggest that they would need a bigger house. It would be clear then without her saying anything, and Matt might take it better if it was his own idea to leave the house in Gardiner Street he cared so much for.

Through a soft and lovely spring with bright days falling into lilac dusks, she could find no fault within her world. The two boys were at the Jesuit school around the corner, coming and going with their satchels on their shoulders, leaving her long quiet days to rest and allow Mrs. Bradley to spoil her. All of them waiting for the little girl.

It gave her immense pleasure when Matt secured for the summer the little yellow house in the terrace beyond Kingstown, for she had grown to love the great expanse of shining strand, with the sun glittering in the pools; the white mail boats canting in and out between the long arms of the pier. And behind them the ever changing bulk of Howth on the north arm of the bay.

In the highest of spirits they all set out at the beginning of July, certain that this perfect summer would go on forever. Celia was so delighted to be free of the burdens of Owenscourt and back in the little yellow house, that she walked all round it touching everything as she had once done as a bride in her house in Gardiner Street; barely remembering to wave the boys away as they clamored out the front door with their shrimping nets and Gracie; into the shining afternoon.

When Matt drove from the city that evening he came into the house with the same look of content.

"B'God, Mrs. O'Connor, ma'am," he said as he kissed her, flinging his hat to Mrs. Bradley who caught it neatly with a smile. "Having a daughter suits you. As long as she's as lovely as you are yourself."

"I'm happy, Matt" was all she said, and he kissed her again. "Where are the boys?" he asked.

"On the shore."

"I'll go down and meet them coming back."

She didn't try to stop him and point out that he had his city clothes on. Matt would only think of that when he was raving about the seawater stains on his fine boots. As if it had happened with no consent of his.

She settled in the bowed window with the velvet seat, to watch the evening light change over the wide water, and wait for the sound of their voices as they came back along the street.

There were four perfect days and then the rain began. A fine drizzle to begin with, no thicker than the clouds that ranged low along the flanks of Howth. In hours it had settled to a steady downpour. Almost every evening the clouds would break to pale streaks of saffron light above the Golden Spears, and the rain would ease and stop, a weak sun glittering in all the puddles as if it did its best to promise that tomorrow would be better. Every morning they woke again to the rain drumming on the outhouse roof, and the sound of water rushing in the gutters.

The boys grew fretful and ill tempered, pressing their noses, complaining, at the windows, and driving Gracie to distraction with their demands for something they could do. Even Matt stopped in the end driving through the country lanes in the treacherous evenings, and came only for the Saturdays and Sundays that were no better than any others, his face increasingly concerned over the letters he was getting from John Julius.

"The harvest is destroyed."

He got up and walked restlessly to the window, staring out at the sluicing rain and up at the remorseless sky, as if by some very godlike power he might bring it to an end.

"It could stop any day," Celia said hopefully, not knowing what else to say, aware of the cold breath of disaster that must hang already over the precarious countryside.

"No matter if it does. Johnju says the crops are rotted in the fields. There's not a potato fit to eat."

"Have you enough stores?" She raised her appalled face to him, still in her heart a farmer's daughter, touched with fear as if the fields lay beyond the door on the streaming esplanade; her only source of life, and Matt's.

"I have. You know I have. But the tenants! There have been some good years. Enough to get them out of trouble and keep them eating. But stores! And money! They have no thought of providing for the future."

At the end of August they came dispiritedly back into city. Every so often there would be a couple of days of fine unstable weather with the high clouds racing from the west, then down would come the rain again, adding day after day to the toll of the wettest summer in living memory. When they were barely back a week, Matt came into the bedroom where she was resting, looking out depressed at the gray remorseless sky. Rain and all, Gracie had taken the two boys to the zoo in Phoenix Park, desperate herself to get out from being shut in the house.

Matt threw a letter on the afghan over her knees.

"I have to go to Owenscourt," he said. "I can't leave them to go through this alone. I have to estimate what we can do to see them through the winter. John Julius needs me. It is too much to ask of him."

Irritably he strode up and down the room, his handsome face creased.

"I can ill afford," he said, "to go there at this moment. There is almost more than I can handle in the Shops."

"Can't John Julius see to it. He is your agent, after all."

He wheeled on her.

"Aren't all the battles in Ireland over the landlords that leave their people to an agent. Wouldn't it shame me that I wouldn't go from here to Galway when they are in trouble."

He ran his hand up through the thick brown hair, and she knew he had not thought of her at all; secure in his mind in the care of Mrs. Bradley and Gracie. She eased herself up into a sitting position and tried to speak calmly.

"What of the baby, Matt?"

"Ah, I'll be back well before that."

Desperately she wanted to weep and cry to him not to go away, that at this moment she needed him more than any of his tenants did. Despite its wonderful start, this baby was not proving happy or comfortable in the later stages, as the other two had been. It seemed restless and awkward and ill placed, forever thumping her where she least expected it; dragging wearily as if it protested it couldn't stay much longer in its prison. She knew she was depressed both by the baby and the rain, and that no matter what she felt she must not show it. He would only be irritable and annoyed, and it was clear he would go anyway. With monstrous effort she tried to let it be with good grace, and, the following morning, stood heavily on the doorstep to see him off in the fragile sun that lay like rare gold along the street.

"Come back in time for your daughter."

He kissed her a little absently.

"Don't ask me to write, pet. If there's anything to tell I'll send you a wire, but that'll only be to say I'm coming back."

"A week, Matt."

"I'll do my best."

And he was gone, clattering off around the corner, the carriage wheels throwing up fountains of silver spray from the puddles of the night. Too preoccupied even for a backward glance. Sadly she laid her hand over the restless child as if begging it to wait, and went back into the house.

At the end of the week there was a wire.

"All going as well as can be hoped for. Take care of yourselves. All love. Matt."

She trudged the stairs with the flimsy in her hand, having grasped it from Mrs. Bradley in the happy certainty that he was coming home. Owen hung dangerously over the banisters on the floor above.

"Mama, Mama. We saw the boy. Is it to say Papa's coming back?"

Emmett's fair head joined him.

"No, boys. I'm sorry. Not yet."

As well as could be hoped for. What was there to hope for. Wasn't it merely a matter of giving John Julius money and filling up the barns with enough to dole out to the creatures through the winter.

She heard the boys crash back into their own room, and went idly into the drawing room where the fire was lit against the gray day that was neither one thing nor the other. What else could they hope for? And weren't they lucky they were on Matt's land and not just left to starve like many others like them at the present time. Mrs. Bradley followed her in and put a cushion at her back, and told her she would bring her a good cup of tea, and Celia knew she barely thanked her; alienated in her dark irritability from even the good soul who was only there to help her.

"I'm sorry, Bradley," she said. "I'm very cross."

" 'Tis no more than natural, Mrs. Matt. Do you stay here now and I'll get the boys out from above. They can go to the gardens for a while and I'll bring you the tea."

Celia wanted to shout at her that no cup of tea would even begin to touch this black weight of introverted sorrow that pinned her down; almost a premonition of some dreadful grief as yet unknown.

"The poor soul," said Mrs. Bradley to the cook in the kitchen. "She's as black and thrawn as if she were fighting all the world. Mr. Matt or no Mr. Matt, there's only one thing will settle her now and that's the baby. Make it good and strong, Mrs. Savage."

When the next telegram came, Mrs. Bradley thrust a penny at the boy and panted up the stairs with it, eager to bring her the good news, certain it would announce Mr. Matt's arrival, and anxious to see the smile it would bring at last to Mrs. Matt's tired face. Celia was as sure as she was, reaching for it gladly, wanting only to confirm the time; eagerly tearing it open.

For a long time she sat absolutely immobile, and Mrs. Bradley could see her eyes moving backwards and forwards, reading it again, her face stiffened into incredulity.

"No," she whispered at last. "Oh, no."

In the silence a coal crashed behind the fretted grate and a train whistled in the murky distance. With the certainty of disaster Mrs. Bradley blessed herself.

"Mrs. Matt! Ma'am!"

She couldn't stand the frozen face, the eyes now fixed on hers, blank with disbelief.

"Oh, ma'am, what's happened to him?"

Still silent, Celia handed her the wire, and the good woman fumbled with shaking hands for the spectacles on a cord around her neck, moving nearer to the one lamp.

"Sorry, my dearest, to have to tell you that your dear mother died today. Will come as soon as funeral is over. Be brave, dear heart, and remember the child. Love and grief. Matt."

"Ah, ah-ah." She moved at once over to the fire, and took Celia's hands in hers, overwhelmed by the responsibility of being alone with her. Celia did not resist, grasping her old fingers and staring at her as if she should know everything.

"He doesn't say what she died of."

"No, ma'am, he doesn't."

"But she was very strong, my mama. Before I married Mr. Matt—" She spoke in a high light voice like a child, that tailed off in the sad recollection of all the hard years for her mother before Matt had come on his white horse to the rescue of them both. And probably, thought Mrs. Bradley shrewdly, not needing the sentence finished, it was those hard years killed her mother now. The whole long tale gathered from here and there across the years.

"Oh, my poor mother. What would she die of? She never said she was ill. Bradley, I must tell the boys. They loved their Grannie. How can I tell them she is dead?"

The thought of their loss brought tears hot and bitter for a few moments to her eyes, but it was her children's loss she wept for, not yet for the mother who had been so close to her. Closer as she got older than at any time before. Growing younger and not older, with the years away from Holly House. Why should she die?

"I am cold, Bradley," she said then. "Cold."

And indeed she had begun to shiver, in the warm room before the bright fire, and Mrs. Bradley reached for the colored afghan that lay across the back of the sofa. Then she shook her head abruptly, going quickly out of the room and upstairs to Celia's presses, coming back to wrap her in a big black shawl, shrouding the warm red of her pleated dress.

Then she raced downstairs again to the kitchen and shook Mrs. Savage from her sleep beside the glowing range.

"Will you get me a cup of tea, for God's sake, for the mistress, and put in as much whisky as you dare and she not to notice it."

Anything, she thought, to break that stony face. Did she cry it would be better both for her and for the child, and a drop of whisky might soften her to that. "Dear God, Mrs. Savage, and do you think we should call the doctor."

"And did you tell me what it was all about," said Mrs. Savage, "it may be I could advise you."

She told her.

"Ah, dear God, the creature," said the cook heavily, reaching for the whisky and the tea caddy. "May Almighty God have mercy on her harmless soul."

But late in the evening, when the boys were weeping into their pillows for the grandmother they had loved, with Gracie telling her beads in the playroom in the lamplight, Celia was still sitting there; wrapped in her black shawl and staring tearless into the fire. She knew that all her household came, one by one, who had never before set foot in the drawing room, to offer her their sympathy and their prayers; staring in anxiety at her black eyes and composed face; and the even voice that thanked them for coming up.

"I'm going to get the doctor," Mrs. Bradley said to Mrs. Savage determinedly at the foot of the staircase. Gracie sat on the stairs halfway down from above, and down in the hall the bootboy stood open mouthed, his thin face pallid in the lamplight, threatened all evening with the race for the doctor.

"G'won," hissed Mrs. Bradley to him from the shadowy stairs. "G'won and get him. Mr. Matt would not be wanting me to take the responsibility." No one noticed that the boy shot out the front door he had never used before, clattering down the steps into the misty night.

"Shock," said Dr. Brice some half an hour later as he came slowly from the drawing room. "Shock. The poor woman. What a time for it to happen. When will Mr. O'Connor be home?"

"As soon as the funeral will be over."

"Days, I suppose."

He nodded his heavily bearded head and not for the first time gave the edges of his professional observation to the Chinese Masterpiece at the bottom of the stairs, wondering what in God's name it was all about. "Let's hope the child doesn't get here first."

He handed Mrs. Bradley a small ribbed bottle of dark-blue glass, the label printed in red.

"Give her three drops of that now in some milk to get her to sleep. But be very careful not to overdo it or you could harm the child. Good night now, and I'll be in again tomorrow."

As Mrs. Bradley opened the door to let him out, the rain had increased to a downpour, drifting in clouds across the spill of lamplight from the hall.

Celia sent her the next morning across the road to the

church to arrange the masses for the dead, and to light the small candles that would burn in the shadows for her mother's soul, and it all had nothing to do with the charming bright-eyed woman with the loving smile, who would never again be waiting for her between the white pillars on the steps of Owenscourt.

The priests came at once, soft footed up the stairs, their long cassocks whispering, and offered everything they knew of consolation, and she thanked them quietly and let them go. The doctor came again and frowned a little and suggested a telegram to Matt to tell him to come home as soon as possible. The children came downstairs, over their first shock now, and awed and curious about the facts of death, that had never touched their lives. Did she die with all her clothes on, Owen wanted to know. And was it true the worms would eat her? Who would make her coffin? Emmett listened to the answers but had no questions of his own, winding his small arms round his mother's neck in silence, offering her a strangely mature comfort that brought tears closer than at any moment yet.

She was loving and forbearing with them, and with all other visitors softly courteous, thanking them for coming and staring at them with great empty eyes as if she barely saw them. Pale and composed and hollow as a shell.

She could hear Bradley whispering to the doctor out on the stairs, saying it was all unnatural and how much better it would be if she would cry. She listened and huddled deeper into her black shawl, resuming her staring at the fire. She could have told any of them that she would cry when and only when she was able to do it in Matt's arms. Counting not only the days, but the hours and the minutes and the very seconds.

But the long gray days stretched on, and by the time the wire came more than a week later, she had sunk into a lonely wordless morass of anger and self-pity, worn by her restless baby; almost beyond reason, convinced in all her lonely grieving and brooding that Matt could have been with her long ago; that something other than her mother's funeral had held him. Mrs. Bradley viewed her with alarm as she stared at the wire with expressionless eyes.

"There, ma'am. You'll be all right now.

"She's in a strange state, Mrs. Savage." Bradley shook her worried head in the kitchen. "You'd think it would lift her."

"It'll take the man himself to lift her now," she said, thinking that at least now there'd be a bit of food eaten in the house by someone other than the children, and beginning to plan what she'd give the master to eat after his long journey in the terrible rain. The mistress in her lost state would take little interest.

Late that night Celia heard the jingle of harness as the carriage drew up outside and Bourdain's voice and then Matt's own, beyond the rain-slashed windows. She didn't move from her chair, compelled by some fearful urge of self-pity to stay where she was, barely acknowledging Matt's existence; unwilling even to lift her morose and clouded eyes from the fire which Bradley had heaped to a cheerful blaze for his arrival. All the lamps were lit and the room was warm and bright. She heard him again down in the hall asking Mrs. Bradley urgently how she was, but she couldn't hear the answer.

As he burst through the door, some part of her was aware of the concern that it had caused, his face anxious, beads of rain on the ulster he had been in too much of a hurry to take off.

"My dearest. My dearest Cee. How are you?"

Deeply she was aware too of the blessed size of him in a room that had been empty; the dear loved face and the smell of the wet night on his clothes. The longed-for reality of Matt. But some other black deep mood, born and fostered by the shock from which she had not emerged, refused to see the Matt she loved. She stared at him from dulled and bitter eyes.

"Where have you been? What have you been about?"

He halted astonished, looking up for guidance at Mrs. Bradley who had followed him to take his coat. She shook her head and left the room. If he couldn't help the poor creature then no one could.

"My poor darling, you know where I have been."

He fumbled for words, not yet knowing how to speak to her of her mother; not knowing how she had taken it so late on into the child. He bent over her and searched for her hands in the black shrouding shawl. He kissed her disinterested face, his own growing appalled. Dear God, it was all much worse than he had feared. Could the shock have turned her reason. Had they had Brice to her, he wondered.

"Celia, there were things to do. I got back as soon as I could. How are the boys?"

"Grieving for their Grannie, and waiting for their father."

"I am sure, but you, my darling, seem to me to be grieving too much. You have been alone too long. Come now. I'm chilled to the bone, and the train was late. Come and eat with me, and I'll tell you everything."

Even as he spoke he realized he was no longer chilled. His head felt strangely hot and heavy and the mention of supper was a mistake, touching him with a wave of nausea. He must be more tired than he thought. But Celia must be coaxed. He held out his hands.

"Come, my love, I get good smells from the kitchen."

He tried to take her hands again and the real Celia looked up at him and struggled to understand the closeness of the dear concerned face, and to tell him that not even death itself could threaten her now that he was back.

"What did she die of," she asked him coldly, tearless, as if she spoke to someone she hardly knew. Nor did she notice that Matt's face beside her looked sharp and tired, the eyes small and a little staring as if he were hopelessly exhausted. He paused a long moment before he answered her.

"Fever," he said wearily.

"Fever!" Her voice was shrill. "And how did you let her die of fever? People like my mama do not die of fever. Did you have the doctor to her?"

She glared at him wildly and Matt put a hand to his tired head. This was beyond him at the moment. God forgive him that he should say so, but he wasn't able for it. The death did indeed seem to have turned her wits. The fire stirred in the grate and the rain lashed down the windows, and she looked at him across the sudden blaze of firelight with a twist to her mouth he had never seen before.

"Or were you too occupied with Peggy Cannon?"

He was not angry yet, only astonished.

"With Peggy Cannon? Why would I? I can tell you this. She was very kind to your poor mother."

"My poor mother!" There were tears in her eyes now. Wild, unreasonable rage, not grief. "If Peggy Cannon was around you'd not have given her a second thought. Any more than you have given me. You could have been home long ago."

Had Matt not been so exhausted; so harrowed by all he had seen and done and suffered since he went away; so touched himself with sorry grief. Above all had he not been so strange and heavy in the head, the shrieking of the unreasonable Celia coming and going from some lost unhappy distance. Had he not been all of these things, he would have brought to bear his natural tenderness and his understanding of Celia's every thought. He would have known that her mind, temporarily unhinged by shock, had focused on the one complaint her wonderful marriage had allowed her.

But Matt stood up coldly, staggering a little.

"I'm very tired," he said coolly. "I don't want any supper." He realized that this was true, waves of nausea touching him now one after the other. "I shall sleep in my dressing room tonight, and in the morning we can talk about it all. Good night, Celia."

He left her there, her fists clenched underneath the shawl, staring again at the fire, and the shocked Mrs. Bradley with expressionless face carried out his instructions about the bed in the dressing room. Matt went up at once.

"Ye can give the dinner to the cat," Bradley said down in the kitchen, "for neither of them will eat a bite tonight."

She told her as much as she knew.

"Ah, musha, isn't that the pity," said Mrs. Savage, thrusting back her straying hair, "isn't that the shame of it, and we thinking the whole business would be right the minute he set foot into the house. Well, Mrs. Bradley, do you call in Gracie and Bourdain and the bootboy, for this dinner is going to no cat."

Upstairs, when Mrs. Bradley had finally left her, Celia lay and stared by the light of her candle at the closed door of the dressing room, miserably aware that she was wrong, but unable to reach below the fathoms of her grief and depression for any gesture that might put it right. Weeping for the first time, slow hot tears of loss she barely understood, she blew out her candle and huddled down in the lonely bed, her arms tight for some small comfort round her restless baby.

It was in the first light of dawn she woke to hear him vomiting. Lurching out of bed, she crashed through the dressing-room door. He had managed to reach his basin and turned to her from it, holding to the washstand for support; bent and ravished with the ferocity of his sickness, his face a dreadful mottled gray.

"Matt!"

She knew she shrieked, but never knew how she got to help him through and into his own bed; aware now in every nerve of her body of her love and trust and all the things she had denied last night. And fear, cold sickening fear.

"Oh, my dearest, dearest Matt."

She smoothed the sheet below his sweating face, and lumbered for the door.

"Mrs. Bradley! Bradley!"

The bootboy was sent once more hurtling out into the lemon-colored dawn, where an almost forgotten sun lay gilt along the streets, and Brice was in the house in twenty minutes. Matt was drowsing into unconsciousness, and when he had finished his terse examination, Brice beckoned Celia from the room. Bradley was waiting on the stairs, her good face drawn with fright, the sun yellow in her gray hair.

"Burn his clothes," said Brice abruptly. "Burn every single thing he had there with him. Don't touch it. Burn it with the tongs. Has he been near a case of fever?"

Celia stared at him in agony, her mouth opening and closing on the knowledge that had hit her like the bolt of death itself, as she saw him vomiting.

"My mother," she whispered in the end. "He told me last night my mother died of fever."

Matt would never have refused to go near her. He loved her and would never have allowed her to die alone, and oh, dear God, last night she had rejected all of it. Would ever God or Matt forgive her.

"Did he sleep in your bed last night?" Brice asked her bluntly and her hand flew to her mouth.

"N-no. No. He was tired and slept in his dressing room."

"Then we must hope for the best. He is infectious no longer, but it could be in his clothes. And how are you, Mrs. O'Connor? You cannot do too much. I'll send in a nurse for day and night."

"I am well, Dr. Brice," she said with sudden calm, "I can do all Matt needs."

And indeed the grief and gloom of the last week had lifted like the mist at Owenscourt before the morning sun, leaving clarity and light and the hopes of the new day. "I am well, indeed."

"Humph," he said, and eyed her assessingly. No point in forbidding her anything. The child was almost at its term, and there would be no gainsaying that if it should start.

As for the fine handsome husband—

Were he alone he would have uttered a sharp furious curse at what would seem the worst ill fortune, but with the two women there before him with their shattered faces; he only sighed and spoke to them gently, giving them instructions for Matt's care until the nurse should come, stamping off into the bright morning with his bearded face creased with impotence.

They drew the curtains against the unfamiliar sun, because the light hurt his eyes, and lit the shaded lamps, so that there was neither day nor night through the long formless hours of his suffering. Sickness and whirling vertigo; headaches so fearful that he shook and chattered with the pain; roaring delirium, and, on what must have been the sixth day of it, the dull purple rash, like a blood bruise creeping over all his body.

Brice came and went, and the two nursing sisters from the convent changed their watch, but Celia never left the lamplit shadows by the bed, dozing uneasily in his times of quiet, driven to some phenomenal strength by the appalled guilt of her unkindness; desperate to seize every moment of exhausted consciousness to replace it in his mind with the image of her love. No one else was allowed in and as often as not she forgot to take the tray of food that Mrs. Bradley left for her outside the door. Brice watched her, and told the nuns to leave her alone, knowing there would be a sad and inevitable limit to what she could do.

After the rash came the coma, when she could do no more than sit in silence, her rosary beads in one hand and Matt's cold one in the other, frantically beseeching God over the battle that her heart already knew was lost; watching the priests come softly to his side with the last rites of the Church; too appalled to pray with them; unable to accept the unacceptable fact that prayers for the dying could be for Matt. His face was already hollowed with the sharpened look of death, his nose a bony beak, and his fine frame so wasted that it barely raised the bedclothes; his eyes unseeing, not quite closed.

On the ninth day he had some brief moments of what seemed like consciousness and she told Bradley to send down the children, but he had drifted off again before they came. They could do no more than stand as she did, helpless. Owen in a storm of tears and protest, Emmett in what seemed like a curious detachment. Only his gray eyes betrayed a fright too deep for tears. She sent them hopelessly back upstairs to Gracie, kissing them, and telling them to pray for their father's soul.

It was in the dead dawn hours of the next day, soon after the landing clock had struck its musical five, that Celia, drowsing in the rocking chair beside him, saw his eyes were open.

"Matt. Dearest Matt."

"Celia."

His smile, and his look of tenderness, were as young and fresh as the day they stood together by Dublin Castle on the banks of the Yangtze River, and in that moment she knew that both God and Matt had forgiven her. It would remain for her to manage to forgive herself.

"Sister!" she cried urgently, softly. Filled with foolish hope. But by the time the nun had come silent from the fire, she knew that Matt was gone.

Down in Owenscourt, Boru shot from his kennel to the length of his long chain and howled and bayed in anguish at the scudding moon. Nor would he be silenced until John Julius threw on some clothes and raced out to him across the farmyard through the windy night. The dog fell quiet then, putting up his paws and laying his great head on his chest with such a human gesture of despair that John Julius only laid a hand on it as he might have with another person.

"Do you say so, Boru," he said, in anguish. "Do you say so. Ah, dear God. May heaven have mercy on his soul."

He took the dog's chain and walked with him down the dark parkland and around the lake to the small bridge, where they sat together in a silent vigil, watching the gray light creep across the quiet water, and then the rosy flush of dawn.

They were still there, nor did John Julius move, when the telegraph boy came pounding up the avenue on his bicycle, his coattails flying, to pull frantically at the front doorbell. A few minutes later, in the first bright light of the new sun, he watched all the shades being drawn down one by one, on the shining windows of the house.

Matt O'Connor, with his elegant Dublin house and his grand estate and his prosperous Shops, his presses full of fine clothes, and all his beautiful possessions, was dead from famine fever. Like any starving peasant from the barren wastes of Connemara.

Two days later Celia was delivered of a dead daughter. Brice could say all he liked about the restless infant and the breech delivery during which it had strangled in its own cord. Celia would never believe other than that the child had died in the moment she felt life leave Matt's hand.

As if the year knew it had done its worse, there was benign gold autumn sunshine as they carried him through the winding paths of the cemetery at Glasnevin. John Julius and Hugh Charles and four men from the Shops where they had made his gleaming coffin. Behind them Owen and Emmett carried their little sister in a small white casket. One tiny wreath of roses, and the wide lilac ribbons hanging quiet round it in the still gold air.

Chapter 10

To John Julius's amazement, Celia asked to see him before he went back down to the West.

He found her ashen pale, the skin drawn on her bones, but perfectly composed, in the pretty, small spare room Bradley had hastily prepared for her and the coming baby, when Matt was taken ill. Only her hands were restless, wandering vaguely over the black ribbons slotted through the ruffles of her bedgown: as if she did not understand why they were there.

"Sit down, John Julius, please," she said. "I would be grateful if you would tell me all that happened." He had to look away, busying himself with pulling up a chair, from the awful bleakness of disbelief lying in her shadowed eyes. "Tell me all that happened, first of all to my dear mama."

John Julius drew a deep breath and would have given anything to be somewhere else.

"There was a man," he said. "One of the farm lads from the cottages down by the back gate. He got a message to say his sister was dying. In some village over beyond Lough Mask near Letterturk. He went at once, I let him go, and he never stopped to ask what ailed her and all the village with her. He brought the fever back."

"And my mother went to nurse him."

"Not him. His wife nursed him and he got the better of it. But the wife took sick after him, and she was a girl had been at Holly House long ago, and your mother had a feeling for her. She insisted on taking her broth and things like that."

"She would."

"The woman died," John Julius said heavily, "and your poor mother, God rest her soul, not long after."

Her wandering fingers closed on the edges of the bed-clothes, gripping them, her mind fixed on Matt.

"If only I had realized he was ill the night he got home."

He looked at her, wondering how much she could take, in this terrible controlled calm.

"Mrs. Matt, ma'am," he said, desperate to dispel even the smallest feelings of guilt that she might have, never knowing of the real guilt that would shape her till the day she died. "Mrs. Matt, Matt was dead before he ever left Owenscourt. All he was, was heart and soul determined to get back to you. There was no more you could have done."

Mrs. Bradley had told him the case of fever was so virulent that even the doctor was appalled. Matt's life had been despaired of from the very start.

But Celia looked away from him to where the autumn sun came flooding in the long windows as if to make up for all the weeks that had gone by. There was one thing her desolate heart knew she could have done for him. She could have made him welcome home.

John Julius told her then about Boru, and her eyes fixed on him as do the eyes of the bereaved, searching for every crumb that was special and different about their own particular loss.

"He's your dog now, John Julius," she said when he had finished, and he didn't dispute it. Boru would not want her or Owen nor any of the children. He was, and always had been, a man's dog, and already padded like a grieving shadow at Johnju's heels.

"Thank you, John Julius," she said. "Thank you for coming to tell me. In a while I will come down to Owenscourt and we will talk about everything. It is Owen's now, of course, but in trust with me until he is twenty-one."

"There's no haste, Mrs. Matt," he said, and knew he could never call her anything else. "There's no haste. Owenscourt will run on until you are well ready to come. Be at ease now, and do your best to get over everything."

He stood up and took her two cold hands and on an impulse kissed them, the message of his own grief for his lifelong friend and benefactor added to her own. She looked at him sadly and did not speak. He felt guilty for wanting to get out of the pretty room, haunted by the trivial role of the black ribbons. The intensity of her determination to be calm shone from the dark-rimmed eyes. She was brave, the creature, brave. And please God it would all ease with her with time.

Hugh Charles came and stood at the foot of the bed uneasily, dumb in the face of her need, jangling the money in his well-cut pockets and repeating over and over again that God help us all it was terrible. Celia watched him wearily and helped him over his embarrassment, and for a few moments knew an insane longing for the arms of the blunt and practical Alicocq to weep in. Fiercely she dismissed it. Tears for Matt would drown the world did she ever let them start. No tears. Only the fierce resolution born through those last long sleepless nights, that Matt's world should continue exactly as he had left it. For Owen. Then all his kingdoms would not belong in the bleak and sickening wasteland of his death. When she was up, in the first black dress that the little dressmaker had raced up for her, the polite and handsome lawyer with the calm eyes and the soft beard came to see her. James Cornelius O'Duffy.

Shrewdly he eyed her and then relaxed. There would be no vapors nor hysterics here. Matt, God rest him, had married a woman of his own mettle. Slowly he took all the papers from his case, and set them before him on the table settling his gold-rimmed spectacles below strong eyebrows.

"There are no complications, Mrs. O'Connor," he said to her. "No complications at all. I read the will after the funeral, and I'll read it again now to you as I have to. But you just ignore the legal talk and I'll tell you what it all means afterward."

He looked up from the document and gave her his quick, singularly sweet smile, and she knew a moment of ease and gratitude that Matt had chosen so well the companions of her loneliness.

The simple terms she had already understood, from a cheerful and dutiful conversation with Matt that had never for one moment envisaged the impossible reality of death. She was the sole trustee for everything for her sons. Owenscourt and Holly House to Owen and all the incomes deriving therefrom. Also the Shops to Owen with the incomes to be divided equally between him and Emmett. To Emmett he had left an income only, divining correctly that beyond those abstracted gray eyes might lie the desire for another kind of life.

"That will is not very old," Celia said, remembering this. "He said he wanted to settle things again, now that the boys were old enough to see how they might shape, and what they might want from life."

"Very wise," said James O'Duffy. Matt had been no fool.

Holly House was now Celia's, in trust for Owen, according to the agreement drawn up at their marriage, that if Matt should die, then the property, with all he had put into it, would go to Celia.

"I am damned," Matt had said to James O'Duffy at the time of the settlement, "I am damned if I am having that pair of rogues unsupervised at Holly House should I die early, after all the money I am going to put into the place. With normal living Hugh Charles will have a lifetime there at my expense and nothing done to deserve it."

"And what," Celia asked now, thinking of it, "what does Hugh Charles think now? About Holly House?"

James O'Duffy looked at her and hesitated. How to tell her of her brother's chalk-white rage that a lifetime at Matt's expense in Holly House had unexpectedly slipped through his fingers.

"He is upset," he said carefully, and at that they both left it.

"You may tell him," Celia said, and the man opposite her marveled at her soft composure, her face nevertheless pathetically pale above the ruffles of the black dress, "you may tell him he will never be asked to leave Holly House as long as I shall live. Nor, I imagine, would Owen ever ask him."

"You will remember that the subsidies from Mr. O'Connor will have stopped at his death."

Her face grew firm.

"I do, Mr. O'Duffy. I do remember. But only a fool could fail to make a living from Holly House, now Matt has set it on its feet. It is land as good as Owenscourt. I cannot give away my children's money to keep my brother. He can work for it."

That'll please him, thought O'Duffy, and bent above his papers to hide his smile of pleasure. Mrs. Matt didn't seem any chicken for the plucking, thank God.

"Then, that is all, Mrs. O'Connor. It is very simple. I take it you'll be keeping on Lind at the Shops and John Julius Cannon. Both excellent men."

"They have both agreed to stay."

"Then you are in good hands."

"Watch for her, James," Matt had said. "Watch for her if anything, God forbid, should happen to me. She'll need someone to guide her."

James O'Duffy was satisfied that at the moment Celia was watching well for herself. Calm and thoughtful, thinking sensibly of guarding her sons.

"You will come and see me at once if there is anything to concern you. Or send your boy round and I will come to you."

She nodded and he got up and left her, bowing over her cold hand, refusing her offer of a glass of sherry, sick at heart like everybody else at the dreadful waste of the death of Matt O'Connor. Sick too, with pity for the turmoil and grief and loss so well contained behind that calm pale face.

Celia would not allow herself even to think of grief and

loss, knowing that if for one second she admitted them she would be lost; and sink down into some black abyss of helplessness from which there would be no way back.

She took every day and every task and asked herself how Matt O'Connor's widow should handle it. This began with her mourning. Matt O'Connor's widow would never have looked a frump. So she summoned the little lame seamstress and Mr. Morrissey as carefully as when she had ordered her dresses for the gay Dublin winters, only bidding Bradley to see that he brought nothing but black. Nor did she know when it was all done, and all the bright colors banished to the attics, that Matt O'Connor's widow in her elegant blacks, her fair hair drawn severely back from her thin composed face, had some impressive quality she had never possessed as a dependent, happy wife.

So she put herself through painfully the first hours. Then the days and weeks, and months, and in the end, unbelievably, the years. Taking task carefully after task and trying to do it as Matt would have wished; in the small things and the big. Trying faithfully to preserve for Owen the kingdom he would inherit. Of Emmett's kingdom she never asked. He was her comfort and her solace through all of the dark time, and never seemed to want anything for himself. If she realized that after his father's death he went to spend long periods with the priests across the road, she took little heed of it, immersed in her own painstaking struggle for survival.

She closed ranks with her two sons, all of them keeping close; lest they expose the intolerable gap that seared them all. Despite her aching need to have them close beside her, Celia decided to follow Matt's plan that they should go away to school, but earlier than he had intended.

"But where, Mother," they asked in outrage. "Where. Why can't we stay here with you?"

"At Clongowes Wood in County Kildare. You know lots of boys there.

"It will be good," she told them, to their protests. Owen's noisy. Emmett's as always, careful and considered. "Necessary, my darlings. I love to have you near me, but it is not good for you to be like this in a houseful of women."

"There's Bourdain and the bootboy," said Emmett practically.

She smiled.

"You need men about you as you are growing up, now you do not have your father."

"They're not men, they're priests," Owen cried rebelliously, and Emmett shot him a considering look.

"Your father would have wished it," Celia said firmly, and that was as the word of God with them. "We will go to Owenscourt for Christmas and then you will go down to school."

"Ah, good," Owen cried, ready to be diverted from anything with the promise of Owenscourt. "Then Antonia can ride the land with me."

"And Mr. Cannon," Celia added dryly. There was no need to press Owen into the understanding of what she asked of him. As of his right, he regarded Matt's kingdoms as his own, wanting nothing but to be earnestly worthy of his father in the same places; willing and anxious, child as he still was, to take his share of the work as his father had done.

"But, Mother," he said now. They sat around the playroom table littered with inky schoolbooks and the dismembered pieces of a steam engine. The white horse was shrouded in the attic with no other child to wait for. "Mother, how can I go down to the Shops on Saturdays if I am away at school?"

She reached a hand to him, so like Matt now that at times she found it unbearable to look at him. And the same high sense of his responsibilities.

"We shall have to get Lind," she said, "to send you a report like Mr. Cannon does, every week. And when you have short holidays you can go down there. You can always work on designs at school."

With careful kindness all the employees of the Shops, led by Lind, had helped the child to sense his position and responsibility; trying to blunt his loss, and theirs. A young artist had been brought in to take over the design, but even he accepted patiently the far from foolish sketches submitted by the child, who obviously possessed his father's talent. He would discuss Owen's drawings seriously, and leave the boy always feeling that in the finished sketches there was something of his own.

Owen looked a little dissatisfied but let it go. He knew his father had wanted him to go to school. His mother was right in that.

Emmett moved over and leaned against his mother's chair, playing with the black bobbles edging the bodice of her dress, saying nothing to object.

"Will you come down and see us?" was all he asked, his opinion of all tragedy and change kept deeply and secretly his own. With this arrangement he was privately well pleased. In the small closed world of a school everything should be quite different, and he wouldn't be reminded so constantly, as he was at home, of all that he had lost. And the priests would be there.

"Of course, my darling," Celia answered him, touching his cheek softly with her fingers, aware of all his secret anguish and aware too that not even she might intrude on it. "It's only twenty-three miles from Dublin. I'll come often."

Often, she thought to herself, smiling at them. Often. For how will I otherwise endure this house without them.

So, against blankness and black loneliness that crumbled her very heart to dust, and in the nights left her in abandoned silence crying upon God for pity, she rebuilt Matt's world about them as closely as she could. As if to tell him, wherever he was, that that one failure was a weakness she would never allow to happen again; trying to close down on the fearful moments of her haunted secret guilt. The conviction against all reason, and against all the doctor had said, that had she looked after him that first night, it might have saved his life.

She offered him Owen, molded in his pattern, to show him that his life had not been wasted; offered him her own ravaged grief and guilt, her anguish and despair that she knew would never leave her all her life.

But like Emmett, all in secret.

When the evening sun would fall across the two velvet armchairs in their bedroom where they had loved to sit, gleaming softly on the empty chair, she would sit down in her own and conjure up the lively figure in the other; or touch the Chinese Masterpiece in passing with an outstretched finger that was a gesture of pain that could not be assuaged. Worst of all she would wake in the dead hours of the night without even the light of day for consolation; forgetting; still half asleep; reaching out a searching arm across the wide bed. Then she would sit wide and dry eyed in the velvet armchair until dawn would come, eating at her knuckles and begging God that she herself might die. Thinking of the spring that would sweep the green land down in the West, and Matt not there to see it. Thinking of all life, and Matt not there to know it.

To the outside world she was the remarkable young Mrs. O'Connor in her elegant mourning, her two fine young sons at her side; a calm picture of the dignity of loss.

Under Lind the Shops ran themselves, nor could she see any falling off in the standards of perfection. Wrapped in her furs over her black clothes, she drove down there every week from the time she was recovered, trying to make them all feel that the family still held the business. Guarding for Owen, with her presence and authority, that part of his heritage.

At Owenscourt itself she knew John Julius would guard it with his very life. He treated her always with a tender respect that touched her deeply. All the accounts were ready for her when she came down, as they had been for Matt, and with gentle firmness, knowing her need for occupation, John Julius made it clear he expected her to look at them; and everything else to do with the estate. Hour after hour she sat in the office and battled with the heap of papers, while Owen rode the land with John Julius and Antonia and set himself to learn all his father's friend could teach him.

"And what, ma'am, of Holly House?" he asked her when they came down that first Christmas. They were coming down the windy muddy pathway from a visit to her mother's grave. John Julius would not let her go alone, fearing that even for her splendid courage, it would be too much. He put an arm under her elbow to guide her round a puddle. "There will be no change there, I take it."

"Do you mean, do I want it? Of course not. My father and Hugh Charles and Alicocq can stay there as long as I will live, or they want it. Alicocq is a great comfort to me, the good soul."

John Julius's blue eyes were evasive, and he didn't look at her as he helped her into the trap. He had not for a moment wanted to suggest putting them out, but he had wanted to suggest putting an agent in, and that himself. He could run both places as easily as one. Even with Matt's money the whole place was going downhill, and any profit that was made wasting away in ill-chosen horses and in gambling. A bad farm next door was a handicap in weeds and boundary fences and diseases. It could all be avoided were the two estates put into one.

He didn't know how to bring it up. Even that might seem to her to be dispossessing her brother, for whom she seemed to have unreasonable affection, although, God knew, dispossessing him was all the man was worth. Hugh Charles caused him concern. There was something furtive and unpredictable about the man; an evasiveness in the little piggy amber eyes. There was no knowing which way he would jump. But Mrs. Matt would hear no word against him, and he supposed in the heel of the hunt that she was right. He had best leave the matter alone.

He shook the reins at the pony, who ambled off down the road, and turned the talk back to Owenscourt.

"We will have to go a little easy on the rents this winter, if you will agree, ma'am. They have nothing to pay with after the failed harvest."

The failed harvest. That had killed her mother and Matt. She glanced back up at the windblown trees of the graveyard.

"Let them go," she said vehemently, her hands a ball of

fists inside her muff. "Let them go. Let them have the money for food. No one else must die."

He gave her one sharp look of pity, and turned the conversation, asking her was she pleased with the new housekeeper they had had to get in when her mother died. Mrs. Bradley had sent her down from Dublin.

"Although I'll say," John Julius said, as they rocked along the ruts, "that in all honesty my wife made a good fist of it for a while. But it wouldn't do. We can't have the county saying the Cannons have taken over Owenscourt."

My wife. Peggy Cannon.

She had forgotten all about her, the sense of guilt at Matt's death so vast and vague, it needed now no central focus. Peggy Cannon. She had angered her very much at one time. Nowadays she never even saw the woman, who had retreated into her white house in sullen and defeated silence, deprived of all the stimulation so necessary to her, in her visits to Owenscourt and her flirtation with Matt.

"I am sure she did very well," Celia said to John Julius. Odious though the woman was, she did everything well. "But I am very pleased with Mrs. Hessian. She is very efficient."

"Indeed, and a kind soul with it."

He turned the trap towards the road home, and they both looked up as they passed the gates of Holly House, along the river to the distant windows. Only Celia saw through the gray blustery day to a prince with a white horse, standing there in the sun of spring, with the dust of kingcups gold on his boots.

She fulfilled her weekly routine of her visits to the Shops, when she was back in Dublin, and moved quietly among her closest friends; and drove down once a month on Sunday across the green stretches of Kildare and up the mile-long avenue at Clongowes to the old castle at the end of it. There were the formal polite civilities with the priests, with the boys shuffling their feet to be away. Then they would go for a drive, scrabbling in the parcels she had brought to refill their tuck boxes; in the late drowsy afternoons sitting over a heavy tea in the gray hotel over in Maynooth. Owen still felt he was wasting his time, and would rather be an apprentice at the Shops, or forking manure down at Owenscourt with the farm lads.

"Your father wished it," she would say to him, over the plates of ham and soda bread and barmbrack, and the huge pot of strong brown tea. "Your father wished it." That was all that was needed to conquer his restlessness, and apply himself to the task in hand with all the single-minded diligence that had been his father's. He was doing well, was popular and good at games, and all his masters were well pleased with him.

Emmett was transparently content. Celia could see his eyes roaming with open pleasure over the old castle as they came back to it; and round the green beautiful acres of playing fields and woods, backed by the far purple shadow of the Wicklow Mountains. It was from Emmett that she learned all the hoary old school jokes. And all the cherished legends, like that of the ghost of the owner some hundred years before, who had been seen walking up the stairs towards the Round Room, in a strange white foreign uniform, at the same moment as he had been killed at the distant battle of Prague.

Wide eyed, he impressed her.

"It's true. Honestly."

"I can well believe it," she told him. Easy to understand loving so much that you could leave your very print on a place at the moment of your passing. Easy. Or on a person. Haunting them till the day of their own death.

It was Emmett too who joined all the sodalities and was hung with holy medals, as Owen said scathingly, like some old woman on a pilgrimage. Emmett who was not academically as bright as Owen; a plodder, but a monitor and everything else he should be, and loved by all the priests.

There were gray winters and rain that all her days she would find an enemy; and the soft high skies of spring; golden summers and the misty autumns she had once so loved. Owenscourt. Dublin. Clongowes. Wherever life asked her to go, she went, calm and smiling, fulfilling with care all the tasks that Matt had left her. Still sitting in the dawns when summer and winter were alike, in her velvet chair opposite the empty one beside the bedroom window; still unbelieving that she must face another day and Matt not in it.

With warm pleasure she saw Gracie and Bourdain married at long last in the church across the road. There would be no more babies for Gracie to look after, but until she should have one for herself, she was staying on as a sort of assistant to Mrs. Bradley, who was growing old.

The boys were on holiday, and Celia gave a wedding breakfast in the house, crowding in the bashful relatives who huddled mutely in the corners until released by the generous glasses of good malt distributed by Owen and Emmett. Mrs. Savage had with great delight cooked herself into a frenzy. For one grand morning, Gracie flushed and proud in the middle of it all, the house had rung with the cheerfulness it had once known, sorrow banished by beaming young happiness.

Alicocq died one spring evening full of light and birdsong struggling to give birth to her third child, and for once, Celia lost her careful calm, battering at her brother in the dark salon of Holly House while Alicocq lay upstairs with the tiny waxen child beside her, little more aloof in death than she had been in life. Breaking suddenly, Celia pounded Hugh Charles's chest with her clenched fists, shattered by a storm of bitter tears, and even through his own dumb grief, he realized she cried like this not for Alicocq, but for Matt, and should have done so long ago.

"But I loved her, Hugh Charles. I loved her."

"That saves nobody."

"There is too much death! May we keep no one?"

"Only who God leaves us," said her brother with unexpected piety, stricken himself with the knowledge that he had been left with two young sons and little else.

From that time on Celia began to cling more closely to him, reproaching herself that she had neglected her brother, who needed her now. The two little boys had been taken away to live at Westport with their grandmother, to be cared for tenderly by the remaining flock of unmarried daughters, and Hugh Charles was lonely and alarmed for his own future.

When she was there, he took to coming frequently to Owenscourt, looking with small envious eyes round the well-kept house and flourishing estate, the full barns and the spotless byres and stables. Often he would slyly question John Julius's judgment, trying to plant doubt; artfully interposing questions as to her financial standing, always cleverly disguised as concern for her affairs.

But he was kind to her, and more affectionate than he had ever been, even coming up to Dublin to visit her in between her journeys to the country; rambling up and down through the house fingering the fine furniture and ornaments with undisguised admiration; even going down to the Shops where Matt had never allowed him go, asking questions of the men and annoying Lind, his small eyes wandering over the expanse of the sheds under the bright sun coming through the long glass roof.

Owen watched what he saw of this with deep resentment, for his uncle gave him none of the love and respect he was used to being given in the Shops, and by John Julius down at Owenscourt. To Hugh Charles he was not the respected heir to all these kingdoms, but merely a precocious child meddling in matters past his understanding. Owen couldn't understand why his mother allowed it, touched by some sense of threat.

"Mother, he is nosy. The Shops are mine, and Lind tells me everything. Uncle Hugh Charles goes down there without being asked, and even you would never do that, and pokes his nose into everything and asks interfering questions, and then treats me as though I know nothing about any of it."

"Dearest, he doesn't understand young people. His own children are too small, and gone away from him too."

She had been about to say he didn't understand children, and drew back in time. At fourteen only Hugh Charles would have called Owen a child. He was long legged as Matt had been, and showed every sign of growing to his height; seeming to suffer none of the awkwardnesses of adolescence save for his unstable voice. Owen's hooter, Emmett called it. His success at school, and the loving responsibilities of the Shops and Owenscourt had endowed him with a fine self-confidence of bearing. Always tempered with the hilarious good humor that was Matt's greatest gift to him.

"Nor does Lind understand young people," he said now, shrewdly. "He is an old man and has never had children. But," he added, "he remembers I am my father's son, and all my father wanted of me."

To his mother he would never speak of the mixture of contempt and pure dislike he sensed from his uncle, who was always careful to control it when she was there. Without understanding it he was aware of resentment and bitterness. This had lain behind the smooth careful surface of Hugh Charles's manners ever since the day that Matt O'Connor had marched into Holly House and sent the matchmaker packing and Joseph Hession with him. Making them all his vassals for immediate money his father had been too grasping to resist. Now the man was dead and all the money with him; waiting for these two spoilt spalpeens to grow up. In every way Hugh Charles felt cheated, not even having the money now for the squireen's way of life he fancied; looking with growing greed and resentment at all that was accumulating, so carefully guarded, for these two strips of boys.

"Does Emmett feel the same about him, Owen?" Celia asked, always willing to listen to Owen, who was rarely foolish.

Owen laughed and spread his hands, his face warm with affection.

"Emmett," he laughed. "Who could disagree with Emmett about anything. He wouldn't even realize."

They both smiled together, acknowledging Emmett's capacity for living in his own world, and let the conversation drop, as Mrs. Bradley came in to tell them the dinner was on the table.

Despite Owen's instincts Celia allowed herself in her loneliness to fall more and more under the influence of her brother, unaware that she was watched by three people, other than Owen, with grave concern. John Julius would have run Hugh Charles off the land and back, as soon as look at him, to his own broken fences and weed-choked drains, and thistled pastures. In the city James Cornelius O'Duffy watched more distantly but with no less concern, having been appalled one day to find Hugh Charles on the other side of his desk, about his sister's business. Daily he framed words of warning in his mind that he dare not put on paper lest the rogue should put the boot on the other foot and drag him into court for defamation. The third one was the small plump Canon Walsh from the cathedral down in Tuam, who had managed quietly to do more than anybody else for Celia's sore and stricken heart. He remembered clearly his impression on the day of her marriage, that that whey-faced pair, both father and son, would require to be watched. Nor did he heed Christian charity or the teachings of his cloth in coming to the sharp conclusion at the present time that Hugh Charles Healey was up to no good. It was not love for his sister that was keeping him hanging around Owenscourt. And the sister, poor soul, in a state to listen to anyone who seemed to offer her a bit of affection and consolation.

There was not one of them did not wish that Owen might be twenty-one tomorrow; before his poor mother was talked into the doing of something foolish.

Old Thomas died. In the wild days of the early year, almost on Owen's birthday. As the scant group of mourners turned from the grave Celia put her hand into her brother's arm, holding down her skirts with the other against the tearing wind. She glanced back at the open grave and then over at the white marble angel that wept above her mother. There were tears on her face as she turned along the flattened grass.

"Not for him, Hugh Charles," she said, and took away her hand to brush them off with her gloved finger. "Not for him. I can't ever remember loving him, even as a small child. He was not a good man. And I would be a hypocrite to pretend love for him, who had no love for me."

She paused and turned to say good-bye to a farrier from Tuam.

"Good-bye, Mr. Daly. Mrs. Daly. And thank you for coming."

"It's just, Hugh Charles," she went on, "that we are the last ones left. Do you realize that? We are not old ourselves but we are the last ones left."

Hugh Charles did no more than grunt, touching his hard hat to the country people who came to any funeral as automatically as they would come to a Fair day. They slipped away like dark ghosts into the gray winter fields, and by the time Hugh Charles and Celia reached the carriage they were alone. She turned and looked into his face and could find no expression in it, the thick lips closed and his eyes creased against the wind.

"And what of the woman?" she asked him as they settled gratefully into the warmth of the closed carriage. "What will happen to her?"

It was she who had nursed the old man with unexpected devotion through his last illness, vanishing like a well-proportioned wraith through the nearest door on sight of any of the family or the doctor. It had saddened Celia on her visits to realize that Holly House was sliding down again into neglect and decay, lost without the firm and ruthless hand of Alicocq.

"What of the woman?"

Now Hugh Charles showed expression, his flat pale face clamped tight with anger.

"Gone," he said. "Gone, before the body was even cold. No trace of her anywhere."

Celia stared at him, unwinding the wrappings of the shawl around her head.

"But how strange," she said, arrested, peering over the black folds. "How very strange. You would think she'd wait to see had we made some arrangements for her. Something she could live on. When all's said and done, Hugh Charles, she served him well. I don't think Mama would have wished her starve."

Her brother snarled.

"She'll not starve."

"You mean she has money?"

"She has now. There's not a guinea left in the house."

"She's taken it?"

"Yes."'

"Did Father have any?"

"He did. He told me so one night with too much drink taken. He had enough, he said, hidden away to bury him and see the farm through a few hard years if needed."

"She would have known everything, of course."

"She would. She had the mattress slit and the money gone from under him before the corpse was even stiff."

Celia had a chill and dreadful vision of the truth. Of her brother and the dairymaid watching for their opportunity in the lonely house as the old man died in the bed above his money. She could not bear to ask how Hugh Charles had relaxed his vigilance enough to let the woman get it first. Suddenly she felt cold and sad.

They drove through the shriveled fields, cowering under the onslaught of the gale, along the avenue of clashing trees towards the house, and she looked in pity at her brother. Good fortune did not follow him. Even in the pathetic contest with the dairymaid it was the woman who had won. Once he had been rescued by Matt, and once by Alicocq, and now he was alone again, faced with the detested hard work of living on the profits of the farm, such as it was.

In her mind she heard herself saying to James O'Duffy that only a fool could fail to make a profit out of Holly House, for the land was the same as Owenscourt. Matt too, long ago, had said he was a bad manager like her father. She sighed and looked at his pale sullen face, blotched with red by the cold, and knew she must be firm about any requests for money. It was not hers to give. She took very seriously her position as trustee to her sons, feeling that at some time it would be her duty to account to them for everything.

As for what Matt had left her, she felt him capable of rising from his grave did she give that to Hugh Charles.

When inevitably he asked, it was the ground for her refusal that drove Hugh Charles to incoherent rage.

"And haven't they enough?" he yelled at her, closed in Matt's small study. "Haven't they enough, and they at the finest school in Ireland and all their grand clothes and Owenscourt into the bargain, and the carriage business too! Haven't they enough?"

"Their money is not mine to give," she said. "I have everything in trust. I cannot part with it. As to what they have, that is what their father left them, and it is sacred to me that they get it all intact."

Not even Hugh Charles had the ill grace to ask her for her own money.

"And if you die?" he said after a long pause, thinking of the trust.

She lifted grave eyes to him.

Before Matt, dying had been for the old.

She felt deeply sorry for Hugh Charles, and could understand both his loneliness since the death of Alicocq, and also the bitterness of seeing both her sons so well heeled while he had not a penny to his name. She sighed. They could not be forever carrying Hugh Charles. Matt had put enough in ten years into Holly House to make it a going concern for anyone with a spark of ability. Most desperately she wanted to do something to restore her brother's pride, and a faith in himself that might rouse him to more effort. As she had said, they were the only ones left now.

She thought about it deeply all through the bright spring days in Dublin, and then one evening down at Owenscourt for Easter she stopped John Julius as he rode in from the fields. In the soft grass-scented evening she was taking a turn down around the lake before supper, waiting for the boys to come home from wherever they might be. She met John Julius on the bridge as he came down the bog road.

"Ah, John Julius." She looked up at him and took his bridle. "Sit with me a moment. It's so lovely here. I don't want to go in yet awhile."

John Julius rolled easily off the horse and looped its reins, turning it loose to crop the long sweet grass around the edges of the lake.

"It's what my mother used to call a pet day," he said. "You'd never get another like it."

In the gentle sun the clouds sailed high, trailing light shadows across the parkland and the fields; over the luminous, incomparable green of Irish grass in spring. At the edges of the water the kingcups were already breaking yellow, and the rushes stood like lances in the shallows, each one to its own shadow.

They sat down on the parapet side by side, and John Julius remembered telling her, dear God was it five years back now, how he had sat there with Boru and watched the lights going out in Owenscourt on the morning Matt had died.

Celia lifted her face to the sun.

"It all goes well, John Julius."

"It all goes well, ma'am." He was happy to be able to agree. Owenscourt was prospering. They had put a stand of timber in too on the edges of the far pasture, which was a new venture and should be profitable. He was able to tell her that all the little trees were doing well.

She turned to him then and there was a small defiance in her gesture.

"There is something I want to speak to you about, John Julius," she said. "You are responsible for Owenscourt and you should know. I doubt it will ever mean anything but it is something must be done. And I want my way about it."

He waited, noticing the moss needed clearing from the parapet of the little bridge.

"I am going to appoint a trustee for the boys lest anything happen to me. I don't imagine that it will, but we have to remember that we never thought Matt would die either. I should have done it long ago, but I could never bear to think of it."

Not that she felt for one second that anything would happen to her. Lightning, they said, never struck twice in the same place, and it had already struck Owenscourt three times in a fortnight. But James O'Duffy had been at her. It was something, he said, that should have been done long ago.

John Julius thought so too, listening to her with relief,

having in these last four years devoted many a long hour of anxious thought to what would happen, if God forbid, Mrs. Matt should die.

"That's very good, Mrs. Matt," he said. "Very wise." No doubt she would appoint that smooth-faced lawyer from Dublin. She couldn't do better.

"I am going," she said, "to appoint my brother, Hugh Charles, as their guardian and trustee."

John Julius never knew how he stifled the words that came racing to his lips. He sat very still, staring up at the rooks circling over the windbreak elms; trying to control his face. He was silent too long, searching for something he could say.

"Do you not approve of that, John Julius?"

Her voice was a little hostile and he fumbled for words.

"Wouldn't you think perhaps," he said hesitantly, almost too appalled to speak, "that someone with a legal qualification might be better. Mr. O'Duffy for example."

"But Hugh Charles is a solicitor."

He had forgotten. In all the fancy waistcoats and the gambling and lately in the whining poverty he had forgotten. He had a strong suspicion the rogue had been worrying Mrs. Matt for money. Solicitor indeed. It took more than that to make a solicitor.

She looked at him and suppressed her anger at the thoughts that lay clear across his face. Patiently she tried to give John Julius some explanation.

"I am tired of death, Johnju," she said, and brought him closer by the shortened name. "I am not old and yet I have seen them all go. Hugh Charles and I are alone now. I know he hasn't been the best of managers, but there is little risk that he will ever have to manage anything. It will do him good just to see that I have trusted him. Since my father died, we are very much alone. There is no one else."

"There is me," John Julius thought fiercely, "who knows as much of the land as Matt ever knew himself, and if anything were to happen, would hand it all over as he intended it."

He was appalled; helpless. The man was not only a fool

but a rogue as well. The only hope was in the unlikelihood of it ever coming to anything. Four and a half years more was no long time.

She echoed his thoughts, smiling at him placatingly.

"I am only thirty-three, John Julius," she said. "And Owen has only a few years more to go. It will be all right. And do good too, I know. Don't concern yourself. I'll see Owen inherit."

"There he is," said John Julius, glad to be able to break the horrifying conversation.

Owen and Antonia were coming across the sloping pasture beyond the parkland, Boru loping stiffly at their heels, ignoring the half-grown lambs that frolicked from their path. In silence they watched as the young pair spurred their horses, and jumped the low iron railings of the park, followed by the dog, who made a poor scrambling job of it.

"Poor Boru," said John Julius, "he is getting old."

Celia looked at the dog coming over to them, having seen John Julius, and knew that it was true. The long hairs of his muzzle were gray, and he no longer was the huge young dog who had so ecstatically galloped the fields behind the heels of the white horse. She laid a hand on his head as he came up.

"Well, Boru," she said, "that was a bit of a struggle, wasn't it?"

Boru was having no woman criticizing him. He went and laid his head on John Julius's lap, looking up as if to say to him that he could really do it better if he tried.

"Ah, Boru," said Johnju sadly, and rubbed the shaggy head.

The two riders had not turned toward them, but with a small wave went up the other side of the lake toward the house. Owen only lifted a hand, but Antonia's strange, lovely face broke into one of the brilliant smiles she kept almost exclusively for her father.

"She is causing me concern," John Julius said, looking after the straight and easy-moving back. He had himself replaced the pony Matt had given her.

Celia looked at him in surprise.

"Concern? She always seems to me most good and dutiful."

Of course, she thought, I never see her with her mother. Peggy Cannon was rarely seen round the estate, at least when Celia was there.

"She is always that," John Julius answered.

How could he describe the rancor and jealousy that filled his house as Antonia grew older; the mother who couldn't accept the beauty of her growing daughter. Especially now, may God forgive him, that she hadn't the outlet of the big house and the shameless flirting with Matt O'Connor. Antonia had always been a silent and inward-turning child, and as she grew older she became more so in defense against her mother's scalding tongue.

There were two people only in the world for Antonia: her father and Owen. And even Owen she held at some prickly arm's length. Beyond them, she didn't care.

"There is a bitterness in her that is wrong in one so young," her father said. "An antagonism to all the world. She feels that it is there for everybody else, but not for her."

"But why? She should have had a happy life here. Especially since she and Owen became friends."

He shook his head and she looked at his concerned face, thinking, as she did so, how rarely she really looked at him at all. He who was the pillar and cornerstone of all their lives; always there in every crisis; who had been more than half a father to her sons since Matt had died. They all took him for granted. His long strong frame had thickened a little and he was a big man, well become by the soft jacket of local tweed and the loose kerchief that he wore around the land. The dark-blue eyes were as arresting as ever in the weathered face, having lost none of their deep color, but threads of gray were showing in the thick black hair above his ears. He held a total air of dependability and strength, and endless kind patience lay in the depths of the observant eyes; that could nonetheless snap like flints when he was angered.

"It is perhaps her age, John Julius," she said, wishing to

comfort him. "They are all a little difficult these days. They are children no longer, any of them."

He shook his head. Antonia's hostilities went deeper than the pains of growing up, and frequently now when he looked into her withdrawn defensive eyes, he was touched by some helpless fear.

He whistled his horse then.

"Come on, Mrs. Matt, the stone'll be getting damp."

They walked slowly and companionably together up through the park, and stood a moment at the white gate by the stables. John Julius noticed the curtains move a little at the window of his house, but Celia never thought of looking. She had forgotten Peggy Cannon, who could no longer do her harm and rarely came her way.

She was more concerned with John Julius himself, looking at him again as she had looked at him on the bridge.

"I think we all forget, Johnju," she said gently, "how much we owe to you."

The blue eyes crinkled in their sun-deep wrinkles and he grinned.

"Ah, go on, Mrs. Matt," he said. "Wouldn't I do it for anyone."

She wouldn't smile.

"I don't know if you would, Johnju," she said, "but you certainly do it for us, and I don't know where we would all be without you."

He spoke soberly now, gently.

"Matt was my friend, and indeed my benefactor. Wouldn't I care for what was his?"

"Some wouldn't. Some might even take advantage of us."

Pity, thought John Julius wryly, you wouldn't see that about your brother.

He let her go, and before he turned into the stables he watched her walk along the front of the house. Four years, and she was out of full mourning now, knowing that Matt would hate her to be forever wrapped in black. She was still very thin and the skirts of a white and lilac print swayed round her as she walked, the sun rich in her fair hair. More beautiful than ever, thought John Julius, and with some new air of strength since Matt had died. God help her, she had proved a good woman and handled the whole business well. And God help himself, he had been more than half in love with her since that first day when Matt had taken him and Peggy off the road. Her wedding day. They had all sat there in the carriage, Matt full of himself and totally oblivious of the anger coming out of his new wife like heat from a hayrick. He smiled to remember it. But it was only her that kept him here. Were it not for her and her children, he would long ago have gone back and tried to get Cannon's Mills back on their feet again. The cherished target of his heart. With the help of God he'd manage it when Owen came into his own.

But how, he thought, as he turned the horse and walked in through the stable gate. How in God's name was he going to try and stop her from this piece of folly about her brother.

He wrote to James Cornelius O'Duffy, a carefully worded confidential letter, and the lawyer, who agreed, appalled, with every word he said, did his forceful best, less hesitant than John Julius himself.

There were silver threads now through the soft bushy beard, but the eyes behind the gold-rimmed spectacles were calmer and stronger than ever.

"Mrs. Matt," he said bluntly, when she had told him what she wanted. As they had expected, she called on him just as soon as she was back in Dublin. "Before making anyone a trustee, especially a sole trustee as you suggest, it is surely advisable, would you not think, to measure their suitability. Would you say that your brother's record in the handling of money would recommend him as suitable?"

He stared at her accusingly over his glasses, but she was ready for him, having been through it all with John Julius.

"No," she said steadily, and smiled at his astonishment.

"Then?" he asked her, and his expression asked if she were mad.

"Mr. O'Duffy," she said, "I am only thirty-four. It is most unlikely that this will ever have any meaning. For that reason I am anxious to give my brother a sign of confidence. I think at this stage of his life he needs it badly."

"Let him get it out of a bottle," thought O'Duffy. He understood Hugh Charles was going there already for comfort in his troubles. He made a noise out through his beard, like one of Emmett's toy steam engines in the early stages of blowing up, and forebore to point out the painfully obvious. Matt had been only thirty-five when he had died, and no one, except oddly Matt himself, had anticipated that either. And this foolish lady would not be so content and well placed now, if Matt had not looked carefully to his possible death.

"Mrs. Matt," he began carefully, wondering how so beautiful and intelligent-looking a woman could be such a fool, who up to date had been so sensible. Or probably not a fool. Just too tenderhearted to that rogue of a brother for her own good. "Mrs. Matt. Would you not at least have someone else as well. There is a great deal of property and money involved here."

She was gently firm.

"I think it would be insulting to do so. It would be no mark of confidence if I had someone else then to watch him. Besides, there is no one else. We are alone."

No matter what he said there was nothing he could do to shake her, and in the end he banged his bell irritably for his clerk and gave instructions for the drawing up of the deed, realizing that if he didn't she would only go to some other lawyer.

His sole hope and comfort lay in her youth and obviously radiant good health. She was right in saying that almost certainly the document would never be implemented. Four years was a very short time until the boy was twenty-one.

The only person she didn't talk to was Owen; unable to face his inevitable furious objections. She comforted herself by telling herself firmly that at the moment she was the trustee and Owen under age, and he did not have to be told every detail of her administration. Almost certainly there would never be need for discussion with him at all.

* * *

They went down to Owenscourt for what seemed a perfect, golden summer, fulfilling all the promise of the gentle spring. It ended with a harvest home for the finest harvest they had had in years. Owen presiding with grace and hilarity, bringing tears to many old eyes that had watched his father from a child.

Never had he been so unwilling to leave his beloved estate, the whole long summer spent working with his own laborers in the fields, learning the trade of his inheritance. He was brown and strong and hard, and bored to indifference by the thought of going back to school.

His mother tried to comfort him, pointing out that there were only two more years of school. She told him, "Your father always said that education makes even a better farmer. After school is done, you can divide your time between the Shops and the land."

Secretly Owen knew his heart was in the land, unable to confide even to his mother the feelings that crept over him when he would walk the pastures of an evening, savoring with every step the rich knowledge that the green land underneath his feet was his. And the square gray house with the low sun glittering in its windows, the tidy sweep of stables at its side. There was nothing else in life he wanted nor ever could be. Not even the Shops, although he accepted them just as deeply as his responsibility. It was the land that held his heart.

Reluctantly he gathered all his books and clothes together, leaving half the job to Emmett, and Celia watched them off in the trap, Bourdain's buttons glittering in the early sun. The street shadows were sharp and black and the light clear on her as she stood and waved until they were out of sight around the corner; in her blue wrapper, the sunlight on her hair, and her hand involuntarily at her side over a small irritating pain that had been nagging her for days.

They had been back to school a week, in gentle gold September weather when winter still seemed impossible. The first leaves were turning red and gold on the Virginia creeper that clothed the castle walls, and across the green acres of the playing fields the football posts were going up and the patient groundsmen tracing the white lines of the pitches.

Owen was faintly surprised when the janitor came to him where he walked in the pleasure grounds with his friends, and told him that Father Rector wished to see him. All his classes were arranged, and the term was set.

"I'd better go and see what the man wants," he said. "Don't go away. I'll be back." In the sunpatched shadows of the front hall, he found Emmett waiting.

"What have you been up to?" he demanded at once, with all the righteousness of the elder brother.

Emmett was unimpressed, the blue eyes accusing in return.

"Nothing," he said, "that I can think of. What have you done? Been drinking the altar wine?"

Owen snorted and they walked together up the curving stairs.

"Probably something Mama forgot," Emmett said, "or something she wants us to know."

In the Round Room, the light gentle on the painted ceiling, Owen scratched politely on Father Rector's door.

They couldn't read his face when they went in, but he had a look of being pale and very careful. His wide desk stood between them and behind him through the open window they could see the long straight stretch of the avenue. In his unusual silence the sparrows chirped in the creeper round the casement frame.

Bleakly and sadly the Rector looked at them, too shocked himself to do a great deal to mitigate the blow. Even with all his experience he sought hopelessly for words. No holy platitudes would help him here.

"Dear boys," he said, and his voice caught on the words. It was a few moments before he could go on, and they stared at him wondering, not yet disturbed, what was wrong. "Dear boys, it is my sad and most hopeless task to tell you that, God rest her immortal soul, your poor mother died at nine o'clock this morning."

Chapter 11

Hugh Charles, gasping with awe and astonishment at his good fortune, for he had never intended to see it otherwise, stalked gently until the funeral was over.

He sent John Julius, who had come rushing from the country with him, down to meet the boys at Kingsbridge station, saying with truth that he could handle them better than he could himself. They had come up on the train that evening, through mellow autumn fields, watching the carefree fishing along the banks of the canal in the low sun; clacking through the straggles of southern Dublin almost in total silence. Not yet in any depth of grief, or even shock; rather in a state of suspended belief. Both of them were convinced in their inmost hearts that as soon as they got there, there would be someone to tell them it was all some foolish error. She would be still as they had last seen her when they turned round to look back at her from the corner, smiling and waving in her blue wrapper. The sun in the soft curls of her hair.

John Julius's somber and compassionate face beyond the barrier at Kingsbridge, and the black formality of his suit, told them even before he could reach them, that there was no mistake. And the unashamed tears on his face as he put an arm round both of them without speaking, oblivious of the crowds pushing from the platform.

"It's true," whispered Emmett, and tears filled his own blue eyes. For once it was Owen who stared, silent, rigid.

"Dear God have mercy on her, yes, it's true," John Julius said. "My poor boys. I'm sorry."

"Why did no one tell us she was ill? Why did no one tell us?"

Owen fixed him with eyes black with pain, outraged by the unbelief of not even being able to say good-bye.

John Julius drew them aside out of the stream of people. Emmett was now crying helplessly, attracting curious and compassionate glances.

"It seems it all happened so very quickly," he said to them, and gave his handkerchief to Emmett, wiping his tears despairingly on the cuff of his sleeve. "A little pain Mrs. Bradley said had been nagging her for days, but nothing you'd make trouble about, they thought it no more than a mite of colic. Then suddenly there was just the one night of dreadful suffering and in the morning she was gone. The doctor never dreamt she would die, never mind so quickly. Mrs. Bradley said to me that it was just as if she suddenly realized it was possible for her to die, and she did."

Emmett looked up with drowned eyes.

"She realized," he said, "that she could go to my father."

They both looked at him dumbly, knowing that he was right, and in their anguished silence Owen knew that all his life he would associate his mother's death with the smell of soot and smoke, and the sound of banging doors along a train's length.

"What was it, then, John Julius, sir," he said. Still calm and stony with control, his arm around his brother's shoulders. "What was it?"

"Something Dr. Brice called appendicitis. An infection, it seems. He said that only when the surgeons manage to operate against it successfully will it be no danger. 'Twas like a boil, d'you see, there inside her, and when it wasn't lanced it burst, and that was the end. Come now, and we'll get home."

Owen followed him because there was nothing else to do, but inside him his mind was crying wildly that it did not seem enough to die of, when you had everything to live for, and were young and beautiful, smiling in the sunshine in a blue dress.

They suffered the ponderous condolences of Hugh Charles and tried to comfort the cataracts of tears from Bradley, their eyes turned upward, waiting in fear and savage, still disbelieving sorrow, for the moment when they were allowed to go into the dark room where four candle flames stood straight and still as the rushes in the lake; and between them she lay under the lace ruffles of her bridal bedspread, beautiful as they had left her, a small serene smile about her lips.

Emmett grabbed Owen's hand so tight, he hurt him, half strangled with his tears.

"Hush, Emm. Look. She looks happy."

"Of course she's happy," Emmett countered as best he could, gulping for his words. "She's where she wants to be, with Papa. I'm crying for us, Owen."

And in still stony silence Owen accepted the age-old truth that it is not the dead we mourn for, but ourselves, for they are beyond grief. He bent over the gentle scent of the little late gold roses Bradley had put around the rosary between her fingers and kissed her cold forehead; and then could no longer stay, rushing from the room and up to the lamplight familiarity of their own playroom.

Belief was bleak and total when they carried her along the same winding paths through Glasnevin to lie beside Matt and the tiny sister. An agonizing funeral, of grief so great and shocked that people could not bear to meet each other's eyes. They said all the words offered by convention and by their own sorrow; desperate then to get away back to their own private lives where in familiar surroundings they could come to terms with shock. They told themselves that they must do something about those two poor brave boys, but for the moment they could hardly bear to look at them, dry eyed now and composed at the head of their mother's pallbearers, and thanking all the mourners at the cemetery gates with somber self-control.

In no time at all they were alone, the last carriage clopping off into the distance, and no more to be done than turn for the sad house, with John Julius and Hugh Charles. Bourdain took care of Mrs. Bradley and Mrs. Savage, both weeping uncontrollably, and his own little white-faced, stricken Gracie.

James Cornelius O'Duffy had preceded them to the house for the reading of the will, horrified beyond words that his worst fears had come true, and so soon. The laddo would have a good run for his money before Owen came to his majority. He sighed heavily, as he drew up before the green door, grieving genuinely for the sad present and the lovely woman, but deeply apprehensive now for the future of her sons.

No guests had come back with them and only Hugh Charles would eat, setting himself solidly to the cold table that Mrs. Savage and Bradley had laid out as their last loving gesture to their mistress. All the others waited for him in numbed silence in the drawing room, warmed by the golden evening sun that Celia had so loved.

Hugh Charles came slowly and steadily up at last, not hurrying nor apologizing, wiping the last crumbs from his wiry whiskers.

James O'Duffy opened the card table, and spread his papers out on it, settling himself to start. Hugh Charles held up a hand.

"Surely," he said, with a cold flip of the hand toward John Julius, "this reading should be restricted to members of the family only."

James regarded him over his gold-rimmed spectacles, the calm eyes icy cold, and thought b'God, he's in a hurry to get the bit between his teeth.

"We have always thought of Uncle Johnju as family," said Owen quickly, giving him the name they had called him when they were small.

"Mr. Cannon," said O'Duffy, "is a beneficiary, and therefore has a right to hear the will. Also those poor souls down in the kitchen, but I think it would upset them more than they are already. I'll tell them afterward, quietly."

Hugh Charles grunted unamiably and subsided into a chair, and John Julius was sick with apprehension, but not for himself.

She had forgotten nobody, as if to protect them all against the possible results of what she did. Lind; Mrs. Bradley; Mrs. Savage; a substantial sum for John Julius, in gratitude for everything that he had been to all of them; a gift to Bourdain and Gracie for their little home. But when all the gentle bequests from her own estate were done, and the balance given into the trust for the boys, the guardianship and care of the entire estate went into the hands of Hugh Charles Healey until such time as Owen should be twenty-one. And Owen, thought John Julius with heavy heart, would not be seventeen until next February.

O'Duffy saw Owen's head come up, his eyes wide and startled. He had assumed, of course, that there would be a new trustee, but had thought, without ever discussing it with his mother, that it could be no one else than John Julius; who knew everything there was to be known and was their father's friend. Life then would have gone on exactly as before, until the time came for him to come fully into his inheritance. He glanced sharply at John Julius, and then at James O'Duffy but neither of them would meet his eyes, and the silence in the sunlit room grew as heavy as the weight of grief that already held the day. Hugh Charles examined his bitten nails.

Slowly and unwillingly James O'Duffy folded up the papers and put them into his gleaming leather case, and then looked formally and with difficulty at Hugh Charles.

"It is very straightforward," he said. "I foresee no difficulties. Things should, without trouble, continue exactly as before in the interests of these boys. Please come to me if anything should arise that you cannot handle. There should be nothing. I know your sister found the trusteeship simple."

It was as near a threat as he dare make, but Hugh Charles stared back inimically at him from his pale eyes and didn't answer. John Julius ran his hands through his thick hair and couldn't bring himself to look at any of them, wondering with a chill of apprehension what was going to happen now.

"I'll go now," said James O'Duffy, "and see these poor good women in the kitchen."

Owen followed him down the stairs, halting him beside the Chinese Masterpiece on the bottom step, and from the drawing room his uncle watched him go with a small smile on his lips, hiding the inward surge of violent excitement that consumed him.

"Mr. O'Duffy."

James turned and looked at the boy with pity. A young Matt recreated, but at the moment all his blitheness stilled by shock. He bent to the lawyer and whispered lest he be heard above. "Mr. O'Duffy, I don't like this. Forgive me, but I don't trust my uncle. He doesn't like me, nor Emmett either."

The lawyer looked at him a long moment, and then was honest.

"No more do I like it, Owen. And no more do I trust him. I must warn you that I am expecting trouble for you, nor do I think he'll wait long to start it. I did my best to dissuade your poor mother."

"Why, why did she do it? Why didn't she talk to me?"

Because you were the one person might have dissuaded her, James thought, but didn't say so.

"He was," he said, "the only relative she had. And she didn't expect to die."

He clapped the boy on the arm.

"Come and tell me what happens to you. I'll do anything I can to help you." Although, he thought gloomily, it would probably be little enough.

He went on downstairs into the kitchen to Mrs. Bradley.

Owen stood a long time and stared at the foolish picture beside him on the stairs. He knew it was the river at Holly House, but had never really understood what it was all about, only knowing it to be symbolic of the love his father and mother had held for each other, and the same love with which they had encircled their sons. The last of it had come to an end today in the flower-piled grave out there in Glasnevin, and he and Emmett were alone. Tears flooded his eyes and he reached out and laid a hand as if for comfort on the small foolish bulk of Dublin Castle. Then he blinked away the hopeless tears and went slowly back upstairs to tackle the void that was their life.

Hugh Charles did not delay, all his avaricious plans churning in his brain since the unbelievable news of his sister's illness and death; trying, for the face of things, to dredge out of his whirling mind even the smallest suitable expressions of grief.

"We had better go back to school in a few days, Uncle," Owen said to him the day after the funeral. John Julius had already gone back to Owenscourt that morning to be about his business, and the two boys were doing no more than breaking their hearts around the empty house. Both of them knew they would be better off at school where they would have plenty to do. As he spoke he tried to suppress his anger at seeing his uncle going through his mother's desk. They should at least have done it together.

His uncle looked up from the piles of papers he was going through, eyes hard as pebbles above round steel-rimmed spectacles.

"There'll be no more of that," he said. "I'll write to them today and have your belongings sent to Holly House."

"No more of what?" Owen knew he gaped at him.

"Clongowes." Hugh Charles almost spat the word. "All that fancy schooling. You're old enough the pair of you to do a day's work on the land and that's what you'll do from this day on. Since you're supposed to care so much for the land, you should be glad to do it."

He was almost beside himself; all the years of resentment

of Matt O'Connor boiling inside him with the heady power to avenge.

"But, Uncle, my father wished it. And my mother."

"They're dead."

"It's their money pays the school fees." Owen flared, seeing already in this flat-faced man all the dangers he had feared.

"Only if I wish it," his uncle said, staring at him with cold venom, and Owen fled before he shame himself with tears. He raced for Emmett and together they went at once to James O'Duffy.

He looked at them sadly over his gleaming overcrowded desk, and there was pity in his mild eyes.

"I'm sorry, boys. There is nothing I can do. Absolutely nothing. There are no grounds to try and have the trusteeship set aside. He is your mother's brother, and in his right mind, and there is nothing that has intervened since she appointed him to make him invalid as a trustee. I am sorry," he said again, "for I think you are only at the beginning."

He put aside his next client and lifted his hat from the mahogany hooks, and took them over to the palm-filled cheerful luxury of Mitchell's. There he bought them chocolate and cream cakes, giving them what bodily comfort he could before sending them back helplessly to face the destruction of their lives.

"Thank you, sir," Owen said, grateful for the kindness, but filled with appalled fear as to what would come next. Emmett stood like a pale shadow at his shoulder, but without Owen's look of fearful shock, always helped by some secret refuge into which he was able to withdraw.

They shook hands with James O'Duffy and thanked him again, and threaded through the thin sunlight over the bridge and on down through the crowds of Sackville Street, toward what had once been home.

Before they left Dublin the advertisement had appeared in all the papers for the sale by auction of the Shops.

"You cannot, Uncle! You cannot! O'Connors had been there for nearly a hundred years."

Owen was ashen, coming to the full understanding of what

was happening. Before it all Emmett had retreated, taking refuge with the priests across the road.

"You cannot!"

"That's where you're wrong," Hugh Charles said laconically, and continued his methodical searching of every drawer and cupboard in the house. A man had already been summoned to list and value the inlaid box of jewelry from which Matt had decked Celia like a cherished Christmas tree in the first days of their marriage. Owen felt he was being tossed helplessly, as in a nightmare from which he couldn't wake, screaming his hopeless protests.

He went racing to Lind, who looked at him with a face as ashen as his own, his old eyes dark with anger.

"I'm off, lad," he said. "Off. Little more than a child I came to O'Connor's and you'll know I only stayed on now to see you into it. I wish you well, Mr. Owen, but before God I see little good to come at this villain's hands. I'll be off tomorrow and there's others like me. Thanks to your good mother, I'll be quite all right."

She had protected everyone except her own.

"Bradley." Desperately he thrashed round him looking hopelessly for someone who might help. He was in the kitchen now, making instinctively for the authority he had known all his life. "Bradley. My mother's necklaces and rings and everything. Her pearls. He cannot do it."

Bradley eased him onto a chair beside the table and her old hands smoothed the strong bright hair so like his father's.

"He can, the wicked villain," she said, as James O'Duffy had, and Lind. "He can. But I don't have to stay here and watch it."

"Nor I," echoed Mrs. Savage, slamming down a skillet as if it might have been in some murderous attack on Hugh Charles himself.

"I can do nicely," Mrs. Bradley said, "with what I've got laid by and what your mother gave us. Mrs. Savage and I were out today with a hired trap and we've found ourselves a good little cottage there at Sandy Cove. There's no need stay another day to watch it. And as for work for him!"

He could feel her trembling up against him with the force of her anger.

"You'll know, Master Owen, God keep you, that I'd do anything in the wide world for you and your brother, but stay here and take orders from that monster I will not. There's a room for you and Master Emmett out there any time you want to come. We saw to that, but we'll be leaving this house tomorrow morning. Gracie and Bourdain are off too."

Her usually pale face was flushed with two patches of furious red, and Mrs. Savage nodded vigorously above the range. Already in a corner of the kitchen they had piled the belongings accumulated in their long years of service to the house.

But in the end they could only think to do what James O'Duffy had done, and set before him good strong tea and hot bread fresh from the oven, dripping with butter as he liked it. All the comfort they could offer.

"Wait now," Bradley said, as he got up to go, a hand on his arm. "I have something here for you do you get nothing else."

She went over to the piled bundles and boxes, and came back with a rolled tube of paper.

"There, now," she said, and her old voice shook, "keep that until the day you can bring it back and hang it up again where it belongs. I put something else in the frame. Unless he gets some expert to tell him, that fella up there would never know one picture from another. It's only something hanging on a wall to him, unless it'll bring him money."

Owen knew he should not allow her to speak of his uncle in the way she did, but he was past caring. She meant well. And he was enemy to both of them.

Slowly he unrolled the Chinese Masterpiece, a little crumpled, thin and fragile without its frame, and the colors slightly faded.

Owen was past tears. Slowly he smoothed it out on the top of the kitchen table and stared at it.

"Did you ever understand it, Bradley?" he asked her.

"I did not indeed," she said. "But it was always very important to them."

"It was them," said Owen, putting a gentle finger to the creases. "It was them."

Rolling it again carefully, he put it up his sleeve lest it be noticed by his uncle before he got it to someplace of safety, although, as Bradley said, he would have small care for it since it was of no value.

In little more than days all the bright promise of his kingdoms broke to pieces under Owen's eyes.

"The house itself?" he asked his uncle, hoarsely, desperately looking at the empty cupboards and stripped walls.

"Auction," said his uncle tersely.

Everything was to be converted into money, the only possible reality to Hugh Charles after all the long hard years without it. And who could dispute his trusteeship until the day of Owen's inheritance came, and he could not produce the value? Nor could he believe even now in the vast good fortune of his sister's death, the day of reckoning four years away comfortably banished from his mind. Not one penny of it all should go into a bank. Not one penny. Liquid gold into his own hands represented the only safety. As he moved around the house giving his instructions for the removal of its contents, he looked at the boys when he stumbled across them as if they were not quite real; nothing of any importance to be considered; a dull fire of excitement smoldering in his small amber eyes.

Owen was beside himself, clamoring against the impossible, sleepless and distraught; yelling his rage and frustration at Emmett through the impossible days.

"You don't care," he shouted to his closed and quiet face. "You just don't care. You were only getting money anyway and unless he turns out a complete criminal, which I have no doubt he will, you'll get that anyway. But mark me, we'll get nothing, either of us, by the time he's finished."

Emmett glanced about him, at the opened cupboards where the crystal and silver had been stripped, and the gaps already in the lovely furniture where the best of it was picked away.

"I care, Owen," he said, and looked with pain and pity at his brother. "But we are helpless at the moment. What can we do? You are only tearing yourself to pieces."

"Is that," asked Owen bitterly, "what they have been teaching you across the road?"

"Yes."

"Then it is no use to me."

They had to go back down to the West in the end before Hugh Charles was finished with his pillage, since there was no staff left in the Dublin house, and the parsimony that was to develop into mania already forbade him to spend good money on a hotel.

Mrs. Bradley and Mrs. Savage had left together in a hired carriage piled around with all their bundles, on a tide of tears and fury, wiping tears of loneliness and sorrow from their old faces, and watched with sour anger from an upstairs window by Hugh Charles as they drove away into the gray day. They took the bewildered bootboy with them to be their general factotum in their new establishment in Sandy Cove. All they had to comfort them was their satisfaction that they had gone before he'd had time to dismiss them.

Gracie went later, and the tight-lipped Bourdain, retreating to their own small cottage away in the huddle of streets beyond the park, where Bourdain professed himself ready to starve before he would drive that thieving rogue around the streets. Both her babies now had had to bend their heads to kiss Gracie good-bye, and she wept uncontrollably for them and for the gentle woman who had seen to it that Bourdain was in no danger of the starvation he threatened. Thanks to her little legacy he could burnish his brass buttons in security while he looked for another post.

"I'll be back, Gracie," Owen told her fiercely. "I'll be back."

Poor Emmett, she thought, looked intolerably tired, never able at any time to be rid of what troubled him by shouting and creating as Master Owen did.

"To be sure you will, Master Owen," she said, and stood on tiptoe to kiss him again, sick at heart at her own helplessness, who had once been able to soothe their every trouble. Then she and Bourdain turned and walked away along the cobbles of the mews as the first flares spat and smoked in their sockets at the big yard doors, and the two boys stood alone in the darkening evening outside the empty house.

"You will go down to Holly House on the morning train," their uncle told them sourly over their supper of bread and cheese. "I will follow in a day or two when I have closed the house."

Owen put down his bread.

"Holly House!" he cried. "What of Owenscourt?"

Owenscourt when they reached it was closed and locked, all the blinds drawn down over its dark windows as if for another death.

"There's only one thing has stopped him selling it," John Julius told the boys, standing below the elms and staring up at the blank rows of windows. Owen was quieter now, acknowledging his helplessness, a light of despair in his brown eyes.

"What's that?"

"He wants the land. He fancies himself as a farmer, the poor man, and he not able to handle the plot of land you would give to a woman for her flowers."

"He'll have plenty of money to throw away on it, anyway," Owen observed bitterly, and Emmett looked at him.

"I don't think he will," he said.

"Why wouldn't he? It's all there in his hands. D'you think he's keeping it for us?"

"No, but I think he'll not want to spend it, once he's got it."

"Ah, go on. There'll be another great splash of hunters and fancy waistcoats and all our good money going in the shebeens of the country."

John Julius looked at Owen curiously, thinking he had

been too young to be aware of Hugh Charles's earlier venture into grandeur.

"What do you know about all that?" he asked him.

"Ah, sure wasn't he the talk of the county. My father thought he was a jackass."

John Julius thought about it, and shook his head.

"I think," he said, "that Emmett might be right."

Like Owen listening to Bradley, he felt some wrong that they should talk like this about their uncle, but they were in the thick of it and must see it as it was. He remembered their mother on the bridge down there, that first day she had told him of the mad idea to make the man trustee, telling him that they were none of them any longer children.

Less than ever now; these two bereaved and bewildered boys must make of life whatever they could.

"You will still be here to oversee it all?" Owen asked him then anxiously, still mindful of the land he felt was his; clinging, both of them, to the one person still steady in their foundering world.

"I'll be here," said John Julius grimly.

He didn't tell them that he had agreed with fury to stay for half the salary that Matt had paid him. Hugh Charles observing parsimoniously that he would only have half the work since he would have no responsibility for the house.

He had tried to point out that an empty house needed more watching than one that was full and warm and cared for, but Hugh Charles had shot him one repressive glance.

"Let it rot," he said.

John Julius did not tell them either of the screaming scene from Peggy, who had tasted grandeur and would never settle again for being poor.

"What can I do?" he asked her, and Antonia looked from one of them to the other.

"You can go elsewhere," Peggy snapped. She was still immaculately neat, but boredom had set in since the bright days of her attempts to captivate Matt and she had put on weight, the light hair falling straighter round a face whose plumpness sagged in lines of sharp ill temper. "Matt O'Connor's agent is a recommendation anyone would take. You can go better yourself."

"And leave the boys?" he asked her. Antonia looked sharply at her mother for her answer.

"They are none of yours," she snapped.

As autumn drifted into cold windy winter, the boys were settled in Holly House, in a bleak half-furnished bedroom that Alicocq had never reached. Downstairs their mother would have had no difficulty in recognizing the house of the very first At Home, as all the furniture in the closed-up salon and dining room fell again to the pale bloom of damp.

The only center of life and any kind of warmth was in the kitchen where they met for poor unfriendly meals ill cooked by some oafish girl their uncle had brought in daily from the village, fulfilling all of Emmett's prophecies that once he got his hands on the actual money, there was nothing that would tempt him to let it go.

Nowhere was there any sign in his way of living, of all the money he had realized in Dublin and that was still pouring into the house in fat envelopes that sent him out at once to harness the trap and drive the long road into Galway to cash the checks in the bank. He could not bear to touch it at all, even for the encompassment of his dreams of grandeur, filled with superstitious fear that it might all vanish as easily as it had come. He began to live as his father had lived, looking at every penny as though it might be his last, indifferent alike toward his surroundings and his creature comforts; meager to the point of parsimony even over what he was prepared to spend on the all-important land.

In time Owen ceased to clamor and protest, only the dull anger smoldering behind his eyes showing that there was nothing of resignation in his quietness. He talked it all over and over with Emmett in the damp chill of their bedroom or as they walked back and forth across the hollied hill. And in the end came to accept the fact that for the moment there was nothing to be done. Four years in February was the day he must live for, and even then he might have to fight for it all, or all that was left and there would be legal costs. There was nothing to do but work on the farm and thank God it was still Owenscourt he worked on; he was at least close at hand and able to try and see the parsimonious old robber provided what was necessary for the land.

His one consolation lay in his closeness to Antonia, the very sight of whom was like a lifting of the black curtain of his griefs and problems.

She was a tall girl now, little shorter than himself, with a thin angular body held with awkwardness, as though unwilling that she herself should willfully do anything to give it grace. Owen alone, grown almost unwittingly into his love, saw perfection in every abrupt gesture and graceless stance.

She was strange with him; clearly as pleased as he was that he was now in Owenscourt all the time, yet equally clearly unwilling to admit it. She was walking every day the five rough Irish miles across the bog to the long stone school in Caherlistrane that the priest had built, where she was learning to be a teacher. But there were saints' days and Saturdays and Sundays, and the gift of the long dark evenings that stopped work early on the farm.

There was pleasure in her eyes to have him there, and yet malicious gladness at his plight, as though it satisfied some long resentment. But she was full of small unexpected kindnesses as awkward as her long body, as when she appeared one day when they were working in the sodden ditches of the avenue, clearing the weeds and mud and dripping grass, the rain falling fine as silver on the split sacks around their shoulders.

She stood above them against the gray unhappy sky, in her dark straight mackintosh, one of her father's caps jammed down over her hair, her hands deep in her pockets.

"Antonia! Why no school today?"

Owen heaved himself out of the ditch, his eyes warm at the unexpected sight of her, her wet face glowing with some chill beauty in the sodden day. Emmett looked up and smiled his detached sweet smile, and went on chipping with his slane along the tangled roots.

"December the eighth," she said. "Holiday of Obligation. Didn't you go to Mass?"

Owen's face hardened. He knew Emmett had been out before dawn that morning, but they no longer talked of it. He didn't feel he owed God much at the moment, nor could he find Emmett's comfort in the priests; nor his sore heart find meaning any longer in the prayers of childhood.

She gave that thin knowing smile that always looked as if she took pleasure in his sorrow, then dug her hands deeper into her pockets.

"I've brought you something," she said, with the warm gentle thought always mixed up in her hostility. "To warm you both inside and out."

From the depths of her pockets she brought out two large hot boiled potatoes and handed one to each.

Owen cradled it between his freezing fingers and smiled at her, longing to put out a finger and smooth the mist from along the edges of her lashes. She looked him up and down, and again the odd light of satisfaction lit her eyes, looking at the dripping clothes that had once been his holiday wear, and the old sack tied with string across his shoulders. He was soaked with the fine rain, and water dripped from the edges of his felt hat. A small gust of wind blew a fresh wave of rain across their faces and she laughed, the blue eyes very bright.

"We're the same now, Owen."

"What do you mean, the same?"

He was wary, always, with Antonia, looking for the meaning underneath the words.

"Well, look at you. A pauper now, like me."

He didn't argue that one.

"Does that make things better or worse for me with you?"

"Oh, better. What did you ever know about anything over in that grand house."

He was stung to the defense of his parents.

"I didn't see you complaining through the years your father was my father's agent, with your pony and your good clothes and everything. I saw little difference between us."

She scuffed the muddy ground with the toe of her boot.

"That wasn't me."

"Who was it, then?"

He wanted to tell her that that person had the same dark-blue fiery eyes and the same thin pointed face that enchanted him now, but he knew she was in no mood to listen.

"That was the agent's daughter."

"And who are you now?"

"Oh, now I'm Antonia again, working for my own one shilling and nine pence a week, and my father is poor again. We are the same now."

Owen gave up warming his hands on the cooling potato and peeled it before it would be too cold to eat, taking a good floury bite.

"Well, I'm glad you can spare the potato," he said coolly, determined to get into no arguments with her, for they led nowhere. "But I'll tell you this, Antonia, I'll be back here as the owner of Owenscourt."

She looked at him as if a child might babble of his dreams.

"And if we have to be the same, alannah," he added, "then b'God, I'd rather have the pair of us rich."

In the wet ditch Emmett threw away the skin of his potato and got back to work.

"You'd better be back to your ditching," Antonia said to Owen with bright malice, "or the uncle'll be after you."

She pulled the collar of her mackintosh up around her tweed cap and went on down the avenue in the rain. Not for the first time he looked after the tall straight back with its air of defying all the world, and wondered why he was so mad about her, and she with the prickles of a hedgehog. And always had been mad about her, he realized, ever since they were small children.

He went back to rooting out the dead ghosts of the flowers that had trailed their color all along the ditches when he had come bowling up to Owenscourt for the summer. And to thinking and planning as to what he could do, penniless, when the four years were up. Not for one second did he delude himself that his uncle's parsimony was in order to save the money for himself and Emmett. But as long as he didn't sell Owenscourt they would have something to start on.

When a day's work was over, and the meager meal eaten, leaving yawning gaps in their hungry young stomachs, Hugh Charles would settle with a look of smoldering satisfaction at the kitchen table with a pile of papers and a stub of pencil, to reckon up his fortune.

Owen was unable to watch, nor yet to endure the clammy chill of the bedroom, and would walk up and whistle outside the agent's house, Emmett already off on the bicycle to spend the evening with the Canon. From the lamplit house Antonia would slip out with Boru at her heels, and as often as not a wedge of bread and cheese or a piece of cold pie, knowing that Owen was always hungry. Arm in arm they would circle the dark lake, the house a lightless bulk up the slight rise of the park; tearing Owen's heart with memories; unbearable in its darkness and its silence, and the longing for the hands that would never kindle light in it again.

"Boru is very old," he said to her one night, when, in the first pale nip of frost and under a glass-white moon, they strolled the long pathway down the crisped grass to the bridge. "He doesn't like the cold. It's great devotion brings him out at all. 'Tis only your father is out, or he wouldn't come."

The dog was close against his leg, clinging always now to those who were left to him, as if he looked for warmth and reassurance in a world that, for him too, had fallen into nothing. Antonia laid a hand on the shaggy head.

"Poor Boru," she said. "You must learn that like all of us, you have nothing."

Owen wasn't going to allow that to start again.

It was enough to have the dark empty house standing like a ghost in the full white moon; Emmett leaving him as surely as if he took the boat for America, for some private world inside his own head; that whey-faced old bandit sitting at his table night after night counting up his stolen money. Loss, futureless loss encompassed him on every side, and he reached out desperately for the one thing he might secure.

She walked beside him in silence, unearthly beautiful to his eyes in the clear bleached light, the black wings of her hair escaping from the bright-red tam-o'-shanter, her lovely face beneath it locked in its withdrawn and secret look. He hoped she was not in one of the senseless depressions that seized her with as little reason as the wind that ruffled the moonlit lake.

He stopped and Boru sat down as if grateful for the rest.

"Antonia." His eyes ran over her face and he smiled with pure pleasure. She was so beautiful. "Antonia." He took her cold hands and shook them a little to try and break the absent look in the blue eyes. "Antonia, you know that I have always loved you. You must know there has never been another girl for me and never will. Tell me, tell me, my love, do you feel the same way about me. Please, Antonia." He took the pointed chin and turned her round to face him. "Don't just look the other way. Tell me yes or no."

He had expected one of her sharp derisive answers and had steeled himself to argument, but he saw her great eyes grow sad.

She laid a cold finger on his lips.

"Ah, Owen, don't say any more," she said. "Don't say any more. I was hoping that you'd never say it. I'd be no good to you or anybody."

"That's for me to say."

Encouraged by the absence of a flat dismissal, he drew her closer. "How could I not say it, Antonia. Things could not go on forever as they were. One of us, or both of us, were bound to fall in love. Please God it's both of us."

His voice was hoarse with all his loss and loneliness, and she looked up at him for one moment, astonishing him by her expression of tenderness and compassion.

Swept with delight, he drew her closer, and when he kissed her, her face was cold with the frosty chill, but her lips under his were warm and willing.

"My dearest love," he whispered against her cheek. "Then it is both of us. Oh, Antonia, my heart."

She laid her head against his shoulder then as if she couldn't look at him, and drew away suddenly, stumbling over Boru.

"Oh, Owen," she cried, and her voice was harsh with despair. "Oh, Owen, my own love, you should never have asked me."

He knew better than to press her then, warmly astonished to have got so far.

Chapter 12

OWEN was alone, plowing the forty-acre field behind the pastures, finding unfailing solace in the space and silence, the steady movement of the horse; watching the chill purple dusk creeping from the edges of the field and knowing that soon he must go in to the savage hostile silence of what his uncle called his home. He turned, and the flock of following birds lifted and beat round his head; the rooks from the garden elms jostling the determined thrushes; one brilliant jay; and even a few seagulls, white against the brown earth; blown in across Lough Mask by some Atlantic storm.

He became aware of Emmett standing up on the railings between him and the empty pastures, waving an arm for him to come, lank and black like a scarecrow against the darkening sky. He waved back and patiently finished his furrow, methodically then unharnessing the tired horse and plodding with it round the long edge of the field to where Emmett waited.

"Are you on your way to the house?" he asked him. "I've just to stable Bonny."

"I've been. I've just come back to look for you. Owen. He's done something else. I don't understand it."

Even in the falling dusk Owen could see his brother's eyes, full of fresh astonishment and outrage. He laid a hand on his arm, and walked him beside the horse, afraid of chilling it in the cold that was rising with the dark. What more, he thought wearily, could the man do? Side by side their two dark lonely figures plodded past the lake and up through the park towards the empty house.

"He's brought all that's left of the furniture from Gardiner Street. A huge dray came with two horses. You remember them. Grattan."

Owen stopped then and looked at him.

"I thought he had sold it all."

Emmett shook his head.

"No. Obviously not. But it must mean the house is gone."

Owen stared into the gathering dark; remembering.

"He just mustn't have had the time to sell it," he said. "He'll probably do it from here. Where have they put it."

"Into the two bedrooms at the end of the upper hall. You know—where—"

"Where our grandfather lived with his dairymaid." Owen finished for him, unemotionally.

"Yes. And all along the hall too."

Almost in silence, both of them filled with their own memories of their home, so brutally dismembered, they stabled and fed the old brown horse, and walked across the dark windy hill to Holly House. Hugh Charles was nowhere to be seen, and Owen lit a candle stump at the kitchen range and went with Emmett up the stairs. It was all there, as Emmett had said, in the wavering shadows of the candle. Most of the contents of the house his parents had so loved; that little Bradley had so cherished, hounding the local girls into polishing until they could use the furniture for the mirrors they had never owned. All there, forlorn and abandoned in the pale light.

"But why?" he asked Emmett. "Why? He could have sold it better in Dublin. It'll perish here of damp."

"Maybe he wants to do this house up and make it as grand as ours was," Emmett said doubtfully, and in the hesitant and disbelieving words hit at the core of the ambivalence of Hugh Charles; who in his secret heart longed for the grandeur that he had strived for for a time. But was always overcome in achieving it by his own cupidity, that would not part with money even for what lay closest to his heart. The furniture had been the last gesture towards his dreams, that he would never trouble to realize. For who was there to help him now.

Owen lifted the candle higher for a last look round and saw propped at the very end of the hall the portrait of his mother that his father had done long ago when she was young; on some Greek beach with a branch of oranges in her hand, impossibly fresh and radiant in the unhappy gloom. In silence they stood and looked at it, until Emmett drew a broken breath and turned away.

Quickly Owen touched him.

"We must hide that one, Emm."

He had seen a pile of his mother's soft satin-edged blankets in the bedroom, and although he could hardly bear to touch them, they covered the picture as closely as they could and moved it into the shadows, heaving a wardrobe across in front of it, both of them sick with the circumstances that must drive them to hide their mother's face.

"God knows what we hope to save it for," said Emmett. For once he seemed devoid of his own inner comfort, his young face bleak with misery in the flaring shadows.

"We'll be back." Owen almost snarled, thinking of himself and Emmett always as one person. In his deep mind, that he never stopped to analyze, he thought of his brother always as too helpless to subsist on his own; and that every plan made must without question include him. Nor did Emmett's amiable compliancy in all matters ever lead him to think differently.

"I still don't understand it," Emmett said again as they went back down the stairs, their shadows long and creeping on the damp-stained wall, and Owen couldn't answer, for he didn't understand himself.

Hugh Charles was in, taking off his leaking boots beside the range. He was too mean to have the boots repaired and the dank smell of his soaking stockings battled with the watery stew. Owen nipped the candle flame between his fingers and both odors were defeated by the acrid smoke of the snuffed wick.

He had intended to say nothing for there was nothing to say, but he could not be quiet before his uncle's blank disinterested face.

"Why?" he shouted at him. "Why?" And did not trouble to say what the question was. "It was never yours to take!"

His uncle arranged his sodden boots carefully inside the fender as if they were the only matter of importance and lifted small pale eyes.

"Mine to take, or sell, or do whatever pleasures me," he said. "Did it never occur to you that someone other than yourself might want a fine house?"

He couldn't, meeting Owen's furious eyes, be sure himself that this was why he had done it. He should have put the whole lot up for auction there in Dublin, and avoided this scene. He had little idea now as to why he thought he might want the stuff, shying away from the simple truth of spiting Matt O'Connor; long years dead.

As if he read his thoughts, Owen said abruptly:

"The house is sold."

"It is. What would we want with it, when we have two houses down here?"

"We!"

Owen was beside himself, hardly able to keep his hands from his uncle, but he was young and at the end of a long day's work in the open air, and his stomach clamored for food. Furiously he slammed three plates onto the table, and the trencher of bread, with such violence that the oil lamp jumped and flared and flickered. He reached for the black stewpot from the fire, and put it in the middle of the table, knowing the withering contempt it would earn him did he try to serve it from a dish.

"I suppose you wanted it all down here to put it round you and play at being our father," he said bitterly, and Hugh Charles glared at him from surprised eyes, caught at the nub of his desires, not sure yet that he had enough strength of character to encompass the ultimate revenge on Matt O'Connor. To take his place. He glowered at his plate, furious that the young whelp should have touched on something he as yet barely admitted to himself. It was, without going any further, some deep triumph to have Matt's fine furniture up there in his house, did he never even sit in a chair of it or sleep in a bed. And Owenscourt closed and going to the dry rot and the damp. Better almost, in his confused and vengeful mind, than if he used the lot of it, as the other half of his thinking demanded.

Emmett stared in silence at his plate of stew, hating to hear Owen yelling at their uncle, no matter what had happened. It made no difference. To him, everything was gone and the struggle done. There was nothing to do now but mourn the savage wounds in silence, and try to carve out some other life. As soon as the wordless and miserable meal was done, he pushed back his chair and said that he was going on the bicycle into Tuam. Owen looked at him in silence and let him go. He must not be stopped from finding his own consolations, even if he himself saw nothing in them to ease the savage raging on his own heart.

Hugh Charles settled himself muttering in the lamplight to his papers, and after putting the dishes in the scullery for the woman in the morning, Owen took his candle again and went back up alone to the long hall. Moving silently among what was there, he touched the lovely things one by one in ravaged sorrow, as his mother had once laid her hand on them in unbelieving happiness; weeping in the end, a man's sore difficult tears, as he had not wept for either of them when they had died.

He told John Julius the next day, and the older man knew from his face that it was the ultimate injury.

"I wouldn't know why he's done it," he said. "He could far easier sell it in Dublin. No one could read that one's mind. And I understand what it means to you to see it all where it is. But, Owen, four years is not a long time. It may all still be there."

Owen looked at him bleakly. Four years was eternity.

"Four years," he said, so furious with bitterness that John Julius thought he might cleave him with the billhook in his hand. "Four years and what do I get then? Two houses, for as God is my witness, I'll put that villain on the roads as he has put so many others. Two houses, falling down and riddled with dry rot and damp, and all the neglected land and not a penny in my pocket for grain or seed potatoes. For mark my words, John Julius, sir, I may get back the property, but that rogue will see to it there's no visible money to recover. Am I not right?"

Sadly John Julius nodded.

"I'll be worse off than I am now," Owen went on. "I'm sorry, John Julius, if I shout at you, but I think about it often and I see no way out."

Not even to John Julius would he speak of the cold dawns when he awoke to the grind of another day, staring at the peeling plaster of the ceiling and seeing nothing but disaster; and Emmett on his hands, regarding everything placidly as the will of God, and never thinking to give even a bit of a push to the will of Emmett. It might comfort him, but b'God such acceptance was no more than another burden for Owen.

John Julius laid a wordless hand on his shoulder, debating whether to tell him that he himself was living on the scrapings from the bottom of the barrel, in order that the legacy from Owen's mother might be kept against the very day the boy was speaking of. It was four years away, and who could know what would happen in between, but he held hard to the money for Owen's future. He himself was working now like any laborer in the fields again, or like the boys themselves, knowing sourly that that was exactly what Hugh

Charles intended, measuring accurately his love for Owenscourt and for Matt O'Connor's sons.

He told Peggy about it all when he went in later for a draught of hot ale against the piercing cold. He told her little nowadays, aware of her bitter hostility to her present circumstances and that almost any word produced an argument. He spoke today for need to talk to someone, trying to estimate the meaning of Hugh Charles's latest caper. She was rubbing goose fat into flour in a brown bowl at the kitchen table, and not even her sullen temper could affect the neatness of her long limp-wristed hands performing any task.

She looked up with sharp sudden interest at what he told her, frowning. Though plumper, she was still beautiful, and the tendrilly hair would never show the change to gray, the aging threads lost in the ash-colored curls.

"Why would he do that?" she said then thoughtfully. "Isn't it money the man always wants? Wouldn't he do better to sell it all. And the houses?"

"He wants the land," John Julius said. "Do you know any Irishman would part with land did he have it under his feet?" And he added, with the same shrewd insight as Emmett, "Unless I am much mistaken, he wants to be Matt O'Connor. He wants the grandeur and is too mean to go about getting it. It's my reading the man is torn in two. A strange creature, God knows. But before all things he's one of nature's misers. He's not one to do it on his own."

Peggy's hands grew still in the basin of flour, and her gray eyes stared at him abstractedly, speculating over what he had said. John Julius was unaware of her, looking wearily into the red depths of the fire. In the last months the white traces above his ears had grown more pronounced and it was rare for his face to light to its warm brilliant smile.

"Were it not for the two lads," he said, more to himself than to her, unwilling to risk her tongue by speaking of what was near his heart; "were it not for the two lads, I'd go off back and try and start up Cannon's Mills. Things are better now in this part of the country, and I think there'd be enough work to make a living."

Peggy's hands dropped to the sides of the bowl as if she needed its support, and she stared at him, her eyes grown enormous and the fury gathering in her face.

"Cannon's Mills, is it?" she cried, when she could control her anger and surprise enough to speak. "Cannon's Mills. And what would I be doing down there at the back of beyond, and your children also?" Although she did not say it, she was crying out already in protest at the deprivation of the bit of life and style that Owenscourt and the O'Connors had given her excuse for; bored to extinction since the death of Matt. "Isn't it bad enough where we are, with the whole place as gloomy as a burial ground, and not a soul to speak to. Cannon's Mills! How long is it since anyone set foot in the place?"

John Julius knew exactly, having counted all the years, his longing to go back defeated by his loyalty to Matt and after his death to his wife and sons. His father had left the Mills in the Famine year of 1843. Only a few starving squatters had been inside it since, searching, as he had intended the day Matt found him, for even a roof above them against the weather.

"Forty-eight years," he said. "And you're right, it's overgrown. But the buildings and the mill wheel are as sound as ever. There is little needed that we couldn't do ourselves. James is a strong lad now."

"You've been there!"

"I went round by Slaughterford one day on my way back from Galway," he admitted.

"When was that?"

Her eyes were snapping with fury.

"It would be a month ago."

When he got the bit of money, it put it into his head, she thought. The eejit. Cannon's Mills indeed!

She slammed into the flour, her lips tight, and the open-faced clock ticked loudly in her angry silence. Then she looked up again, across the warm room to where John Julius sat hunched before the turf sods, as confused and unhappy as Owen himself about the future.

"I'll tell you this, John Julius Cannon," she spat at him, and her rounded face was sharp with the force of her temper. "Do you go to this misbegotten place, then you go alone, for I'll not be with you. There is nothing to keep me."

John Julius sighed. He knew well that her need of such freedom from his wishes was the reason she had never been willing to marry him. Should he not please her, then she was as free to go as the gypsies that had mixed up with the broken-down D'Arcy's and given her a measure of their blood. Retorts crowded to his lips, but he held them back. Long ago he had realized he would be better off without her; slowly disenchanted from his first enthralled love; then disgusted by her vindictive jealousy of Celia; by her shameless pursuit of Matt O'Connor for no more reason than to upset his wife. And if rumors were true, there had been many others since Matt's death that had given her more genuine satisfaction. They were sniggering through the estate, behind their hands, about the very cowman, seen coming constantly to his back door, with as many cans of milk, if they were full, as would feed all the starving west of Connaught.

But he would not be the one to tell her go.

She shot a glance at him from the long-lashed eyes, that at one time he had found so irresistible himself, wondering that he had not answered her.

Glumly John Julius continued to stare into the turf sods, knowing there was no answer he could give. There was no decision to be made about his going to Cannon's Mills. He was trapped where he was. The beautiful young woman who had left him the money that would set him free, had tied him at the same time by leaving him her sons.

He set his tankard by the hearth and got up, shrugging on his coat and facing out again into the misty fields without a word. Through the casement beside the door Peggy watched him go until he had turned from the garden and was out of sight. Her eyes were heavy lidded and speculative, touched with the light of some sultry and determined excitement. She turned round abruptly to the red wooden flour bin against the wall as John Julius vanished from sight, and lifted the lid, taking the scoop to double the quantity of flour in her mixing bowl. Then she moved over to the fire and took the bellows, vigorously blowing the turf into a hot scarlet glow, a small catlike smile creeping round her lips.

Two days later John Julius asked her at night to give him a bag of meat and potato cake in the morning and a jar of ale. He and the boys were off to the far edges of the bog, to get in turf that should have been long cut and stacked. It would be a waste of time to come home for anything in the middle of the day.

"Though it will be so wet," he said, his mind on the turf, "that it'll take two years before it's fit to use. That fool cannot see he is ruining the whole estate by getting rid of so many men. If he's so heart set on the land why doesn't he learn to look after it. There's more than the few of us can do. Put in plenty of food," he added. "I'm taking James."

Any other time her mouth would have twisted in contempt at his transparency, knowing that the plenty of food was meant to cover the hunger of the two scarecrows from Holly House. Today, however, she slapped the calico bag, bulging with potato cake and pie, onto the table with alacrity.

John Julius pulled on his big frieze jacket and tugged his cap down over his brows, yelling for James from upstairs, too preoccupied with the day's work to notice an air of tension and excitement that Peggy was doing her best to control.

"You'll not be back till evening," she said to him as James came clattering down the open stairs, and then he looked at her and thought only of the cowman, his mouth tightening with distaste.

"What else would I be taking the food for?" was all he asked.

She watched them go, out into the clinging pearly mist of early day, and then whipped round her daily housework humming, with the same small enigmatic smile about her soft mouth.

The house as shining and clean as it was her undeniable nature to make it, and the evening stew already on the side of the hearth, she got out the flatirons and laid them up against the red bars of the range to heat; going then into her bedroom to rummage with thoughtful pleasure in the presses.

Over in Holly House, Hugh Charles had had nothing to eat but bread and cheese, both of them stale, and the cheese touched with pale furry spots of mold; slapped before him indifferently by the slattern from the village before she raced for home.

As he gathered up the last unrewarding crumbs, staring morosely at the range for which he must go out and get more turf, the front doorbell jangled through the house.

Matt had been saddened when Alicocq had had it mended. Holly House, he had said, was not the same.

For a few minutes Hugh Charles went on sitting, his sandy brows drawn down, debating as to whether he should allow the caller to go away, distrustful of anyone he had not himself summoned. In the end he rose unwillingly from his chair and lumbered along the dank and mist-filled hall to drag open the protesting door.

Between the pillars of the doorstep stood John Julius Cannon's wife, smiling at him gently, with a basket on her arm covered with a white cloth. The red lining of her hood cloak framed a soft face glowing with the cold of the day, her long lashes and the pale escaping tendrils of her hair beaded silver with the mist.

"Mr. Healey. We haven't met since the sad death of Mrs. O'Connor. But you'll remember me. Peggy Cannon."

He remembered her well enough and had often wondered what she made of the present scheme of things. She with shameless eyes in those days only for Matt O'Connor, although the whispers had it that she was anybody's almost for the asking. But mostly they were afraid to ask for fear of John Julius Cannon. The very memory of her, in her low-cut gowns over the fine bosom, set his body to reminding him with sudden urgency that with all the other farradee, it was a long, long time since he had had a woman. His tongue moved slowly and involuntarily over his pale lips.

"Will you come in a while," he managed to say at last hoarsely, only a small part of his mind still managing to ask itself what it was in hell she wanted; mesmerized by the soft smile and the enormous, deep, inviting eyes.

Sweetly she indicated the basket.

"Just," she said modestly and even a little shyly, "to your kitchen." The long lashes dropped over her eyes, as if with shame over the impropriety of even thinking of coming further. "I thought you might be lonely with only those two boys for company, and not very well looked after. I came to bring you some food. I hope you don't find it impertinent of me."

Chapter 13

It was a mild winter. Before Christmas was long over, Antonia was able to go searching for primroses and violets along the mossy banks of the avenue. Lambs were early in the fields, and the first pale sheen of winter wheat over the soft brown land.

For Owen and Emmett the gentle weather meant that in the bleak uncared-for state of Holly House, they did not have the added misery of bitter cold, and Peggy, in her many careful, secret journeys over the hill, was not hampered by mud and ill weather.

After the first astonishing visit, which left Hugh Charles staring into his meager fire, bemused and beaten with excitements and desires he thought long forgotten, they arranged it all with care. Delicately dropping her long lashes, and seemingly appalled at her own impropriety and forwardness, Peggy soon had Hugh Charles begging her to come, full of stuttering apologies on his own part that he should let her do it, and not be riding himself to the agent's house, to offer his respects. At the thought of confronting the strong and uncompromising John Julius his puffy face grew gray with fear.

"You'll take care you're not seen!"

"And who's to see me, and both places as deserted as the grave!"

Her mind and eyes were flicking all the time round Holly House, for she knew that even she would never get Hugh Charles to Owenscourt, where he would be stalked by Matt O'Connor's ghost. God knew it was all in a sorry state, for all the efforts of the high-nosed Alicocq with her mincing ways. But now, Peggy knew, Hugh Charles had money to spend on it, no matter that John Julius was saying he had become more of a miser even than his father. Her little catlike smile curled at her lips. There were ways and means to get what you wanted out of any man, and Hugh Charles was not proving difficult in these early stages.

Slowly she prized from him most of the secrets of what he had acquired, for he regarded his villainy as a triumph and was filled with astonished pleasure that this warm enticing woman sitting across the range should agree with him.

"Sure Matt O'Connor and those boys always had too much," she said, and he hastened, his blue eyes bulging, from indiscretion to indiscretion to agree with her. Peggy smiled in soft admiration, and her mind was working as steady and deliberate as a clerk on his high stool in a countinghouse.

"And I have most of the furniture now," he said in the end, unable not to tell her everything; not yet with deliberate intent, pursing his thick lips with satisfaction. Before God, it was good to have someone else to talk to, and with the same opinions as himself of his sister's husband. Too large for his boots altogether.

"The furniture?" Wide eyes as if she did not know it.

"From the Dublin house. Come on with me and I'll show it to you." He could barely control his triumph.

She went with him up the stairs and in the gray shadows of the winter day, ran her appraising eye over the jumbled collection of fine furniture, thrusting down the surge of excitement that overcame her, carefully keeping her face cool and blank.

"Very fine," she said. "Very fine indeed, Hugh Charles. You must look forward to creating yourself a beautiful home."

He looked at her in the wintry light, and for a moment seemed about to speak, then his lips closed as if in protest at the threat of indiscretion. He led her in silence back down the stairs to the hall.

Saying good-bye to him, she took her time and he stood beside her, his eyes on her face and his fingers moving in small involuntary twitches. Against his will they longed to touch her. She was always careful to keep herself a little distance from him, sitting on the far side of the range, and never being quite within reach of those twitching fingers if they should forget themselves.

Her shapely arms lifted to touch the careful curls on the top of her head, revealing the plump but still alluring lines of her body in its tight bodice, hiding her smile as she saw Hugh Charles move restlessly; sliding his eyes away but unable not to bring them back, his tongue on his dry lips.

"I have to go now," she said, and swung her hood cloak to throw it round her shoulders. It was too much for Hugh Charles, who lurched towards her, his hands reaching for her waist.

"Hugh Charles. For shame on you."

Deftly she slid away from him, making the most of tying the strings of her hood below her soft chin; shaking her head at him, and taking her basket; full of gentle and proper outrage.

"I will bring you another pie on Tuesday."

Grinding his teeth, his pallid face suffused, Hugh Charles was forced to acquiesce; shamefaced, pretending that for him too, the pie was all that mattered.

"Take care now, coming," he said hoarsely, and from the windows of the hall watched her turn up into the shadow of the hollies. Facing into the chilly wind, she pulled up the hood over the pale curls that had begun to tantalize him.

She was always careful to be home before Antonia came in, with her sharp assessing eyes that let nothing past them. And if in those weeks John Julius saw the small tight contented smile about her lips or heard quick snatches of unaccustomed song about the house, his mouth twisted with disgust, and he closed his mind, setting it to the presence of the cowman. To him alone did Peggy feel it wise to explain her absences, for he watched her with a greed as pressing as Hugh Charles's. She said to his sullen importunities, that she was caring for a sick woman on the far side of the estate; placating him, unwilling to lose him lest she fail and get no better.

One evening near Owen's birthday, when the first gusty winds of spring were sweeping from the west across the land, touched by the salt of the distant sea, she was late.

Dusk had already fallen as she came swiftly down the bare hill and skirted the stables to the house; the men in from the land. Owen and Emmett were with John Julius, for Owen to look at some records of the previous farming of the estate, there being no longer an estate office, but merely a drawer into which John Julius had crammed all he could save, hoping that in some better time in the future, it might be of use to Owen.

Young James was there, and when the four of them came in, they seemed to fill the whitewashed kitchen, and bring with them the cold breath of the windy evening, and the damp smell of the land. Antonia gave them her light evasive smile, allowing her eyes to rest a moment longer on Owen.

"Where's your mother?"

John Julius looked round frowning as he shook off his frieze coat and hung it up behind the door. He looked round the kitchen, puzzled. Peggy had many faults, but never in her duty to the house. He did not understand the fire dying in the range and the smoking lamp, just kindled by Antonia. She blew on it to clear the smoke and turned up the wick.

"Is she upstairs sick?"

Antonia shook her head.

"I looked. But I don't know where she is. I'm only in myself. James, do you take the bellows and blow up the fire. Where do you think she might be, Father?"

"I don't know," her father answered with truth, for he had never known her other than at home. He himself had learnt, in order to avoid trouble, to keep regular hours of coming and going. She might not then expose him to some situation he would be more pleased to ignore. Now he didn't want to make too much of her absence, never sure of her; afraid of stumbling publicly on something he would not wish his children know. But he was concerned. No matter what she did in the hours he was gone, he came home each evening to the lamps lit and the supper on the range above the glowing turf. Her good housewifery as much part of her nature as her wantonness.

"I imagine she's visiting somewhere," he said easily, and deliberately cleared the anxiety from his eyes. "Sit down, Owen. Sit down there and I'll get you what you want to see."

He went on through into the big sparsely furnished parlor, and they could hear him riffling through the deep drawer.

The two boys sat down at the long kitchen table, and Antonia moved to pull the black iron kettle round above the heat, as James blew the dying sods to a warm red glow.

She touched it with her hand.

"It's cold," she said. "She must be long gone."

She turned, still holding it, as the door opened on a gust of wind, and Peggy came in quickly, closing it behind her with some slow deliberation, putting her basket on the floor. Although she didn't speak, there was something in her attitude that made them all look at her in silence. John Julius came to the parlor door, the papers in his hands, the easy questions dying on his lips, and in the silence the wind battered at the door behind her. Something more momentous than an unexpected evening visit lay in the trimphant brightness of her eyes; the quick eager movements with which she moved the basket from her way and turned to hang up her cloak, the long fine fingers smoothing back the windblown tendrils of her hair.

With some strange finality she stood and looked at them all as if it were for the last time, the wavering lamplight on her face.

"Where were you?" said John Julius mildly, trying to ease some atmosphere that was beginning to creep into the room, dark and tangible as the lamp smoke.

It was to Owen and Emmett she spoke when she did, her voice husky and excited, a little unsteady. Even she must search for courage for what she was about to do.

"It's well you two are here," she said to them. "It will all concern you as much as anybody else."

"What will?" John Julius came forward and laid the papers on the table, his question not so easy; apprehensive of some unformed threat; fearful suddenly for those he loved who might be at the mercy of Peggy D'Arcy. "Where were you?" Something in her bright provocative attitude was disturbing, and a deep sense of trouble stirred him.

"Where were you?" he said again, and saw Antonia watching her mother closely, sensitive to her unpredictable moods as he was himself. Peggy moved over to the fire, and he realized she was wearing one of her best gowns, unsuitably low cut for anywhere she might want to go within walking distance in the middle of the afternoon. She stopped to rearrange the kettle, as if she sought a moment before she turned and faced them all, the gray eyes wide with challenge and some dark light of excitement.

"I have news for you all," she said, with a little catch of her breath. Then she drew herself up and her eyes rested only on John Julius. "I am going to marry Hugh Charles Healey, of Holly House. Your uncle, yes," she said in answer to a grunt of sheer astonishment from Owen.

It was the only answer she got, all the young ones staring at her in dumb amazement. John Julius alone moved, turning abruptly and walking away from the table, over to the dark window; as if he had been struck; staring out into the gusty night.

Antonia spoke in the end, her face gone thin and sharp with shock, carved with sudden shadows above the lamp.

"You are getting a divorce from my father?"

It was a word that none of them clearly understood, nor how it could come about. A word belonging to the fast society of Dublin and of London, where it seemed now marriages could be broken and reshaped at will.

Before Peggy could answer, John Julius wheeled from the window, his handsome face ravaged.

"No, Peggy," he said. "No!"

She looked at him as if he were nothing, understanding clearly that it was not the marriage he objected to, but the words that trembled next on her lips. Her eyes were full of contempt.

"And why not, John Julius Cannon," she said. "Did they not have to know sometime?"

"No," said John Julius painfully, and they looked from one to the other across the room, the shadows of the lamp moving on the ceiling with the draft.

"Did you think, John Julius," she asked him with sudden venom, as indifferent to her children as if she were alone, "that I was willing to go back to being the wife of"—she laughed shortly, bitterly—"of a half-paid laborer with the clods never off his boots? Or to Cannon's Mills where no one has opened a door for fifty years? You got up once and should have stayed up, if you wanted to keep me."

John Julius looked at her long and steadily, and the last of peace drained down from his face. Owen moved round and stood close beside Antonia, but she didn't look at him, her eyes on her mother. The lamp flared and smoked and threw dark savage shadows over all their faces and no one moved to trim it. On the hob the kettle suddenly began to sing; small impossible common sound. All their faces in the flaring light were bleached with shock and wary with the expectation that there was worse to come.

Except for Peggy, who held to her place before the fire, where the turf glow set her hair to a gilded nimbus round her head, her cheeks flushed and her eyes blazing.

"Tell them," she said. "Tell them, John Julius. Tell them for yourself."

He made a gesture of sick distaste. But better, he thought then, that I do tell them, than that she fling it a them like an insult.

"Antonia," he said, and his voice was sad and bleak as the night wind that keened beyond the windows. "James." He paused a long moment.

"Yes, Father," Antonia said, as if to reassure him that they would accept anything from him.

"What your mother wants you to know is that she is free to marry Hugh Charles Healey or anybody else, come to that, as she wishes. She and I were never married."

Antonia gave a small choked cry and Owen instinctively put an arm around her, mad with fury at the crudity of the woman standing so assured before them; sick with a surge of unbearable compassion for the girl who, for some secret reason of her own, found life difficult enough already.

She flung him off and moved over to face her mother over the bright rag patches of the rug. The light grew dim as the unheeded lamp globe smoked and blackened.

"You are telling us," she asked her mother, her voice hoarse and strained, "you are telling us that we are a pair of bastards, my brother James and I."

John Julius closed his eyes, and Emmett gave one long pitying glance at young James, who appeared too shocked even to understand what it was all about. Then he looked down at his clasped hands in his lap.

"What else?" said Peggy, and all those watching could see with pain the mean satisfaction granted by the wounding of her daughter. "And I never married to your father?"

She smiled then, a secret satisfied smile, and her teeth glinted in the growing shadows. As if she thought of more to come, but for the moment let it go.

"Then what of us?" Antonia asked carefully. "What of us. Do we go with you to your new home, James and me?"

Not once did she look at Owen, even though the question she asked was whether they were to live under the same roof. He started to speak, but she held up her hand, waiting for her mother to answer, and her mother looked at her levelly, loosing all the dislike and jealousy of years.

"I'll take James," she said, and for the first time James stirred.

"You will not," he cried vehemently in his young unstable voice. "I stay with my father and Antonia."

Peggy looked slowly around them all and her eyes gleamed with the pleasure of her last blow.

"Would that be entirely proper now," she said, "seeing that Antonia was never his child at all."

There was a moment of silence in which Antonia's fall of black straight hair and the brilliant dark-blue eyes so like John Julius's came before them, and in that one instant there was no one in the room who did not think her lying.

Except Antonia, always open to the nearest wound. Owen felt her gasp beside him, and grasped her arm, but she hurled him off. No one would face this but herself. In the gray smoky light John Julius's face was ashen and he moved towards Peggy, his shadow monstrous on the white wall behind him.

"Did I hear you aright?" he asked her hoarsely.

Owen moved towards the door, suddenly ashamed to be there at the moment of their most private sorrow.

"Emmett," he said. "John Julius, we'll come back tomorrow."

John Julius gave him a brief glance.

"Stay where you are. Isn't the damage done."

At the back of his outraged mind he knew that Owen would be the one for dealing with the damage to Antonia. Ah, dear Jesus Christ, what would this not do to her, already at odds with all her world. He turned back to Peggy.

"Well then, madam." His voice was sharp. "Well then, madam. Tell me who she is."

Antonia was staring, eyes as large and black as coals. Peggy gave her one glance and examined her fine nails.

"She's a bye blow of Bunaffrey," she said lightly.

"Bunaffrey!" He was disbelieving. "I never saw him on the land."

She smiled and shrugged.

"He was never one for visiting his tenants. Didn't we know him well from the days we used to sell him horses."

John Julius was unable to argue. He had taken her, mad with love, from an old broken-down house beyond Claremorris, where the rabble of D'Arcys had lived like tinkers. What did he know of them or of Lord Bunaffrey either. What did he know other than to be soft with gormless pride when Peggy had told him she was with child. He turned away from her with a gesture of disgust. For her, and for his own green-sick stupidity that would have believed her every word.

Owen was groping in his mind. Bunaffrey. Lord Bunaffrey. The land beyond them to the north. Up Claremorris way. From all he had heard of him it must have been quick advantage he had taken of Peggy D'Arcy, for the man had the name for never setting foot onto his lands. The woman was telling Antonia she was the bye blow of a lord, but Owen knew that for the girl, that would not make it one whit better. John Julius was the pillar of her sad, uncertain world and no one else would do. Desperately he longed to take her in his arms and tell her that for him it made no difference at all, nor ever would. To shelter her from any further blows the woman might have yet to give. But he knew Antonia would not even let him touch her, standing rigid before her mother, all the lovely planes of her face sharp with shock.

John Julius was advancing slowly on Peggy.

"Then," he said thickly, "you were lying with Bunaffrey after—after—" Was it a quick toss behind a hedge, his mind was wondering, or the privilege of my lord's bed for the afternoon and a guinea tossed into the bargain.

"Ah, yes," she said calmly. "After I had come to live at the farm with you."

"Bad cess to you," John Julius said between his teeth. "The D'Arcys were always a cheap poor lot, but before God, never as cheap as that."

Owen realized it was only the going out of the lamp that

saved her. John Julius's fist was up to smash the smile from the self-satisfied face, when with a last small flare they were plunged into smoky darkness, no thicker than the driven feelings in the room. Below the singing kettle the turf glowed in serene, indifferent calm.

It was Emmett, always the watcher, who stood up quietly and got a cloth to wipe the lamp globe, relighting it with a spill from the range. John Julius, his brief rush of violence spent, showed up in the new light collapsed in a chair, his black head in his hands. Antonia moved over as if she walked in her sleep, and laid a hand on his shoulder; not in any reassurance but rather as one might say good-bye. Briefly he laid his hand on top of it, and then stood up, master of himself again.

He stood before Peggy, and although they could not see his face there was something in it that made even her flinch, and drop her eyes.

"Then you can go, madam," he said very quietly, but the words dropped like stones into the room. "You can go to your new lover."

Something flickered in her eyes as though she would protest. It was only by playing the lady and holding the fellow at arm's length that she had got the offer of marriage at all, and he as randy as a stallion.

"You may go," John Julius said. "Neither I nor your children will hold you. But before God, you will go now."

"Now?"

She had not expected this, planning to shuck them all off so that she would never be bothered with them again. But her leaving was to be in her own time, when she was ready and with all her belongings packed. To slip off with Hugh Charles one afternoon when all of them were in the fields.

"I cannot go now."

"Madam, you will go now. Or I will have the pleasure of throwing you out myself as you deserve. Nor will you come back for anything you own."

From his gray granite face she knew he meant it, and she

looked for one flurried and astonished moment round the others, but none of them would meet her eyes. For the first time she had failed to call the tune.

"You have as long," John Julius said, "as it will take me to put the horse into the trap. I'll leave you at his door as I should long ago have left you somewhere."

As he moved to go out, Boru came anxiously from the corner where he had watched the scene with puzzled eyes, and put his nose against John Julius's hand.

"Not now, Boru," he said. "Not now. Wait here and I'll be back."

Boru put his front paws up against the window, and watched him off into the shadows, sure of nothing in this strange uncertain night.

That had misfired, Peggy thought furiously, flinging clothes pell-mell into a valise. John Julius had produced an unexpected strength which his seemingly indifferent compliance had not led her to expect; giving, as she had, no thought to other than her own desires. She had done as she liked for years and not a word from him, and she was furious he had chosen this moment to stand against her. Petulantly she scrabbled through the press for what there was time to take. She had no doubt, suddenly, that when John Julius stood ready at the door, he would come in and take her physically from the house if she did not come herself. Then she relaxed and again the small smile curved her lips. It did not matter. Played properly, Hugh Charles would buy her everything she wanted. Or get nothing he desired.

As she passed them all wordlessly in the kitchen, standing where she had left them, she knew a small moment of unwonted shame; catching on James's face a look of abject loss; as though he and he alone might protest her going.

John Julius did not speak or even look at her, sitting immobile in the trap in the light streaming from the open door; his handsome face set like stone; allowing her to hand in her own valises. Nor did he speak on the short drive round the hill to Holly House beneath the scudding moon, the cloud shadows racing on the bare fields. At the door of the house he waited with the same stony indifference while she got herself out of the trap. No shred of light was apparent, the house pale and ghostlike in the windy night, all the windows of the long hall blind and inhospitable under the gibbous moon.

She stood a moment looking at the darkness and the silence, and a thread of fear touched her lest Hugh Charles prove not to be as certain prey as she had thought. The bleak-faced man clicking at the horse to turn the trap would never give her shelter again. Then she drew herself up, tossing the hood of the dark cloak back from the silvery hair. As she reached for the handle of the doorbell, John Julius was off down along the road by the river without a backward glance.

"John Julius," Owen said as soon as he came back into the kitchen. He could hardly bear to look at the pain that darkened the face of the older man, and with it the humiliating burden of shame. "John Julius. Might Emmett and I stay here until we can find a cottage or something. We cannot go back there."

John Julius passed his hand across his eyes as if to wipe away some image. Antonia had gone without a word up into her own room, and Emmett was slowly and painstakingly laying out the buttermilk and cold potatoes that were all he could find to eat. Gently he took James by the arm and steered him to the table.

"All those pies and things we had," he said to Owen. "They came from here."

"I know. Can we stay, John Julius. I'll find money to pay you."

John Julius gestured that aside, knowing the impossibility. Here was something else for their mother's legacy to cope with.

"I was coming in myself to tell you stay," he said. "Take the trap over in the morning and get such as you have. Where is Antonia?"

Owen gestured up the open stairs.

"Gone up. She wouldn't talk."

"As well. Leave her a while, Owen. She'll have need to be alone. There's a lot for her to accept."

"John Julius, sir, I don't accept it."

John Julius shot him a warm look of affection and even gratitude.

"Nor I," he said. "But who can prove against her mother's word."

In silence they drank the sharp clean buttermilk, and plastered the cold potatoes with salty butter to make them edible, and felt the better for it. Only James, with the resilience of his fourteen years, showed any desire to talk of what had happened.

"Leave it, James," his father said to him quietly. "Leave it. 'Tis best not spoken of."

When they were done eating, he crossed the room to the press beside the fire and from it took a long dark-necked bottle, richly labeled, and four glasses of the precious crystal they had kept for company. Formally he poured them all a pale golden drink, even the boy, who eyed it with astonishment.

"Papa," he said, awed. "That's your Napoleon."

"It is. Your father," he said to Owen and Emmett, "gave me this bottle the Christmas before he died. God rest his soul, he would never know for us an occasion more rare and special than this. If only I knew what I was celebrating."

They had in the end, in the light of the sinking lamp, to carry him to bed, the tall dark bottle empty and the dreadful evening done. Emmett walked with James out to his little attic up above the dairy, through the thick darkness when the moon was gone. He thought the child might want to talk, but by now James was exhausted both with shock and unaccustomed brandy, his eyes in the light of his small candle at one moment large and dark with all that he had seen, and in the next one, fast asleep. Emmett stayed with him a while, sitting on the hard chair with his own head bent above his breast, and then he got up quietly and snuffed the candle, going back across the yard into the house, and the room that he was going to share with Owen.

"Thank God," said Owen, dropping his boots on the floor, "for our father and his Napoleon brandy. And thank God for John Julius knowing what to do with it. 'Tis God's pity we weren't able to give some to Antonia."

In spite of his sick and desperate concern for her he was already falling into sleep, as John Julius had intended for them all. Only Emmett lay awake a long time, listening to his brother's deep and even breathing, wondering did he really hear the sound of weeping in the darkness, or did he merely know in his own sorrowing soul that it was a night for tears.

Antonia was down before them all in the morning in the gray chilly dawn, ladling out the big bowls of steaming stir-about on which John Julius and James were accustomed to go for the day's work. Despite her pale face and repressive silence, and the terrible air of chill determination that held them all, Owen and Emmett could not resist a glance at each other over the warm steam from their wooden bowls, in each of which was a good tablespoon of cream and a big lump of butter melting in the hot oatmeal. Better, they told each other silently, than the stale bread or piece of yesterday's pie they had become accustomed to.

Owen tried patiently and carefully to speak with Antonia, but she would answer nothing save about the food or the plans for the day, her long black hair still loose, shielding her face; her eyes blank, communicating nothing.

"Do we go, sir," Owen asked John Julius, "to my uncle still for orders about work or what?"

John Julius snorted from his chair beside the fire where he was lacing up his heavy boots. He looked up at Owen and his face was sardonic.

"He'll have his hands full, the man. He'll not go far wrong with his land do you do as I tell you. Or," he added, with the first smile he had shown since Peggy left, "or if I do as you tell me. You're the owner."

When Antonia was leaving for the school, Owen raced

over after her from the stables, to catch her up at the top of the avenue.

"May I walk to the grand gates with you?" he said gently.

In the look she gave him there was no rejection or reproof. No hostility. There was nothing. The dark-blue eyes looked back into his as cold and empty as an open grave. Involuntarily he shivered.

"Antonia," he said, and took her hand, frantic to give her some comfort; feeling an imperative need to avert some tragedy he didn't yet understand, but that lay overt in her empty gaze. "Antonia."

Quietly she eased her hand away. "I would think it better," she said, "that you do your work."

And she was gone, off down the weedy gravel underneath the trees, her black scarf wrapped up to her tam-o'-shanter against the cold, its end lifting in the wind; her neat buttoned boots choosing steady footsteps in between the ruts.

Owen frowned helplessly and then turned away. As she said, it was better get on with his work. And for her too. She would need time, as her father had said. Where did it leave all of them, John Julius and Antonia particularly? It would be little use to say to the girl that no one else believed what her mother had said. If she believed it then that would be enough, and she could turn any way. He took the bucket from the lad who cared now for the horses and went over to the well, trying to put it all from his mind. The stables needed a good cleanout. One of everything now was the policy of Hugh Charles. One man for the cows, one for the horses, one for the land, and the two boys and John Julius and James to fill in all the gaps, that showed on every side in the inevitable neglect.

When the stables were done, he went away, going quietly through the deserted yard where the threshing machine stood shrouded in its tarpaulins against the harvests of the years. At the kitchen wing of Owenscourt he stood awhile and watched all round him carefully.

The boys came back to the agent's house in the middle of the day for bread and cheese, and when they were all sitting,

Owen went over and laid two golden sovereigns on the table, before John Julius's astonished face.

"What's this?"

"That's little enough to pay for us to stay here."

"Where did you get it?"

"John Julius, sir, that's my affair. All I will say is that it's my own money. Neither my father nor my mother would ever have intended Emmett and I should live like paupers crawling on your charity. You have little enough now as it is." His face creased. "I don't see clear," he said, "the morals of what I do, but were it for ourselves alone I wouldn't take it. But I cannot see you go short for the sake of us."

They both stared at him, speculating, and levelly he met their eyes, nor would he back down.

"There's plenty more where that came from," he said evenly, "but I'll take no more than is needed."

"Do I know?" Emmett asked him across the table. Emmett had lost his bland blond look, the fair hair now falling limp and ragged over his thin face.

Owen looked at him gently.

"No," he said. "You don't know. It's my sin."

John Julius clapped him on the shoulder and with no more said, they fell to the bread and cheese.

They passed the evening in unhappy silence, Antonia completely unapproachable by either Owen or John Julius, her pointed face pinched and stiff, and her eyes dark with secret grieving. It tore Owen's heart to watch her but she made it clear there was nothing that she wished to say to either of them. Only to James was she gentle. Before she went up early to her bedroom, she told them she would be taking the mail car into Galway in the morning to buy some books for the school, and would be gone until the late evening. She bade them good night, and they looked after her baffled, unable to help her since she would give not the smallest hint as to her feelings. Nor could they speak to each other of it, both of them wounded by her turning away from them.

On her return the following evening she got as far as

Tuam, climbing stiffly down from the hard seat of the mail car into a chill blue dusk, full of the pipings of hopeful birds; bare trees awash with the faint amber shadow of new life, against a sky the clear blue of a thrush's egg. She stood a long moment and looked all round her as if she marked forever what she saw, and then she turned across the road towards the farm where she had left her bicycle.

At a livery stable on the outskirts of the little town she turned and wobbled in across the ruts into the stables, looking for the owner.

"And what," the man said later, coming thoughtfully into his warm kitchen picking his teeth, a dubious frown on his face, "what would you think the daughter of the agent's house at Owenscourt is doing wanting an outside car at six in the morning. And not to the house either, if you please, but down at the grand gates. To take her into Galway."

His wife looked up sharply from her knitting at the fire, her round face glowing in the warmth. She had heard a few odd murmurs about Owenscourt that very morning, and she down to get a few things in the chandler's and the blood for the black puddings from the butcher.

"She could have a man," she said speculatively, "or she could be running away. Has she the money to pay you?"

He looked a little ashamed that he had asked.

"I asked her that," he said. "She said I could have it now."

"On the other hand," his wife said more charitably, "the whole gillivrang of them could be off somewhere in the morning. Although," she added darkly, "I have heard the Peggy one is off somewhere of her own already."

He didn't rise to her.

"Is it any of my business?" he asked her, his kind face crumpled with some anxiety he couldn't put a name to, conscious of the strained and even tragic face of the girl who had booked the car. There was nothing there to suggest it was, God help her, for any happy purpose.

His wife answered him.

"It is not indeed, any of your business," she said sharply. The gentry and even the half gentry like those in the agent's house were queer cattle when all was said and done, and not to be understood by the likes of her. "She wouldn't thank you," she added, "for interfering in her affairs."

"No," he said unwillingly to himself. "But her father might."

He gave way to the easy habit of letting his wife make all his decisions, and settled in the high-backed chair on the far side of the hearth; so that when Antonia stood alone in the bitter black before the dawn waiting at the grand gates where the noisy brood no longer clamored at the carriages that were gone forever, there was no one to see her but a surly and half-sleeping driver; taking her away unquestioned into the darkness with her bundles.

It was always John Julius, and always had been, who was first up in the white house beside the stables, padding round with his candle in the chilly dark to wake the others; and then down into the warm kitchen where the cat stretched lazily and Boru thumped a feathered tail to greet him from the hearthrug, where he had been allowed to sleep as he grew old; taking the bellows to blow the faint pink turf-glow into heat, and pulling the pot of stirabout that Peggy would have left ready, over above it from the hob. The brief solitary quiet of the morning was precious to him; a space of breathing, alone in the dark and empty house before the day began.

This morning in the thick darkness he crashed into the boys' room, the candle wavering in his hand, tilting light across the ceiling. It was to Owen that he came, shaking him furiously, and grease spattered on his face.

"Owen," he cried. "Owen!"

Owen grabbed his blanket underneath his chin and tried to cling to sleep.

"For God's sake come awake, man," John Julius shouted. "Come awake. Antonia's gone!"

Slowly Owen drew himself up in the bed and looked at John Julius over the candle flame, finding time to ask himself in anguish why all his life at the present time seemed to have the aspect of taking place in darkness.

Chapter 14

THEY traced her easily to the livery stables, where the poor man's face crumpled with contrition, not daring openly to accuse his wife but darting reproachful glances at her face. She stood indifferent.

"Ah, I'm sorry now, Mr. Cannon," he said. "I said to the wife that maybe I should have told you. Then I thought maybe it was for the whole lot of you, and you off somewhere, that she was getting the car. Has she vanished entirely?"

As far as you could take her, thought John Julius bitterly, but clapped the man on the shoulder and told him it was no fault of his. It was still early, the first cold sun glittering in the ruts and puddles of the yard, and the turf smell strong from the newly banked fire inside the house.

"When did she go?" he asked him.

"Six of the clock. And I know," the man added, as if it justified something, "that the driver was punctual. I was awake early with my stomach that does give me a bit of trouble, and I heard him going away there from the yard."

John Julius thanked him, and turned for the gate and

Owen with him. The man stood a moment, with concerned and doubtful face, before going back into his house, looking at his wife; but she only shrugged her shoulders and went on over the yard with her steaming bucket for the feeding of the hens.

"Galway," John Julius said heavily to Owen as they climbed into the trap, and Owen understood him at once.

"Has she money?"

"Enough." John Julius shook the reins and turned the trap for the Galway road, urging the pony to a trot. "I gave her some money some time back for keeping for herself."

He didn't say to Owen that he had long feared for Antonia's security at Peggy's hands, and wanted her to have something to turn to if, God forbid, anything should ever happen to him.

Almost in silence they drove the long beautiful miles down to Galway City, through the dark brown empty bogland and along the wooded slopes of Corrib, where the light flashed on the vast expanse of water as if it were the ocean that already haunted both their minds.

In the bustling city they stabled the horse, and then began their urgent walking through the crowded cobbled streets, from one small shop to another where the bright posters advertised the sailings to America. Offering new life for a pittance, and new hope to the starving and the hopeless. With controlled patience John Julius waited at every counter and asked his question.

But tall thin girls with long dark hair were as familiar as the stones in the west of Ireland, and in every crowded shop they were looked at with pity or impatience.

"Ah, God ha' mercy on you," cried one old woman in the end, and said it for them all; peddling her steamer tickets to another world between the bags of meal and the hard lye soap, and the candles, in the back shadows of her shop. "Isn't every other one that comes in here the measure of that," she asked them impatiently. "Is she gone?"

The two men stood in silence in the bacon-smelling gloom, unwilling to admit it.

"She's gone." John Julius said at last.

"Ah—ah—ah." The old woman gave a wordless sigh of compassion and blessed herself with a wrinkled hand, her old heart sick for the young ones who came in every day with stony faces and their few bits of scraped-up gold, to buy their tickets to prosperity. "May the Blessed Mother take care of her," she said, "for they tell me 'tis no place to have a girl alone." She scurried off, her old shoes flapping, to where two farmers stood beside the porter barrel, leaning on the stained counter, waiting for the first thick dark-brown swallow of the day.

They went on then, almost in a panic, down to the quays, thrusting their way through the people in the narrow streets, between the gray houses, who took many a speculative glance at their two set and silent faces; tall, both of them, even in this city that bred the tall men of the West, and handsome enough in their set urgency to attract attention.

They found a tender moored beside the quays, the steamer standing black in the distance against the open glittering sea.

"Ah, God," John Julius said, and came to a halt. "We should have come here first."

The passengers were pressing down towards the tender, already gone on the first steps of their long journey, separated by a wooden barrier from the friends and relatives who had come to see them off.

Grief rose like a storm from those left behind, crowded along the quay in an abandonment of sorrow. The bright spring sun sparkled on the water and the seagulls wheeled and cried, and along the quayside milled the old ones and the ones too young yet to go; given over to such power of lamentation that Owen and John Julius stopped, shaken with pity for them. The young ones wept and waved at those already gone, knowing that their own time was short and as soon as they were old enough, they too must go. Old men, bent and crippled from their half-starved lives, tried to hold white-haired fainting wives who had just watched their last sons to the tender. The lifeblood of its youth, pouring out of

Ireland, as from a batch of mortal wounds. The bright air dark with mourning and the aching sorrow of partings that the old ones knew would be forever. They stood, the tears wet on their ravaged faces, unwilling to move away until the last trace of the steamer would be gone from the open sea.

"God have mercy on them," John Julius said, not yet willing to admit that he was one of them himself. "Come on, Owen."

Gently but quickly he made his way between them, his strong face soft with compassion, down to the two jersied men at the barrier. Urgency took him again. He seized one by the arm.

"Is that the last tender? Can we get onto it if we're not traveling?"

"It is. And you cannot. Do you go on that 'tis to New York."

"When does she go?"

"Any time now when she's full."

John Julius shot him a glance.

"Can we get a boat anywhere?"

"You can't go far in it, but me brother has a bit of a boat down there at the Spanish Steps."

He did not add that his brother waited there at every steamer with the boat, for just such as John Julius who had the sorrow and the money for one last look.

"Ye want to see the tender going past, is that it?" said the brother when they raced up to him through the archway at the Steps, as if it did not happen every week. "I'll have you out there in no time at all. That's what you want?"

"It is," John Julius said, and they scrambled into the inches of water in the bottom of the old boat. With wiry and unexpected strength, the brother bent to the oars.

Cold with the realization of loss and shattered by the abject grief all round him, Owen had no wish to go. Her father should know Antonia. Were she on that dark hulk of a rusty tender, heaven and earth would not get her off it. And in his sore and rejected heart he knew that she was there. Or already on the steamer waiting out beyond the bay. Even in these few short hours he knew that there would be no life for him until he got her back. The dream of Owenscourt that had filled his every waking thought, became without her as barren as a pauper's grave.

Dutifully he sat with John Julius, the rowing boat balanced on the chill and choppy sea, and scanned the wan sorrowing faces as the tender passed, all of them staring back towards the gray city drawing away into its ring of grape-blue hills; and towards the shrinking figures left behind them on the quay.

"There now," cried the brother. "Is that close enough? It does get a bit rough further out. Sure the lot of them are sick before they ever reach the steamer, never mind New York."

In silence John Julius nodded.

It was close enough to be stricken again by the uncertainty and grief that packed the rusty craft now churning past them.

Close enough to know that Antonia was nowhere they could see.

They rocked a while in the wash, watching it draw away, and then the brother rowed them back to the Spanish Steps, his wizened face disappointed. He could usually count on the entertainment of a good bit of tears and upset, but these two sat stony faced as if nothing had passed at all.

By the time they climbed the Steps and looked back, the tender had merged into the dark outline of the steamer on the edges of the open sea.

In the chill dark of early evening they got back to the agent's house to sit in heavy useless silence in the big kitchen that had seemed somehow lighter for the going of Peggy, but was bereft without Antonia. Owen's mind was barely with them, as he thanked Emmett absently for the mug of tea which was all the comfort he could offer, dominated through all his consciousness by the spread of dark water that was stretching wider every hour between him and Antonia. Emmett had managed to cook a meal, grimacing over it doubtfully on the range, his face flushed like any cook's. He looked up at his brother, sensing his thoughts, and there was compassion in his gray eyes.

"You don't know yet that she's gone," he said gently.

Owen shook his head, and John Julius stared into the fire, his whole body weary and defeated. He shook himself suddenly as if to rid himself of weakness.

"We must get a woman for the house," he said, his eyes on Emmett probing carefully in the big iron pot with a wooden spoon.

"It'll not be as bad as that," Emmett said, trying to lift the stony gloom from his face. "I think I'd be quite good at it. You'll get no satisfaction from the village women and we haven't the money for a good housekeeper. I was thinking, in fact," he said diffidently, "that maybe I could stay here and keep the house. You all know I'm no great fist on a farm."

He grinned at them both, unabashed, and neither Owen nor John Julius could help smiling at his artless face. Driven to agree with him that they had to do again most of what he did about the land.

John Julius objected.

"It's not fitting."

Owen lifted his head, answering somberly.

"There is much that isn't fitting," he said, "in our lives at the present time. Someone must do it, and it could be Emmett as well as any other."

Obscurely, he understood his brother's wish, knowing he would be happier. Unsuited, as Matt had long ago realized, to the practical life of the land, Emmett shot him a grateful look, across the bowls he was laying on the table, unable to explain even to him how eagerly he grasped the chance of the solitude of the empty house through the days. Even if it meant sweeping floors and peeling potatoes to get it. Leaving his mind free in peace and silence to make the journeys that had become so necessary to it.

"Get on out of the way, Boru," he said, taking John Julius's unwilling silence for consent. "You and I will have to stay at home and be the women of the house."

The old dog moved slowly back to the hearth from where he had risen laboriously at the sound of the bowls rattling on the table, and settled again, laying his long grizzled nose on his paws, and who could know what he remembered. Silence fell among them all, as though even for Boru this was an evening so weighed down with change and sorrow that there were no words left to help it pass. Only the barren comfort of bright-lit memories of the life they had all once shared, and that it seemed would never come again.

To Owen the loss of Antonia was a new dimension to his almost blind and hopeless obstinate struggle. In all his dreams and in his grim determined plans, when he had got back Owenscourt and stood as master on the pillared portico looking towards the lake, Antonia was standing at his side. Her hand in his and the sun gleaming in her black hair. Even his young courage found it hard now to sustain the dream at all.

"Well, come on then, woman," he said to Emmett. "Let's have it even if it poisons us. I'm truly clemmed."

A few days later the Canon came to call from Tuam, clopping up the weedy avenue on his undernourished horse, his black coattails flapping in the wind, rusty in the searching sun, Holy Mother Church having little generosity in stipend to either man or horse.

Beyond the elms the weeds sprouted round the portico and the shuttered house looked forlorn and abandoned in the sunshine, bypassed by the universal surge of spring.

The little priest sighed, and took off his round spectacles to polish them on a corner of his coat.

God help them they had it hard here. But it was no more than he had ever feared at the hands of Hugh Charles Healey, and Matt, God rest his soul, had feared the same.

Emmett diverted him, opening the door to him in one of Peggy's aprons. Boru came out slowly and sniffed at his coat, raising his gray muzzle as if to apologize for not being as he once was. The priest laid a hand on the dog's head and peered at the apron through clean glasses. Emmett grinned at him unperturbed. In the few moments he had watched him before he opened the door he had decided to say nothing. The Canon would know it all before he came.

"Somebody had to do it, Father," he said. "And do you stay to the dinner, I'll show you what I can do to a bit of bacon and cabbage."

The priest shook his head.

"It suits you better than a spade," he said shrewdly, and the boy nodded.

"It does."

The clear sunlight that caught the rusty lights in his clothes caught also the marks of the years on the good priest's face. The cheerful bubbling young man who had married Matt and Celia was gray now below the rim of his round hat; the merriment of his face dimmed for long lack of anyone to laugh with. But the eyes still shone bright and wise and rested thoughtfully on the tall fair boy in the pink apron. Long ago he and Matt had talked of the strong independent spirit that lay beneath his amiable nature, and it troubled the priest that Owen in his strong imperiousness didn't seem aware of it. In all he did and planned, he assumed he planned for Emmett also, unaware of his brother's strength. Certain, in all his own sweeping determinations, that they were shared by Emmett.

"Will you not come in," Emmett said then. The smile he gave him was one of deep trust and affection, as though he spoke to the small man on a different level from their words. "I can give you a dish of tea," he said. "I have the bread baked. Yesterday's was like the stepping-stones in the lake, but today's has a head on it. I shouldn't get it thrown at me."

"I'll take the bacon," said the priest, "when it's ready. Can you tell me now where to find John Julius Cannon?"

What he had to say to the man, he thought, would be better said in private than before these boys around the table; never knowing that Peggy D'Arcy had said it all before him.

"He's on the hill pasture. Will I stable the horse for you and you can go across the yard?"

"I'll do that."

He let Emmett in the apron lead the horse round to the stables and he himself set off across the farmyard, past the well and over by the back of Owenscourt, until he came to the first slopes of the green hill between it and Holly House. The far curve that faced into the sun was given over to the sheep and lambs.

John Julius moved among them, a collie at his heels. He saw the Canon beginning to tackle the gate leading onto the hill field and waved an arm to tell him stay, coming on down to him with the long loping stride that hadn't changed since Matt had first employed him.

"You're well met, Father," he cried. "Did you go to the house?"

He shook his hand, his weathered face creased with genuine pleasure. He had seen little enough of the good man for years. God knew it was another world when they had all the cheerful card parties in the evenings there in Owenscourt. A priest, even Matt's cousin, was not a guest to be encouraged by Peggy, and for a long time there had been no more than the passing greeting at the Sunday Mass. But John Julius knew that after Matt's death, Celia would hardly have survived without him and his gentle consolation, and from all accounts young Emmett was the same.

The Canon smiled.

"I did," he said, "go there. And the woman of the house told me where to find you."

John Julius grimaced.

"It isn't fitting," he said as he had said before. "It may be," answered the priest.

"So his brother says."

They left the matter of Emmett then, and his apron.

"What can I do for you, Father?"

John Julius was curious, having no illusions that the Canon had ridden all the way out to the house either to pass the time of day or for the sake of his immortal soul. The man had too much sense.

"Mr. Cannon."

John Julius heard the change of tone and stared at him, seized suddenly by the unbelievable notion that the man had come out here to ask him to take Peggy back. His fists clenched at his sides.

"I had two visitors yesterday," the priest went on, "and I may add," he said, with mild malice, "they were both dressed as if to go to the Viceregal Lodge itself." The fists began slowly to uncurl. "Mr. Hugh Charles Healey and the lady who names herself Miss Peggy D'Arcy."

He shot a sudden sidelong glance at the carefully impassive face of the man beside him, and looked back up the hill.

"They want," he said then to the sheep and the lambs, "to get married."

"And what's stopping them?"

The sun was turning from the hill and the first bite of the evening wind no colder than John Julius's voice. He looked straight down at the priest, demanding that he ask the question he had come to ask, and the priest turned away from the possessed black fury of his eyes.

"It's my duty," he said mildly, gently, "things being as they are, to ask you did you ever marry the woman called Peggy D'Arcy. She's a very respectable lady, it seems," he added, keeping the irony carefully from his voice, "and for Mr. Healey it's marriage or nothing."

As he had intended, he eased the rage in the other man, and John Julius leaned suddenly on the gate as if he were exhausted.

"We were never married," he said. "And I'm sure she was never married before I took her. Bedded, yes, God knows, but never wedded. She is free to marry Hugh Charles Healey, and I wish them the good they may do each other. Come on in now and we'll see what the woman of the house has for dinner."

As they walked through the chill encroaching shadows of the farmyard, the priest looked up again at John Julius.

"Do you mind my asking," he said diffidently, "why you never married her? 'Tis always useful to know the reason for these things."

"She never wanted it," John Julius said indifferently, thrusting away the anguish and insecurity of the years of besottted love when he had feared to lose her. How many times, although it shamed him to his heart, had he been glad of her infatuation for Matt O'Connor, because it kept her at his side. "She never wanted it."

Not even to his good-natured friend would he speak of Antonia, or of the fresh searing wound, come with the thought that maybe Peggy had never married him since her true heart, if she ever had one, had gone to the father of her daughter. Had she ever hoped to marry him? 'Twas not beyond her to hope to be Lady Bunaffrey.

In silence he opened the white gate for the priest, and they could smell Emmett's bread and bacon from the garden. From the dark lake Owen was riding up the park, away all day around the boundary fences.

Canon Walsh performed the marriage ceremony between Hugh Charles and Peggy D'Arcy three weeks later, looking down on them with unsuitable somberness from the steps of the high altar of the cathedral; unable to exclude from his mind the soft bright day when his cousin Matt had stood there with Celia; and all the years of happiness that everyone had hoped for. There was no one from his family to stand up for Hugh Charles, only a few horsey friends dredged up from the past. And on the woman's side of the church, no more than a gillivrang of drunken D'Arcys in their gypsy finery, hotfoot over from Claremorris for the drink.

Sadly he looked at them over his prayer book.

"We are gathered here together . . ."

He was aware even in his celibate mind of the finery of Peggy's dress, and the brilliance of the bridegroom's waistcoat and his satin stock. From the window of the vestry he had seen the spanking-new yellow carriage in which she had arrived. Hugh Charles for the pretense of propriety that brought sardonic grins to the faces of the watching villagers had come a few minutes earlier in his own trap, a beautiful bay horse between the shafts. Clearly she had managed to open his purse strings before they were even married. It was all the priest could do to walk out along the few steps of carpet to the altar, sick with the recollection of how Matt's two sons had fared in Holly House.

The news of the grandeur at the wedding filtered up to the agent's house, and with it the rumors of the Italian honeymoon and the men brought all the way from Dublin while the couple were away for the refurbishing of Holly House.

They spoke little of it, the two boys hesitant to speak of Peggy to the man who had lived with her so long as his wife, and all of them unwilling to bring the matter up at all to Owen's blanched and furious face.

"You realize what this new caper is going to mean," he said to Emmett bitterly in their bedroom. "Not a penny will be left. Not one single penny. Does she not get enough from him, she could drive him to the selling of Owenscourt."

The bones were strong now in his young face, giving him so close a likeness to his father in his anger, that for a moment Emmett blinked and looked away.

"No," he said then reflectively. "Not that. I don't understand it, but there is something would never allow him to sell Owenscourt."

"Our father would come back and haunt him," Owen said dourly.

"Something like that."

Emmett's answer was sober and considered, and Owen looked at him and grunted, understanding. But not understanding that he was haunted as closely as his uncle was, by the ghost of perfection that had been Matt O'Connor.

Nor did either of them know how their young mother had looked at Peggy Cannon on her wedding day with the unhappy premonition that she would bring trouble to them all, never thinking it would go on far beyond her own grave.

"I'll get it back from the thieving bastard and live in it," Owen said fiercely, "even if it be on the bare boards, and tilling the fields with my fingers."

What he really meant was that he would not rest until he had recreated it exactly in his father's style, even thinking often in his brooding dreams that he must have a dog to run at his heels, and that poor Boru was past it.

"Holly House is yours too," Emmett reminded him.

"They can do as they like with that." His father had never been concerned with Holly House. "Think, Emm. No matter what he did, our mother would never have us run her brother out of Holly House. But I want Owenscourt."

And Antonia with it, said the sad part of his mind that thought of little else, and Emmett reflected, with reason, that their mother's brother had not thought twice of running them out of Owenscourt.

The long summer dragged, from the green fields through to the golden harvest. In the long blank days Owen and John Julius each pretended with bleak endurance to the other, that they didn't live only for the hour when they could come back from the fields into the house, and ask Emmett if there had been a letter. In the end they stopped asking, if only to save Emmett the pain of saying no.

There were not many occasions now when the old postman came toiling out to Owenscourt on his high bicycle, his canvas bag across his shoulders. No more than the occasional kind letter from James Cornelius O'Duffy, reassuring them that he was always there to help them; the neat tall script of Mrs. Bradley, who would appear to do no more than sit in her small cottage out at Kingstown, watching the mail boats keeling in as Celia had once done, and dreaming like them all of days gone by. At increasingly long intervals came a blotty and half-literate scrawl from Bourdain, for Gracie couldn't write, full of messages of love for the tall young men she still thought of as her children; and of her joy and pleasure in her own small son. "We do thank God every day," wrote Bourdain painfully with his uneven pen, "for the bit of money that did see us threw."

Owen would lay the letters aside in silence and walk out onto the land, sitting always in the end where John Julius and the dog had sat the night his father died, looking up at the gray ghost of his home.

Hugh Charles came as little as he could.

"And why does he come at all?" Owen asked bitterly. "Doesn't he know this land is in better hands than Holly House?"

When he did come, he was careful to seek out John Julius alone and avoid the boys, as if before them even he knew shame at his costly mount and bespoke breeches, and his fine new shining boots. If Owen saw him he would turn away, and go at once to some safe distance where he would not be threatened by the black rage that would in a second of provocation have torn the man down from his horse and pummeled him into the ground that he had stolen. Hugh Charles never made an effort to follow or to speak to him, aware of the stories that must be reaching even the isolation of the agent's house, and seeing in his brief glimpses of the young man a new and uncompromising strength that was alarmingly like his father's.

They heard all the stories, mostly from Emmett after his sallies into the town to buy provisions. Soirées and card parties, it seemed, and the stables full of priceless bloodstock and conniving D'Arcys. Holly House ablaze with lights at the end of the river road, and carriages full of Hugh Charles's drunken friends and Peggy's family stampeding through the sleeping town in the small hours of the night. And Milady Peggy now too grand to buy as much as a spool of thread in the local shops. Even the servants that came and went like Punchinello in his box were brought down from Dublin. Tuam saw nothing of her save the fine rigs and flashing gowns and feathered hats as she drove through the street with never a glance to left or right. As if it were the Prince of England himself that she had married, and not Hugh Charles Healey from the broken-down house that he was only putting together with Matt O'Connor's money, and she herself no more than half a tinker from that lot beyond Claremorris.

Poor they might be, in the shabby town with the manure along the dusty street; counting their few pennies in the tiny cabins, with the children and the hens together on the beaten floor; but they still saw Peggy D'Arcy as beneath them, and like Owen and Mrs. Bradley, their hearts turned always to the past.

What they didn't see they made up for with what they heard, mainly from the outraged and disgruntled servants dragging their valises to the mail car on their way back to Dublin; slamming behind them in fury the grand new wrought-iron gates of Holly House. Swearing to a man and a woman that they had for Jesus' sake, never been so treated by a jumped-up madam in all their days of service, and the so-called master no more than a dog there for the licking of her patent leather boots.

Owen's face grew darker and tighter, and he refused for any reason to go anywhere near Holly House, avoiding even the town as much as possible, unwilling to see anything he didn't have to. Even through his own sad loneliness John Julius was concerned for him, watching the hardening set of his wide mouth that like Matt's had smiled so easily, and realizing that he was growing unnaturally silent for a young man of his age.

Where, he often asked himself, would be the end of it all for them. And what chance would there be now of sorting out the inheritance with all the goings-on at Holly House, and Hugh Charles Healey with all his own resentments, firmly in the grip of a woman who would take pleasure in ruining the boys simply because they were Celia's sons.

Like Owen himself he saw no answer, and thought sadly of the passing time and Cannon's Mills still lying beneath a shroud of weeds and nettles, the elder trees beginning to threaten the fabric of the walls. Did that go on the cost of setting up again would be twice as great. To add to his frustration, the harvest had been good now for years and the country round was doing better. There'd be work again there for a mill. Could he, he brooded, persuade Owen to come and run the mill with him and the money they made could be put back into the land when the time came. Above him as he walked up the park was the gray bulk of Owenscourt almost lost in the dank mist. He shook his head. Owen would never leave it. During the first months since his mother's death he had been quiescent, almost in a state of shock, numbly working the land in the conditions at Holly House. As though he had not yet begun to think. Lately there was a new ferocity, almost violence, in his attitude and John Julius knew he would never be able to shake his singlemindedness. For Owen there was only one thing. To stand again as his father had stood, on the portico, looking out across his land through the brown trunks of the elms. He read him so closely and so clearly, yet well as he knew him, and knew his feelings for Antonia, he did not understand that now it was only half the dream, and that without Antonia it would be nothing.

Owen was in Tuam that damp October day with the horse and cart; unwillingly; getting supplies for Emmett, who had a fever. The rain that had spilled down all night had eased away but the day was hung with chill gray mist and the unmade street of the little town was still awash with sheets of water. He came out of the chandlers, fusty with the smell of meal and salty bacon and full of women with the rain beaded on their black shawls, doing their meager buying.

"Did you hear!" one of them had said to him at once, "Did you hear the news? Didn't it come on the mail car!"

He must say to her first that he had heard nothing. Only then would she tell him, relishing her drama of delay, her black eyes bright.

"I've heard no news," he said, and almost added that he didn't want to. It would almost certainly be no more than something in the way of a new tidbit about the Healeys.

"Parnell is dead," she said. "God save his sinful soul."

Charles Stuart Parnell. A vague memory of a rolling hoop and a man with a big black beard and his father talking about the one hope for Ireland. Well, it had all in the end come to nothing and Ireland stayed where she had been for centuries, under the heel of England. He realized he had thought nothing of the troubles of the country for a long time back, his own sea of sadness having swallowed him to the point where he cared for little else. With a sense of guilt he recalled the emigrant steamer and the young ones pouring from the land where they were starving.

"Look after your own," his father had always said, and that was why there were never troubles on his fields. A wry smile touched Owen's lips. No one could say that at the moment he wasn't looking after his own. With his own two hands and the strength of his back.

He eased his sack of goods across his arm and was thinking of Ireland as he walked out again into the street. Heaving the sack into the cart he made to get around the puddles, over to the small shop that held the mail, since the car was in; in the regular hopeless hope that there would be a letter.

Down the long curve of what was virtually the only street came flying a dark-blue phaeton with its hood up, two smart bays racing in the shafts, the hens pecking hopefully in the puddles scattering squawking underneath their hooves. Muddy water from the road took Owen in a shower from head to foot, and as he leapt back cursing, he caught one second's glimpse of the woman at the reins; and of the contemptuous smile he hadn't seen since she stood that last evening before the fireplace in the agent's house, and named Antonia a bastard twice. Well she knew who she had drenched, and it had given her pleasure.

He was still standing, staring after the vehicle and trying to control the rage that shook him, when little Tessie Nolan ran out from the mail house, a blue letter in her hand.

"Mr. O'Connor," she cried, breathless with the second sensation of the day. "I have a letter here for Mr. Cannon. From America," she breathed, so racked with eagerness that she was standing in water to the hem of her skirt and didn't know it. "Will you open it?"

'Twould be from the Antonia one, no doubt, and she able to tell all of what struck his face as he read it.

Owen took it, and knew that even were it addressed to him, he would barely have the strength to lift the flap. But it was inscribed to Mr. J. J. Cannon. The writing thin and flowing. A girl's hand.

" 'Tis not for me," he said to her crestfallen face, "but thank you."

He put it in his pocket and was never aware of the miles below the dripping trees to home, wondering all the time would John Julius be there, and if he wasn't, would he have the strength of mind not to open it.

John Julius was there, drying his feet before the range, and took the letter with a curious deliberation as if he had lost control of his fingers. They stood over him as patiently as they could while he read it, and Owen clasped his hands behind his back to keep from snatching it, walking away in the end to look out the window.

"She is well," John Julius said at last, "and has found herself a job in New York."

"Doing what?" Owen asked harshly.

"She doesn't say."

"Is there an address?"

John Julius looked to the top of the letter.

"Care of Mrs. Miller. Fifty-two Frankfort Street, New York."

Owen looked as if a weight had fallen from his shoulders, but John Julius could hardly speak, handing him the letter to read for himself. It began, "Dear Friend," and was touching in its directness and simplicity, and made little mention of her own life, or of herself. She wanted, she said, father or not, and behind the few words lay all the anguish of coming to terms with that—she wanted to say thank you to John Julius for all the years of love and care. She remembered him always in her prayers.

"I love you all," she said at the finish, down at the end of the thin blue paper, and desperately Owen searched to find in the words something special for himself.

"Fifty-two Frankfort Street," he said to himself.

"Yes," John Julius said, "we can write to her."

Owen laid the letter on the table and looked from him to Emmett.

"It's not that," he said. "It's something I have been thinking of since she went, and I came to my decision some time back. I've been waiting only to know where she is. Now we know, we'll go to America ourselves. Emmett and me. There's money to be made there, and do we work all hours then we should come back in a state to deal with everything. There is nothing for us here at the present time. We will only go from bad to worse."

The sun broke through the mist and fell through the window on Boru, stretched on the rag rug, his eyes going from one of them to the other.

Neither Emmett nor John Julius spoke, staring at Owen, clearly full of their own thoughts, and in their doubtful silence his eyes darkened.

"We're going," he said, and never thought of Emmett as being separate. "But I'll be back. And bring her with me."

Chapter 15

THEY argued all through the gray afternoon, Emmett's cold pie forgotten on the table. He himself sat and looked from one of them to the other, and did not speak, as if completely ready to acquiesce in anything they might decide.

Owen was adamant. John Julius simply did not want him to go. While his heart ached for the efforts to find Antonia, it was not in his experience that people who went to the States came back in four years' time with pocketfuls of money. They would only the pair of them finish up in a far worse state than they started out. But he had no answer to Owen's impassioned ravings on his hopeless poverty, and the impossibility of staying where he was, falling at every turn over his uncle and that wanton gypsy squandering all that should be his. Nor this time did he try to spare John Julius's feelings.

"And I will bring back Antonia," he said to clinch the matter, and the older man fell silent, his face stony.

"And where," he asked in the end, knowing that what Owen said about Peggy was true—murder had been done for less—"where will you get the money to go?"

He was ready to offer it, since the young man had made up his mind.

"I'll get the money," Owen said. "Before it is too late," he added grimly, as though that possibility lay high in his considerations.

Clear in all their minds were the golden guineas laid down in challenging silence on the table every fortnight for his own and Emmett's keep.

John Julius sighed and straightened in his chair. He, too, had come to his decision.

"Well, then, Owen," he said. "Do you do that, then I'll go back to Cannon's Mills."

At his feet, on the patchwork rug, Boru stirred and lifted his long head, looking into his face.

Owen was taken aback. As long as he could remember, John Julius Cannon had been at Owenscourt, although vaguely he recalled some difference about the early days. In all the dark nights he had lain sleepless, planning, he had envisaged him, in his absence, still watching over Owenscourt, guarding it for his return. With difficulty he forced himself to be reasonable, suddenly realizing he would be almost impertinent in such a demand. When all was said and done there was no reason why the man should stay. He had done already far more than decency demanded. Cannon's Mills. The place held John Julius's name exactly as Owenscourt held his. And both of them in ruins, he thought ruefully. How childish of him not to have thought before that the reclaim of the Mills might mean as much to the older man as the estate to him. Shame flooded him that they had so long held on to his comfort and protection, and in a few silent minutes, with Boru lying between them, Owen acquired some measure of the maturity he would need. "I wish you well, John Julius," he said soberly at last, and the warm crinkle of the dark-blue eyes told him the man had read his every thought and approved it.

They said little then for a while, the warm lamplit kitchen too full of memory and loss, all of them grappling with the full understanding of what they were about to leave.

Boru sat up stiffly and laid his head along John Julius's leg, and he leaned down to rub the shaggy neck.

"Don't fret, old lad," he said. "We'll not leave you behind. I'll take you with me."

"I want to do it at once," Owen said then, looking at Emmett as if it was an order. "I don't want anything to happen to stop me."

It was as if Peggy and Hugh Charles had walked into the room.

"When?"

"We'll go tomorrow night. I've found the steamer times and there's one the day after tomorrow. Please God we'll get on that; otherwise we'll lie low in Galway and take the next one. I was only waiting for the letter. I'd rather not delay in Galway if it's possible."

John Julius didn't ask him why, knowing it would concern the passage money and where he got it. The less he knew of that, the better. He rubbed Boru's head and let Owen talk.

"We will leave everything, John Julius. Let them sort it out. Stand up and take what's yours and James's and be gone. And God speed you. Emm, we'll take the good clothes we haven't had on our backs since Dublin. We'll need them for finding work."

Emmett nodded. He had said nothing, and his face held none of the excitement of great decision that brightened his brother's eyes, nor even of the slow astonished pleasure kindling in the older man's.

James came in, still carrying the lantern he had been using in the stables, his coat and cap rimed with the cold mist.

"There's good beef spoiling in the pot," Emmett said then and laid it on the table without further comment while they told James what was going to happen. He blew out the lantern and peeled off his wet coat, his young eyes bright.

"I'd rather go to the States with Owen." His voice cracked with excitement. "Father, could I not do that? Please."

They all laughed at him and it lifted the sorrow that weighed down the decisions. In the end they all sat round the lamplit table almost in a mood of celebration.

Yet that night Owen couldn't sleep. For all the months of thinking of it, apprehension of the totally unknown crept over him, and he knew himself as sick with doubt and sorrow as any of those he had seen crowded at the rail of the tender that day in Galway. In the cold pitch darkness, with Emmett's even breathing coming from the other bed, he lay and listened to an owl hooting dismally in the pines between him and the stables. All he could think of was of the acres of Owenscourt lying around him in the black night, and the shrouded house beyond the white gate. He tried to resist them, but his mind raced with brilliant pictures he could not control. His father always on a white horse and there was some joke about that with his mother, Boru his shadow loping at his heels. Poor Boru, he must wonder what had become of life, and now another strange home for him. He was old, poor dog, and deserved better. He saw his mother, a straw hat tied with ribbons on her fair hair, driving the little basket trap with Emmett, stopping the fat white pony on the bridge so that she might gather the tall flags that grew along the edges of the lake, and they were the same color as her dress, blowing in the wind. Antonia. And he could not know which longing was the greatest, as he thought of her, astride her shaggy pony like a boy, her hair a dark flag.

His eyes opened wide.

"I'll be back," he said fiercely to the darkness and the moaning owl. "As God will help me, I'll be back."

He thought of the picture Mrs. Bradley had given him from the bottom of the stairs in Gardiner Street. The strange muddle of Dublin Castle and the Chinese country. It was already packed with their crumpled, unworn clothes from Dublin.

"I'll bring it back when I am twenty-one. I'll hang it on the stairs in Owenscourt."

Recreating, like a child bereft, the one small part of the pattern that was left with him.

John Julius woke him quietly in the first pale light, and didn't go away, standing beside the bed, his shadow crawling enormous on the wall behind him.

"What is it now?" Owen asked, and couldn't think what else might befall them. What fresh bad news that always seemed to belong to the dark dawn.

"Poor Boru is dead."

"Ah. Ah, the poor fellow. He knew we were going to leave Owenscourt. He didn't want to go."

John Julius nodded.

There had never been a time without Boru.

"He was older than I am," Owen said. "I remember him taller than I was myself."

Emmett woke, and together they all went down and looked at him where John Julius had found him, stretched on the rug at the range, as peacefully as if the decision to die had been his own.

"I don't think," John Julius said, "that he ever had much use for any of us since your father died." He alone remembered the anguished dog, baying at the racing moon.

They all told each other it was better as it was, but could not even settle to eat their breakfast until they had chosen a grassy slope beneath a beech tree by the lake. There in the damp morning, they dug a man-sized grave and laid him in it gently, filling in the earth and putting back the green sods; leaving him to Owenscourt, to lope forever in the sunshine at the heels of a young man on a fine white horse.

Owen felt no shame for the pricking tears on that gray morning, for all the life that had been Boru's, and his own and Emmett's with him.

Emmett found a paling in the yard, and carved on it the dog's name and set it in the grass below the tree, hammering it in deeply so no wind or storm would ever move it.

When the silent and inconclusive day had darkened into dusk, Owen had one last task, nor would he let Emmett share it. Alone he walked out and through the white gate, round the back of the house to where thick darkness lay across the kitchen yard.

There were certain things, thank God, his uncle Hugh Charles Healey didn't know when he had sealed the house up like a tomb, and thought no one but himself could get into it and the secrets he had placed in it. Owen reached up his full height to a niche in the stone wall and brought down a heavy brass key for the kitchen door. Put there long years ago when they had a half-mad cook, convinced the whole world was out to rob her. She was always locking the kitchen door when she went to sleep of an afternoon, and forgetting where she had put the key. They had six cut, Owen remembered with a small smile, to try and keep pace with her. But his mother wouldn't be rid of her since she cooked like an angel. His father would have kept her were it only for the brandy snaps.

He needed no light to thread his way through the pitch-black house, and only at the center of it in the inner hall did he set down his little lantern and kindle it.

Grimly he closed his mind to the ghosts that walked the curving stairs and to the memories of laughter rising through the tall house. Did he give way now he would never go at all. And he must go, to come back.

But he asked his parents' pardon as he laid the lantern carefully on the table in his father's study. There was a picture on the wall above the desk which his mother had never liked. Gloomy. Two dead partridges and a bottle of cloudy wine in some dark-curtained corner, with a few dead leaves.

"But I have to leave it here, Owen," she had said to him, "because it is part of this. You should know about it, lest anything happen to me." She had laughed as she said it, and now in the icy shadowed room, he could recall her perfume.

By one edge she lifted the picture as he did now, held to a clip, and underneath the red damask wallpaper seemed to lie unbroken, but pressure in the center of a flower opened a door so exactly fitted that not even the closest search revealed it.

"Does anyone else know?" he had asked her.

"Your uncle. I thought he should. I am very much alone, Owen," she had added as if she ought to apologize even to him for her weakness about her brother.

When they were all speculating as to where Hugh Charles was putting away all the money from his illicit sales, Owen had come here at once. Bags and parcels of golden guineas, all labeled in his uncle's neat crabbed writing, the labels reading like a record of his father's life.

Now he broke one labeled, Stock from the Shops.

He had thought about it all. Did he take the lot, as he was tempted to, the man would surely pursue him. Did he take enough and no more, he would be glad to see him gone.

He took two hundred guineas. Five dollars to the pound. Two steamer fares and enough to see them both safely into work in a strange city and some to spare lest for any reason either of them could not work. Like a father to Emmett, he had calculated it all, and his face held little of its youth in the small glow of the lantern as he carefully closed the safe and felt his way from the house.

John Julius drove them in to the Canon's house in the trap, where they would say their good-byes to him and then catch the night mail car into Galway at eight of the clock. Even in the darkness John Julius marked the place where Matt O'Connor had stopped his bridal carriage and taken him for the first time to Owenscourt. Penniless he was then and almost in the same state he was leaving it. He would like to have stopped and tried to think about it all. To get, before he left forever, as his heart told him he was doing, even some vague understanding of the ruthless tide of misfortune that had struck them all. But he would not burden the boys with his thoughts, for they in all God's truth must be like plants ripped from the soil. He shook the pony on.

The mist of the day had turned with dusk into a streaming rain, and so their good-byes in Tuam, that should have held all the solemnity of years of love, were hurried, all of them already soaked; the water streaming from their hatbrims, silver in the small light that spilled against the rain from the Canon's curtained window.

As John Julius drove off and left them, standing together, no more than shadows in the pouring rain, he could only ask God sadly to help them all, the two of them and his own daughter, for nothing in the world would persuade him that Antonia was otherwise.

The plump little priest rose reluctantly from his fire. It had been a hard day as were most days in his parish, where the consolation of human suffering outweighed most other parish duties. Who, he wondered, could be so troubled now as to bring them to his door on this disastrous night.

When he opened the door he kept the surge of anger carefully from his face. What fresh indignity had brought the two of them to this, the rain running from their clothes and blowing past them in gusts into his little hall? Clearly on the run, valises in their hands, incongruously the fine strapped leather of their Dublin days, dark with rain.

He asked them no questions but took their dripping coats and sat them at the fire, sitting down again himself opposite them. He had need to look away from the gaunt misery of Owen's face.

"What has happened?"

"Antonia has written," Owen said, and the priest waited patiently for more, for that surely should be good news and nothing to drive them out like this with their belongings in the pouring rain.

Reluctantly Owen put more words to it. Now that the decision was made he was tired of talking and giving the reasons that had driven him past the point of any more patient endurance. Occasionally he glanced at Emmett for support, but his brother stared into the spitting fire and didn't speak.

"We haven't much time," he said. "We are catching the mail car to Galway at eight, and going to the States, I hope tomorrow."

The rain drummed down outside and the priest put his hands across his eyes.

"With what is going on in Holly House, there will be no money left by the time I am twenty-one. There's money in the States, they all say, and we can come back with enough to handle Owenscourt."

The Canon's throat was thick. Circumstances were driving them out. What use to break their hearts and their confidence by telling them of the poor, brave, barren letters he was given so frequently to read, always full of hope that by the next letter there would be work. And money. The creatures starving as easily on the streets of Boston and New York as in the crowded cabins on the Irish hills.

Full of grief, his eyes rested on their drenched faces; trying to hold at bay the sorrow that could destroy them all. He was old enough to fear in these uncertain times that every parting could come to be the last.

"Have you money?" was all he asked them and Owen looked at him directly. His father's straight uncompromising look.

"We have," he said, "and I must tell you, Father, where I got it. It is my sin, not my brother's."

The priest listened and his eyes held Owen's quietly.

"I'll not think," he said when he had finished, "that almighty God will be after either of you to get it back."

Owen smiled for the first time, but Emmett lifted up his head suddenly, sharply.

"I'm not going," he said.

Both of them stared as if they didn't understand the words. He pushed the sodden hair from his forehead and there was neither anger nor exasperation in his expression. He spoke quietly, but even before he finished they knew there would be no argument.

"Always, Owen," he said, and his eyes rested without resentment on his brother, "you have thought that I am you. But New York is not for me any more than the estate. I would be no more than a millstone round your neck, and you will be far better off without me."

Owen opened his mouth on a torrent of furious protest, as much upset and disbelieving that the compliant Emmett had decided something for himself, as at what he had decided. Even as he began to speak he realized that it would be Emmett who would be better by himself, and wanted nothing else. In the warm dim room with the rain hissing on the turf, loneliness yawned suddenly as wide as the ocean itself, the long solitary journey in an instant real. He stared at his brother as if he had changed into someone else, but knew that was not true either. Emmett was being Emmett. Quietly and without ever the making of an enemy, he would do exactly as he wanted. He closed his mouth on protest.

Emmett looked grateful and relieved that there had been no storm, and a faint suggestion of his former bland contentment crept across his face, but his brother was pale and shaken, faced so suddenly with another parting he had not expected.

"But what will you do, Emm?" he said bewildered. "If you want to go to Cannon's Mills why didn't you stay with John Julius and James?" A wild thought crossed his mind that Emmett might be going to make friends with his uncle.

Emmett looked over at the priest as if from him he was certain of understanding.

"I am going back to Clongowes," he said. "Since I have no money I will go in as a lay brother, giving them the strength of my back and the use of my hands."

Both of them realized that had been the reason behind his calm acquiescence in the kitchen work of the agent's house. Owen had no words, staring at his brother, trying to fit his image into all these new shapes of thought. Even in the astonished moment, he knew he should have been aware of them. They were all there, had he looked. But anger flared in him again, knowing that if his brother wished to be a priest, then his parents would have wished him do it properly, and not to go into the back door of his old school like a servant. He subsided, suspecting Emmett didn't mind. There was much to Emmett he hadn't understood, and now it was too late to understand.

"You will take half the money I have," he said.

Emmett shook his head.

"I'll take my train fare to Clongowes," he said. "That's all, Owen. I'll catch the mail from Galway in the morning. It's all arranged long ago. I wrote to them. I said I would come when I could, but I didn't want to leave you."

Owen ran his hands through his russet hair and Emmett smiled at him.

"Now you will have Antonia and a new life," he said. "So I can go."

There was no time to examine the astonishing proposition that Emmett had been stronger than himself, had been watching him with compassion. Waiting for the moment when he was fit to be left.

"Did you know about this?" he asked the priest, and the Canon shook his head. He had felt it would come someday, but not yet.

Owen looked at the old kitchen clock that ticked and clacked against the wall.

"It's time for us to go," he said.

Emmett had chosen his moment well. No time to argue now. All the time in the world in the weeks on the empty sea to try and understand it.

"Do one thing for me, Owen," the priest said. "No, two things." He looked up at the gaunt young man, standing there crushing the memories that threatened to overwhelm him; freshly shattered by what amounted to the loss of his brother. His heart bled for him, but there was nothing to do but be practical.

"First buy yourself a money belt, for you'll not last a week with all that gold stuffed in your pocket. And second, take Emmett's passage money now and don't go on a coffin ship. Take a decent steamer and go second class. You'll be little use to Owenscourt being shot across the railings in a canvas bag."

Or to Antonia, thought Owen in sudden fear; appalled.

In the tiny hall they knelt on the polished floor with the rain battering at the door beside them, and with a hand as heavy and reluctant as his heart, the Canon blessed them for their journeys.

"God go with you both, my sons," he said, but it was on Owen that his glance lingered, and he turned quickly to open the door into the streaming night so that he might say it was the rain that blurred his glasses.

Chapter 16

OWEN was young, and in such surroundings, loneliness and anger and grief were not able to haunt him long.

For the first three days, when the gray skies of Ireland still hung above the steamer and she reached and yawed through terrifying seas, he was withdrawn and brooding. Keeping not only to his cabin but to his bunk, where he could haul close his curtains against the dark pitching world, pretending to anyone who tried to intrude that, as with most other passengers, his trouble was his stomach. He had taken the Canon's advice and bought a second-class ticket on a reasonable boat, struck suddenly, with little short of terror, that having left everything behind him, he might never reach Antonia. On the coffin ships, he knew it to be true, one died in four, of fever, before ever even seeing their land of promise.

Darkly he lay and brooded, trying to come to terms with his still astonished and affronted grief at Emmett's going. In the gloom behind his drawn curtains, striped with swinging bars of light from the lamp outside, he came to recognize the first tarnish on his determined bright self-confidence; the first unbelievable warning that everybody might not go his way. Could he not be sure of his brother then who could he be sure of? Was this whole journey going to be for nothing. Stubbornly he brought it back to Emmett. He had always been soft, even when they were children. Too much with Mama and the priests. It was Emmett and Emmett only. No one else would let him down. In such thoughts he did not even dare to formulate Antonia's name.

On the fourth day the sun came out and the waste of gray water turned to deep dark blue and foaming green. The wind was fresh and sharp with salt and with the changing weather Owen's spirits lifted to the future. He grinned shamefacedly at the three young men with whom he shared the cabin as if he had never set eyes on them before, and from then on set himself to making the best of his voyage.

After all his fears and anxieties through the months since Antonia had gone away, it all turned out unbelievably simple; from the first cold dawn when he stood at the rail to watch the United States darken the long arc of the winter sea.

At Castle Garden he was treated easily by Immigration. The food had been little to boast of on the steamer, but the weeks at sea had rested him. He looked healthy and his clothes were still good, and he was able to show them gold in his pockets, and not the flimsy useless paper money of some godforsaken country that so many of these poor souls hoped to trade for dollars. He got as near a welcome as Immigration gave to any of the thousands like him.

There were good-byes. He had been well liked, freed from the treadmill drudgery of the land, and able to find himself again; recapturing the easy natural charm of the boy who had been the heir to Owenscourt. He had his father's singing voice, and learnt to use it with shy pleasure, enslaving all about him in the evenings in the cramped saloon.

One of the young men sharing his cabin had been a priest, not long ordained, going out from Rockwell to one of the houses of the order in Philadelphia. To him Owen had confided that his one chief anxiety was of finding somewhere to live in a city the size of New York when he didn't know one street from the next. On second class were a few of the legendary ones, coming back after a trip home to visit their families with every immigrant's dream of a handcase full of dollar bills. These ones had warned him of the flophouse touts who would be waiting to pounce on the quayside; trying to ensnare him into some hell of filth and bedbugs that he might have difficulty getting out of, did he not lose everything he had almost before he had the blanket on his head.

"Well, now," the priest had said, cocking his red head, little more than Owen's own age, and the look of the farmyard still about his boots. "I have a sister here, married, in New York. She came out five years ago. She can tell you surely where to get a lodging."

"You'll be going to her place yourself?"

The young priest shook his head.

"I have no holiday," he said. "There's a father to meet me, and then we go on down to Philadelphia. But my sister's to meet me at the quay, and you can talk to her there."

"Not one day, when you haven't seen her for five years?"

"Not one day. Isn't God good to me that I'll get to see her at all?"

There was neither rebellion nor resentment in his gaze, and Owen left it, thinking of his brother, who was perhaps halfway to this detachment before he entered anywhere.

Yet he could hardly bear to watch either their greeting or their poignant parting when at last they found her under the bright wintry sky, on the swarming quay. Already Owen's eyes and ears were drawn to the clamor of the city out beyond the sheds, numbed with the knowledge that somewhere in it was Antonia.

The sister had a baby in her arms and two small ones clinging to her faded skirts; beside her, her young husband, his long fair face scalded by the wind, the thinness of the starving years still showing in his cheekbones.

First she went down on the cold pavings to kiss her brother's ring, and when all the kissing and the hugging was done, and the messages from home that brought the tears, the poor small packages handed over, and the children admired, they talked as best they could in the jostling crowd; all pushing and stampeding like animals towards their new life, with never a notion where they would find it.

Father Tom explained who Owen was, and she turned and looked at him with tear-washed eyes as blue as Connemara's lakes. He could feel the callouses on her hand when he took it.

"Sure," she said, "I'd take him myself, the lad, but I tell you I have the baby in a drawer and one of the young ones sleeping on two chairs. Isn't that God's truth, Seamus?"

Seamus agreed it was indeed God's truth, and were it not for that she would take the lad herself.

"But," the girl said, "we'll take you back in the cart. And I can show you where a woman is has lodgings. I know they're not the best, but clean. She'll probably take you."

"The cart?" Father Tom asked, astonished at the sign of wealth.

"Isn't Seamus an oilman," she said with pride. "And the finest thing to be since it's winter work." The words meant nothing to Owen at the time. "At least," the sister added, "he does work for one, and the man being an Irishman himself, and with proper respect for a priest, he said we could bring the cart down today to see Father Tom."

Seamus nodded with solemn pride. There weren't many men on the quays today with a horse and cart. Nor did Owen yet understand the heartbreaking hierarchy of New York. The ones with work, and the ones without. "Mind you," added Seamus, "I'll have to work to midnight to make up for it."

The final agonizing partings done, Owen found himself making the first long-dreamed-of journey into the middle of the city of New York on the back of an oilman's cart, sitting on the red-painted rake in the reek of paraffin beside the drum, and behind him the brooms and mops and the shelves with wicks and mantles and hard yellow soap, the scouring powder and the bathbrick and the Reckitt's Blue that young

Seamus hawked around the crowded tenements of the city.

He jogged and shook along the rutted roads and tried to keep his valise and his overcoat out of the slopping paraffin, watching with bright eyes and rising excitement the rattling, thickening traffic and the crowded sidewalks, trying to make some comparison with Dublin which was the only other city he had ever known. Understanding, with a stab of compassion, the bewilderment and fear that must beset those come to it without knowing anything else; straight from the sky-filled spaces of Connemara, or the stony fields of Clare.

He found lodging as the young couple promised, not far from where they lived, after many promises to go and see them. With difficulty he managed not to recoil from the worn drugget and the greasy walls up the narrow stairs, aware that the slit-mouthed woman with the Belfast twang was taking malicious pleasure in his shock, eyeing his good clothes and his costly luggage.

"Were you perhaps thinking it was the Waldorf Astoria?" she asked him sarcastically.

He took it, realizing it was the only bed he knew of in New York, and five others with it in the room. But they looked clean, and the price was right. Or so the oilman Seamus had told him. Only a flophouse would be less.

"No one is allowed in the bedrooms before ten of the clock," she said as she took his money. "The times of meals is downstairs in the hall. And keep yer money on yer body," she added almost with pity, as if she didn't think it would last long anyway.

"Would you by any chance know where Frankfort Street is," he asked her. The one thought above all others.

"Frankfort Street? Isn't it where I lived myself when I first came here. Put yer clothes in the chest at the end of the bed and see you lock it. You can try hiding that fancy valise underneath it."

And God help it even there, she thought. He wouldn't have it long. Somehow the ones that clearly had had a bit of decency behind them were always the most pathetic. Wet behind the ears and as innocent as babes.

In spite of her directions, it was almost dark before he found Antonia's street, after what seemed like hours of wandering. All the streets looked alike except when regularly he stumbled on some long straight thoroughfare of big houses and hurtling traffic that could be no place Antonia would live, and each time he turned away again to plunge into the warren of the back streets. By the time he found the house the last streaks of a wicked sunset were flaring scarlet westwards and the gas lamps hissed and glowed over the small shops. He was tired. His lips were dry and his mind light with unbelief as he lifted his hand to the black japanned knocker and understood that Antonia might answer it.

For moments he stared at the slatternly little maid as if he didn't know what she was.

"Miss Cannon? Miss Antonia Cannon?"

"Ye're not allowed in; no callers."

The door slammed in his face and he stood bewildered and annoyed, looking at its peeling paint. The narrow streets all looked bustling and cheerful with the small bright shops scattered in among the clapboard houses. Close to, there was nothing that was not poor and dingy and in high need of a coat of paint.

When the door opened again, Antonia stood against the murky gaslight of the hall.

"Owen."

There was a draper's across the road, naphtha flaring at the corners of its windows, and he saw her in the yellow light, chalk-white with shock. She tried to speak but no words came and a sudden disastrous terror took him that she was not pleased to see him.

"Alannah! Antonia!"

He tried to feel she was more beautiful than ever, but honesty told him she was thin to the point of gauntness, the dark-blue eyes enormous, ringed with shadows.

Suddenly she gulped and began hopelessly to cry.

"Dear heart!" He leapt to the top step and took her hands in his. "Am I such a dreadful sight?"

Clear in her face was the effort she had to make to control

herself, but she did, and smiled then, the same sharp smile touched with startling sweetness, her eyes drowned.

"Oh, Owen, I am so happy to see you. Truly. It was just so unexpected."

"Bedam, it was a fine way to greet me, and me after coming three thousand miles to find you."

"To find me?" Some shadow passed across her face. "Was that all you came for?"

"What else?"

She relaxed again, as if postponing something.

"Ah, Owen, how good of you. And how is John Julius? And James? I miss James dreadfully."

"All well," he said. "Well. Can we not sit down somewhere and let me tell you everything?"

"Not here. Wait. I'll get my coat. You can't come in here, it's for women only."

He saw her lips crease with some distaste, and thought of the lodging to which he had only given a cursory glance earlier in the day. The drab paint with the marks of greasy hands around the beds, the small high windows covered with wire like a chicken run, to stop the customers, he imagined, putting their boots through them or worse. He would have all that, and maybe worse, to come to terms with, and God alone knew what this high-strung and intelligent girl was putting up with in beyond the half-lit hall. The sooner he had her home the better.

Once again the door closed in his face, lest, he thought wryly, he spy out the scenes of luxury behind it. The last red flails of light were gone, and under the cold black sky the small streets stirred with the fresh surge of life that struck the city once the dark had fallen. Gas jets roared and spluttered into life above the shops that would be open half the night, and a jig blared already behind the frosted windows of a green-painted saloon he had passed back on the corner. Along the gutters trudged the street vendors with their carts, fruit and vegetables, fish and ice and secondhand clothes, naphtha flaring over their tired heads. A big coal dray passed him and blocked out the lamps. The narrow street was urgent with the stir of life, and he thought the faces mostly Irish, filled under the harsh light with an intentness of purpose that chilled him. He had seen it before today, in the face of the young oilman, thanking God and all the saints that he had winter work. The intentness of survival.

Antonia came then, running down the broken steps, and he smiled to see the same green tam-o'-shanter she had worn in Owenscourt.

"Everyone will know you're Irish."

"So's everybody else round here."

He had been nervous as to how she would receive him, sick with a deep fear that so lovely a girl would have someone else by now in a city acrawl with lonely men. But she appeared to have recovered from her first shock, and it was she who slipped an arm into his, turning him along the littered sidewalk.

"Ah, Owen, it does my heart good to see you. Tell me everything now, about everybody."

The air was turning bitter, frost gathering with the dusk, and Owen realized suddenly he was both cold and tired. Too much had happened in the day, and he realized he was in little mood to face back, even if he could find it, to what the Belfast woman might call dinner. And yet the noises of the street in the frosty air were no sharper than his own exhilaration. Never in all the dreams that had consumed him in the long dull hours aboard the steamer, had he envisaged he would find Antonia so soon. The city had proved bigger, noisier, dirtier, and more confusing than anyone had been able to make him understand, and yet here he was in little more than hours since he had landed, with her arm through his, and no sign of rejection in her grave and gentle face.

The rest seemed almost simple, his mind racing ahead to their marriage and but three short years of making money before their triumphal return to Owenscourt.

"Did you have your meal yet?" he asked her.

Again the grimace of distaste.

"No."

"Well, d'you know somewhere we could go? And eat and

talk. A chop or something?" As he said it, he realized his mouth was watering for a piece of fresh meat after the weeks of salt beef on the crossing.

"Have you money?" she asked him and he wondered would it ever be taken for granted again that he had. He grinned at her and squeezed her hand.

"For a while," he said. "Is there somewhere?"

"Well, it's not Delmonico's," she said, but leaned a little closer and steered him along the street and round a couple of corners, on both of which saloons spilled light and music in their path. Shrieking children played tag in and out of the shadows and between the horses' hooves, and below one of the few lampposts, his hat in his hand, a blind young beggar with a sweet nostalgic tenor tore his own heart out with the "Londonderry Air."

"Oh, God," said Owen and felt in his pockets, that held no more than the clean unbroken dollar bills he had got in exchange for some of his gold. Antonia pulled him on.

"He's only one of thousands, Owen," she said. "Keep your money for yourself. You never know. You could be like him tomorrow."

He looked at her incredulously and laughed, but she didn't return the smile. Her toughness shook him, she who had never been further in her life than Galway City for the day. Then he remembered the hollow cheeks of the young oilman. And he had work. For God's sake, he thought, he wasn't some peasant from the sod. He had education, and still some good clothes. He would have no trouble finding work. It would be different for him. Yet the clear sad falling notes followed him on the frosty air like some chill warning; dimming his total confidence.

He shook himself. Nothing could go wrong now that he had found Antonia.

She took him to an Irish chophouse, clean white cloths below the hissing mantles that even had the shamrock on their globes. The wallpaper was dark-green and gold, and huge paper shamrocks fanned out across the wall above a roaring fire. *Erin go Bragh* ran the legend in huge green letters, on a white banner put up above the bar. Owen felt sure there were times it was paraded in the streets.

"Have we come to the right place?" he asked her teasingly as they sat down on the bentwood chairs, but Antonia was having no jokes about New York.

"It's best each keeps to his own here," she said, and he caught in all her comments and many of her expressions an edge of suffering. Well, please God, it was all over now.

They gave their order to a grinning waiter who gave them a few steps of a jig, as if he thought it was expected of him, or that he might not get his wages if he didn't do it.

They settled quietly in their corner.

"Now," Antonia said. "Everything."

She had so disciplined herself to forget that she felt weak and sick to look at him actually across the table from her, the gaslight taking red lights from his hair; the wide strong shoulders and the quick smiling mouth and lively eyes. These she had known before, but not the look of almost fierce determined strength that lay behind the ready smile. He looked grown up and steady, and his eyes were wise, sadly wise beyond his years, still darkened by the shabby outrage of his uncle's treachery.

"Bad cess to the pair of them," was all she said about her mother.

He talked eagerly now of all his hopes and plans, even though the hoarseness of exhaustion was growing in his voice. He felt he had lived a lifetime of experience since the dark hour that morning when Father Tom had dragged him from his bunk to greet America with the dawn. But the only reality now was Antonia, opposite him, going steadily with the same appetite through the heap of mutton chops and swedes, and big floury potatoes such as he hadn't seen since Owenscourt; slapped down steaming on thick white plates by the jigging waiter.

Nor did she object to anything he said, looking at him intently over her plate, the dark-blue eyes watchful but refusing nothing; touched now and then with a glowing tender warmth.

They took a long uncounted time, eating and talking, and after the meat they had big steaming cups of tea, thick with sugar. Suddenly, abruptly, in the middle of a sentence, Antonia said, "Let's go out and walk."

Even as she spoke she was gathering up her gloves and purse and making for the door.

Startled, he paid the bill, childishly pleased by his first transaction in dollars, and followed her out into the cold night.

They walked still in the patchily lit streets, alive now with more people than he had ever seen. It was dangerous, she told him, to walk the dark ones. After a little while in silence Owen began again where they had left off, speaking of the time when they would be back together at Owenscourt finding it all, for some strange reason, more close and real to him on the streets of the foreign city, than it had been in the long, deprived months when its shuttered bulk had been every day before his eyes.

"Owen."

She had stopped without warning and in the hustling crowds she turned to him as if they were alone. One hand remained in his, the other she placed slowly on his chest, part benediction, part symbol of rejection.

He refused to see the rejection, ignoring something in her look that frightened him; chilling him more than the cold of the November night. He took the gloved fingertips and kissed them.

"What is it? Am I hurrying you? Bedam, I'm in a hell of a hurry myself, when you think I was only off the boat this morning."

A gas mantle flared and died above them, giving a small sudden patch of gloom.

"Owen. I'm not coming with you."

He was back in the Canon's parlor on the streaming night in Tuam. Emmett's voice. Dear God, he thought sickly. Did no one want him?

He could hardly frame words.

"What do you mean, you're not coming with me? What else d'you think I've come so far for?"

"Money for Owenscourt," she said. "God help you."

"True for you." He did not see the pity. "But, Antonia, alannah, what is all the money in the world without you? Or Owenscourt without you? There's nothing else for me. No other meaning."

He was stuttering now, his bright bubble of exhilaration shattered to another lonely gaping void, clasping her two hands in his. For minutes it went to no and yes and back again before he thought to ask her why.

"Why, why, why? Oh, my dearest love, oh, why?"

Her face was showing the heartbreak of her refusal, white in the dim light, the great eyes pools of sorrow, full of tears.

"Why? Oh, dear God, Owen, you know why. Did you have to come all the way here to New York to remind me of it? Isn't it enough to be what I am without you—without you—"

The tears choked her and he stared stupidly and then turned away his head. Jesus Christ. Not once in the entire time since he had set out to find her had he given thought to the scene that had driven her from the agent's house. Certain in his thickheaded conceit that it would be enough to find her and she would fall at his feet. God forgive him for an unthinking selfish boor.

He said the only things he could think to say, and it was what he thought.

"Antonia." He pulled frantically at the fingers over her face, aware of a small gathering knot of curious passersby. "Antonia. It doesn't matter! It just doesn't *matter*!"

It was the wrong thing.

"Matter? Why should it matter to you? The O'Connor child—no matter what has happened since, no one can take that from you. You are your father's son." Her eyes in the pale face were black with passion and old resentments. The same unreasonable jealousy; fed now by her lost love for her father and hate for the woman who had smashed her world. "What do you know," she was going on, her voice hoarse.

"What do you know about being a bastard? Sure, I know I'd be a bastard anyway, but I was proud to be John Julius Cannon's even if I was born in a stable."

That took him aback. How long had that mattered? Everyone knew she had been born above the stables since the only cottage was still tainted with the typhoid. What matter that either?

"So was Our Lord," he said, trying to lighten the dreadful tension in her face, but she never even heard him.

"Were I John Julius's, I'd still be his child. I've *been* his child. As it is I'm no more than a bye blow that belongs to no one. Some drunken night behind a haystack or milord's bed if she were lucky. What is there there for Owen O'Connor of Owenscourt?"

He tried to take her hands; to tell her that all he wanted was to make it up to her; that nothing was healed by insisting on fresh sorrow, flaying herself with her in-turned griefs. Alone. Three thousand miles from anyone who loved her. His heart bled for her and he could have wept himself with weariness and disappointment and pity.

"Antonia. My love!"

But she snatched her hands away and wheeled from him.

"Leave me alone!" she cried at him, eyes wild and dark. "Leave me alone, Owen O'Connor. Don't you realize that's all anyone can do for me. Leave me alone!"

She whirled and was gone, running, tacking through the people on the sidewalk, and he knew better than to try and follow her. It was the shock of seeing him. He had been clumsy and impetuous, and gone at the whole thing like a bull at a gate. John Julius would curse him for a fool.

But she would surely come round; cool down. He was sure, no matter what she said, that she loved him. She would come round.

"I'll come tomorrow," he shouted after her.

Beside him in the darkness a thin youth in somebody else's hand-me-down suit eased a toothpick from his mouth and gazed after the vanishing shadow that was Antonia.

"B'Jasus," he said, and the soft slur of Connemara held his

voice. "B'Jasus, but I'd say you were better off without that one. Willya reely go back in the morning?"

He didn't go back in the morning for she had told him she had a job in the cash desk of a draper's shop, and didn't get back in the evening until seven.

He went instead the same time as on the previous evening through the last trails of the frosty sunset, and had to wait outside the house because in his anxiousness he was over an hour too early.

In the end, when she should have long come, he hammered on the peeling door. When the little slattern came, she took some mean pleasure in being able to tell him that Miss Cannon had taken her bags that afternoon and left.

Chapter 17

By Christmas, in the most bitter winter New York had known for over twenty years, he had newspapers wadded underneath his shirt like any hobo, and newspapers lined between the meager blankets of his bed in a desperate attempt to keep out the cold; worse than anything ever imagined; persistent and penetrating and remorseless as a sickness.

Nor had he work. Now he fully understood the look of relief and gratitude on the faces of those like Seamus the young oilman, who had been fortunate enough to find winter work. In the biting cold the jobless thronged the streets like a gray shuffling tide, turned from their lodgings during the day and with nowhere else to go; glad even of the next snowfall for the couple of dollars they would earn shoveling the snow along the proud sidewalks of Fifth Avenue and Park Avenue; clearing the roads of ice to make safety for the spirited horses of the rich; warm under their blankets that would comfort a whole immigrant family.

In eight inches of unswept snow, the wind like a knife along the straight streets from the east, he ran into Seamus, plodding along beside his rough old horse, both of them swathed to the ears in ragged blankets.

" 'Tis all very well," Seamus said to his grin, "did we not have to take them off at night and sleep under them, and, before God, by then they're even colder than ourselves. Let me tell you. I took the horse yesterday to be shod down there at Phineas Gratten's, and believe it or not, it was so cold, he had to break the ice on the trough beside the fire each time he wanted to harden the shoe. That's God's truth. And it frozen again before he could reach it with the next one. Have you work, Owen?"

Owen almost asked him would he be tramping the streets all colors with the cold if he had, but he could not speak so to the thin concerned face, the skin on it flaked with the wind. They had been good to him, Seamus and Annie, and given him what Christmas they had had themselves.

"I have not, Seamus. It doesn't seem there'd be work for God himself. And those that have work have no wages, I'm told."

"God help them all, 'tis always the same in the winter. Owen, why wouldn't you go down to the City Hall and get a shovel for the snow. 'Tis always a bit of money?"

Owen realized that Seamus thought him a weakling, and even too superior that he didn't do it. He didn't want to explain to him that while he had guineas still warm and gold around his waist, he wouldn't take such work from the ones who had nothing.

He had started high, unconcerned and optimistic in his search for work; going first to the offices and banks and the countinghouses; and the countinghouses of the grand shops, and the publishers and newspapers; learning with varying degrees of unkindness and profanity that while there were decent Americans needing work, no immigrant Mick need apply for such positions.

He would come out snarling from these encounters and rebuffs, and try and comfort himself by walking up the swept and spotless sidewalks of Fifth Avenue and Park Avenue and the smart exclusive streets between them; reminding himself that none of the fine houses set back behind their wrought-iron gates were one whit bigger or more splendid than his own at Owenscourt. Watching the endless flurry of fine turn-outs from single curricles to racing coach-and-fours; assessing them with a critical and knowing eye; lost in admiration for the horses in their traces, but able to tell himself with satisfaction that much of the coachwork would never have been allowed out of his father's Shops.

He realized humbly that he was fortunate. In spite of having had, more than once, to thump off fumbling hands about his waist in the middle of the pitch-dark stinking nights in his lodging, he still had money. And, with care, for a long time yet. He was grateful for some prudent instinct that had stopped him from going out to search for better lodgings. The food was edible, and the bedrooms no better nor no worse than any others for the same money. Every day he was able to add to his crude feeding with a hot meal against the cold, in some pie shop or chophouse or saloon; keeping always, as Antonia had warned him, among the Irish. Two black eyes and a cut lip in a Polack eating house had taught him she was right.

But he had lost Antonia.

Every single place he went he asked about her, for all the Irish hung together and there seemed to be always someone who knew someone who knew anyone you might want to find. But blank eyes and shaken heads met every query.

"Even though," said one landlady to him at the door of a woman's lodging, "you'd think that with a strange name like that someone would surely remember her. Was she foreign or something?"

No, thought Owen bleakly, as he turned away into the piled-up frozen, dirty snow. No. She was as Irish as myself and maybe we should both have stayed there.

In his pocket he carried Emmett's letters, calm and staid and content, implicit with all the security of life in the smooth green country of Kildare. Also John Julius's. His life was full of struggle like his own, but the letters in his strong easy hand were full of enthusiasm for the reshaping of Cannon's Mills. His own dream. The mill, he hoped, would be ready for the next harvest, with the help of God.

Harvest, Owen thought. The golden sweeping fields with the harsh cry of the corncrakes in the sun, and the high-piled carts lumbering into the stackyard with their load. The old thresher roaring and belching and spewing out grain, and old Boru going mad about the rats. That last harvest home with Mama, and all the people looking at him as though he was his father come again.

The heir to Owenscourt.

He kicked at the hard-packed snow, and looked at the blue-black skies above the city, lowering with the threat of more to come, and tried to thrust aside the memory of the last letter from John Julius. Clearly he had been held only by the distance, and by pity for his loneliness, from cursing him for the eejit that he was. To have found Antonia and handled it so clumsily that he had lost her. Nothing her father said could be worse than his own fury with himself, and disappointment and dejection pursued him all through the long dreadful winter.

Through the most impossible weather when the blizzards drove along the straight streets, soaking his thin clothes, he passed a lot of time in the library, where they were powerless to eject him despite his shabbiness. Unlike most of his half-starved and frozen countrymen, he was able to read.

With the bitter turning of the year he was still workless, trudging the snowbound streets under the icy skies, brooding on Owenscourt; seeing the brown fallow fields starred with the white of drifted seagulls. Antonia coming bright eyed from picking the first small flowers of spring along the avenue, and Christmas only past. Her smile sweet with pleasure above the small bunch in her hands.

He waded through the running slush when the snows began to melt, wet to his knees, and thought of the green sheen of winter wheat across the Irish land. And began slowly to know the immigrant's terror. Would he have to spend his return fare in order simply to live; cutting himself off forever from the land where he belonged? The end of the endless promise to go home. With pockets full. The final agonizing parting that came with the last hoarded dollar.

In April the birds sang even in the stunted trees of the neighborhood, and day and night his mind was full of the sound of the rooks cawing and fighting and building in the windbreak elms.

In blind sad recollection of security and love, he would go back even further to the beautiful house on Gardiner Street, filled with light and laughter and beauty. To the picture at the bottom of the stairs and all it stood for; locked with all its fading promise of the future in the tin box stapled to the floor at the foot of his bed in his lodgings; where the walls sweated in the growing heat, and the cockroaches fled like a defeated army before the candlelight.

In late April, the snow gone, the streets of Upper Manhattan swept like a ballroom, and the city clamoring into new life after its long hibernation, he found himself work. As a runner in the kitchens of the Fifth Avenue Hotel, for twenty dollars a month and all the food that he could eat. He counted himself rich, and paid the Belfast woman only for his bed, and hope began to flicker again around the edges of his mind.

The work was all hours of the day and night, but he was willing, glad to be out of the packed lodging where, he told Emmett and John Julius, he had gradually counted fifteen Greeks, ten Austrians, ten French, six Turks, and various Dutch and Spanish and Italians. All proving that what Antonia had said was true. "There isn't a night," he wrote, "that most of them don't come home drunk on cheap liquor and the fighting is not to be believed. Hardly a week passes that old Mother McClintock doesn't have to call the police and have a few of them hauled off to cool their heels in jail."

Spring drove on into the high heat of summer. Sweat rolled down him in streams in the hot clamorous kitchen, and when he came home to his lodgings late at night, all the smells of the small streets were trapped, unable to escape, beneath the windless, humid sky. The good feeding in the hotel, be it whenever they could find time to eat, was filling out his big frame, and the dark brooding of the winter was receding. He knew himself handsome now, and enjoyed unashamedly the bright inviting eyes of the girls when he sang and danced with the best of them in the ceilidhs at the corner saloons; courteously evading the eager approaches of their mothers, desperate to see their daughters wed and settled in the alien land. He was in the upper hierarchy now. The desirable and enviable. He had work. And slowly, painfully, he was saving money.

Yet, when the last drunk had snored and mumbled himself off into sleep in the lodging at night, he would lie in his lumpy bed and stare disconsolately into the darkness, the chicken wire like a prison against the night sky; listening to the heavy breathing and the restless groans, and often the muttered, anguished prayer that couldn't be suppressed.

It was not enough. Were it not for the gold still buckled at his waist he was working for little more than survival. There was nothing here to help go back with the money to reclaim Owenscourt. Winter in New York was as barren for the immigrant as the bare flanks of the Joycelands hills.

And he had lost Antonia. Were it not for her, he would go West. San Francisco, they all said. That was the place for money. And who knew, he thought defeatedly, while he struggled and searched here, she might be there before him.

There was money in New York, God knew. It only needed a walk uptown, or the glimpses he got of the upper regions of the hotel to tell him this. The names of money floated through the kitchens, Rockefeller, Carnegie, Frick, Jim Hill, Vanderbilt. These were the names that owned the fine houses set in their own grounds, and the glittering turnouts that whirled through their iron gates. As he himself had once whirled through the grand gates of Owenscourt in his parents' carriages.

In poverty and gnawing loneliness he fretted on into the full heat of summer, the high days of July, when at home the dog roses would be festooned like garlands on the hedges. Here the sky hung brazen over the sweating city, and the heat, like the cold had been, was more than he had ever known. The rich were gone, out to their estates at Newport and along the Hudson River, the big houses shuttered and the gates closed on the graveled drives.

After it had all happened, he was staggered by his own ignorance and lack of thought. He had been so many months in this city, knowing that even the Irish from his own part of the West were divided into factions; and the same feuds broke and simmered in the hot streets as had in the starving villages at home. Yet always he had been brought up to think of himself as simply Irish; Catholic by long tradition of his family. Never once had he heard his parents say one word of disapproval of anybody who was not. Many of their Dublin friends had been Protestant, going into the Church of Ireland in Kildare Street, as they had gone to the Jesuits across the road. Never a matter of importance. As for down in the West, they had more minds there for filling their poor stomachs, and asking themselves were they O'Flaherties or O'Malleys, than in asking a man what foot he dug with.

Prejudice and fanaticism had never come within his range of thought except in the flaring faction fights between the families, and the men battling in them were the best of friends when it was over. When he awoke one July morning to the monotonous and somehow threatening throb of drums, he asked what it was. Then gave little heed to the answer. Parades were parades, be it St. Patrick or the Knights of Columbus, St. Hubert or St. Nicholas or the Orange Lodge. A welcome chance to break the dull sweat of work that never earned enough. An exciting day for all the family, out with their own kin and kind, and for the man of the house the right to get riotous drunk when it was all over; fistfights and maulings through the streets, and hands shaken and songs sung at the end of it over a bottle of American beer.

He frowned slightly, listening. The drums for this one seemed to hold no sense of celebration. Only the dull monotony, little short of menace.

Parade or no parade, he had to get to work. Lateness even once would be the end of his employment, and he left the house soon after seven o'clock. The day was already suffocatingly hot, and under the brassy sky the unbroken thunder of the drums grew nearer. They were obviously cutting through the small roads to the main avenue to form up some procession for the march through town. The street was empty and the shutters still up on all the shops, which puzzled him slightly, used as he was to the passing word with the early ones out cleaning windows and holystoning down the doorsteps.

When the procession came round the corner behind him, it filled the entire street, the straggling body of its supporters pouring along the sidewalks in the deafening noise. Owen turned to look. Packed across the whole width of the street were the drummers in their hard hats and orange sashes, bent backwards under the weight of their gigantic drums. Their fists were already lacerated, running with blood back down their wrists from the fury of their beating, and blood spattered the drums. He saw the banner of King William swaying against the hot sky, in his long wig, his white horse rearing underneath him. Behind him the vengeful message in letters a foot high. Remember Aughrim. Astonished, as they surged and pressed round him, he was aware of a fanaticism he had never known. This was no cheerful day off work, with the women and the children running and singing along the edges of the band. There were only men, hard eyes dark and possessed with the wordless message hammering from the drums; echoing from the shutters and closed doors.

They were on him and all around him, swarming in their own dustcloud, before he could do more than acknowledge a sudden flooding sense of danger. A few paces away he caught the intent eye of his coming assailant, realizing he was not one of them. A thin man, his cap too small for him over his bony skull, advancing with a fixed, aggressive glare, his wiry body poised like a spring for the pleasure of violence in the name of God. The first blood of the day, and Owen knew there was no way of avoiding that it should be his.

He shouldered roughly up to him, others milling round him.

"And what fut," he demanded, the North hard in his

vowels—he was almost dancing—"and what fut de *yew* dig with?"

Owen sighed. There was going to be a fight anyway, and he outnumbered by about three hundred to one. The senseless hostility angered him.

"The left," he said, "and be damned to you." And hit him first. "And to your King William, whoever the hell he was," he added as the man fell.

It didn't last. Nor did Owen have any idea for how long he had been lying there, before darkness began to stir and break away before his eyes. There was something big and pink against the painful sky above him, and a taste of dust in his mouth.

"He's coming round."

It had a voice, the pink thing, and slowly resolved itself into a round red-veined face with bright dark button eyes; a fringe of sandy hair above them. All attached to a fat man in his shirt-sleeves with his suspenders dangling at his waist, and a small crowd gathered behind him.

"Are you all right now?"

Owen sat up slowly and didn't know which piece of him hurt most, gazing vaguely at the blood on his shirt. He ran his tongue around his teeth and gratefully found them all still there. Someone gave him his cap.

"Are you all right?" asked the round face again. His voice had a certain ring of authority.

"I am. Give me a hand up."

Slowly he got to his feet and the hot street spun and tilted to the sky.

"Ouch," he said wryly.

"And in the name of God," cried the fat man, and had been clearly waiting to say it ever since he had rushed out to him. "In the name of God, what part of the world do you come from not to have the sense to stay off the street with that gillevrang coming through a Catholic district. Aren't they best left alone to get on with it."

"Galway," said Owen numbly. "I didn't know."

"God help us," the man cried to the little crowd, stunned

by such ignorance. "My father was from Lettermullet. Come on into the house and let the woman give you a drop of tea to steady you."

It seemed he was a policeman, thankfully off duty for the day, grown up in the city where his father had come with him and his little sister in his arms, their mother dead on the coffin ship behind them. With the soothing influence of the tea, Owen's battered brain began to work again, and as soon as he realized he was a policeman he told the man about Antonia.

"Did you ever see a girl like that?" he asked him, leaning back gratefully in the plush armchair. The bleeding Sacred Heart above the mantelpiece still swam red if he should try to move his eyes. One of his shoulders seemed to have come apart, and he was sniffing blood.

"Did you ever see a girl like that?"

The policeman eyed him, the small black eyes full of pity.

"In a city crammed with Irish," he said, "doesn't every second girl look like that. But it's a strange name."

Hazily Owen remembered the old woman in Galway saying the same thing, and wanted to tell him how different Antonia was to all of them, but the wife came in quickly from the kitchen, wiping her hands on her apron.

"Did you say Antonia?" she said. "There's not many would be called that. Antonia?"

"Yes," said Owen and it was nothing to do with his beating that his breath was difficult. He set down his tea in case he spilt it.

"There's Mary Brennan, you'll know her, James, and a good decent woman doesn't deserve the things they say about her, she'd give you the coat off her back, and she has an eating house on Franklin Street. Old Mother Brennan they call her, and she a decent widow woman no older than themselves, the eejits."

"Get on with it," cried Owen silently. "Get on with it."

"Didn't she have a waitress of that name, James? And didn't it annoy her, although she was fond of the girl. Too grand altogether for a waitress. Isn't that so, James?"

"I do believe it is," said James, as though he had never heard it before, nodding his round head, the thin sandy hair smeared across the scalp.

Owen was already up, trying to steady the tilting world. His job was gone. There was nothing to keep him.

"Franklin Street?"

"Do you know it? Have you enough tea? Are you all right?"

"I do. The other side of Broadway there. I'll get along there now and thanks for all you did for me."

"Well for the love of God, if you hear the drums get inside somewhere. At the end of the day's drinking there'll be battery on all sides and neither side better than the other."

He opened the door for Owen, his uniform cap and jacket swinging on a nail on the back of it like a talisman.

It was only when he was halfway to Franklin Street, the drums throbbing safely in the distance, that his head began to steady and his body collect itself, listing its injuries. He frowned, trying to decide about some unnatural lightness about his waist, then with slow sick understanding felt beneath his tattered shirt. His money belt was gone.

Quickly, stiff with a cold, numb acceptance, he searched an inside pocket of his jacket, unbelievably made by a Dublin tailor who thought that even young gentlemen might have things they preferred to keep in what he called a confidential pocket.

He stood, immobile in the airless street, oblivious of the curious who stared at him; shaken by his beating, ashen with shock and undeniably close to tears.

Three twenty-dollar bills and no employment. And Owenscourt three thousand miles away across a sea he could not pay to cross.

Blindly he made, like a damaged animal, for Franklin Street.

Like all Catholic eating houses on the Twelfth of July, Brennan's was closed, the wooden shutters up. He went round until he found a side door and hammered on it, nor did he stop until a window was flung up farther along the wall and a cross face under a tangle of rag curlers thrust itself out to look at him.

"Are you daft?" the woman cried. "Can't you see we're closed. Closed!"

She made to pull down the window and Owen put a hand through it.

"I can see you're closed," he said. He squinted, still finding it hard to focus, vaguely aware that the friend of the policeman's wife was a young woman, and comely underneath the curlers and the temper. "Mrs. Brennan?"

"What if I am?" She looked as if she would slam the window on his hand.

"Mrs. Brennan, I'm looking for a girl."

She cackled suddenly.

"Aren't the lot of you," she said. "But not here."

He was too shocked and battered for her pleasantries, too anxious to get her answer. "No. Antonia. Antonia Cannon. She was here, they said."

"Antonia, is it." He realized the plump face had softened. The woman had said she was fond of her.

"What d'you want with her?"

"I'm a friend from home. I've known her since we were children."

There was a long silence while she decided to believe him.

"Well, she's not here now," she said, and it was the last intolerable blow.

"Do you know where she is, then?" he managed to ask her, and did not know what he would do if she said no.

"I do indeed—weren't we great friends." She had decided now to trust him, and warmed to the romance of the handsome young man coming looking for the girl, although it was God's truth he looked as if he had been in some sort of barney, and got by far the worst of it. A fine young fellow for all that.

"She got the offer of a grand job down in the country," she said, "and took it, and wasn't it wise of her, and she with as little flesh as wouldn't stave off a gripe."

Thin, his poor love. Always too thin. And what could he offer now but more poverty? Would she want him, with her grand job?

"How long ago?"

"Ah, three months or more."

"Do you know where?"

"Tanglewood, New Jersey. People called Turnbull."

He thanked her, and when she had gone, slid down the wall and sat a long time on the sidewalk in the sun, trying to come to terms with his sore, bruised body and his change of circumstance.

The winter had been hard on clothes and he had few left, and those outgrown. It had never occurred to him that he would grow. He owned as little now as he could tie into a bundle in a shirt since he dare spend no money on a new valise.

"Going somewhere?" asked his neighbor in the next bed as he gathered his things together in the following dawn.

"The country," Owen answered, and even the word was a relief after the sweating stinking city and the broken-down house with its streaming walls and fleeing cockroaches; the grieving drunks and beggars so plentiful that now he no longer even heard them, when they sang their breaking hearts out in the swarming streets. The last crushing injury of being robbed. If he had to be poor, better be poor on the land where he could breathe God's air. He was a country man and a farmer, and surely could find work where he belonged. And if God was good, he'd have Antonia.

"Argg-g-h."

The man spat on the floor with an expression of disgust and disapproval.

" 'Tis no different."

Owen was sure it would be different, only half hearing the man mumbling of his failures in both city and fields, confronted by the problem of the Chinese picture in its long roll. Too long to be accommodated in a folded shirt.

"What is it," cackled the man, leaning up on a grimy elbow. "What is it? The title deeds to your estate?"

"More or less," Owen answered, and with every crease a physical pain, he folded it slowly back and forth, across the gray painted stones of Dublin Castle.

When he left to walk to Barclay Street for the New Jersey ferry to Hoboken, the landlady refused to return him any of his money, even though he was only a week into the month.

"What happened to your job?" she asked him, eyeing his rumpled and dirty clothes. In the same go-down now as all the rest of them, and it hadn't taken long.

He didn't bother to answer her and as if she grudged it, she handed him a letter with an Irish stamp. It was from Canon Walsh in Tuam, telling him, among the other gossip of his poverty-stricken parish, that the life of luxury and grandeur continued unabashed in Holly House, and that his uncle, the poor fool, was the object of pity and derision over all the country, and the woman there flaunting herself still like a duchess.

He picked up the bundle by the knotted sleeves of his shirt and set out to walk across Lower Manhattan to the ferry.

And from dreams and ambitions that had been blasted out of him, to the town of Tanglewood in New Jersey. The heir to Owenscourt could do no more now than take one day as it came and do what he could with it, like any other workless Paddy three thousand miles from home.

Chapter 18

ONCE again he stood before fine wrought-iron gates; but unlike the ones on Fifth Avenue and Park, these stood open to the curving drive of sycamores, heavy with the dark leaves of the advancing summer. In the distance between the trees he could see the brilliance of many flowers, and, one word on each pillar, was the name of the house, engraved on gleaming brass. Glendon House.

He stood and stared, and all he could think of was that it should hold Antonia.

He was more cautious now, shorn by disappointment of the happy certainty that he would find her. Touched with the first creeping doubts that he would manage to keep her if he did. There was nothing he could do about his clothes, not improved by a night in a roadside barn, but inside the gates he found a bush and hid his bundle underneath it, and tried to pull the holes in his socks down below the level of his boots. It would be difficult enough without her thinking him a hobo.

His broken boots crunched up the swept gravel and amazingly no one came at the noise to turn him back, until in the end he stood on a wide space before the house, banked on all sides with flowers and with a clump of birches in the middle. Beyond stood the house.

Not as big as Owenscourt, he thought with satisfaction, and it was comfort for the dirty outgrown suit and the shoddy boots that had come apart in the long walk from New York. By damn not as big as Owenscourt, but a handsome house nonetheless. With sheep-dotted parkland spreading away beyond it for satisfactory acres and ornamental gardens falling at the side down to a small lake. When he got back to Owenscourt, he thought, he'd add a garden. It did a lot for the gentling of a house.

This one was mellow light-gray stone, full of nooks and gables, mullioned doors, and windows heavily framed in handsome-looking timber. At one end was a sort of tower with windows all round it and a pointed roof, like pictures he had seen of castles over in Scotland. The timber looked well cared for and the stone clean, all the big windows glittering in the sun. A strong sound house, with all the evidence of care and money.

With a wry shock he realized he had been standing looking at it, and the land round it, with the instinctive assessment of all he had been reared to. It was the heir of Owenscourt who stood at the edges of the trees among the flowers, examining with critical respect a house much like his own. With a surge of anger he remembered that to anybody looking out, he was no more than a vagrant with four inches of wrist and ankle protruding from his shabby clothes. A guard with a shotgun would be all he'd get.

Antonia too, he thought bitterly, would be at the back of the house where all the servants belonged, her very position in danger probably for attracting such a follower. Resisting the temptation to march up and heave at the glittering brass pull of the front doorbell, he made off discreetly round the side of the house, where he could see the road run on down to a vast stable block a quarter of a mile away. The size of the stables staggered him. Or maybe garages as well, he thought, for a man this rich might well have one of these newfangled motors.

He felt vulnerable and exposed now, impressed by the long sweep of beautifully kept parkland on this side of the house; feeling it urgent to get first to some door and state his purpose before someone got to him and threw him out before he had a chance to open his mouth.

He found the yard door and then what seemed to be the back door, almost as grand as the one at the front. The house stretched vast on all sides of him from the doorstep, drenched with the heat and silence of the heavy afternoon. No bigger than my own, he told himself fiercely to restore his self-respect. No bigger than my own. So that when the door opened suddenly on a tall negro of incredible stillness and presence, it was again Owen O'Connor gentleman, who glared at him in a brief moment of authority. A small spark of interest kindled in the black eyes.

"Sir," he said smoothly, never betraying to the scarecrow outside that to answer the back door to anyone was beneath his dignity. But he had happened to be passing when the bell was pulled. It was the veiled and questioning respect that brought the young man down to realizing how he looked, and a shadow of pity touched the butler's eyes. He stood waiting for the young man to speak, expecting no more than the usual request for food or work.

"Antonia," said Owen confusedly, too suddenly thrown back into his poverty by the steady waiting gaze. It would have been easier to have been put out at once. Given him something to fight about. He took a deep breath.

"You have a girl working here, I understand. Antonia Cannon. Is she still here?"

He had, he realized miserably as he spoke, nothing to offer her but the impulse that had brought him here as fast as his sore feet would carry him. If she was still here, what in God's name would he do? Take her from her secure job to sleep in a barn with him and watch him shaving in a pond? A sense of total failure encompassed him, and he was suddenly overwhelmingly tired.

"You are Irish?" said the butler. Curious. The girl too had been something out of the ordinary. No common servant.

"I am," said Owen, and in his hopelessness almost asked him what the hell it was to do with him. "Is she here?"

The negro butler was so impeccably experienced and trained, from his shining dark pate down to the toes of his highly polished patent leather boots, that he would not flaw his own performance, even to what seemed like a beggar at the door.

"I am very sorry," he said courteously, "but she has left."

He saw the light go out of the young man on the step.

"How long?" The heir to Owenscourt was gone, leaving a tired young man who had walked here from New York, every penny he owned in his pockets; his clothes ragged. Swept in that instant by a desolation bleak as the snow-laden winds down the straight streets of the city. He tried for very pride to keep his shattered disappointment from his face. Somewhere inside the house a woman began to sing.

"Only days," the butler said. "Only days. There was no reason for her to go. She gave complete satisfaction."

A strange unapproachable girl, nevertheless, he thought, and her sudden disappearance unsurprising. She had made no friends among the other staff and seemed often withdrawn to the point of melancholy.

"She just came and told me," he added. "That she wished to go."

"To avoid me," thought Owen bitterly. Three months here and three months there and how could he ever trace her? It was only the ill luck of having his ribs kicked and his money stolen that had brought him this far.

"You'll not know where she's gone?"

"Mr. Jolliff," cried a voice from somewhere in behind him, but the butler ignored it. He had a mannerism of complete stillness that gave importance to his smallest gesture.

Gravely he shook his high-domed, balded head.

"She told no one."

They stood a long moment and looked at one another, carefully restrained compassion on the dark face and on Owen's a blank and mute despair. He made an effort to gather himself together.

"Well, thank you all the same."

He realized the man had been very civil. Most would have run him out of such a place after one glance.

"Good day to you," he said and turned quickly away from the too observant eyes, catching the loose sole of his boot and almost falling down the steps. He was halfway across the paved and spotless yard with lines of laundry hanging limp in the airless sun, when the man spoke behind him.

"Son," he said. "Do you want work?"

Owen turned and stood, facing back to a sympathetic understanding of his state and at the same time a boundless and severe authority; inherent with critical standards that would demand as much back as he had given. And with it all a fine sense of his own position.

"Yes, sir," he said, and knew the "sir" was expected. "I need work."

The thin black face was now an aloof and distant mask. In one second the relationship had changed.

"Follow me," he said. In a remarkable pantry lined with drawers and cupboards of gleaming mahogany, paneled with beveled glass, he took a brassbound telephone off a hook.

It was a yard boy that was needed, down at the stables, and when Owen realized, he almost turned away to take his chance back in the city with his less than sixty dollars; shamingly filled with the recollection of the shaven-headed youth with a ringle eye, who had been the yard boy in Owenscourt. A village lad, not bright enough for anything else.

He felt the man watching him and forced his shame down as if it were a sickness. There would be a bed, and probably a decent one in a place like this. Food. And above all time to think.

"Yes, sir," he said.

Owenscourt was more unattainable than on the very first day Hugh Charles had closed it and ordered them to Holly House.

"My name is Jolliff. Mister Jolliff."

"Yes, Mister Jolliff."

He went back down the shady drive, past the bees ravening in the colored flowers, and retrieved his bundle from underneath the bush. Then, following instructions, he walked for the first time down between white fences on the carriage road sweeping in a splendid curve through the green parkland from the house down to the stables. The L-shaped block was almost as large as the house itself, of the same stone, and with the same well-cared-for solid and costly finish. Around at the back of it, safely away from the horses, several garages had been built. Over to one side were more buildings which he later learned were the bowling alley, the swimming pool, and three lawn tennis courts. Shame was still gnawing at him as he came to the huge double gates in the stableyard wall, and he turned and looked back at the gray solid house beyond its green lawns. His mouth tightened. Didn't he own one bigger? And if the only thing he could see at the moment towards getting it back was to be a yard boy, then a yard boy he'd be, and let the devil himself try and look down on him.

Quickly he came to realize that the job meant doing any outside work that no one else wanted to do, and he also rapidly acknowledged that the whole thing was going to be an education to him. It was an estate of a size and complexity that would have dwarfed Owenscourt even in his father's heyday.

Although the work was menial he found himself gradually more content than he had been since he first lost Antonia, realizing it was because he was back close to the land. The nightmare of the smells and dirt; the cockroaches and the fighting drunks; the ever-present griping poverty clamoring on all sides of him. All of it began to recede like a fading nightmare in the clean air and familiar surroundings. He had recovered his vision. With the presence of the gray stone house, drowsing in its flowers across the parkland, he began to feel closer to Owenscourt than at any time since he had left it. And more determinedly reconciled to the long slow battle to get it back. The present was only a temporary defeat.

There was little to encourage him; sweeping and cleaning

and shoveling; at the beck and call of everyone. But it was a space; in which to breathe and think and collect himself.

All the outside servants lived in dormitories either above the stables or the new garages and ate in a long clean mess hall with oilcloth tables and bentwood chairs and hissing with gas lamps; with its own kitchen and rigorous protocol in the placing of the servants at the long tables. Owen at the very bottom was watchful and civil as the newcomer, but set out coolly to make it plain to some of them that yard boy he might be, but he was six foot two and growing into it, and the small turbulent streets of the city had given him a pair of fists readier than most in the answering of coarse jibes about Paddies. He earned slow respect by the strength behind his amiability and his cheerful acceptance of his position.

The chauffeur was away with the family and most of the other stable staff in New Bedford for the summer, and Owen had the staggering pleasure of the garage dormitory to himself. The chauffeur was still in a minor position in Glendon House where there was as yet only one motorcar, so advanced that no one except its owner regarded it as much more than a joke. The stables held some of the finest horseflesh in the state, and the car was a rich man's passing fad.

When Owen first came hesitantly down the curving road on Jolliff's instructions, he stood respectfully while the outside manager outlined his work to him. He regarded the man carefully from underneath his lids and tried to comprehend the twist of life that had him like this before what was no more than John Julius, who in two years should have been formally in his employ. The man, whose name was Ossie Tendon, surveyed him in return with shrewd experienced eyes and reflected that there were some rum ones in these immigrants. This one was no yard boy. He watched him keenly for any hint of what he would call side, but the young man looked back at him with quiet respect, and the scarecrow clothes and broken boots spoke their own message of the need for work at any price. Good luck to him.

There were weeks of quiet with only a skeleton staff in the stables, the estate slumbering in the hazy sun. Owen was careful not to ask questions, but gathered his information piece by piece, mostly from the two girls in the kitchen who were clearly delighted with the tall good looks of the new yard boy, and only too glad for any chance to chatter to him.

The house was owned by Mr. Phineas G. Turnbull. The *G* was for the Glendon, which was his mother's name. Something, they told him, to do with Wall Street and business and those stocks and shares, and if he wasn't a millionaire six times over then there was no one this side of China would ever be one.

"Rich," said the little Irish girl with the thick red hair packed in under her cap. She rolled her great blue eyes; beyond words.

A good man, they said, and kind, and treated all his people well. There were few ever left once they had come. Owen thought of Antonia, who had left only to get away from him.

He had offices, they told him, somewhere in the city and a suite in one of the posh hotels along Fifth Avenue for when he was entertaining in New York, for the lady wouldn't have a city house.

"The Waldorf Astoria," put in the cook. "I've seen it myself when I was working in the city. It's a fine big place."

Glibly they talked of a world they had never known except along its fringes and in the chatter of their fellow servants, taking it as much for granted as they had once taken their peasant homes in the far countries of their birth.

"The lady." He had come in for the kitchen refuse and been given the privilege of a mug of scalding tea at the huge scrubbed table. He remembered the grease and the fleeing cockroaches of Mother McClintock's. It was a dark rosy Polish girl who was talking, up to her elbows in potatoes in the stone sink. "The lady is half an invalid, although no one ever seems to know what is wrong with her. I was in the house, see, for a while, but I like it better here. I came from a farm," she added in her thick accent, and Owen wondered what memories haunted her in the long nights.

"She's from New Bedford," the little Irish girl chimed in.

"Mrs. Turnbull." She poured him another mug of tea from a huge red enamel pot, her blue eyes sharp with knowledge. She had been there longer than any of them. "Something to do with her family used to catch whales. It's very important, anyway, and it's her estate they have there by the sea."

The elderly cook nodded sagely above the range. No immigrant she.

"Old money," she said. "Old money. None of your robbers' rubbish. Old money."

It was some time before he assembled even vaguely the picture of the shrewd and brilliant and aggressive man, with a finger in almost every venture in the jungle of the city; and a frail, beautiful and apparently ailing wife, proud descendent of one of the first whaling captains of New Bedford. Revolted by what she considered the vulgar world of new money where her husband plied his fortune.

When he got to know them all better he asked them had they known Antonia, and they shook their heads.

"She would have been inside, you see. We never see them. There's inside is Mr. Jolliff, and outside is Mr. Tendon. And they're not pleased to have you running up and down."

He was more patient now to wait and see what news John Julius had of her, realizing he could waste every last dollar trying to find her. When she was determined not to be found.

Up at the distant house the bright massed flowers of summer gave way to the golds and yellows of the coming fall, and the first faint changes crept into the heavy trees. There was no cultivated land. Only a gentleman's park, landscaped exquisitely with specimen trees; dotted with spotless sheep to keep the grass down. Over past the house and the lake, and a stretch of woodland, there was an immaculately kept farm and a fine herd of black and white dairy cattle with narrow horns. Imported, Tendon told him, finding him interested, especially from Holland.

He would wake in the cool nights and get up simply to look out the open window without chicken wire, seeing the spread of pasture falling away below the stables in the white radiance of the harvest moon; slowly shedding the memories of New York as he would shed a sickness. Thinking of Owenscourt and Antonia; of Emmett and John Julius. Expanding in the solitude that was his until the chauffeur came back.

"You'll not have much peace then," the girls told him and the old cook clicked her teeth.

Owen was shoveling up the rubbish where they had been stripping beans and peeling potatoes in the golden sun outside the kitchen door.

"What's wrong with him?"

He had their names now. Molly was the Irish one, and the Polish girl, Mariza.

"There's nothing wrong with him," said Molly quickly and Owen grinned, understanding at least that he was personable.

Behind Molly, Mariza lifted a bottle in pantomime to her mouth, and Owen groaned. He thought he'd left all that back there in New York.

"He's the terror of the village," Molly said with a note of pride. "Jacques his name is, and he came from Paris itself with the motorcar, and no one else can do a thing with it."

He cherished the quietness even more after that; a breathing space between all the sorrow and the suffering that had gone before and the long unplanned effort of the future. Carefully he hoarded away all he could of his three dollars a week, starting towards he knew not what.

Only the end lay beckoning unchanged. The gray bulk of Owenscourt and Antonia beside him.

"I almost feel myself again here," he wrote to Emmett and John Julius, "but I'm sure the feeling will fade once the real owner comes back!!"

He came back on a clear mellow day touched with the first hint of frost and all the parkland hung with the blazing colors of the fall. For a week or more there had been frenzy. The windows of the house thrown open and not an hour that delivery vans did not go spanking past the stables labeled with the best names in New York; from the back gates that Owen had never found.

Every time he thought of that he was touched with sweat. Had the house not been empty and someone seen him, he would have been put off those front lawns with a shotgun.

Every immaculate flower bed was reweeded and reraked and the already spotless empty stalls in the stables were hosed out and bedded with fresh straw and hay piled in the racks. Since it was no one else's job, it was given to him to sweep out the huge garage and personally polish all the meaningless tins and bottles and drums ranged on shelves for the mystic service of the motor. He could not help being caught up in the sense of expectation. The house and estate were waking again after the long slumbering summer.

"They'll be here now till Christmas," Molly told him, busy in the big storeroom outside the kitchen, sorting all the extra food. He lifted a heavy box of jam onto the table for her.

"And what then?"

"Palm Beach," she said laconically, as if it were across the street. "For the Christmas."

"And where else?"

His parents had been thought quite grand for their annual migrations between Dublin and Kingstown and the West, with the occasional sally into Europe.

"Up to the Catskills in the spring." With half an eye on the trim ankles as she climbed on a chair, he handed her the stone jam jars one by one, reflecting that it was far from jam he had been in Mrs. McClintock's. "Jamaica, when they'd want a change from Palm Beach. Ah, sure, anywhere they'd fancy they'd take a house."

He found the huge double doors of the coach house open for the first time and ventured inside, wandering up and down the tiled floor he could have eaten off, staggered at what he saw.

A barouche; a phaeton; a single-horse victoria and a bigger one for double harness; a single curricle and a gig. And every one of them with silver fittings and silver finish to the harness racked along the walls on polished wood. Yet the great spaces of the spotless building were still half empty.

He stood in sun-striped gloom, shafts of light soft in

gleaming paintwork; around him the half-forgotten smell of polish and good leather and the faint whiff of fine oil. He was back beside his father in the coach house of the Shops, seared with a longing for him that he had not felt for years. And for the simple whitewashed spaces of the coach house in the yard at Owenscourt, the cobwebs hanging from its ancient rafters and under them as many fine rigs as he had ever thought a gentleman would need. Were they there still, he wondered, or had Hugh Charles and the woman remembered them and got them out?

"They have all the big ones with them," boasted a passing stable lad, thinking his stillness and silence were with the shock of something he had never seen before. "And as many more like this at the other house. And sulkies there too for the ponies."

Owen shook his head.

"And all he can think of," the boy went on, "is that bubble he has out of France."

"Bubble?"

"The motorcar. The Renault, they call it."

Owen was full of curiosity to see at close quarters the machine that could take a man's mind from this grandeur and the horses to go with it. He had seen a few of them in New York, churning along the streets, roaring and sputtering and flinging horses into a frenzy; he thought them poor temporary things.

It was like an invading army when they came streaming down the road from the house a few days later. The traveling coach, and once again Owen could not but be sick with longing for warm drowsy journeys on the soft cushions from Dublin down to Galway. Three baggage wagons and two wagonettes that had carried all the servants. Every one of them was in the same clear dark blue as the vehicles in the yard, the grooms in long brass-buttoned coats in the same color and fawn top-hats cockaded in the blue; immobile on the boxes with a dignity that had become habit; too fiercely disciplined even to acknowledge their friends until they were off the road. Splendor and training set against the green perfect parkland. Owen was deeply impressed, feeling humbly that he had a lot to learn and none of it had to do with being a yard boy.

Two days later he unlearnt it all, hearing the motor in the distance rumbling up the front drive and knowing from the talk that the boss was home in it. It had been put on a special flatcar from New Bedford. To New York and out again. Expecting even more splendor and discipline than before, he couldn't understand the grins round him as it advanced steadily down from the house, dark blue like all the carriages, set high on glittering silver wheels, headlamps splintering the sun. The groom beside the driver sat with all the formality of the previous day, but when the driver saw the group at the gates, he tore off his peaked cap and the goggles with it, and waved them in the air, the motor weaving dangerously in his one hand.

"Ah, my frens!" he shouted, half rising in the driving seat, scattering the friends as the car swerved toward them. Owen had a glimpse of a thin face and a wide hilarious grin as the young man sat down and grabbed back his controls, steaming past them all and round into the garage yard.

Life for Owen was never going to be the same again. Jacques was back, and with him the bottle of anis beneath his bed and the advent of the first friend Owen had made since coming to the States. He was everybody's notion of a Frenchman, gratifying them that they had always known what Froggies would be like. Huge expressive eyes and the droll face of a clown. All the girls adored him and he had never made an enemy, gathering everyone into the warmth of his own inexhaustible good nature.

Owen he drew at once into a web of irresistible conspiracy.

"You are my fren, Owen," he said about a month later, the big eyes sunk in the shadows of the night before. "I have never had a fren here before."

"Then who," Owen wanted to ask him, "put you to bed when you were too drunk to do it yourself? Who dragged you over the walls with the stable ladder when you were so late the gates were locked? Who shoved your head under the yard pump to get you fit to go behind the wheel and begged black coffee from the kitchen?" Time and again rage grabbed him and furious exasperation, but they always died before the abject eyes and the torrents of apology.

"Ah, Owen, I get you out of bed again. I am so sorree. But she was so beeutiful I could not leave her. Plees forgive."

"Dammit, Jacques, where do you *find* them?"

Rumor had it he had been through every willing girl in the house, both inside and out of it, and must by now be scouring the dark countryside at nights.

"You will forgive me, Owen?"

And Owen always did, charmed like everybody else by his unfailing good temper and generosity. In return Jacques gave him the greatest gift that he could offer and taught him all about his beloved motor. To his amazement Owen, dedicated heir to the Shops and reared to his father's passion for fine rigs and horseflesh, found himself a natural mechanic; readily fascinated; becoming as fanatical as Jacques himself about the cleaning and oiling and greasing of the machine, until Tendon demanded sourly who had promoted him from yard boy to assistant chauffeur.

He was more careful after that, but had no intention of resisting Jacques's determination that he should drive it. Round and round the huge yard built to hold the twenty motors that Phineas Turnbull was sure he would one day own. Dizzy with the power of it, his eyes blazing with excitement. Astonished at his natural success.

In the long winter nights when Jacques was sober enough, they talked the dark hours down in the cold dormitory with its empty beds, their one candle throwing flaring shadows in the bitter drafts. Jacques told him of his childhood in Paris where his father had been an engineer working on the first development of the automobile, and he had been allowed beside him from the time he was big enough to hold a wrench.

Like me, Owen thought, huddling the blankets under his chin. His memory surged with the smell of wood and resin and fresh varnish and his father at his side, but when Jacques asked him in turn about himself he was evasive, saying only that he was a country boy. Unable to frame for anyone the gaping loneliness that still tore him for his home and family. And what, in any case, he thought, would Jacques do but laugh at the idea of the yard boy owning Owenscourt.

Jacques looked at him in the small light with shrewd black eyes and let it go.

Snow blanketed the park and as Owen scraped and shoveled at the yard he remembered the frozen filth that had passed for snow in the city, and marveled at the untouched beauty. His very contentment began to alarm him. He had good food and a clean decent bed and a friend; a dollar or two going carefully away every week, and by God a rich man's motor for a plaything. His careful hoard was rising towards the size of a steamer fare, and then he knew he must make a decision, touched by fear that he was settling too well and would lose sight of his goals. By the time he had some money, maybe John Julius would have some news of Antonia.

"I saw my employer close at hand for the first time," he wrote to John Julius and Emmett, "when he came down to wish us well at our Thanksgiving dinner which is something they have here like Christmas only on the third Thursday in November. They are off now to Florida for Christmas, with all the servants and the lot of it loaded onto private railcars in New York. You'd never see such a performance. It only surprises me they don't take the house as well. The motor hasn't gone this time so I am having a lot of lessons from Jacques. That's the chauffeur I was telling you about.

"A fine decent-looking man my employer is, about forty years of age or a little more, but there's something in his face tells me he'd be a hard man to cross. Were it not that I have other things in my mind, I would be very contented in this place, although God knows it is months since I set eyes on a book, and must be turning into a total ignoramus."

Emmett sent him books then and he plowed reluctantly through the horrifying tales of the Jesuit martyrs in North

America and the tender poems of Father Matthew Russell and small meaningful volumes that clearly showed Emmett's concern about his soul.

Jacques looked at them on the chest beside his bed.

"*Mon Dieu,*" he said in horror. "Let us go out and drive the motor."

When he was coming close to his decision to go, with the young lambs leaping in the pastures and the cherry trees white with blossom on the road up to the house, there came the inevitable morning when he failed to get Jacques from his bed.

He had dragged him, feet trailing, down the stairs to the pump, where the cold water had only thrown him into violent vomiting, and he could do no more than drag him back again, ashen and sweating and barely conscious, and throw him soaking on his bed. Sweating himself that the noisy performance might have caught Tendon's eye; thankful that by now everybody else would be in at breakfast.

"I am dying," Jacques moaned weakly, and Owen had to admit he didn't look far off it. "Owen, I am dying."

"You're drunk," Owen said callously. "You have to get up. Tendon will miss you."

"Tendon." Jacques's eyes opened wide, black as pitch and full of horror. "*Sainte Marie,*" he whispered and rolled them round to Owen, too weak to move his head. His pallor was frightening, and Owen wondered should he get help. "Owen, *mon Dieu*. Today it is not Tendon." He could barely speak. "Today at nine thirty. The house. Mr. Turnbull."

He kept passing out. Desperately Owen shook him.

"Jacques. It's your job. You'll lose your job."

And mine too he thought, am I not seen somewhere soon.

Jacques's face was all eyes, wet hair plastered to his narrow skull.

"I know," he whispered.

"Can't you get up?"

"No. Everything is everywhere. I have no legs. *Mon Dieu* but I am so ill."

Owen stood over him in despair.

"Owen." He had come round again. His voice was little more than a whisper. "Owen, you must go instead of me."

"*What!*"

"Owen, I promise. I promise. You do this for me and I will never drink again. Never. On my oat'. I won a lot of money last night. I give it all to you."

"How can I go? It would be both our jobs!"

"You can drive the motor. Take my coat and cap. With goggles he'll never know. He wants to drive himself."

The sort of thing, Owen thought furiously, that Jacques would do himself, laughing every inch of the way and getting away with it. But he himself! Before God he'd surely make some mess of it. Tendon wouldn't miss him, though. He'd be off by then on his rounds of the estate. No. He couldn't do it.

"Don't forget," Jacques mumbled, "to stop every fifteen minutes. To let it cool."

And he was gone again. Nor this time could Owen rouse him.

He had trouble starting it, cursing himself all the time for an insane fool, and in his impatience he nearly broke his wrist on the kickback. But he couldn't stop exhilaration from seizing him as the Renault finally hissed and rumbled up the road below the cherry trees. There was a brilliant blue sky and the white petals scattered in a soft wind, falling like snowflakes on the blue bonnet. The sun was hot and in the blossoms small birds sang and whistled, and he was filled with power and excitement to have the motor to himself; almost careless of the consequences. It was time for him to go in any case.

"It's as well to enjoy it," he decided, "for before the morning's out I'll be back on the road, and the fool Jacques probably with me."

The long blue dustcoat was loose, and took his bigger bulk, and he had diligently burnished the brass buttons with his sleeve. The peaked cap and goggles, as Jacques had said, covered his hair and half his face.

But the moment the man spoke to him he would be lost.

"Sair," he said to the trees, and the sputtering car. "Plees, I am here. Good mornin', sair."

It was useless.

He drew up carefully and cut the thumping motor outside the front door where he had not set foot since the first day he had come looking for Antonia. For Christ's sake, now did he pull the bell or squeeze the horn or just stay where he was? The man would have to be unconscious not to have heard the thing arrive. He could feel his palms sweating inside the gauntlets.

Erect as a ramrod, as he had seen all footmen sit, he sat and waited, his hands stiff before him on the wheel. It was hot. Hotter, he thought, than it would ever be in Ireland at the time of year. Two liver-and-white retrievers sat idly on the top of the stone steps, limp in the sun, waiting, like him, for their master. Bees thrummed in the banks of flowers below the windows of the house and blue jays were going mad in the birches that formed a little island in the middle of the gravel sweep.

The cooling engine cracked in the quiet and no sound came from the house. The comfort of his seat and the old familiar smell of warm fine leather gave him an atavistic sense of comfort and security. It seemed in the warm silence as though life itself had stopped, offering him a moment of time to breathe and be himself. Twice he caught himself as his chin cracked down to his chest, and thought in sick panic that, Jesus, that's all he would require. Fiercely he sat up again and stared ahead, keeping himself awake by his anger at his friend. He had been up half the night trying to struggle the fool to bed, and missed breakfast dealing with him this morning.

It was hot. Damnably hot. The goggles made a rim of sweat round his eyes, but he didn't dare remove them. Light splintered from the glittering mountings of the car and he could feel sweat gathering down his spine. Jacques could have told him that in such weather he would wear nothing but his underclothes and boots below the heavy dustcoat. He yawned cavernously, and again, and the rummaging bees seemed to have come closer. The next time his head flopped down it stayed there, and a fly crawled idly across his goggles.

"Ferrier."

He heard the voice and recognized Jacques's name. Nothing to do with him. He drew a deep beautiful breath and waited for the voice to say O'Connor.

The next second he was out on the gravel sick with shock, and still more than half asleep, standing beside his employer, and behind him Jolliff, holding his cap and goggles, impeccably without reaction, regarding Owen with dark expressionless eyes.

He had only had the one sight of his employer close at hand, and that at the crowded tables of Thanksgiving. He found himself standing beside a man of his own height but slender to the point of being cadaverous, a strong square jaw that reminded him of his father and a head of thick reddish fair hair going gray along the sides. Forty to forty-five, and an impression of power and alertness that might turn easily to aggression. No idea what he would be like when he smiled. No time for smiling. His eyes assessed the situation without visible comment.

"Sir," said Owen and didn't know what else to say. He had forgotten that he should be French. The two dogs circled with waving tails and sniffed at his trousers underneath his coat, drawn by the smells of the stables. Frantically he shook the sleep from his eyes and saw his death knell in Jolliff's impassive face.

"Thank you, Jolliff," said Phineas Turnbull. He took his cap and goggles from the butler. "That'll be all."

Jolliff bowed and went back up the steps, into the house, closing the double doors behind him silently.

"You—you wish to drive, sir? Shall I start it?"

"Sure, do that."

Mercifully it sparked at the first try and his master, in fawn dustcoat to his ankles and fine light leather gauntlets, put on his goggles and his cap, and took the wheel. Turnbull whistled the two dogs, who jumped at once into the back-seat, and Owen leapt no slower into the front, barely knowing what he was doing, half his mind cursing Jacques from there till the end of eternity. He sat erect, like a footman, staring straight ahead, hands on blue-coated knees.

With his hand on the lever ready for advance, and the cylinders thumping like a barrage, his employer spoke above the noise.

"You're not my chauffeur."

Owen felt light-headed. There was nothing to lose. Everything had been lost already, and what happened to that fool Jacques was his own doing. He turned round and looked Phineas Turnbull in the face.

"No, sir. I'm the yard boy."

"The *what!* And you know what you're doing with this machine?"

"Yes, sir."

I *was* the yard boy, he thought, and Jacques *was* the chauffeur.

"The yard boy," his employer said again as if he didn't believe it.

"Yes, sir. From the stables."

Phineas Turnbull let it rest at that and gave his attention to getting the machine round the birch trees and down the drive beneath the sycamores in a series of leaps and lurches and great gouts of steam. In the backseat the two dogs barked wildly at the noise and slavered their excitement down Owen's neck. As the motor careened out through the gates, missing the stone post by less than half an inch, he shouted again.

"Can you drive this thing better than I can?"

"Yes, sir," Owen yelled back, too frightened to dissimulate. His employer grunted and below the goggles a smile touched his lips.

"Sir!" shouted Owen after ten minutes of lurching along the country road. Jacques had said fifteen minutes but by another five they might well be dead or in the ditch or up in flames. Jesus Christ! He ducked his head as they roared past big studded gates in a brick wall and he had a snatched picture of two horses rearing on their heels and a coachman on the box of a victoria, purple faced and roaring. From somewhere behind him there were female screams. The noise was shattering.

"Sir!" he bellowed. "Sir!" And now pure fear made him indifferent. "Ferrier said we should stop and let her cool!"

The radiator cap with its gold mascot was scalding in his hand even through the gauntlet, and the jet of steam shot into the blue quiet air. The cooling cylinders snapped like fireworks, and Jesus, but Jacques would murder him. The machine must be ruined, but how could he stop the man.

He marched back round to his seat, and found his employer watching him intently, his goggles pushed up above his checked cap, exposing strange green-brown eyes with yellow lights in them. Like peat water in the sun, thought Owen after meeting his glance for one trapped, astonished moment. He climbed in and sat down in his footman's pose, staring straight ahead and waiting for the knife.

"Now," said Phineas Turnbull mildly. He took off his gauntlet and flexed his hot fingers. Nothing was said of Jacques or why Owen was with the car. "Will you spend the time telling me why you are working as a yard boy?"

Owen in turn pushed up his goggles and gave the older man one startled look and then, meeting the steady, waiting eyes, he forgot his footman's place. Between the green hedges of the country road, under the arching trees of spring, the jet of steam still drifting from the bonnet, he spoke for the first time since he'd set foot in America, of Owenscourt and all that he had lost. Not from any desire to excuse or impress, but from some strange certainty that only the truth would do for the man who watched him unblinkingly from the other seat. He spoke of the long desperate struggle he foresaw to get it back. And of Antonia. His gauntleted fingers knotted between his knees, crushing sorrows he had not admitted to for eighteen months.

Chapter 19

In retrospect Owen had difficulty in chronicling his progress in his new position, or even in defining what it was. Nor would Phineas Turnbull ever say why he had given it to him, other than, laconically, that he knew a good thing when he saw one. Owen was to find all his decisions were similarly taken; with deep, concentrated attention to anything that anyone had to tell him. Having asked for information he always had the patience to listen to the end of it, his strange tiger's eyes fixed immovably on the speaker. Decisions came at once from his own brilliant shrewdness, and his ability to assess everything put before him, brooking no arguments after that one moment of decision. He could be obstinate then and unwilling to change his mind, no matter what came later. It was said by the envious that Phineas Turnbull would go down in Wall Street history as the Man Who Was Never Wrong.

All this Owen came to understand later, but at the start he was pitchforked from the stables with only the haziest idea of his job.

"Just be there, boy," Turnbull had said. "Just be there, and it will all turn up."

Was he to be a secretary? There already was one; a soft-faced young woman called Bess who moved like a shadow of quiet efficiency at Turnbull's heels. Owen noted that most of his staff seemed to be young. Was he to be a valet? There was an English one, Peters, with a deeply developed sense of his own importance, and ruthless ill manners toward what he saw as a young Irish interloper into his master's life. A companion? The man was rarely alone. He spent Monday, Tuesday, and Wednesday in the uproar of his New York office, with its bank of telephones and the sweating top-hatted messengers racing in and out of the stock exchange. In the country for the other days, guests came and went in a boil of activity without which he seemed unable to live. Business was still at fever pitch, even if moved to the beautiful house run by Jolliff, apparently with the minimum of interference and direction from the quiet woman with the watchful eyes who was Turnbull's well-born wife.

He asked Bess, who seemed the one most disposed to be kind to him—already poised, her hands full of papers, to go after her boss—and she smiled at him.

"Just be there," he said to her. "What does that mean?"

"It means just that." She had a lovely husky voice that went well with her face. "There was someone else, you know. A man older than himself. He'd known him all his life. He died last year, and I think you should be flattered. Mr. Turnbull has been waiting ever since to set eyes on the right person to replace him."

Owen felt appalled and overawed. What dead man's shoes was he supposed to fill, not even knowing the size of them?

"I think," went on Bess, "you must always be there when everybody else is gone. You must be half his mind. Fill all the gaps so that he can give his thoughts to other things. You must listen when he is only talking to himself. Anticipate everything. As he said, just be there. That is what Gene Andrews seemed to me to do."

"Good God," said Owen, and she smiled at him again, thinking the good-looking young Irishman with the lively eyes would be more pleasure round the place than the aging Gene, lugubrious with sickness.

"I'll help you all I can," she said, and he looked down at a list in his hand that Turnbull had given him that morning; the yellow eyes daring him to say he couldn't handle it. He had better not ask Bess to help with that, lest in some way it filter back and be a mark against him. He realized it was a test.

"Thanks, Miss Gibson," he said, and she moved off down the corridor toward the office that looked out on the rose garden.

"Call me Bess," she said over her shoulder.

The list was of the finest tailors and haberdashers in New York, with a covering letter of introduction to all of them, and details, supplied, he suspected, by the antagonistic valet, of what he must buy to equip himself for the job of being always there. All of it to be put down to the credit of Phineas Turnbull. The test came in finding the courage to present himself in his scarecrow clothes at these emporiums, and to impress them sufficiently not to find himself straight back on the sidewalk. Indeed even to manage to get past the uniformed guardians of their gilded doorsteps. In the little he had seen of his new master, he suspected a wry delight in creating such a situation. Nowhere must he fail.

Several of these hallowed shops he knew, from the days of his defeated tramping round the streets of New York. Suits from Wetzel's. That was a gloomy establishment with a cockaded doorman guarding a studded door as heavy and defeating as a medieval castle's. One day when it was standing open, he had seen a suit of armor at the foot of the red-carpeted stairs. Thirty-fifth he remembered. He wouldn't have to look for that one. Just off Fifth Avenue.

Sulka for shirts; the restrained window full of silks worth a king's ransom. He had seen that too.

Peal's for boots. Made to measure.

Kaskel and Kaskel for what was discreetly called his haberdashery. There was enough there to equip a regiment.

And enough money to keep him in a modest hotel until all of it was ready.

"You never thought, I suppose, as many would," John Julius was to say to him long later, hearing the whole remarkable story, "of simply taking the money and using it to get a steamer ticket back home?"

Owen had looked at him, profoundly shocked, gripped from the very beginning by the sense of obligation that was to shape the rest of his life.

The first test came with taking the telephone off the hook and winding the handle to call the stables; asking for a trap to take him to the public coach into the city, and suffering the incredulous resentment in the face of the groom who came to the front door to pick him up.

The second test, and he could almost see the wry critical face of his boss watching him, came in entering, in his workman's suit, the conservative portals of the Fifth Avenue Bank, bringing to an astonished halt all the deferential business at the rolltop desks before the open fire; in the opulent gloom of paneled walls and Persian carpets.

He came out damp with sweat and angry, but with his money in his pocket, and after that the shops were easy.

In the time he had to spare between collecting all the merchandise and putting it on in a sort of somber delight before his bedroom glass, he thought a great deal about Antonia. Staring out into the swarming streets and wondering if once again the same city held them, no distance from each other. Sadly he felt it pointless to search without a grain of lead. He longed to tell her of his change in fortune, and yet doubt touched him over that. She would probably do no more than look at him with the old distaste twisting her lovely mouth, and carp at him for being back among the rich.

In his quiet moments he tried to decide what he felt about it all himself. Immense pleasure at his sheer good luck. And what had happened to poor Jacques, who seemed to have vanished without trace? He could not resist a deep excited satisfaction that, good luck or not, the pauper days were over. Unless he made a complete fool of himself, he knew himself in all honesty better suited to being whatever it was to Phineas Turnbull, than he had been as a yard boy.

And he would see, he thought grimly, that he didn't make a fool of himself.

He settled the glossy white collar above his Sulka shirt and knotted a pure silk Kaskel tie, pulling down the points of his gray foulard waistcoat; regarding his image with the new haircut in the glass with unabashed satisfaction, seeing again after a long gap, the Owen of Owenscourt and Gardiner Street. He had come back into his own. Owenscourt. No mention had been made of salary, but he could not imagine it being mean. By the time he had discharged sufficient years for the man to have got back all his outlay, then he should with care have saved enough to make Owenscourt an easy task.

Two years until he was twenty-one. Probably that would be too soon to go back. Already his forehead creased with his sense of obligation. But at least once it was legally his, he could put the robbers out whenever he chose. Or could he ever put his mother's brother out of Holly House?

In faraway New York, the gray misty problems of Ireland filled the comfortable room, dominating even his excitement, and then deliberately he shrugged them off. Plenty of time to think about them later. He eased himself into his silk-lined jacket with the fashionable high lapels and only one button closed, setting his derby at an angle, and, picking up his gloves, set out on an evening stroll down Fifth Avenue in the golden sun. Not quite believing in himself, and yet aware that it was all more real than the stableyard had ever been, or the fruitless winter tramping in the snow. He resisted the impulse to go on down to Lower Manhattan like a returning hero, and press money into the grimy hand of every beggar that he met.

His position was even more demanding than he had envisaged, and more rewarding. His task to be everywhere at all times, and to think of everything, freeing his master's mind for the all-important business of making money. His place to remind Phineas Turnbull that in the heat of a deal he had torn off his tie, and must not go like that into the street. At the other extreme, to sit when all the moguls and the brokers and consultants had gone away, acting as a sounding board for his master's thinking while the gas lamps hissed in the deserted office, and the hot night came down like a weight above the city. Phineas would stand up abruptly, and Owen knew a surge of surprised pleasure to realize from his face that he had not completely failed him. Through the gaslit streets, dank with the whiff of the motionless river, they would walk on down to somewhere like Charles Rector's on Broadway, to eat great quantities of lobster Newburg and drink White Seal champagne. In the presence of the kings of money that frequented these places, Owen struggled to keep his head and his intelligence, bewildered by a scope of living beyond his wildest imagination. He was careful never to ape them, holding always to his own young dignity; Owenscourt looming always as a sort of measure of stability in the background of his mind; finding an unexpectedly gratifying reward in the level, faintly approving gaze of his master.

In the plush and chandeliered splendor of the Waldorf there was a sitting room for him and Bess, and a bedroom of curtained elegance that made him feel embarrassed, wandering from place to place at first and trying to decide where he should put his clothes, New York roaring along Fifth Avenue below him, as strange from this height as if he had never set eyes on it before.

"I'd imagine," he wrote to Emmett, "it was a dam' sight less splendor than this brought about the French Revolution. You should see the boss' sitting room. It would fill the ground floor of Owenscourt and enough grandeur for a palace."

From Emmett's letter back he could feel that he was troubled about him and his sudden rise to fortune, with many barely veiled references to the dangers of worldliness. He grinned. He was able to assure Emmett that it was all far better for his immortal soul than either starving or being yard boy.

As Turnbull got used to him and didn't find him wanting, it became his habit after a long day of wrangle and discussion with problems yet unresolved, to arrive in Owen's bedroom in the middle of the night, preceded by the rich smell of his Havana puro. He would stalk the bedroom floor, barely aware of where he was, only aware of his need to clear his mind to his audience of one, whose quick intelligence had not been long in grasping what it was all about, and who had begun to make clear thoughtful comments of his own. Never daring to point out the time, earning often a sudden pause and silence as the cigar glowed in the darkness, and beyond the draped windows dawn crept in pale over the sleeping city.

By six o'clock Turnbull would be at his desk again, his mind clear, calling for Owen, and for Bess, who would come quietly from her own room as though she had been up all night; smiling with the gentle fresh simplicity that was hers alone, belying her sharp intelligence and infinite capacity for organization.

Gradually Owen realized he was everything he had thought he might be. Valet. Nursemaid. Never without a pocketful of pills for stomach or for headache; sounding board and increasing confidant; and slowly, slowly as the months piled up, with gratified pleasure: friend.

In Glendon House for the last days of the week, he entered a dream world of old masters and French marquetry, velvet padded chairs and Persian rugs and Ming vases stacked with hothouse flowers. He entered, watchful, as if treading on glass lest he make some mistake, the world of Corona cigars and jewels from Tiffany. Revillon furs and Dom Pérignon champagne with Huntley and Palmer biscuits. To Abercrombie picnic baskets fitted with silver in the wagonette for hunting trips with English-made guns. Into the world of Baccarat glass and Paris fashions and fine bone china made in Staffordshire. A world of such discreet and dreamlike splendor it made the warm family comfort of Owenscourt seem like a memory of simplicity.

The flowers were the pride and passion of Mrs. Elvita

Turnbull, tall thin lady with a strong narrow face, who spent a great deal of her life lying on her beautiful sofas without visible ill health, or dimming of her large, intelligent eyes.

"I am well enough," she said suddenly to Owen one day when he made formal inquiry after her health. "Well enough for all my own ends." Giving him as near a grin as her patrician face would allow. Meaning, he assumed, that she was well enough to do exactly as she wanted but never well enough to be pressured by Phineas into the social scrimmage of New York. Always able to make the apparent struggle to the city to the productions of grand opera in the Academy of Music in Irving Place, where the very possession of her box proclaimed her exclusiveness. Always too frail to accept any invitations afterward except to the discreet family receptions of a close enclave of people exactly like herself. Then she would look at her husband with exhausted eyes and proclaim her need to go back to the country first thing in the morning, lest her nameless ailments overtake her. Owen liked her, and did not think himself wrong in surprising gleams of pure mischief in the dark, languid-seeming eyes.

Nor would she subscribe to any of the habits of the Lobster Palace Society, such as footmen too heavily laden with their great powdered wigs and the gilt dangling from their livery, to be able to pass a platter of terrapin. In Glendon House the footmen wore a plain livery of the same blue as the carriages and the grooms, with cut silver buttons and their own hair. Presided over by the unearthly perfection of Jolliff, who regarded Owen with a liquid expressionless gaze, never betraying by word or gesture his secret satisfaction that this amiable and efficient young man seemed to have got his merits. Having reached the top in his own world, he had no jealousy or malice in his impeccably controlled being toward the good fortune of anybody else.

Owen learnt the astonishing pleasures of traveling to Florida on the Turnbull Pullman, where Jolliff reproduced almost identically the luxury and calm of Glendon House; tried not to gape at the Spanish ranch house on Ocean Boulevard in Palm Beach. Acres of grass and palms and cypresses; blazing gardens running down under the endless sun to the snow-white beach and the warm milky sea.

Emmett wrote to him as he described each new opening splendor in his life, not wishing before God to pass judgment, but clearly of the opinion that his head was being turned by little less than a life of sinful luxury, and the motives of a man who would pitchfork him like this into it, must be watched with grave care. I am not sure, he added, that all that sea bathing is beneficial to the limbs.

Owen smiled affectionately. He knew he could never get Emmett to understand that even with every luxury of great riches and all the apparent self-indulgence, the life of Phineas Turnbull and his quiet wife was of a rectitude and respectability that would not have disgraced Clongowes itself or all Emmett's fellow priests. For Phineas Turnbull and his friends the ultimate in sins were high stakes in poker games and a good taste for Bourbon whisky.

In February 1895 Owen's twenty-first birthday was spent in the white-colonnaded splendor of the Antler's Hotel in Colorado, where they had come by hooking the entire entourage onto the right-of-way of the Rio Grande railroad. Mrs. Turnbull in Palm Beach had decided that she was not yet ready to go back to the rigors of New Jersey in the early year, and sufficient of Phineas's business associates were already in residence at the hotel to allow the conduct of affairs to remain virtually uninterrupted.

He was deeply touched that they gave him a birthday dinner as they would give to one of their own. The beaming waiters flocked round with the terrapin and roast grouse and *bœuf Mirabeau*, all washed down with Dom Pérignon, while the string orchestra scraped away at birthday music behind the potted palms, and in the end it seemed the entire smiling restaurant knew the day. Phineas beamed from his yellow eyes with the same pleasure as he might have beamed on his own son, and not for the first time Owen was struck by the chilly certainty that he had made a commitment he could not easily undo.

It was late night before he stood at his window looking

down at the lights shining on the sculptured snow, a flash of color still here and there on the swept walks, and the tinkle of laughter in the black shadows. He thought of Phineas Turnbull and all he had so deeply committed himself to.

It had not all been easy. Turnbull had not reached his riches without being a hard man to please, and at the beginning had treated Owen often with deliberate lack of consideration and even downright rudeness. Owen refused to rise to it, remaining steadfastly his own man, but making it clear he would prefer the stables to any kind of purchased subservience. When his master found he could not be nudged or jostled, a gleam of satisfaction would lighten the deep-set yellow eyes, and gradually it all stopped. It was from that point that Owen knew it would be hard to go away.

Looking out at the great round Colorado moon, he thought of Owenscourt and of Antonia and picked up again the cables from Emmett and John Julius and the Canon, and the lawyer James Cornelius O'Duffy. They wished him well and said no more, but as clearly as if printed, they asked him what he was going to do now. Papers following, O'Duffy's said, and he thought wryly it would take time enough to get them out of his bastard uncle.

He could go back now. The most surprising thing about his apprenticeship as Phineas's aide, as he had learnt to call himself, was that they had uncovered his own sharp acumen with money, and his natural talent for the world that Phineas lived in. The result of this was that even in so short a time he had multiplied all he had saved. And in honesty, the life both satisfied and excited him.

He could go back now, although it would fill him with guilt to do so, take his inheritance, and start the lonely struggle of restoring Owenscourt. There was nothing to prevent him. He turned from the window and looked at the lamplit room behind him; firelight warm on the dark-green walls and the snow-white drapes; glittering in the knobs of the elegant brass-railed bed. The cupboards full of handsome clothes; the silk dressing gown from Paris into the pockets of which he thrust his hands. It was a present from Mrs. Turnbull.

Phineas had given him a gold chiming hunter, and he knew there would be jokes about it when he staggered heavy eyed to his suite at six o'clock in the morning for a couple of hours' work before breakfast on the papers that had come in on the night train.

There was much to keep him there.

On the crested stationery of the Antler's, he wrote next day to John Julius and to Emmett and to James O'Duffy.

It was the same letter, in effect, to all of them, saying that after much consideration he would not come back to claim Owenscourt at the present time. The first reason being that he did not feel he had yet quite enough money to put it in order as he wished, or to establish it as a profit-making entity on its own for many years. Nor did he imagine Hugh Charles would have left much intact of what he had taken.

In this matter he instructed James O'Duffy to do nothing, as he did not believe in throwing good money after bad, but at the same time he gave John Julius what was virtually his only instruction. That he be good enough to go to Tuam, and find a good man who would change every lock in Owenscourt and seal the shutters so that the house could be opened only by force. This way, he said, it must stay till I come back.

The second reason he gave, came to his own mind first. He would not mind pinching the pennies in Owenscourt. What else had he been living for? But he knew he could not yet leave the man who had virtually taken him from the streets and done so much for him. Some years' service would be the least he could do in repayment. In the meantime he could go on building up money for the reopening of the estate.

To James O'Duffy alone he gave instructions for the reclaim of all the remaining deeds of what belonged to him. He had not needed to grow as old as he was to know his uncle at heart a coward, who would only steal when he had the law apparently on his side.

Although it had come now into his possession, his uncle could continue to live in Holly House, as he knew his mother would never wish him turned out. He could, if he wanted, continue to farm such of the Owenscourt land as he was farming. Even bad cultivation was better than no cultivation at all, and he could be put off easily enough when the time came. This was to apply only as long as the house was securely closed and locked.

He paused there and thought about his uncle and his character and knew that he had read him right. Please God, he had moved fast enough to catch him. Probably the man thought that by now he was gone forever.

When he was done, he put down his pen and stared out at the glittering snow under the dark-blue sky. The decision had been a hard one that had troubled him for months, and now that it was done he did not wish to think of it at all. But it was made. He rang for a footman and gave him the letters and turned again determinedly to the splendid world of Phineas Turnbull.

In the following summer he had a letter from John Julius, who had debated with himself for many days before he wrote it. He thought Owen right to stay where he was while he established complete financial security. The lot in Holly House had drawn in their horns and might as well not have been there, and he didn't want Owen now to come stampeding back on any wild-goose chase that might gain him nothing.

In the end he wrote, Antonia had come back to Cannon's Mills. She had been ill in New York. The Sisters of Charity had cared for her through the worst of it, and then while she still had the money she had come back to the only place she knew to come. Father or no father, it was the only home she had. He did not speak of the wordless sick delight that her decision had given him, or the clutch of sorrow when he actually saw her. So dreadfully thin and with such an air of strain, the enormous eyes looking as if they had been pressed into her face with dirty thumbs.

She remembered well the house where he was, and had enjoyed working there but had been afraid he might find her. He must be having the great life.

He looked up from the letter, sensing the cynical flare in the blue eyes. She would never want him now.

John Julius emphasized this.

"Do not," he instructed, "come racing back for her. It would do no more than break you, for she is as bitter as ever about her mother and her position, and would never consent to marry anyone, although," he wrote, "God knows, Owen, if it were anyone it would be you."

With that end to the letter died the flame of hope that had risen when he saw that she was back. But he knew John Julius right. If she wouldn't hear of marrying because she was a bastard when they were both struggling in New York, how much less would she hear of it to Phineas Turnbull's well-groomed aide, with his Wetzel suit and his shining boots from Peal's beneath the table.

He felt he had everything and yet he had nothing, neither Antonia nor Owenscourt, and in the busy and prosperous years that passed before the turn of the century, nothing was different. Only that he was able to write to her regularly for the reward of an occasional stilted letter in a hand as spiky as herself. As he became more and more woven into the very fabric of Phineas Turnbull's life, it became more impossible to suggest that he might leave, nor in all honesty did he wish to. Owenscourt had become a phantom at the back of his busy mind.

"Plenty of time for that, my boy," Phineas would say to him if he should ever broach it. "Plenty of time for that. You're young yet. And you'll need money. Now look, tell me what you think of this."

And they would be back again in Phineas's world. Lead, biscuits, shipping, banking, boots, and railroading. Any option that would make money. And for a safety hatch a gigantic herd of dairy cattle out on the wide prairies of Indiana.

He was twenty-six, and the century new, when he left his room in the Waldorf one evening, hastily adjusting his cuffs and tie, to attend a dinner party given by Phineas for some party of visiting lords from England.

Normally he would have arranged it, discussing the menu

with the redoubtable Oscar, terrifying and unapproachable headwaiter at the Waldorf. He would have run his eye down the list of guests given him by Bess, for anyone to whom he or his employer should give particular attention. At the last moment he would have gone to the private dining room to check that everything was in order and to cast an eye over the seating that would have been done by Mrs. Turnbull's girl.

Tonight was men only and he was late. He had been down to Chicago on his employer's business and the long journey back through the snowbound country had been interminable. New York was freezing under a sheet of glittering stars, the ice cracking like gunshot beneath the carriage wheels as he was driven from the station between ramparts of snow. Under the mink lap-robe he remembered his first winter, and the newspapers underneath his clothes, and his own frozen grief at losing Antonia; no less harsh and unforgiving than the weather itself.

He sighed. There seemed as time went by to be less and less opportunity to think about her, or about Owenscourt; never mind to come to any sort of a decision.

Phineas was warmly glad to see him. There were no ladies tonight and they had gathered as was the custom in such circumstances in the men's bar on the ground floor; all the ambience and dignity of a gentlemen's club.

"Owen! Dear boy, I thought you snowbound somewhere in the wastes of Indiana. I'm glad you got here. There sure is someone you'll be glad to meet."

"Who are they all, sir?"

Very English from the sound of their voices and the old-fashioned high-chested cut of their tailcoats.

"Party of Irish landowners, believe it or not. Taken conscience about the condition of their country and come over here to study farming methods. They want to see my herd."

"In this weather? And Irish?"

He listened to the high clipped English voices, and felt some atavistic antagonism. These were the people who had filled the coffin ships, and the slums of New York he had come to know so well. He forced himself to be reasonable, knowing that few people, listening to him, would think he was an Irishman. And if they were indeed trying to better the lot of Ireland now, then more power to them.

"They're going south and coming northwards with the spring," Phineas said. "The snow is late, you'll know that—they've been here a week eating their heads off. Sure are nice fellows. Here—this"—he laid a hand on the arm of one passing gentleman, a round florid face pouched over his gleaming collar—"is the man you should meet. Perry! Perry, come a moment. I'd have you meet Owen O'Connor, who's my right hand and indeed my left one as well. Owen, this is Lord Bunaffrey. Comes from your corner of the world, I'd think."

"Sir."

Phineas moved off, and limp with shock Owen stared at the man who had turned to him, quelling the bitter anger that nearly blinded him; searching in the round, self-assured face for any trace of the delicate features engraved forever on his mind.

"I am from near Tuam," he heard himself saying. He sensed the man didn't give a damn anyway. "I understand your land is over near Claremorris."

The smile was stiff on his face, his memory ripping back to Antonia's expression that evening in the flaring lamplight in the kitchen of the agent's house; his mind so hazed with unforgotten fury that he hardly heard the man's answer, only knew that he was his employer's guest and he must not insult him.

". . . never set foot in the place until a few years ago, when my son Giles there decided it was the fashion to be Irish. Always hated the blasted country and everything to do with it, except, ha ha—the rents."

The crowded room with its heavy mahogany and gleaming mirrors swung and tilted before Owen's eyes and settled again into place, leaving him staring into the robust face, the slightly protuberant blue eyes filled with little more than the lifelong pleasure of being Bunaffrey.

"Where, then," said Owen. Someone had given him a glass

and he put it down carefully on a marble table, not trusting himself to hold it. He tried to make the question have the necessary idle politeness. "Where, then, did you live, sir?"

A flicker of the rounded eyes asked whether this youth was even worth answering.

"Place in Berkshire."

Bunaffrey was bored. Being stuck for the evening with the company of men was not his idea of pleasure. Dam silly jaunt the whole thing. But there had been a filly in the lobby in a dress of rose silk cut rather lower than most. He stared over Owen's shoulder and out through the arches of the bar in the hope of seeing her again. Promising. Fine eyes.

"Very civilized," he said to Owen then, measuring Berkshire against the gray barracks in the wet fields of west Galway that his son seemed to set such store by.

"And you never came to your Irish property at all?"

Owen knew he was risking a rebuff, but he had to have it cut and dried. Spelt out for him so that his racing heart would know that there was no mistake. Bunaffrey's chilly glance told him he disapproved of being questioned, but he answered impatiently.

"Never," he said. "Never. Born in Berkshire. Stayed there, thank God. None of these damn bogs and savages for me. Pardon me, my boy."

He was off, to take a turn outside in the lobby in the hope of seeing her again.

Owen walked out of the smoke-filled bar and over to one of the long windows in the front lobby. Between the velvet curtains he could see hazily through the lace drapes; the gleaming lights of the hotel entrance falling on the swept street; glittering on the banked and freezing snow; the constant procession of fine carriages, closed against the bitter night, to the steps just out of his sight; the first drifting flakes of a new snowfall.

He was aware of none of it, seeing only a thin desperate face and hearing her young voice full of anguish.

"Sure, I know I'd be a bastard anyway, but at least I was

John Julius Cannon's. I'd have been his child. I've *been* his child. As it is I'm no more than a bye blow like she said."

All that shock and sorrow and bitter grief. All the years they had been apart. And none of it was true.

Sick anger tore him like a physical pain, and he could not know if he cried out.

He turned abruptly. Phineas would be missing him.

In the morning after little sleep, he went to him, where he was settling to his breakfast in the vast sitting room of the suite. The chandeliers were lit and the fire crackled warmly in the grate, cheerful counterpart to his night of sorrow and regret.

"Ah, Owen. Come and have some breakfast."

"Thank you, sir. I had it with Bess."

The sky of the new morning was brilliant blue and the icicles were beginning to crack and fall outside the windows. The thaw had come.

"Sir," said Owen, unable to bear the distraction of trivial conversation about breakfast. "Sir. I want to ask you for a month away. I have to go to Ireland. And when I come back I shall be bringing my wife."

This time it hadn't even occurred to him that he should stay there.

Chapter 20

HE heeded neither the thundering seas of spring, nor the comforts and company of the *Olympic* in which he crossed; beginning to gain true consciousness and understanding of where he was going only as they were drawing into Queenstown, past the outthrust arm of the Old Head of Kinsale, and the incomparable green of the soft hills along the shores of County Cork.

Ireland. Half New York would give its immortal soul to be where he was now.

After a great deal of thought he had decided not to tell them he was coming. Lest before he could say anything, Antonia would disappear again. He spent a night in Cork City within earshot of the bells, and slowly wandered the wide streets, savoring the Irish accents and the half-forgotten haunting smell of turf. Like the returned wanderer he was, he lingered over the bacon and cabbage at his dinner in the gloomy cavernous hotel dining room; the smoke of wet turf filling the room like a fog. He thought unbelievingly of the warmth and luxury and the glittering chandeliers of the Waldorf, and turned back to the two big cups of scalding tea, and the rough brown bread and salty yellow butter with the taste of the bog in it. Smiling at himself, he knew he was behaving like any returned immigrant, and went off to find out about trains for the morning, before he began to buttonhole some unfortunate fellow guest with his traveler's tales.

There was a long wait at Limerick Junction in the morning, cringing from the wind that raked across the flat green fields, and trying to make himself understand that by evening he would be with Antonia. Never for one moment did he doubt that all would be well between them as soon as he told her what he had found out. But the woman must confirm it. Herself. She must be made to admit to her lies to John Julius. Only from her, he sensed, would Antonia believe the truth.

After the change of trains he watched, with pleasure he could hardly differentiate from pain, as loved landmark after loved landmark appeared on what was once the voyage of delight down to the West; and Owenscourt. The stone walls threading up the green-and-yellow hills, touched with the shadows of the sailing clouds. The low-lying sedgy fields from which the cattle lifted slow soft eyes to the noise of the passing train. The thistles still spangled with the glittering webs of a passing shower. Athenry; the flat plains stretching away into the misty distance beyond the dark hulk of the old castle. The first of the sea; reaching into the green land with shining fingers at Oranmore. And in the end, unbelievably, the gray city of Galway, that he had left seven years before in loneliness and grief and pouring rain.

When he reached Oughterard in his hired trap, it was almost dark, the last light of the limpid evening trapped in the shining lake; the birches on the islands trembling black against an opal sky.

He turned the trap quietly down the river lane at Slaughterford, in full dark night, peering about him, not knowing where he must go. He had last seen it some time when he was little, and out on a journey with John Julius and it had been a ruin. Now the mill loomed high above him in the darkness, and as he passed it and turned in an open gate into a yard, lights glowed behind red curtains from a long low dwelling. As he stopped he could hear the stir of horses in the stables and the rush of the waterfall beyond the mill; smell the dank chill of the pond.

Antonia. He felt his breath come short as if he had been running all the way from Queenstown.

He fumbled the reins into a ring beside the door, and knew that this time there would be no mistake. Above him was a big lamp, bracketed to the wall as in a city street, and when Antonia opened the door to his knock its light fell on both of them. Giving him the unquenchable memory of the flood of bewildered joy that lit her face, that died as quick as it had risen, like a turned-down lamp, and she was warmly and correctly welcoming, but he had seen it, and it had armed him.

"John Julius!" Even in the emotional moment, Owen noticed that she didn't call him Father anymore. Well, they would change all that. "John Julius," she cried. "Come and see who we have here."

He heard John Julius's voice asking wasn't it Jerry Fineghan he was expecting, and Antonia took his hand to lead him in. At her touch he wanted to fling his arms about her, but her cool and correct affection held him at bay, leaving him clinging to the recollection of her face when she had seen him first. John Julius came then, from some inner room, and at once provided all that was lacking in a warm spontaneous delight at seeing him, wrapping him in a great bear hug, and unashamedly wiping the tears from his cheeks.

"Owen, boy! God bless you! Let me look at you. You're a sight for sore eyes. Why didn't you say you were coming?" He held him off at arm's length, and his eyes creased in a wry smile. " 'Tis clear you haven't come home for the lack of money to stay out there."

"Oh, John Julius!"

Nothing had prepared Owen for the depth to which he was stirred, to see again the steadfast weatherbeaten face.

The thick black hair was no less, but streaked with gray, and the man looked tired at the end of his day, but there was a deep contentment and satisfaction in his eyes that had not been there before.

"John Julius, I am glad to see you."

Owen spoke from his heart, and wished he could speak as warmly and as easily to Antonia, to whom he wanted to say everything and could say nothing, pushed into her own attitude of cool affection.

There were all the questions and answers of welcome then, and again why hadn't he let them know? To that he gave the straight answer, and looked the girl in her evasive eyes—that he had not wanted to give Antonia the chance to run away again. Even she laughed then, turning up the lamps to light his welcome in the warm room and whirling away to go and get James and his young wife from their cottage beyond the stables.

Owen watched her go with grave eyes and would have sold his soul to be able to say that she was looking well. Honesty compelled him sadly to acknowledge that she was little more than a bundle of awkward skin and bones, her eyes enormous under the shining sweep of her black hair.

John Julius followed his gaze.

"John Julius, she is very thin." For all there was to see and talk about, he could think of nothing else but her. "Very thin."

The older man passed his hand across his hair as if to try and smooth away some perpetual trouble.

"She devours herself," was all he had time to say before she was back with James, grown fair and square and steady as he had promised, with a little plump blushing wife more suited, it seemed to Owen, to the schoolroom. B'God, he thought, he must be getting very old himself.

There was how was the Canon? And had they heard from Emmett? And willya listen to the Yankee accent. They laughed and mimicked him, but when the talk came round as it must do to Owenscourt and Holly House, John Julius said let them for God's sake be sitting round the table to do the talking, for Owen must be famished. "Had Antonia," he asked, "enough to go round?"

"Of course," she said. "Do I not always give satisfaction as your housekeeper, John Julius?" The bitterness of the small remark stilled the happy room. But Owen sat down without speaking, leaving them all to think, as they clearly did, that he was here to take back Owenscourt.

James's little wife went racing back to the cottage for buttermilk and barmbrack and cheese, and miraculously there was a goose roasting in the range.

"I wouldn't tell the others," Antonia said, repenting her unkindness. "But I knew you were coming."

For one moment their eyes met, filled with all that was left unsaid, and this time she did not look away. B'God, thought Owen, it was like coming to grips with a cobweb.

John Julius got out the tall black bottle of whisky, and the good glasses from the agent's house, that Owen last remembered on that night of sorrow he had come here to undo. He held his up to the light, savoring the rich gold of the good malt, and thinking it fitting they should be using them again tonight. Full, rich, excited welcome flowered in the lamplit room, heady with the smell of the roasting goose; a big farm kitchen like any other, but with touches of imaginative comfort like the dark-red curtains at the windows and the red cushions on all the polished chairs. These, he knew, would all have been made by his difficult and prickly love. Please God, it would not be long before she was making a home for him.

In the end it had to come, when all the chatter died.

John Julius pushed his plate away, and leaned back before the spent carcass of the goose.

"Well, Owen," he said, "I've no doubt you've come back to Owenscourt and there's no one will bid you welcome like myself. 'Tis time the house was opened up. We did all you said about the locks, and as I told you, the house was sealed on the morning I had your letter of instructions. B'God that's five years back."

"Thank you, John Julius."

"To the best of our knowledge," John Julius went on, and Owen could feel all their eyes fixed on him—the landowner come to take his own—"there's no one been inside it since. Either James or I go over every week or two and I'm afraid, Owen, it will need a lot. The whole place is in poor fettle, even lichen growing on the stone of the house. It'll need—"

It was all obviously on the top of his mind, all his thoughts ready as to what needed to be done; waiting only for the coming of Owen, and now Owen was here. It was Owen who stopped him.

"No, John Julius," he said, steadily, and set down his glass. "I haven't come back to take Owenscourt. Not yet."

The combined astonishment and disappointment in their faces was like a blow, and he felt shamed to do it to them.

"Well, then?" John Julius managed to say in the end.

All their eyes were fixed on him, the room still.

"I have come," said Owen, knowing the next blow would be even greater than the last, "to marry your daughter."

Antonia leapt from the table immediately and made to run, but he grabbed her by a fold of her blue dress and held her tight.

"Listen to me, all of you." Thank God for the whisky that had loosened his tongue a bit. "I mean your *daughter*, John Julius."

Still holding to Antonia's skirt, looking round the ring of their mesmerized faces, he told them the story of the bitter winter night, and his extraordinary encounter with Bunaffrey. In the warm, simple room, full of the smell of roast goose and baking bread, he found it difficult, himself, to believe in the brilliant crowds and the glittering chandeliers and the velvet spendor of the Waldorf.

"Is that true, Owen?"

It was John Julius who spoke at last and his voice was hoarse with emotion and with curdling anger.

"Would I come half across the world," Owen said, "to tell you a lie?" Beside him he felt the rigidity slowly fading from Antonia, and then she slid suddenly down again into her chair, her face buried in her hands. Owen leaned over gently and eased them away, and his fingers were wet with her tears.

"Don't cry, my love," he said to her. "It's not a time for crying."

She looked at him with great swimming eyes full of love and gratitude, and with an astonished lurch of his heart Owen felt his troubles to be over. Phin Turnbull had promised him the white clapboard cottage on the far side of the lake. They could put a family in it.

John Julius's face was like stone. Too stricken at the needless cruelty to turn yet to Antonia.

"You are right, you know," he said. "I never knew man or woman yet who had set eyes on Bunaffrey. . . . The mean, double-dyed, deceitful—"

"Father," said James, and John Julius let go a long breath and smiled.

"My darling girl," he said to Antonia then, and Owen had to look away from the tenderness in his face. "I never for one second believed it and you know I didn't."

"Nor I," said Owen.

"Nor I," echoed James.

"So there was only you. Running away from nothing."

Owen grinned at her, and still poised on the edge of tears, she managed to smile back.

"It was enough," she said.

"True for you." John Julius hit the table with his fist, his anger not yet spent. "True for you. And the woman herself must admit to the lie."

They looked at him, considering this.

"Yes," Owen said then. "We'll go over tomorrow."

In the charged moment he could not yet know how he would feel about going to Holly House when he had decided not to go to Owenscourt, but such a woman was not to be trusted with one person alone. She could say anything. Also he was afraid that were he alone, John Julius might give way to the violence inherent in his clenched fist and knotted forehead.

Antonia stood up then and cleared the table and busied herself about the range, coming back with a great dish of apples, sweet with dark brown sugar and awash with cream.

"I am going too," she said.

"No," cried Owen and John Julius together and she looked from one of them to the other, the big spoon in her hand.

"She told the lie to my face," she said, "just to see me suffer. She can admit it now to my face, and may the good God help me keep my hands off her."

The following afternoon it all seemed to Owen as vague and distant as a remembered dream, when he turned into the gates of Holly House with John Julius and Antonia beside him in the trap.

John Julius's face was still stony with rage, brooding over all the years of security and love, with him and also with Owen, that had been denied to the girl who had sat white faced and silent all the long drive through the misty afternoon.

The bogland was haunted and lonely, hung with damp, the curlews calling sadly from the invisible distances; but up on the higher road toward Owenscourt the young leaves were breaking on the trees, hazing the branches with yellow, and the ditches were tall with grasses in the first green rush of spring.

Owen had skillfully held off all talk about Owenscourt, and was deeply glad that along the road, it was Holly House came first. The tall ornamental gates stood open, a lack of care in the shrewd eyes of both men, and the small lodge beside it was empty, its garden untended and its windows blank. The drive along the river that had been so sprucely graveled was unraked, and weeds sprouted in the deep ruts.

"I have been hearing from the Canon, these last five years or so," said John Julius sardonically, "that the honeymoon is over."

Five years, thought Owen, and smiled with grim satisfaction. Since his birthday and the locks on Owenscourt. He looked up at the rise of holly-crowned hill that lay between him and his own house, and wondered sadly what state it was in, not even having had the benefit of a few years of prodigal spending; then put it firmly from his mind as John Julius whirled the trap to a halt before the portico.

A very young and cheeky maid opened the front door, and would have kept them waiting in the long hall were it not that John Julius swept her aside with one of his big hands.

"We know where we are going, thank you."

Owen could scarcely bear to look at it, oppressed with memories of cold and hunger and bitter grief, but he was compelled to give an admiring glance to the character of the long hall, warm now with velvet drapes and buttoned ottomans and small tables. But it was cold and the furniture looked uncared for.

"All in the same go-down," John Julius said crisply, but there was no time to think of it. Already they were at the salon door. With an instinct to protect her, although, God knew, the damage had long been done, Owen moved close to Antonia and took her arm. Impatiently she shook him off, and side by side they followed John Julius through the double doors he had flung open. Nor did Owen trouble to close them at his back.

Peggy was sitting with a shawl around her shoulders playing patience on an elegant baize-topped cardtable beside a fire of smoking turf. With a sick lurch of memory Owen recognized it as one on which his mother used to play with him and Emmett in the long lost world of Gardiner Street. The woman herself looked staggeringly no different, the gray in the tendril hair the same as the silver it had always been. The body underneath the shawl was heavier, but the hands placing the cards had lost none of their limp-wristed delicacy. Only the lines of petulance and discontent were new, graven deep on the still lovely face.

As they came in she looked them all over for one second and then carefully turned over and laid down two more cards before she gave them her attention, her lashes shrouding her fine eyes. She surveyed them then as if it were yesterday she had last seen them all, and under her gaze Owen remembered the phaeton whirling up the village street, splattering him from head to foot with mud. She would do the same again, her look said, and with pleasure, did she ever get the chance.

"Well," she drawled, and carefully laid down another card. "What brings the happy family here?"

John Julius's fists closed but he held on to himself and told her quietly, knowing that anger would give her no more than pleasure, what brought them there. She showed no reaction at all other than to flick a provocative glance up and down Owen's clothes.

"I'd heard," she said, "you went to the States. You would seem to have found the pot of gold."

John Julius looked round the chill-looking dusty room.

"Which is more than you did, madam," he said coldly. "Or if you did, you failed to hold on to it. You will tell us now please that what you said about your daughter was a lie. No more."

Peggy looked exasperated and more than a little bored.

"Of course it was a lie." She spotted a sequence and moved over the cards. "To my knowledge Bunaffrey never came near his lands. I'd have said anyone." Antonia made a choked inarticulate sound.

"Why?" she managed to say. "Why?"

"Why?" Now she lifted her eyes and gave Antonia her full attention and there was not in her face one hint of love or even concern for the dark, lovely girl who was her daughter. "I wanted rid of the lot of you. All this talk of going back to Cannon's Mills. I wanted something better."

"And you," she could have said, but didn't: "You were growing more beautiful beneath my eyes while I grew old, and I could not endure it."

Once again John Julius looked round him.

"You could have done worse than Cannon's Mills," he said. "I see your fine man has closed the purse strings again. He was never one to keep them open long."

Her face turned to John Julius was sharp with venom, and Owen knew he had hit the nail on the head. She was as poor as she had ever been, surrounded by all the fading grandeur of the last fling of Holly House. She should make the best of it. It would never come up again while she was in it.

Antonia could not leave it alone.

"How," she demanded of Peggy. "How do we know this time it is the truth? How do we believe you?"

Peggy laid down the cards slowly and her smile was something to recoil from.

"Your father should remember."

Lifting a pale finger she beckoned to John Julius, who went reluctantly to stand beside her at the fire. Again she beckoned until he put his head down close to her, thinking that by God, she was never done yet with the dregs of the Paris perfumes. Never for one second did the woman take her eyes from the girl, and looking steadily at her, she whispered to John Julius some suggestion of memory so lewd that he blushed scarlet to the edges of his hair, and Antonia turned and raced from the room. Owen would have followed, but for the terror that did he leave John Julius alone with Peggy there could be murder done.

Somehow he dragged him out the open doors and past the gawping maid, and at the table Peggy moved another card.

In the trap they sat silent all the way back down to the grubby crested gates, not wanting to meet each other's eyes; every one of them feeling ashamed and sullied by her, Owen sick with rage that what should have been Antonia's triumph had been turned into some fresh dreadful damage, that he could not yet estimate. She had been wrong to come.

Fiercely John Julius pulled himself together. With the help of God, it was the last any one of them would see of her.

"Come on, now," he said. "Put it all behind us and we'll go on to Owenscourt."

Painfully Owen had to explain to them that he didn't want to. That he could not bear to, although he didn't say that. With difficulty, the trap standing in the middle of the muddy road, he had to tell that he was not yet ready to come back. Apart from the way the fascinating tendrils of his different life had closed around him, he had as good as promised

Phineas Turnbull five years more in return for the gift of the cottage beside the lake.

Then he and Antonia, with, please God, another heir, would come back to Owenscourt together. If he went now to look at it, he would never bring himself to leave it again. Nor was this a good moment for talking marriage to Antonia. Although it must be done quickly. There was little more than a fortnight, and Emmett to see, before he must head back for Queenstown and the *Olympic*, in the time that Turnbull had given him.

He gave a tug to the reins.

"Turn the trap the other way," he said to John Julius, who was staring at him in perplexity, trying to make the best sense he could of what he was saying. Antonia stared away into the misty afternoon as if she had never heard of Owenscourt, or even of Owen, her withdrawn face buried in the collar of her coat. John Julius's eyes flickered with a new, thoughtful understanding over Owen's beautiful tweed suit, and the fine highly polished boots. Not only, as that fiend of a woman had said, did he appear to have found the pot of gold, but the end of the rainbow might be proving more attractive than Owenscourt. Matt, God rest him, would be rolling in his grave, and Celia too.

The heir to Owenscourt and ready to settle a thousand miles away.

"The other way," Owen cried, and John Julius would never know what it had cost him. "The other way. We'll go and see the Canon."

There was so little time for anything. Although this time the hopes and plans could surely suffer no defeat.

No time at all for the astonished shock when once again Antonia rejected him. He had walked her out and up along the river road on the soft loam below the arching beeches, just beginning to throw the first solid shadows of their new leaves. Across the boulders at the ford, and then back along the other side of the river to where the peat-brown water turned into a gleaming sheet as it hissed and sang down the falls before the mill. They settled, Antonia with a sort of gentle patience, in a sheltered spot in the sun, hidden from the house and mill on the other side of the dark pool, by a copse of alders in the first golden flush of spring. Owen looked about him once again, touched with almost unbearable pleasure at the unforgettable green of this, his half-forgotten country.

As in New York, there had been nothing in her gentle acquiescence to warn him. Not one word said about the scene of yesterday afternoon, all ugliness forgotten by the evening of wonderful conviviality provided from his small stores by the aging Canon, who had unashamedly wept when he found who was pounding at his door.

All Antonia's problems, Owen now assumed, were solved. God in heaven, he thought with a certain self-righteousness, he had come all the way from New York to solve them. And gone all the way there in the first place for the same reason, although so much had happened since that he had begun to forget that.

Yet she refused him once again, her voice tight, her dark head bent, refusing to meet his eyes, stripping a long sharp blade of grass so fiercely, she brought blood to her fingers.

"It wouldn't work, Owen."

"But, Antonia! Look at me." He put a hand under her chin and lifted the unwilling face, and still the blue eyes slid away. "Antonia. You know you love me. You know you do. What is it?"

The big eyes came round to meet his in the end, pools of such sadness as made him cry aloud.

"Antonia. My dear love. Tell me what it is."

Surely most girls were pleased by a proposal. He was clean and respectable and had enough to keep them well, and even her father's wholehearted approval. And he knew she loved him. What in God's name was on her?

"Why, my darling, why?"

"It would never work."

"For the love of God, why not?"

"Well, look at you."

"What's wrong with me?"

"That suit you have on must have cost a year of a man's life. And the silk shirt—and—and you'd ask me to go back there and live in the house where I was a servant, and the butt I'd be of all of them."

"We'd have our own house, Antonia. And our own servants. And I as much as promised the boss. Anyway they all liked you there. They knew you were no real servant. They'd be no trouble. Anywhere. I promise you. We'd live our own lives."

Even as he said it, he knew this was not strictly true. She, as well as he, would be drawn into the affairs of the big house. And carry it all off perfectly, if only she would get rid of these nonsensical ideas.

"But I was a servant there, Owen. I was. I was. And I'd be no use as the wife of a posh New York dandy. Nor come to that, for the heir to Owenscourt."

"The owner of Owenscourt," he corrected her, and then said, "for pity's sake. You'll be telling me next again that you were born in a stable."

"Well, I was."

"Well, you know the answer to that one."

He remembered her when they were small children, railing at him that he was too well dressed, and different from her. Jealousy? Or, more likely, heartbreaking insecurity even then, at the hands of her deplorable mother. Pity for her racked him like a physical pain.

"Antonia."

He took her hands then, and pulled her close to him and kissed her unprotesting face, where he could taste her tears salt on her cheeks. Encouraged by her lack of withdrawal his mouth moved down to her lips, and for one moment of sweet complete surrender, he held the willing softness of them underneath his own. Without warning, she burst into a torrent of tears and scrambled to her feet, flaying her blind way out through the thicket of young trees.

Kneeling up, he watched her go, but did not try to follow her.

In the morning he drove over to Tuam to seek the advice

of the Canon, for he felt himself out of his depth. His aging, balding little friend could only shake his head and give him little help.

"Well, the days are gone, Owen," he said sadly, "when you could fling her on a horse and drag her onto the boat after you by force. The poor girl is deeply unhappy, I think, and is terrified she will pass on her unhappiness to you and ruin your life. She regards herself as a danger to you."

"Doesn't it occur to her that I might pass on happiness to her?" He stared out the window, and half his mind noticed that the sky above the village was a strange sulphurous yellow. "She cannot," he said, "seem to admit the existence of happiness."

"It does not seem to her a possible idea," the priest answered. He looked tired and a little old. Not old, Owen thought. His father would have been fifty-two, and his cousin was no more than a few years older. Worn, rather, by vicarious hardship and sorrow in his poor struggling parish. Owen felt guilty for touching him with his troubles when, God knew, his work brought him enough of his own.

"I'm sorry, Father," he said. "You have no magic wand to wave for me any more than anybody else. I shouldn't have troubled you."

The priest looked at the tall, vigorous, and handsome young man, clearly on the crest of a successful life, even if it was not what they had all expected for him. And yet as poor and distressed as his most deprived parishioner, because he still couldn't gain what was closest to his heart.

"You should indeed have troubled me, Owen," he said. "Try and get her to marry you, son; everything else should follow, including happiness. It's amazing what a child or two could do. God bless you both. I'll pray for you."

No more, thought Owen, pulling on his gloves beside the trap. No more than he could reason out for himself, but how was he to bring it all about. In any case, for the moment, the thing was to get home before all the skies opened, for now that he was outside, the day had the look of something terrible.

As he drove from the last streets of the town, the countryside was bathed in a sick greenish light, turning the young grass livid; giving the budding trees some ponderous artificial weight, deadly still against the sulphurous sky. He whipped up the mare and as he raced along the empty road, he noticed that no wind stirred. In the farmyards the dogs were silent and the people stood outside their doors and stared up at the yellow sky and blessed themselves as if it were the Day of Judgment, or raced to the fowl runs to close the hens in shelter. In the fields the cattle already huddled underneath the trees, and all the birds had joined the eerie silence.

"Jesus!" said Owen, and looked fruitlessly around the well of the trap for an umbrella or a coat.

The yellow sky was turning black, and a sudden wind thrashed through the budding trees. He realized he must turn back now for shelter or face the open wastes of the bog. He was reluctant to go back. Help of God it wouldn't last long, and a bit of a wetting would do no harm. Whipping up the mare, who was as anxious to be home as he was, he set off briskly over the bog road.

By the time he reached the lanes leading to Slaughterford, his Wetzel suit that had annoyed Antonia was black with water, and the hair was plastered down the sides of his face below his cap. Water ran in streams from the horse's flanks. The bottom of the trap was truly a well, and the narrow road he had turned into, a muddy rushing torrent. Several times on the drenching journey over the bog road, he had had to stop, because he could see nothing through the driving wall of water, and was terrified that horse and trap and all would finish in the black depths of the bog. He was gasping with the effort of getting his breath in the ceaseless onslaught of the rain, but there was nothing now but keep on going.

At the ford the water was above the mare's fetlocks, and he had difficulty getting her out up the slippery bank at the far side; knowing his first moment of real fear. Aware of the yellowed water tearing past him towards the falls a quarter of a mile away. But there should be no danger to anyone.

John Julius was in Galway and the rest of them would be safely in the house or the mills.

The roar of the falls was deafening as he drove into the yard, and at first he didn't realize what it was. He put the frightened mare, trap and all, into the open sheds that lined the yard, and saw that James had done the same thing with the dray, backing it in and taking the big horse from the shafts; leaving it tied to a ring in the wall, rather than make the race round for the stables. He didn't wait to unharness the mare, caught suddenly by some dreadful anxiety, born of the silence and closed doors of the house and the thunder of the water beyond it; the groaning cracking strain that he realized was the mill wheel trying to drag its lashing; over everything was the baleful black-and-yellow sky and the remorseless streaming water.

There was no one in the house when he crashed in the front door. "Antonia," he yelled. "Antonia."

There was no sound but the rain hammering on the thatch and on the streaming windows, and he raced out again and across the yard and round the stables to the cottage.

James was there, and young Mary Anne, white with fear.

"I've had them lash the wheel," James yelled against the noise. "Does it come loose in this torrent, it will tear the mill down. And I've had the men drag the sacks from the ground floor. The river's coming in."

Owen could find no concern for the mill.

"Mary Anne, where's Antonia?"

"Antonia?" Her soft young mouth was trembling with fright. "She took the old punt up the river to get moorhens' eggs. Will she be— I never thought!"

James and Owen looked at each other for one appalled second but Owen was away first. He took the old dray horse, still in her traces, and grabbed a coil of rope off the wall. While James was still struggling to get the mare from the trap, he had the astonished animal going out of the gates at a canter she had not reached for years, taking the waterlogged road along the side of the river. Sliding on her wet back, he was pouring out an urgent torrent of prayers and pleas and curses to keep her moving.

Flossie, they had said they called her, this big one. Dear God, Flossie. He crashed his boots into her solid flanks and yelled into her ears and the water poured off both of them as if they were driving through a wall of it, his frantic eyes all the time on the gray mass of racing water that had been the gentle river of yesterday.

He found her in the end about half a mile above the ford, where the river widened enough to be called a small lake, dotted with the green rushy islands where the moorhens loved to lay. Most of the islands were no more now than the green tips of the rushes above the tide of water, and the punt was lodged against one of the biggest and the last of them. Or had she had the sense to steer it there? Already it was bumping and sliding on the submerged grass as the water rose to take that island like the rest. In a few minutes it would be flowing over it, and nothing then would stop the punt from the dark race headlong to the falls.

"Antonia," he yelled from Flossie's back and leapt off to throw the reins around a bush. God help the poor old thing, she was too astonished and winded to move anyway. Owen crashed his way as if they were matchwood through the alders at the river's edge, already halfway under water.

"Antonia!"

She was kneeling in the front of the punt, staring away down the river towards the falls, and in the moment that she heard him and turned her face to him, he knew with cold terrible certainty that she was not glad to see him. The enormous eyes in the blanched face stared across the roaring water at him, and he knew that if she came with him at all it would be unwillingly; that he would be dragging her away from something beckoning more winningly than any life that he could promise her. He felt colder than the rain that soaked his suit; touched with the chill of pure horror.

"Antonia! The rope!"

His voice was hoarse with his desperation, knowing her

capable of sliding away there before his eyes into the monstrous yellow day. But when at his third attempt the end of the rope crashed into the punt, she moved like a sleepwalker and took it; and secured it expertly then to the painter.

Owen raced back to Flossie, chattering inanely at her long willing face, and tied the rope to the hames on the top of her collar. He licked the streaming rain from round his mouth so he could even breathe, and began to lead her.

"Come on now, girl," he said to her. "Easy, easy."

Carefully he led her away from the riverbank back into the trees. Nothing happened. And nothing. The damned rope was too long, he thought. Antonia hadn't tied the knot properly and the punt had cast adrift and there was nothing he could do. Clean panic was beginning to fill his mind when he felt the chuck of the rope as it took the strain, and then he let himself look round.

"Go on, girl," he said to Flossie and slapped the streaming flank.

Slowly, agonizingly slowly, the punt was turning, the rope holding, and Antonia was paddling with her hands to help it round.

"Pull, Flossie. Pull!" he yelled at the old horse, and seized a branch to belabor her. "Pull!"

Steadily old Flossie plodded over the road and into the trees, glad to find something to do that she could understand, and the punt crept steadily across the race that fought to turn it and drag it off towards the falls.

James was there then, on the mare from the trap, to plow into the bushes and take the straining rope, steering the heavy old punt until it was wedged among the alders, where she was able to haul herself in by the slippery streaming branches until she could reach her brother's hand.

Owen said little, speechless with shock; not so much from the risk of her death as from the sick moment when he had felt certain she found it preferable to him; searching to summon back his confidence that there was no trouble they would not solve, were they together. That it was enough that she loved him.

He had recovered by evening, when the blackbirds fluted in the dripping trees and the gentle sun glittered in the puddles of the yard, denying like a forgotten dream the violence and horror of the afternoon. Owen came to search for her and found her scattering grain for the bewildered white doves, in her little garden along the bank of the swollen river. She looked pale and quiet, but smiled at him as he came across to her from the house.

"Thank you, Owen," she said to him. "You saved my life."

He took the bowl from her, and scattered the grain himself among the white birds milling around their feet, demanding all her attention, to what he had come to say.

"Thank me?" he said to her, and she looked at him surprised by something in his tone. "You are going to do more than that. You are going to marry me."

Immediately the defensive shadow crept across her face, and she looked down at the birds, and would not meet his eyes.

"Why should it make any difference?"

Owen took the lovely turned-away face by the chin, and forced her to look at him, and even her reluctant eyes softened at the determined love in his.

"Because, Antonia, my dearest love," he said. "I didn't pull you out of that goddam river for anybody else."

Chapter 21

In that year after they were married, Owen thought incessantly about Owenscourt. Having at long last got Antonia at his side, then both halves of the dream were now attainable. He would indeed, as he had so long planned against all defeats, go back to his inheritance and stand on the portico of Owenscourt, with Antonia beside him, and look down towards the lake and know it his. Now, to his passionate delight, the picture was enlarged, for Antonia was almost immediately with child. By the time they went back, there would be another heir, some four years old, to stand beside them. To ride as he had ridden, on a shaggy pony at his father's heels; a new Boru running at their side. Learning, as he had learnt in his time, all the ways that Owenscourt would one day belong to him.

Like his mother before him, he never doubted for one second that his firstborn child would be his son.

He had been deeply touched by the pleasure and affection, tinged with surprise, with which he had been received back by Phineas Turnbull and his quiet wife after his time away.

"Did you not think, sir, that we'd come back?" he asked Turnbull.

"Well, son, who could blame you if you didn't? I know I have a mighty powerful rival in that heap of stones across the ocean."

"I said five years, sir."

"Thank you, my boy."

He was touched by the older man's gratitude, aware long ago that every man of Turnbull's wealth and interests had an aide similar to himself. But that very few enjoyed the unspoken, total confidence of the intimate family life that Turnbull had given him.

"Sir. Mr. Turnbull." He put it into words. "I think I am mighty fortunate to be able to come back. And Antonia with me."

Turnbull smiled slightly and bent his head in acknowledgment.

"The cottage is ready," he said. "She's a beautiful girl. You make a fine young couple."

To his deep relief Antonia had taken the return to Glendon House quite calmly in the end. As though the gray day of the flooded river had at last washed away her stubborn prejudices. And Jolliff was his impassive and uncritical self, in welcoming at the front door the girl who had walked out the back.

Only Phineas Turnbull would have called the house a cottage, with its four bedrooms and a little annex at the end of the old-fashioned garden, for two servants. There was a colonnaded porch all along the front of the house where they could sit and watch the blaze of color change in the gardens of the house up the gentle slope above them. On that side of Glendon House a circular pillared portico led from the drawing rooms down flights of marble steps into the formal gardens, where from their distance the fountains were no more than a haze of tossing mist. Cast-iron stags as large as life with spreading antlers guarded the archway from the gardens on to the long slope down to the lake. Privacy on both sides was defended by a holly hedge along the palings of the little house, thick and rich as Christmas itself.

When Phineas was at home for the last three days of every week, Owen would walk up the slope of grass and into the house through the gardens, rarely failing to lay a hand on the flank of one of the cold iron stags, thinking how he and Emmett would never have been off their backs had they been at Owenscourt. They would be here for the little chap that was coming.

He brooded a little on the idea of Emmett being an uncle, wondering if even a child would penetrate the smooth cocoon of almost meaningless urbanity that now surrounded him. As though the realities of his life were for him and for him alone, and no glimpse must be given even to the outsider that was Owen. It irritated Owen, still feeling in his heart that Emmett's withdrawal had been unnecessary, and that soreness caused by his smiling smooth disinterest only faded gradually as he settled back into the march of his own days.

"You know," he said to Antonia one morning as he kissed her good-bye at the white gate in the holly hedge. The sun was blazing even so early in the day, and the thrumming bees gorged themselves in the banks of blue delphinium and scented phlox. He was looking up at the house, sunblinds out on all the windows in the same color as the servants' liveries, heavily fringed with white. It looked rich and well cared for and splendid, opening to yet another day of its gentle sheltered life. "You know, when I first stood up there with my toes out through my boots, I told myself it was no bigger than Owenscourt. I'd only seen the middle bit at the front and after that I was damned if I'd admit that I was wrong. We could lose Owenscourt in the garden wing. It's as well we'll have the boy back there before he remembers this and thinks we've cheated him. What is it?"

Antonia had wheeled away from him towards the front door, rubbing furiously with the end of her sleeve at the brass door knocker.

"This is enough for me," she flung at him, across her

shoulder and he shrugged and smiled and shut the gate, thinking she must be feeling the heat or the baby or both.

It was the first sign of the old prickly hostility that she had offered him. She was always sharp and tart of tongue, but often with it so hilariously funny that their little house was full of laughter. To Owen alone she showed the sweet and tender disposition behind her diffident smile; bringing to him, now she had capitulated, a love so tender and so humble that often he longed to shake her and tell her for God's sake to put a proper value on herself.

His love for her had consumed him most of his life, even before he was aware of it, and still it grew with every day they were together. Secretly he thanked God that his worst fears were not being realized. She would seem at long last to be content.

In that summer they were to have as near a honeymoon as possible, apart from the journey on the *Olympic*, furrowing its way back through mountainous spring seas. Phineas Turnbull, furious and resentful of a heart that was beginning to give a little trouble without instruction from himself, had been ordered that his summer vacation at New Bedford must indeed be a vacation; all work left behind.

"That means you, if you would wish it, Owen," he said. "I realize you only had the time standing on your heads on the steamer since you were married. You can have the place to yourselves."

Owen grimaced. The whole business of the wedding had been so helter skelter that neither he nor Antonia believed in it for a long time, and were certain that the entire *Olympic* had decided they were a couple in sin; an impression much helped on by their own bewildered and bemused expressions.

"That's good of you, sir. Will that be all right? I know Antonia would prefer it. She's not very comfortable with the child."

"I'll not need you for going fishing and sitting in the sun, and that seems all I am to be allowed."

The kindly gleam of the yellow eyes told him that even

these harmless pastimes would have been more acceptable were Owen there, and the young man was touched. Turnbull had been thin before. Now he was gaunt, the heavy veins traced purple on his bony temples.

"Have a good summer, son."

They waved the cavalcade away when the household left; the carriages and the wagonettes and the luggage wagons, and now a De Dion Bouton and a Daimler, and a Bugatti and one of the new Cords, all rigorously correctly chauffered. Jacques was no more than a wry memory.

The summer was theirs to while away, the whole estate at their disposal for drives and picnics and rowing on the sun-drenched lake. Antonia picked over with a noncommittal smile the elegant fittings of the Abercrombie and Fitch picnic baskets, and insisted on bringing her own lunch in a paper bag, and in his turn Owen strove to make no comment. Resolutely she declined to have anything to do with the big house or the staff that remained there, coming home from their outings through purple evenings to cook for Owen in their own kitchen in the white house beside the lake.

Yet, in the burgeoning summer, with the child growing within her, he congratulated himself that she seemed at last to be achieving the serenity he had always craved for her.

They drowsed one sultry afternoon on the glassy lake, the oars shipped and the boat immobile in the windless day, one of the offending picnic baskets between them, and Antonia delving firmly in her paper bag. Through his half-closed eyes Owen looked up at the sloping splendor of the formal gardens, the pinks and blues of high summer giving way to the autumn golds, darkened by the bulk of cypress and clipped yews, ranked around the marble steps. Before the archway the cast iron stags took the sun in their antlers, and seemed horned in light.

"I'm sorry for Phin Turnbull," he said absently.

"*Sorry* for him?" She stared at him amazed, a sandwich halfway to her mouth, too astonished to protest that the man had enough to feed a starving town. "*Sorry* for him!"

"I know you think he has too much," Owen said. "But I would never grudge it to him. He has worked as hard as any man for everything he has. I admire him."

Antonia snorted.

"No." Owen pursued his own thoughts and among them was a small disloyal one that they would have got a better picnic from the kitchen of the house. Antonia always seemed to want to behave as if they sat together at the bottom of the guillotine, and might be needing their last lump of bread when the dreaded aristos were dead. "No." He waved a hand over the sun-drenched scene. "All this and no heir. No one closer than a second cousin to have it all when he is gone."

"It may be he'll do something wise with it."

"Such as?"

"A convent or a school or something."

Owen felt saddened. She was quite untouched by the careful and loving creation of so much beauty. Turnbull had never been a spendthrift, and gave immense sums each year to charity. He wondered should he try and tell her of the real extravagances of the robber barons of the half century before. Of Jim Fisk and Diamond Jim Brady who would put a Christmas tree to shame. Or Bet-a-Million Gates, willing to wager that very sum on a fly going up the window of his railroad car.

Turnbull had never been such as these.

He gave it up before her closed and disapproving face, and bent over the picnic basket, merely observing that he thanked God he was going to have an heir for all he owned.

She clapped her hands over the baby as if to protect it from some terrible fate.

"What do you mean?"

"What do I mean?" He looked up, the sun catching the red lights in his hair. He was shocked to find still such a difference between their thoughts. "Antonia, dearest. You know that our child, and I am sure it will be a son, will be the heir to Owenscourt. And, please God, with it, all it will take to keep it up."

She stared at him, her eyes gone dark, her hands still clasped protectively across the child within her, and her lovely face sharpened with the old defensive look.

"That is something," she said slowly, "something that I try to forget."

In the silence, a cloud seemed to have fallen over the bright lake and the colored gardens, a chilly formless darkness of sorrow yet to come. Owen would not let it get a grip on him. As lightly as he could, he said:

"Well, you must remember it, Antonia. There is nothing will change it. In four years' time we will be going back to Owenscourt."

She said nothing, turning abruptly to hang over the side of the boat and dabble her hand in the water, the ruffle of her blue sunbonnet coming between him and her face.

All through the autumn he felt uneasily that she was using the baby as a shield; legitimately making it an excuse on all the occasions when she should have been at his side in the many social functions in the house. Both of the Turnbulls had made it clear to Owen that now he was married, they wished his wife to take her place in the pattern of their lives exactly as he had done himself, and it embarrassed him deeply to see their generous offers flouted; for all that she did it with a kiss and an evasive smile, and always the unarguable excuse that it was because of the baby.

Only with Christmas did the open trouble come, with the first snowdrifts curling like breakers down the slope above the lake, and packed along the top of the hedges. Owen had to go the long way round to the house now by the swept paths. Over along the lake road to the stables, and then up the carriage road.

It had taken him a long time to broach to Antonia the matter of Christmas, deeply sad himself that their first one should be spent apart, but knowing the necessity. Knowing too how difficult it was going to be to get Antonia to admit it.

"My love." He stood before the roaring fire in their snug white-painted sitting room, feeling the blood steal painfully back into his hands and feet after the numbing walk across the park, in the purple dusk. The lights of the big house had been blazing above him on the hill, his own gleaming its own special welcome among the snow-laden trees along the lakeshore. "My love, you do understand I must go to Palm Beach for Christmas. I cannot be let off again. There is too much on hand."

She looked up at him from a lapful of white sewing for the baby. Sharp. Already resentful.

"But you know I cannot travel. The boy is due in January."

"Not until the end of January," he corrected her gently, "or even into February." He was full of pain to see the familiar bitter look contracting her lovely face. "We feel it will be perfectly safe for you to stay up in the house with the housekeeper, who will look after you as I would myself. I will be back long before the end of January. Phin says I may come before them."

"Phin!" she echoed him, her mouth twisted with mockery. "And who else is 'we' that must discuss the coming of my baby?"

"Bess, of course. We have to arrange everything."

He spoke reasonably, not yet aware of the pit of jealousy into which he was falling.

"And who is Bess, to arrange everything for me? And what will be going on down there anyway, that that flat-faced dragon cannot handle without you?"

He turned away to look into the fire, sickened by the senseless description of the gentle, loyal, and remorselessly efficient Bess.

"It's only for this year," he said, to try and mollify her. "Next year you will be able to come too. And the child."

His look was soft at the thought of the faceless small one before the magic of the giant Christmas tree in the white airy house on Ocean Boulevard where Mrs. Turnbull held her Christmas with all the faithful tradition of her snowbound childhood in New Bedford.

The argument went on all evening, and ended in bitterness. With it, on Antonia's side, unconcealed contempt for people who would go across a continent for the pleasure of their Christmas, and the folly of Owen who would go with them. Just the same contempt as she held for the sort of man who would own Owenscourt and pass it to his son. And so want to call her child its heir.

"Well, what do you want, Antonia?" he shouted at her in the end. "What do you want? To have me go back to a shovel in the stables to satisfy some inferiority of yours?"

And was at once appalled and contrite, for she burst into tears and, heavy with his child, went lumbering from the room, gasping with uncontrollable sobs. It was long into the night before he had her quietened, and lay beside her wide awake, staring at the white reflection of the moonlight on the snow and asking himself where for her sake, for he loved her beyond bearing, did their future lie.

If maybe Phineas Turnbull would let him go before the agreed five years were up. He had money enough now. Surely if he got her back to Ireland and to Owenscourt she would be happy.

With Owenscourt. And the child.

He slept only as the first streaks of blue-and-scarlet dawn were drawn across the white slope of the snow, his arm protectively across Antonia, and disappointment and anxiety drawn even in his sleep across his face.

Although nothing occurred during his time away, he felt that she had not forgiven him. She smiled and spoke to him sweetly and agreed that she had been perfectly cared for and given a lovely Christmas. But her eyes would not meet his, sliding away from him, and he felt with a mounting anxiety that only her body remained with him. Her mind had retreated to one of those dark worlds of her own where none could reach her.

Desperately he reproached himself, and at the same time felt exasperated with her. He was not the only man who had to go away occasionally because his work demanded it. She was more fortunate than many, who would have been left alone completely, and for the birth of the child as well, to manage as she could. She had herself known the dreadful hardships of the west of Ireland. Indeed, for God's sake, were it not for his own father she herself would have been born on the roadside, or in Clifden Workhouse. She had also known the bitter grinding poverty of the city, and what it was like to bear a child in some tenement with two other families to the room. He expected her to be like he was; grateful without end for good fortune, and to the man who had dragged him out of all that; so that when the time came, they would be able to go, still young, back to their own life as well heeled as it demanded.

He tried to curb his exasperation and spoke to the doctor, who patted his arm and told him not to be anxious; such hostility was quite common in the last stages of pregnancy and would undoubtedly disappear with the birth of the child. Owen listened and hoped that he was right, remembering as he lay awake in the bitter nights, watching the firelight flickering on the ceiling, how this same senseless cold detachment had been apt to come into Antonia's eyes as long as he could remember her. And with as little reason go away, he comforted himself.

Through the dark frozen days he tried to jolly her along as he would coax a child and found her eyes on him often with contempt, as though his pathetic efforts were an insult to her intelligence. Almost with panic he felt that every day she went farther from him, and sick with helpless apprehension he could only wait for the coming of the baby to put everything right.

Matthew came on a brilliant day with the sun glittering on the snow, and the water for a few hours dripping from the icicles outside the windows. He was a healthy, perfect child, with a great shock of black hair and his mother's dark-blue eyes. In the moment of looking at him Owen forgot all his fears and apprehensions; wild with delight; seeing all he had longed for, and swept with certainty that this small scrap would have all the power to make his mother happy.

"Darling, Antonia. You're the greatest girl! My son! My heir!"

He looked down once more at the composed morsel in his arms, minute hands clenched.

"Look at the fists on him. The heir to Owenscourt, Antonia. The heir to Owenscourt."

Never had the fulfillment of all he longed for seemed so close.

In his exuberance he thought it was only because she was tired that the white lids dropped over her eyes and she turned her head away. He gave the baby back to the nurse, and came over to kiss her. She didn't open her eyes.

"I'll come back," he whispered. "I'll come back when you are rested. Antonia. We have a son."

During the next few days he began to feel almost sick thankfulness that the doctor had been right. She was all gentleness towards him and amazed and tender with the baby, as though astonished that she could have produced anything so perfect.

If she was unnaturally quiet, he put it down to her reasonable exhaustion after what had been a fairly difficult birth. Her room was filled with gifts, banked with flowers from the hothouses of the house, soft with perfume, and alight with Owen's happiness. Almost in silence she lay and looked at it all and at the baby's crib beside her bed, and except when he roused her by talking to her, her eyes were strange and lazy. As if only a small part of her mind was concerned with these outside unimportant things. All the rest of it turned inwards to what concerned her more deeply.

Owen only saw what was good, too blissful to notice anything else, only catching the warning flare of anger that told him he must tread carefully with all the plans that came tumbling out of him for the child and for Owenscourt together. She would be herself again, he thought happily, with the turn of the year. Once the weather changed and she was able to be out in the sun with the baby the last lingering troubles would go. She was so much better.

He could already see them in his mind, Antonia with the sun in her black hair, pushing the new basket carriage that already waited in the hall, a gift from Mrs. Turnbull.

He said all this to her, and she smiled with her old sweetness and agreed with him, but her eyes looked through him, vague and dark.

Nothing could touch Owen, his step as light as if the spring were already come, his brown eyes bright with excitement and delight and pride. He had Antonia, and he had his son. And in four years time they would have Owenscourt, and all the money they would need to restore it. The old world could be recreated. In the gray snow-laden days that brought a fresh fall with almost every dusk, he could find no fault with his world. Antonia would be fine now that the child had come.

It was a black and bitter day, the light gone even from the snow, when the house telephone rang beside him in the middle of a busy morning. The wind scoured the brittle snow along the slopes of the park and whistling round the eaves of the house. In the big hearth the fire blazed and the room was warm and comfortable against the cold outside, Bess at her big desk opposite him.

It was the nurse down at the cottage.

"Mr. O'Connor." Her voice was strangely calm and flat. "Mr. O'Connor, I think you'd better come down right away."

"What's wrong with him?"

"Oh—there's nothing wrong with the baby, sir. He's fine."

It never entered his head that anything could go wrong now with Antonia.

"What's the matter?"

"Mr. O'Connor. I just think you'd better come down right away."

He put the telephone back on its rest and stared at Bess as if he'd never seen her before.

"There's something wrong."

He didn't seem able to move, his legs bound by fear.

"Then you'd better get going, Owen."

It was she who got him his coat and helped him into it in silence and saw him out the side door, answering his look of mute appeal with the equally mute promise that in time she would do all she could to help with anything that had happened, but for the present, he must go alone.

There was no going across the path and he must take the long way round, beating against the wind, his ulster and face covered in a fine freezing snow. Shelter only came when he turned along the lake road, underneath the trees, and could already see his house, looking like a haven of comfort and security, the lamps all lit against the dark day.

The Irish servant girl was crying in the hall, and he took one look at her and raced for the stairs.

In the warm white bedroom with the dancing fire and pretty muslin drapes, Antonia appeared to be asleep, the lace bedspread hardly disturbed by her tall body, her dark hair spread across the pillows. Her eyes were closed and her beautiful face composed and tranquil in the lamplight, without sign of trouble or distress. The baby was gone from her side.

He stood there beside her, feeling no surprise, or as yet no grief, washed by the sick hollow certainty that he had failed her. The nurse held out a dark-blue bottle, and he became aware of a sweet heavy smell in the room. Laudanum. The doctor had given it to her before the baby was born when she couldn't sleep. Vaguely he looked at it.

"How much?" he asked her numbly.

"All of it."

"How did she get it?"

He was asking all the right questions. Postponing the moment when he must be still and silent, and know it true.

"She got out of bed sir." The girl was crying now. "She got out of bed while I was downstairs. I didn't think she could. She was still very weak. I didn't think she could for one moment."

He touched her on the arm.

"Don't reproach yourself."

She would have got it one way or the other, or if not that something else. He wheeled round suddenly.

"The boy?"

"He's perfectly all right, sir. It just didn't seem proper to leave him in here."

He stood a long silent moment looking down at her, at peace now from some long uncomprehended battle that belonged to her alone. There had become too much for her to fight.

"No note?" he asked the nurse.

"No, sir."

She struggled not to weep again, professional detachment not proof against the mortal sorrow in his face.

No note. Too preoccupied with her own flight into safety even to say good-bye. How did he fail her, that he could not have held her back?

"Get the doctor," he said to the weeping girl, and when she had left the room he knelt down beside the bed and laid his face on the limp, already cooling hand, letting the scalding tears come, knowing that she was not the only loss.

With her went the dreams of his life. There could never be one without the other.

When all was done and the house quiet in the evening, he stood with his small son in his arms and looked out the window of his little room, at a great sickle moon rising above the whirl of drifting snow. He looked down at the small crumpled face, drowned in sleep.

"It's all yours now, my son," he said sadly. "All to wait now for you. I could never go there without her."

Chapter 22

I'M sorry, Pop. I just don't want it. I sure hate to hurt you, but I just don't want it. I'm an American. I've planned my life and all I want to do. I've been very lucky to get into Harvard and I'm going there and then I'm going to settle down and marry Clancy."

Owen snorted.

"Clancy! What a name for a girl."

"It was her mother's maiden name," his son said patiently.

Anything would do as a target for Owen's irritability at the moment, plunged deep into the bitterness of his final disappointment over Owenscourt. He sat side by side with his son, Matthew, on two steamer chairs; on the sunny spotless upper deck of the *Mauretania* on her first day out of Southampton towards New York. He himself sat back, clutching the rug a little against the teasing breeze, but Matthew was sitting on the edge of his chair, watching restlessly the group of young people in white flannels and tennis dresses gather noisily farther along the deck where it was laid out for sports; their laughter carrying on the wind. He was dressed to join them. Only his affection and respect for his father, and his patient good manners, were keeping him where he was for another session of the argument that had been going on fruitlessly for weeks.

"You're only eighteen," Owen said. "How can you be so sure what you want?"

"How can you be so sure for me?" Matthew answered reasonably.

"It's your duty," said his father, and did not say what he thought. That the inheritance of Owenscourt should be in the young man's blood.

Matthew was still respectful but struggling hard not to lose his patience. His father simply would not understand. He tossed back the lock of black hair that fell so constantly down over his forehead.

"It was *your* duty, Pop," he said. "Owenscourt was your duty and you didn't want to take it. I can't see now why you want to wish it on me, when you never wanted it."

Never wanted it.

Owen was silent, staring out at the sea, touched with shock that this was how it appeared now to his son. The dream of his life that had always evaded him, relinquished in anguish when the boy's mother had died. Still cherished all the more strongly for the day when he would be old enough to take it over, and bring it to reality in the heel of the long hunt.

Now the boy sat there, as he had sat on other chairs for the last weeks, calmly and patiently, but with growing restlessness, saying that he didn't want it.

"Why don't you retire now, and take it over?" Matthew asked then. "You don't have to keep on working. It's time old Phin gave it up anyway, before he drops in his tracks. You take Owenscourt and settle down in it."

Sea gulls still screamed about the ship, and a gust of laughter came from the young people who were picking sides for games. Determined walkers passed and repassed along the deck, throwing the occasional curious glance at the obvious tension between son and father. Matthew looked over at his friends and his face creased with the effort to suppress his irritation. It was the first fight he had ever had with his father, who was asking something he was not prepared to give. His whole life! It was not fair of him.

His father answered him a little brusquely. He knew the answer.

"Because," he said, "your stepmother would never leave the States. You know that."

That had been the final severance. The payment for the solace of Bess in his loneliness. In any case, the restoration of the estate now was a young man's job. Past him now, he knew sadly.

"I suppose not," said Matthew wearily. No way out that way.

His answer was almost without interest, his eyes on the beginning of the game. The argument had gone on too long. His father made an angry gesture.

"Go on," he said. "Away and play your quoits or whatever it is. It's of more interest than what I have to say."

Matthew was too polite to agree with him, or to point out that he had said it all already. He was up and off along the deck; giving only a moment to thinking that all the fun of the crossing sure was more important to him than his father's fearful plans to bury him in this moss-grown ruin in Galway.

"Hi! Wait for me," he shouted at them, and they parted at once to admit him, acknowledged even in twenty-four hours as one of their leaders.

"C'mon, then, Matthew! C'mon and play. Come on my team!"

Owen watched him go with sad disappointment, feeling little of his usual pride in the boy's tall, dark good looks, so like his mother's. And in the easy charm that made friends for him wherever he set foot. At the moment all he could think of was the obstinacy that was causing him such astonished sorrow. The obdurate refusal to take the inheritance of Owenscourt. It wasn't as if he had taken the boy by surprise. He had talked to him all his life of Owenscourt and of the day when it would be his, never understanding that to the boy reared in New Jersey, it was little more than a fairy tale;

a saga of his grandparents and of his father's youth, that had no connection with the realities of his American life.

Matthew's statement that he himself had not wanted it had hurt him to the depths of his passionate love for the house, and all it stood for. The winds of circumstance had taken him and blown him by need or obligation of one kind or another away from all he so longed for. Matthew had no such ties. Only the clear choice either to take Owenscourt, with all the resources of the trust funds Owen had set up for him when he was twenty—wealth enough to restore it to all that it had ever been—or to ignore everything that had gone to make him, and remain in the States, one more faceless O'Connor among how many hundred thousand, no matter how successful he might be.

Owen stirred restlessly, almost in pain. It had never even occurred to him that the boy would not want Owenscourt once he had seen it. That the very stones of it would not beckon him. But Matthew had been coldly disinterested and then clearly appalled when he was told what was expected of him. The only person to raise excitement in him was the old gentleman in the place called Cannon's Mills, with the shock of white hair, and penetrating dark-blue eyes.

"Pop, I'm real proud he's my grandfather. He surely is a very special person. Why," he said regretfully, "did we never get to know him sooner? Was my mother like him?"

Yes and no, thought Owen, brooding on it all, his eyes on the gentle rise and fall of the mahogany rail against the sun-lit sea. Yes and no. He had not even thought of trying to take Matthew earlier to meet his grandfather; saving it all carefully through the racing years for the final drama of the boy coming home to his inheritance.

"Leave him alone," John Julius had said now, when Owen came to him full of his astonished bitterness. "Leave him alone. Don't push him. He's an Irishman all right. God keep him, he's a fine boy, Owen. It does my heart good to have known him. Antonia's son. He's an Irishman, only he doesn't know it yet."

"What can I do?"

"Nothing." John Julius was definite. "Nothing. If you push him, you will only drive him further away."

But Owen had been unable to resist pushing him, and this one now was only the last of many scenes.

Should he, he wondered, have taken the boy when he was younger? Got the idea into his head. There had been the war, he reminded himself, when no one could have gone to Europe without very good reason. And he was too busy anyway. The troubles in Ireland itself were only now simmering in an uneasy peace.

His mind ran over all the disappearing years since the night of Antonia's death, when he had vowed Owenscourt to the baby in his arms. Nearly twenty years, and he had barely felt them go; buried in the life of Phineas Turnbull, steadily amassing his own fortune; building up the trusts for Matthew so that he would be able in comfort to realize the dream he himself had laid aside.

When Matthew was twelve, Owen had married Bess. He knew almost with guilt that he didn't bring her love like he had brought to Antonia. No man was blessed twice in his life with such a passion; and rarely once. He brought to Bess respect and deep affection and the desperate needs of his own unassuaged loneliness. Bess, who had loved him since the first day he had walked into Glendon House, took all these things to her warm generous heart and forged of them a marriage that filled him with grateful pleasure, and slowly infinite depths of a different kind of love.

He smiled to himself remembering it.

He had been concerned about Matthew, who had had him to himself for twelve years, and with careful words had spoken to him about the idea of a new mother.

Matthew had regarded him with direct blue eyes.

"New mother, Pop? How can I? I never had an old one."

"She was yours, not mine," his attitude seemed to say, and Owen winced, but the boy raced on, his thin face bright with pleasure.

"But I'd sure like a mother, and I guess we couldn't do

better than Aunt Bess. I think it's great being married. When I grow up I'm going to marry Clancy."

Even then he had said it, Owen reflected now. At the time he was delighted to have his fears and anxieties blown away to nothing, and he and Bess were married in the little parish church of Tanglewood, and driven home in an open carriage for which Phineas Turnbull had procured two snow-white horses, drowned in the smell of roses and lilies of the valley, Matthew grinning among the flowers on the facing seat. Waiting at the house was a wedding breakfast that would not have shamed a prince, all provided by Phineas Turnbull, who recognized his own good fortune in the joining together of the mainstays of his empire.

Owen and Matthew and Bess lived in the greatest contentment in the cottage by the lake, where the bittersweet ghost of Antonia was at last laid to rest and serene, unquestioning happiness filled the rooms like sun.

Two years past Mrs. Turnbull had died of her vague and unnamed ailments with the same gentle dignity as she had lived. Without her Glendon House had grown quiet, apart from the needed entertaining for his business, hosted for Phineas by Owen and Bess. The old man, his brain still needle sharp, buried himself in his work as he had buried her in the marble vault out at New Bedford, and the grand entertaining in the house was seen no more.

He, and Owen with him, had not been bypassed by the remarkable profits of a world at war, moving astutely now through the unstable tangle of its aftermath. They had been emotionally removed from it since Matthew was too young, and Turnbull's only relative was a childless nephew not long younger than himself.

Owen stirred in his chair, not for the first time touched by a sense of guilt, that such a holocaust had almost in some measure passed him by. Yet he did not think he could have withstood it, had it lasted only a few more months and taken Matthew, who had been drilling, ready for it, with his corps at school. Ready to go without a thought, to one of those nameless graves in Flanders that they were tidying only now into neat rows across the mangled fields.

Ireland too had been marked and scarred by its own savage war, the beautiful Dublin of his childhood battered and blackened by the violence of the Easter Rising; the streets hung like a cloud with the tension and hostility. The green beautiful countryside was marred by the blackened shells of burnt-out houses and police barracks; the marching groups of the irregulars, their rifles slung. Around Owenscourt the country had been quiet, most of it in Irish hands from long back, although he heard Bunaffrey, poor harmless foolish man, had had his house burnt out above his head one wild December night. The influenza that had scoured Europe like a plague in the winter after the war had carried off the old Canon, God rest his soul. And Hugh Charles Healey, to whatever judgment he might have to face, and never a word spoken between them as to what had been done.

Owen sighed. Often he asked himself should he have pursued the man with all the might of lawyers his money could afford, but always the thought of his mother and her gentle excuses for him held him back. "Whatever he was, Owen," he could hear her saying, "he was my brother." She would say he had enough. Leave Hugh Charles alone. Now Hugh Charles was dead, and Owenscourt there for the taking.

Peggy D'Arcy, they told him, had long gone back to her own mess of gypsy relatives at Claremorris, having given up Hugh Charles as useless. Rumor had it that some of the finest horses in the new stables behind Holly House had gone there with her and everything she could in decency take out of the house. Hugh Charles had spent his last years living in cold and poverty in Holly House, with his two sons, exactly as he had lived there with Owen and Emmett. As if he had never had one penny of all that he had grabbed. And did he, growing old in loneliness, ever stop to think of all that he had done?

For a moment Owen smiled, relishing the end he hoped might still come to it all, and then stood up with an abrupt gesture, stopped again by Matthew's refusal to take his proper place.

He began to walk the polished deck, tilting gently as the great liner plowed over the blue spring sea. As he passed the young group in white he heard them all shouting at his son, crying encouragement in some game; as if his was the only name they knew, the girls' voices up above the rest. With a surge of warm pride he knew that it was always the same. Matthew, the easy and self-assured center of any crowd. He paused and turned to the rail, looking out over the distance of sunlit water. Although Matthew looked like Antonia, and a little like John Julius, he had the open and compelling character of his paternal grandfather. Owen's face grew soft remembering how, even as a child, he had been aware of the way everybody smiled when his father came into a room, and people turned toward him as if he was the light. By the time he was Matthew's age, he thought, his father had been seven years dead.

Angrily he banged his flat hand on the polished rail, and turned away from the sea.

What was the matter with the boy that he wouldn't go ahead and recreate it all?

At forty-five Owen had lost none of either his good looks or his good figure. The dark red hair was brushed now here and there with gray and his friendly manner had the patina of maturity; giving him a control and watchfulness, masked by his ready smile; a commanding presence that easily held its own. He had the world in his hands. Yet his son refused the one thing he had lived for since the day he had been born.

Pacing along the deck, he was oblivious of the many glances that followed him from among those speculating on the possible stars of the glittering social life that would throb through the ship in the days and nights to come. Admiring his good looks, knowing his name, fitting him hopefully into their plans.

He was still lost in his own problems that Matthew had

brought to a head, looking back on all the things that had kept Owenscourt empty through all these years. Nagged not with guilt but with grief that it should have been so. Telling himself it could not have been otherwise. Lack of money first to fight his uncle. When he was twenty-one he would have had just about enough money to open the doors and plow a field or two; and then back into the same dead grind of poverty. For who dare count on what his uncle would have left him. And that woman. Then his sense of obligation to Phineas Turnbull, and, in all honesty, the life he had given to him when he had been nothing. Then Antonia. Over her, the cold finger of sorrow touched him even to this day. He could never have gone back without her. She would have walked beside him at every step and dimmed his life with grief. Who knew whether he would have held to his vow as time passed had he not in loneliness married Bess? Who had become so much more to him than he had ever dreamed. Bess would never leave the States, nor indeed leave Phineas Turnbull while he lived.

Always through all his heart searchings he had looked with warm confidence to the day when Matthew would be old enough to take his place. Now the time had come and he rejected it as lightly as if it were a bag of proffered sweets, never seeming even to appreciate the value of the inheritance. To him it was no more than a run-down old house he didn't fancy.

What now? thought Owen, and remembered how he had sailed the same sea to bring Antonia back with him. What now? Should he sell it? With a violence of recoil that made him step aside as if from a physical blow, he rejected the idea. To sell Owenscourt would be to sell his own childhood; to sell that wonderful and special atmosphere in which he had grown as long as they were left to him; the atmosphere which in maturity he recognized as for the loving passion that it was, lying between his father and his mother. Touching with its richness the very air that filled the house. It would be selling his father on the white horse with Boru loping at his heels; selling the sun on the lake and his mother's voice about the rooms; selling all the memories that had never left him through the empty years.

People spoke to him and he stared at them blankly, oblivious of the fashionable morning parade beginning to fill the decks. Blindly he struggled to think of renouncing all these things after he had cherished them so long, with all the passion of the poorest immigrant, recalling in anguish the green fields of his home with the knowledge that he would never know them again. Struggling not to go back down the deck and take his handsome laughing son, and shake him until he had shaken him into reason.

Clancy would be at the root of it. She was dominated by her mother and her home, and Matthew would know that, shaping his life to the laid-down pattern of hers. Clancy would be no wife for Matthew, who needed to get back to Ireland, and come to grips with the massive task of Owenscourt, and in the end marry some suitable Irish girl, who understood the land as he would himself. His face softened a little. There was nothing wrong with Clancy for the right young man, and all his instincts told him that her mother would be aiming far higher than Matthew when it came to finding a husband. Were they not just about crossing on the ocean now, as she and Clancy set off to do the London season, and Clancy to be presented to the Queen of England no less, and the mother all prepared to lay her money out like flypaper in the hopes of catching an English lord.

And a neat and competent little wife Clancy would make him, straight and strong as a little tree, with her shining fair hair and beautiful teeth and her sharp clean American look. Born on the very same day as Matthew in the vast white Palladian house on the adjoining estate, which was owned by a second-generation Irish-American, whose father had made his pile in the silver lodes of Colorado; leaving his son to come East with it all when he died, in search of what his wife called a measure of culture, and of a less arduous way of making money.

Though having little on the surface in common, the two families had remained always on good terms, the door in the wall opened between the estates so that the two nursemaids had joined each other to push the children side by side in their carriages almost as soon as they were born. Matthew and Clancy had taken their first steps together; mounted their first ponies together; learnt their first lessons together until they had gone away to school.

For some reason there had never been another child to the McPartlands, so that Matthew and Clancy had grown together like sister and brother.

Until they were sixteen, when predictably they had fallen in love.

Owen dismissed it irritably. Calf love. They were too young to know what they were doing.

From among the crowd of young people Matthew watched with half an eye his father walking the deck and stopping in short irritable spurts, and knew exactly what was going on in his mind. His young mouth set with a firmness that matched Owen's own. All this stuff about Owenscourt had been great when he was a kid; stories told to him, sitting against his father's knee with the fire blazing and the snow heavy on the trees outside. He had loved the tales of the big gray house and the green parkland and how his grandfather always rode a white horse and a dog following him as big as a small pony; and how his own mother and father had ranged the estate on their own ponies, with their food in a calico bag, and he didn't know what a calico bag was, but he understood or thought he understood, when at the end of every story, his father would say:

"And one day, Matthew, it will all be yours."

It had seemed then like a promise of a magic kingdom. Like Camelot that he read of in King Arthur and his knights, but it all began to fade somewhat when his father married Aunt Bess and he went away to school, and real life took over. It had been downright impossible when his father suddenly produced it as a fact, one night in Greece, early on their tour. They were sitting on the terrace of their hotel, the moon shining unbelievably on the columns of the Parthenon, when his father had told him he was expected to give up everything he had come to care about, and take over what proved to be a moss-grown house, sad with emptiness, in the middle of acres of neglected land.

A year with Ossie Tendon round the Glendon House estate, his father had said, would teach him all he would need to know to set it up again. A year with Ossie Tendon. And he a summa cum laude from St. Peter's.

He had been quite glad to see it all, even down to the dog's grave with the name above it and the date that had been the day before his father left Ireland for the States. Glad to meet his strange detached uncle in his black habit, in that place where he and his father had been at school. And sure delighted to get to know the dynamic old gentleman in the mill house who was his grandfather.

And strangely, and here he grew thoughtful and forgot the game, strangely after all the beautied and fabled places of Italy and Greece, he had been drawn to the green, beautiful, war-torn country itself as if it were the only place he had seen. He had found Dublin touched some note of deep excitement in him. All ruined and blackened buildings and the wide streets full of uniforms and the narrow ones of barricades; the sense of tension that filled the soft air and the sporadic rifle fire and acrid taint of smoke and burning.

He would have been glad to stay, hoping desperately to see some of the real action, but his father had been anxious only to get out of it; there only on his way to reach his brother, and go searching for some old servants who all seemed to be long dead or gone. The same sense of tension and watchfulness hung over the soft country at the turn of winter when they had hired a car and driven up from Galway, warned anxiously that every hedge could hold an ambush and that the trigger-happy lads behind the walls were not too bothered to see it was the right motorcar before they opened fire. In the villages soldiers guarded the barracks of the RIC that were not already blackened ruins, and all the people rushed into the muddy streets to see the strange motor and speculate for weeks on who it was. The charred skeletons of big houses rose like ghosts at the end of their abandoned avenues, brooding over the harmless fields.

Matthew realized his father was nervous to the point of fear, and asked him why he had come there at this time.

"I wanted you to see Europe before you settled down," he said, "and for all the good it has done me, I wanted you to see Owenscourt while you were still free to take it." His eyes were on the stone walls that lined the darkening fields as they came near to Oughterard along the edges of the still-gleaming lake, refusing to acknowledge his deep fear that if once Matthew had got to Harvard he might never get him to come back. Just as he himself had never gone back, pulled always on some other road.

Resolutely he refused to take the estate and there was strain between him and his father that there had never been before. Yet after all the arguments that had run through hotel rooms and motorcars and around the neglected fields of Owenscourt itself, he knew some astonished sadness as he watched the green land of Ireland fade into the sea, leaning alone on the rail at the back of the steamer taking them to Holyhead and then for a couple of weeks in London before going on down to Southampton for the *Mauretania.*

"Matthew. Matthew. Wake up. It's your turn."

He came back to the cheerful crowd around him, and flung himself into the game, as he was to fling himself for the rest of the crossing into the unparalleled luxury of life and entertainment that Cunard provided for its passengers; trying to avoid his father, and evade the purposeless discussions that need only come to a head when in the autumn he either went to Harvard or buckled down for a year with Ossie Tendon as he demanded. The thought came unbidden that if he was to do this impossible thing, he would rather learn all he had to learn at Owenscourt itself, from his lively old grandfather.

Clancy would be home before the autumn, from her London season. He was serenely unperturbed by his father's certainty that she would have hooked some English lord. How often had he told him that he had fallen in love with his mother when she was a little girl, and had never loved anybody else. Even Bess was different. He wondered desperately why his father, after his own experience with his mother, couldn't see that it was exactly the same with him and Clancy. Dismissing it woundingly as calf love, when he had in his time so often spoken of his own young passion that had never left him, even beyond death.

Sadly and shrewdly he realized that his father did actually understand about him and Clancy. But regarded their love as a danger; drawing him towards all things American, and away from the Irish future he had planned for him.

"Too bad, Pop," he said to himself. "Just too bad."

The long hot blue summer passed slowly at New Bedford, in the sea and on it in his own proud sailboat; games and parties and beach picnics and formal dances in the big houses in the evenings, soft with the excited faces of sun-flushed youth. There was a cruise on Phineas Turnbull's yacht that made no effort to outclass the vulgar splendor of a Vanderbilt or a Gould, but nonetheless of a luxury and excitement to thrust away into dimness the memory of a moss-grown house where he was supposed to settle down.

When he thought of it now, it was with disbelief, bringing him almost to laughing, and all through the splendid days of holiday, he and his father were carefully polite, never mentioning their dispute, setting it aside; but with a strain that saddened Matthew, having never known anything before to lie between him and his father. Bess watched them both with loving eyes and gave advice to neither.

When they were only a day back home in the cottage below the house, and all the turmoil of their arrival settling down, Owen met his son, leaping down the white stairs in immaculate flannels and a striped blazer, a silk scarf at his throat and a tennis racket in his hand.

"Where are you going, Son?" he asked, thinking that very soon their disagreement must be clinched. It was time for the boy to get ready for Harvard.

Matthew beamed and clearly had no thought for Owenscourt or quarrels or anything else.

"Clancy came home last night. I'm going to take her to play tennis at the club."

Owen fell silent. The battle was on. At his expression Matthew's young face hardened.

"Don't you think," said Owen, after a long moment of silence when the grass cutter rattled past on the lawn outside, "don't you think you should just call first and see how things are? She's been away a long time. It's possible there may be changes."

It's possible, his father was saying, that she may by now be engaged to someone else. And hoping it was true.

Matthew thrust back his hair with his familiar gesture and his expression was cool and careful.

"Nothing will be changed between me and Clancy," he said. "Nor," he added, making himself clear, "about anything else."

Time was running out. His father just had to understand he had no use for his outworn memories.

"Someone," said Owen, stung to tartness and to the age-old threat of parent against child, "someone will have to pay for Harvard. What if I refuse?"

Matthew stood at the bottom of the stairs and his racket fell slowly to his side, the light gone from his face, staring at his father in the first chilling realization of his power; and of the fact that after all the loving years when he had been denied nothing, he might be facing the refusal of the one thing he wanted most.

All because he refused to live the life his father himself had abandoned. Founding an existence on his memories. For God's sake, he was building a store of memories of his own, and there was not one of them that did not include Clancy. Anger rose in him where before there had been patience and no more than irritation.

"We can forget it then, Pop," he said, and already Owen's face had crumpled with regret at the hasty words that had caused the first real gap between them. They had argued interminably but they had been still together. Now hostility yawned like a darkness, the boy's face bitter. "You have given me a good education. I can easily find a job. Old Phin will help me."

Still Owen couldn't stop himself.

"And do you think Clancy McPartland would be allowed to marry some young jobbing broker? Let me tell you, I doubt the son of Owen O'Connor, in the best of circumstances, is thought good enough."

Matthew thought again of his mother and the love that had driven his father to America to search for her and all the way back again to find her.

"We'll manage if we want it enough," he said bravely.

Owen turned away before his aloof young face, running a hand through his hair, appalled at what had happened. It should all have been encompassed in friendship and reason. Where was Bess? He must find Bess. She would know how to handle it and put it all back as it had once been. His mind turned to her as if he were a child with a broken toy. There was nothing Bess could not make right.

Matthew went on out the front door, as sick as his father that it had come to this, but upheld by the rightness of his rebellion. He was an American, and his father had no right to try and make him anything else. Unbidden into his angry mind came the memory of the surge of sorrow he had felt looking back from the steamer over the darkening sea to the white houses of Kingstown, lambent in the soft purple dusk; Howth black against the last light and the cone of the Sugar Loaf touched to gold by the lingering sun. He hadn't known the names of all the places, only that it was beautiful and it had tugged at his surprised young heart and he had felt he didn't want to go away.

The tennis racket was flung into the backseat of his yellow Model T, and he roared off along the lake road and round the corner of the stables and up towards the main gates of the house. He felt better to be on his way. Now that Clancy was back and they were together, they would be stronger in everything. No doubt, he told himself as he swung through the tall iron gates, his father would come round. He had never refused him anything yet. By the time he was bowling along the road, the trees overhead heavy with the first touch of fall, he was smiling, his mind only on where he was going. On Clancy.

Amiably he waved at the guard who opened the tall gilded gates, and churned on up the long curving drive, darkly overhung with pines and larches until it opened suddenly onto the manicured sweeps of lawn before the huge white-pillared house that made even Phin Turnbull's look small.

Bounding up the white curving stairs to the front door, he had forgotten everything except the sheer sick excitement of seeing Clancy after almost a year, and he didn't wait to ring any bells, going straight in through the huge open double doors of polished oak, pushing through the inner doors of glass that led into the house.

In the vast hall, floor checkered black and white and soft with the colors of priceless rugs, marble staircase sweeping up on either side in perfect curves, a butler materialized like a careful wraith from somewhere at the back.

Matthew didn't pause.

"Don't trouble, Beckwith, I'll go through myself. Miss Clancy is expecting me."

Expecting him from the day she had gone away.

The man Beckwith, in his impeccable tailcoat, inclined his gloomy English face and didn't permit himself a smile, even though he had known Matthew since before he could walk.

"Miss Clancy, sir," he said, "is in the solarium with her mother."

"Thank you, Beckwith."

Already he was through the long doors of mahogany and glass that folded back the length of a wall when needed, to throw the reception rooms into one with the hall, a long vista of rich and spendid salons, one beyond the other to the back of the house. Matthew raced through them, long familiar with their splendors, until he reached the doors from the back hall that opened out into the colonnade.

The solarium was built onto the end of one of its long curves, an addition for the pleasure of Clancy and her mother, set there with many complaints that it spoiled the look of the whole house, but James McPartland could refuse his women nothing. It was built in panels of glass with yellow blinds to draw against the sun they had invited; filled with flowers and flowering plants and big pale colored chairs; looking out onto the gardens and the swimming pool.

Along the marble colonnade Matthew's tennis shoes made no sound and he came unheard to the open doors at the end of it. Only then he halted in his rush, suddenly aware that inside among the palms and the orange trees and the sharp tang of the new chrysanthemums there was what Clancy would have called the father and the mother of a row going on.

Clancy's mother was yelling like a fishwife and his immediate idea was to turn and creep out as he had come, for very shame for Mrs. McPartland, who would never want anyone to know her careful refinement could crack like that. He felt a certain pity for her, and the desire to save her embarrassment, but even as he turned to go, he heard what she was saying, the Irish out in her as if she had that very morning left the ship.

"—and I tell you, you will not, by Jesus himself, be marrying the likes of Matthew O'Connor, and the sooner you accept that the better it'll be. We'll not have it. Your father'll not have it. Nor I. Didn't we do better for you than that. And you having laid the finger of destruction on a whole season in London with your pining and moping and no one good enough for you, even the Eyetalian Count himself—"

Clearly Matthew heard a hoot of derision from Clancy and his heart leapt to her. God love her shining head. Clearly she had waited for him too.

"—and all that good money down the drain and even the Queen herself." In her fury she was getting confused. Matthew could see neither of them behind the banks of palms, but he could imagine the small plump woman scarlet in the face and swelling in her tight dress.

"—and all the devil you wanted all the time was to get back here to young O'Connor. 'Twas us made the mistake in the first place in letting him inside the door, and I'm telling you now he's been in it for the last time."

"And what's wrong with Matthew? I'm going to marry him."

His heart lurched to hear her clear defiant young voice, although he knew already the sick certainty that the defiance would do no good. They could not fight both their parents.

"You are not that, going to marry him," Mrs. McPartland said flatly.

"Why not? What's wrong with him?" she said again, and now there was a note in her voice that was piteous. Matthew moved towards her instinctively, and then stopped again as her mother burst out.

"What's wrong with him? Isn't there everything wrong with him for you? D'you think after all we've done for you and all your father is, that we'd allow you to marry the son of an Irish peasant for when all is said and done, that's all Owen O'Connor is, not matter all Phineas Turnbull has done for him. Didn't he take him up from the sweeping of his own stables? Didn't he? Didn't he? And is the son of a nobody like that someone our daughter should marry?"

Matthew stood now, too sick to move. How often had he heard his father tell in public the story of the day when he had taken the chauffeur's place and finished up as Phin Turnbull's aide. Never hesitating to tell of it, in his own certainty and knowledge that he had never been a yard boy in reality.

Now this was how the McPartlands looked at it, although young as he was he knew that Clancy's grandfather had come over starving on a coffin ship, and fallen on the silver boom in Colorado when no more was needed to make a fortune than a tough character and a strong back.

Shame and outrage and pure rising fury for his brilliant father pinned Matthew where he stood behind the palms. He could hear Clancy crying now and almost could have wept with her, knowing it was the end for both of them, but also that he would only make it worse for her by charging in.

Vaguely he sensed the bitter disappointment and frustration that was powering the rage of Mrs. McPartland, who had spent a fortune peddling Clancy all round Europe only to be defeated by the unsuitable boy next door.

"He's not for you nor you for him. D'you hear that? Not your father nor me neither want your peasants here, and do I see him near the place we'll lock you up. You'll marry who we say, miss, or there'll not be a penny piece to you."

So had his father said or words to that effect. They could both do it. And he knew no girl reared like Clancy could live on what he could make alone. The ultimate threat.

He turned then and walked away, and as he went soft footed down the long curve of the colonnade, the wound he had half ignored began to hurt. Son of an Irish peasant. Phineas Turnbull's yard boy who had made good, and nothing more than that. It was the first time he had heard it said in spite and jealousy and as though it were the whole truth. His father, he knew, would do no more than throw back his handsome head and laugh, but Matthew was neither old enough nor strong enough to set it aside.

And it had cost him Clancy. He was under no illusions that either of them was capable of being poor. Nor could he ask it of her.

Poor. Without warning he was shaken by a storm of resentful anger, shaking him with its unexpectedness, assailed suddenly by furious loyalties he had struggled to disown.

"No peasant's house, Mrs. McP!" he said aloud to the Persian rugs and empty hall. "No peasant's house."

Blindly he climbed into the sun-warmed seat of the Model T and drove slowly home along the walls of the two estates under the same trees where his father had long ago stopped the steaming Renault and told Phineas Turnbull about Owenscourt. Under the blowing black hair his face was a mixture of anger and confusion, echoing his mind; taken unaware by the image that, since Mrs. McPartland's shouted words, had been slowly thrusting its way into his thoughts. Of a gray square house, moss grown and neglected but that surely could be cleaned; with a long gentle sweep of grass that would take no time to restore, down to the soft shimmer of a lake.

But it would not hold Clancy. None of his future would hold Clancy. His bright American future. Bleakness swamped him. It was only indulgence that had allowed them to stay together so long. The patronization of parents who had allowed the children to play, until they decided it must stop.

For days he walked in a silence that alarmed Owen; sending him rushing to Bess for comfort and reassurance that he had not driven the boy too far. Bess smiled serenely and kissed his forehead, lamplight gold in her graying hair.

"Don't disturb yourself, Owen," she said. "No one will drive that young man anywhere. He is too much like yourself. You must just wait and see what he has decided to do."

"He seems to have decided something," growled his father. "I wonder when he'll be good enough to tell me."

After a week of uneasy silence and careful evasive conversations, when Owen trembled a hundred times on the brink of launching an attack, caught back always by Bess's admonishing eye, Matthew came formally to his father in his office. The tart autumn smell of chrysanthemums filled the room from gigantic blooms waist high beside the fireplace. The year was passing and the time short and Matthew had said nothing.

"Am I bothering you, Pop?"

The young face was very careful and without expression.

Owen looked at him and sighed a little, aware that something important was going to be said, and hoping desperately it would not force them farther apart. He didn't look too intently at his son's face, carefully laying a blotter over his papers. What matter if Phin Turnbull didn't double this investment for another fifteen minutes.

"No, Son," he said. "Why should you be? What is it?"

There was silence, no sound save the ticking of the clock held up by gilt cherubs on the mantel.

"Pop," said Matthew then, and his voice had a strained, don't-you-dare-to-comment ring to it. "Pop. D'you think we could compromise? Could I go to Dublin to college instead of Harvard?"

No promise there. Only the hesitant step that cried aloud that it promised nothing. Owen felt his throat grow thick. For a few moments he said nothing.

"Why, sure, Son," he said then at last as though it was only of the smallest import, shuffling his papers as if he was anxious to get back to work.

Then he looked up fully at his son.

"There's a very old man there," he said. "In law practice in Dublin. He'll help you all he can. Name of James Cornelius O'Duffy."

Chapter 23

In later years Matthew was to look back and smile at the pigheadedness that made him say he was going to college. And that made him stick a year of it in Trinity before he admitted to the decision that had so strangely seized him by the heart that day, as he looked through the potted palms and the hydrangeas at the weeping Clancy and her mother. If he could not have her, then there was suddenly only one other thing he wanted, his attitude sharpened by Mrs. McPartland's contempt for his father.

She had sheared his pride to furious resentment, and he could not yet reduce himself even further by capitulating at once to his father, as he knew he was compelled to capitulate to her over Clancy. For the healing of his pride, the time of going to Owenscourt had to be decided by himself. Alone.

He spent his year living in a students' lodging in a small tree-lined road off Stephen's Green, and studying in the distinguished halls of Trinity. Caught up in all the tension, and the inevitable side-taking of a city racked by civil war. As he ducked into doorways with the bullets flying in the barricaded street, and the armored cars roared toward the action, he was caught by the excitement and the plain challenging fear of such living; learning in the air of hatred and the smell of battle and the throng of foreign uniforms in the Dublin streets, the one lesson most needed to pull him back completely towards Owenscourt. That he was an Irishman, as fierce for his country as the shabbiest Sinn Feiner crouched behind the barricades with his rifle and his bawneen cap; heartstricken for his country that it should have come to this to gain its freedom. Desperate now to know and walk the green acres that were his own; remembering what his father used to tell him of his grandfather. That such an estate was a responsibility. That it was not necessary to carry a gun and defy authority. Look after your own, apparently his grandfather had told his father, in the far days when it had seemed automatic he would inherit Owenscourt. Care for your own, and if everyone does that, then there will be no unrest. He longed now for Owenscourt, but was not yet ready to say so.

Still slow to admit it to his father; held back by something he could only recognize as obstinacy, or as simple as a trailing childish unwillingness to do directly what he had been told.

Yet in that year he sought and found again the house in Gardiner Street and stood outside it with his back to the church that his father would say, to this day, had stolen his brother Emmett; looking up and down the narrow frontage and at the shabby green door, trying to recreate the family that had gone in and out; recalling all he could of the tales told by his father. About everybody in it from the two loving women down in the warm basement, to the snow-white rocking horse harnessed in scarlet leather and golden bells, up in the sunny playroom at the top. All pervaded by the atmosphere created by two people who came through to him in his father's words more as an active presence of happiness, than as living flesh and blood.

Grandfather. Grandmother. He tried the words, standing there in the dusty street, the crack of rifle fire coming sharp from somewhere over towards the park. The words had no meaning here, and a face had come to watch him curiously from a window on the first floor. He turned and walked away.

He went down Baggot Street on a day when smoke was rolling dark above the city from half a dozen fires, and stood before the plate-glass windows of the garage and showrooms that had replaced the Shops, shabby already like everything else in Dublin. Only the fine mahogany door and the bowed windows of the office remained of all his father had remembered.

In a gray gentle rain on a silent day, he stood in Glasnevin cemetery before the marble angel that Hugh Charles had been shamed into raising, weeping its cold tears over the inscription to Matthew James O'Connor and his wife Celia Mary; and their infant daughter Louise. Brooding, as he had never brooded before, on their early and tragic deaths that had changed the whole course of his father's life. And with it, his.

He went out to Kingstown on a windy day in spring and found the little yellow house, so faithfully described that he had no difficulty, in the terrace near to the Martello Tower. He stood, as they must have stood, beside the seawall and watched the mail boat keeling through the arms of the harbor, and the light changing with the evening on the long flanks of Howth.

Even he went once more where he had gone with his father, to make another forlorn attempt in the little empty house below the castle, where his father had hoped to find his nursemaid, who had married the groom with the strange French name. His good clothes were too conspicuous and he found himself watched with hostility, beggars clawing at his hands.

Emmett he saw often. He received him always with the same urbane pleasure that gave no clue to the thoughts behind his unlined and seemingly ageless face. Nor did he ever ask him, sitting there in the cold parlor at Clongowes, why he had come back to Ireland. Matthew prompted him shamelessly and led him to tell stories of Owenscourt and their childhood, and found them singularly different from his father's. The house and the estate had never dominated him, as though even at an early age his interests had been already in some other world. When the time would come for them to say good-bye, his uncle would leave him with the same measured smile, and Matthew was never entirely sure whether he was welcome or merely an interruption to carefully ordered days.

All these things he did, consciously or unconsciously, trying to gather round him the reality of a past that would in turn give reality to the future he had decided on in his heart. Almost against his will.

When he came to the end of his academic year, he sent a wire to his father to say he would not be coming back to the States for the summer in New Bedford. He went instead down to Cannon's Mills, and spent the slow gentle months with his grandfather, working beside James like any other workman in the mill.

Not once did he mention his intentions, and old John Julius regarded him with his wise faded eyes and walked with him in the soft evenings on the bank above the river, and talked to him of his other grandfather, who for him would never die. Not once did he mention Owenscourt as it was now, or that it stood an easy hour's drive away across the country.

In the autumn Matthew left quietly, without a word that he was not going back to the university as expected. His uncle and his grandfather stood in the mill yard and watched him as he turned out of the gate with a flick of his black hair and a wave of his hand.

"That's a deep one," said his Uncle James, as the clamor of the motor died at last into the stillness of the early day. "That's a deep one indeed."

"So was your sister," his father answered, but he took his pipe out of his pocket, and his expression was content, as if he saw more than James and was well pleased with it.

In battered Dublin, Matthew didn't go back to Trinity, going instead to the Shelbourne Hotel, and leaving all his belongings in the trunk of the motorcar and hoping that no stray bullet would set fire to it in the night.

In the morning, calmly, with everything ready that he wanted to say, he went down to the rich old offices as his father had instructed him, and saw James Cornelius O'Duffy, shrunk to a rail behind his vast mahogany desk, but still upright and formidable and alert, his mane of hair and beard snow-white against the dark-red walls. Matthew was touched by the tears in his old eyes when he finished speaking.

"It does my heart good to see you here, Matthew," he said, and there was no age in the strong voice. "It puts right for me the day I saw your father and your Uncle Emmett lose it all, and I could do no more than take them over there to Mitchell's and fill them up, God help the pair of them, with sugar cakes."

Matthew grinned.

"I like sugar cakes too, sir."

O'Duffy banged the desk bell for his clerk.

"How old are you now, Matthew?" he asked him then.

"Nineteen, sir. I'll not do anything substantial until the spring when I am twenty, and my trust funds come to me. But I would like to put it all in hand."

The old man's eyes gleamed.

"Your father and I have had it all in hand since you were born," he said, and Matthew found to his astonishment that all resentment was gone. He was doing exactly what he wanted to do, and since it pleased his father also, well and good.

James O'Duffy took a big box-file from the curious clerk who was sliding glances round the corner of his glasses at Matthew. The name O'Connor had been a legend in the office since as long as he could remember. This would be the grandson, no doubt.

"Thank you, Houlihan," the lawyer said testily, and the old man hastily put down the file and scrambled out.

There was little to be done, save to sign all the papers that Owen and James O'Duffy had laid aside between them, and when Matthew stepped out again into the fine drizzle of the day, he had the one set of keys of Owenscourt in his pocket. John Julius had the others.

He turned in his hired car, and bought himself a small tan-colored bull-nosed Morris in the garage that had been the Shops', piling all his belongings in the rumble seat, and heading out through the fine rain towards the west.

"I was expecting you," was all his grandfather said, coming out of the house to meet him as he drove into the yard, and for a moment in the soft evening with James's children clamoring round the car, he wondered did everybody always know what he was going to do, before he knew himself.

There was one thing, he thought with satisfaction, that his grandfather, however percipient, wouldn't know.

Half the night they talked, sitting round the glowing range, all of them caught up in the excitement of something waited for for thirty years.

"For the winter," Matthew said, "I just want to camp there, and survey it all. Live in the kitchen or something. Get in the help."

"Get the ground ready for planting in the spring. You could do it easy, Matthew. And come to that, you could live in the agent's house."

For a moment John Julius and James looked at each other, caught by memory.

"That would do you well," he went on, "did you get a good woman from the village to come there and live in for you."

"We had a good woman once, there, living in," James said and grinned, thinking of Emmett in his apron.

"He did well," John Julius said, and would not smile, the anguish of it all forever too real.

"Grandfather," Matthew said. He looked round at the three of them, expecting objections from James's wife. "Grandfather. Would you come with me?"

He got the immediate objection he had expected, Mary Anne crying out in protest. James's father was an old man, she said, and not to be taken off to spend the winter in a cold house that had been empty since anyone could remember. It would be the death of him.

John Julius silenced her with a gesture.

"Why, son?" he asked Matthew. "Why would you want me?"

Matthew pushed back his hair, and the gesture was so like Antonia's that the old man could barely stand it. He blinked and steadied himself. The wind was getting up outside and in the pause the turf roared scarlet in the range.

"Advice, Grandfather," the boy said. "Your advice." James was quiet, saying nothing. "There's very little here for you to do now. James has it all in hand."

"True for you. I'm on the shelf now."

Amiably, father and son grinned at each other. Under James, Cannon's Mills had moved back into steady prosperity.

"I want your advice about the land, Grandfather," said Matthew. "You'll know it better than anybody else. I want to get it back as fast as possible into good fettle. I can pay all the help we want, even now. In the spring we can open the whole place up."

"But the house!" cried Mary Anne. "The agent's house. It'll be a ruin."

John Julius shook his head.

"Like everything else at Owenscourt, it's soundly built. It's a good house. Give Matthew a couple of weeks getting the jackdaws out of the chimneys and roaring up the fires, and it'll be as warm as it ever was. There's Mary Sheehan over there in our own village, with her man dead and she a childless woman. I've no doubt the position as your housekeeper would come to her as a godsend."

My first dependent, Matthew thought dazedly. Look after your own, his grandfather had said. So soon. No time for savoring it all alone. Responsibilities began at once.

"If Mrs. Sheehan was looking after father, he could well go," Mary Anne conceded. "But not until the house is warm."

"Be off with you, child," said John Julius.

He stared into the roaring range. Owenscourt. He had broken his heart to get back to Cannon's Mills and broken his back to put it into shape once he had got there. But the boy was right. James had the mill now to all intents and purposes, and he was well liked around the country. There was little he himself could do now without making himself a nuisance.

But Owenscourt again. A second chance. Where the boy needed him. To see it come back under his hands to all it had once been. In his old age God was being good to him. And the boy Antonia's son.

His voice was a little rough as he spoke.

"Wouldn't Matt be glad to see it," he said, recalling the last time he had been taken on at Owenscourt, from the middle of the Tuam road on Matt's own wedding day.

"We'll open the house properly in the spring, and go on from there," Matthew said, his young face plain with the relief of having John Julius at his back. "But, Grandfather." He paused and then spoke more slowly. "I'll get you all the help you want, but I want you to care for the land. I will have something else on my mind."

"And what'll that be?"

They were all looking at him expectantly in the lamplight, James with his glass of porter halfway to his mouth.

"Horses," said Matthew, and his blue eyes flashed with sudden brilliance. "Horses. Breeding horses. That's what I'm going to do at Owenscourt."

Three and a half years later Matthew had his first winner with a young two-year-old filly in a novice chase at the Galway races. Her dam had been the first horse he had ever bought, in that chaotic spring when they were back in Owenscourt, and he barely had a loose-box ready to receive her.

True to their arrangement, during the mild wet winter John Julius had been surveying the land and hiring help; trundling everywhere in the little old basket trap they had found still intact in the coach house.

"It was always for the infirm," he said wryly, "like babies and women with child. But it's better for my knees than a horse."

It suited him well, and took him everywhere he wanted to go, his old eyes bright with a contentment that he knew would last him out.

In the early morning after the first foal was born, he stood with Matthew in the loose-box, before going off around the fields. Matthew was wild with triumph and excitement. He had been up most of the night with his stable lad because the delivery had not been easy, but now the mare was on her feet again, great eyes soft with pride in the shadows, the little long-legged foal nuzzling at her side.

"Perfect, Matthew," John Julius said. "Perfect. The best of life to it. It's a lovely little horse."

"Didn't I pay enough for the sire!" said Matthew. "Phelan says we have a winner there and he could be right. Will you look at those back legs. If they wouldn't jump a cathedral, I'm not myself at all."

But he was looking at the little creature with something else in his mind, his blue eyes dark with a sorrow that still came to them, and stayed in them, too easily.

There was something about the foal. Its beautiful perfect youth; a freshness; a straightness; and the clear blue-white of its beautiful eyes.

A look already of strength and elegance combined with sheer shining beauty that tore at his heart with its familiarity.

"Clancy!" he cried. "B'God, we'll call her Clancy!"

"A strange name for a mare," his grandfather said, and as the first streaks of sun came in through the stable door, in the middle of the smells of manure and sweat and leather, with the land already sown out there beyond, Matthew thought of the white, sunlit deck of the *Mauretania*, when his father had said something similar. And he had sworn he would never take the house.

"I always thought it a strange, *nice* name for a girl," he said, and his grandfather's heart stirred with pity, getting the first faint idea as to why he had changed his mind and come back after all. Not that it wasn't right for him. He was both happy and absorbed. He had a shrewd eye for the land, and an eye for a horse that was one of nature's gifts. Even in the time they had been there, Owenscourt had changed beyond recognition; everyone who worked for Matthew, fired by his own energy and enthusiasm.

Matthew was absently stroking and petting the mare, who nuzzled at his face, staring down absently at the little foal.

He had never tried to see Clancy again, nor had she written to him about the afternoon in the solarium and what was said to her. Beckwith, he realized, would have told them he had come in, and she would know that he had heard it all. Both of them had acknowledged defeat, and withdrawn, but for all that he was now the new darling of County Galway, and the eligible target of every mother west of the Shannon, no other girl had ever even touched a corner of his heart.

He envisaged Clancy long married to some wealthy character of her mother's choice, and what matter, he still thought bitterly, were he the greatest savage unhung, so long as he had enough money and preferably a handle to his name, so that Mrs. McPartland might talk in her refined tones, God help her, about my daughter the Lady So-and-So or the Vicomtesse.

He snorted and John Julius concentrated on the mother and the foal, understanding his need to be left to himself.

There had been no news even generally of Clancy's family for a long time. Six months back Phineas Turnbull had gone down in his office like a felled tree, dead before he ever hit the ground. True to his character he left everything so organized that the transition to the new life had been almost effortless, and both Owen and Bess in their hearts had been ready for it. Phineas Turnbull's heir was a lanky desiccated lawyer from Philadelphia, with rimless pince-nez, and a long nose down which he appeared to look with faint distaste at all the machinations of his uncle's financial empire, while showing little reluctance to inherit the results. All the office staff were at once in need of other positions, but Phineas had foreseen this and provided generously for them all. To Owen and Bess, with touching words of appreciation apart from a substantial endowment, he had left a charming clapboard house that he occasionally used as a refuge, on a gentle slope near the wilds of Barnegat, where the lighthouse filled their rooms at night with shining light.

When all the arrangements were being made, Jolliff came to Owen and asked him if he might come with them and look after it.

"But, Jolliff!" Owen was conditioned by the years of perfection in the running of huge Glendon House. Astonished. "Jolliff. Would you wish to? It's only a small house."

The tall negro smiled gently.

"I'll only be a small man now, Mr. Owen," he said. "I've been with Mr. Turnbull for forty-two years and I'm too old for new employers. I'd be truly pleasured to work for you and for Miss Bess. I'll try and get the cook to come with me, and that's all you'd need with a couple of young ones."

Owen, dazed by the excellence of their arrangements, wrote often to Matthew apologizing for not going over to see what he was doing at Owenscourt, because he was too occupied in rearranging all his own affairs and settling into the new house, where he and Bess, with all their years of specialized knowledge, were going on, on a much smaller scale, with the satisfactory and methodical multiplication of their money. At fifty years of age and with Bess five years older, Owen felt a deep relief to be free of the pressure that had killed his employer, and turned with enthusiasm to the administration of the ten acres of land that came, wooded and gentle, with the clapboard house above the sea.

"I'm a little busy," he wrote to Matthew, "getting used to running my own estate, although you could lose it in one of the fields at Owenscourt. When we are settled down, and Bess is happy to be left for a while, then I'll come and visit with you."

Matthew folded the letters as he got them, and put them aside in his desk in the small room at the front of the house that had been his grandfather's office. He sat back with his hands behind his head and looked out the window at the line of men clearing the thistles from the slope down to the lake. He was delighted that the strain was gone from between him and his father, and delighted he had stopped the mad race of work before he went the same way as old Phin. It was always good to hear from him, but at the same time he knew, with a certain relief, that he wasn't yet ready for him to come to Owenscourt.

He took a step towards being ready when the young mare won at Galway, on a day of high cloud with the salt unseasonable wind blowing in across the green fields from the sea and whirling the discarded tickets on the racecourse; the young horse pounding home two and a half lengths from the remainder of the field and the crowd going mad fit to be heard down in Cork City, and some fellow behind beating him on the back, step for step with every stride she took.

He took his own arms from round the neck of the man in front of him that he had been half throttling on the last run in, and turned to John Julius at his side, tears unashamedly coursing down his face.

"Didn't she do it! Didn't she do it! Grandfather. Ah, God love her, me little Clancy!"

His brogue was so thick he might never have seen America.

They fought their way down then, through the roaring cheering stand, almost eaten alive by everyone who knew them, and from all the proffered flasks and bottles Matthew was already half sheets in the wind by the time he got to lead his mare in, a beatific grin on his young face and the steam rising from her like a cloud in the cool day.

There were all the proper celebrations, foaming with champagne in the Owner's Bar, and all the wise ones saying that young O'Connor was a man to be watched, didn't they always say he had it in him? All the horsey men of the county looking with interest at this new young fellow who had done so well on his first time out, but b'God of course, he was no new young fellow at all, but Matt O'Connor's grandson, God rest his soul, and didn't it look as if Owenscourt was back in business, and as grand as it had ever been.

Gradually the level of Matthew's celebrations fell away.

There were the stable lads and their friends and all the laborers on the estate, and the people over in Tuam who had all taken him to their hearts for his father's and his grandfather's sake, and not one of them who didn't have a few difficult shillings, or even their last hopeless halfpenny on the little mare; who had come home before God at ninety-nine to one, and a fortune in drinking made for the lot of them, and no one worth celebrating it with but Matthew himself.

Gradually Matthew had progressed from celebration to celebration growing after each one a little wilder in the eye and more willing for the next, followed by John Julius like a sort of benign old nursemaid, his own old eyes bright with rejoicing and his legs far less steady then they should be. Matthew was pushed and pulled on the tide of excitement and good black Guinness, until he found himself at last in the general refreshment tent, surrounded by what seemed like half of Ireland, all their pockets well filled and anxious to show their unending gratitude to Clancy.

He had no recollection himself of how he got there, only of John Julius watching him with an amiable grin from a bench along the canvas wall of the tent, and he himself with a bottle of Guinness in his fist and his hat gone somewhere, up on one of the tabletops giving his best of the "Londonderry Air" to a sea of grinning faces down below him, and the good black porter flowing there like water.

The sun had taken over from the fitful clouds, filling the huge tent with a dim yellow light that seemed no more than the distillation of the haze of smoke and alcohol, and Matthew's contribution was little in the sea of noise, for it was now two races later, and the end of the day. The place was filled with the riotous celebration of the winners, and the angry litany of complaint from the ones that drowned their sorrows.

"Give us another one, Matt!" they all yelled round him when he stopped for breath and a long encouraging draw at the bottle of Guinness. Old John Julius was getting a bit hazy over there by the doorway, where the fresh air looked like another world. Matt felt no unwillingness to go on singing, b'God he could sing till Christmas, the darling little horse, and a bit of a dance too, with Phil the Fluter's Ball.

"Ah, that's a grand one!"

"Get on with you, Matthew! There's another bottle for you!"

They joined him in the choruses and they milled and roared round him and the ones not in the party never even gave them all a glance, it was so normal an occurrence.

Beside the door old John Julius sat near the only breath of air and wondered vaguely how in the name of God he was going to get him home. James fought his way over to him, a glass of porter in his big hand, and even his normally placid face was glowing scarlet, his pockets full.

"He's drunk as a fiddler's bitch," said James, and collapsed a little unevenly on the bench beside his father.

"Why wouldn't he be?" said John Julius. "Did you make much money?"

"Did I not? Didn't I have Cannon's Mills on her!"

John Julius grinned and Matthew pealed out into his favorite lines.

"There was boys from every barony and girls from every art,
And the beeauutiful Miss Brady in a private ass and cart."

From the door John Julius and James watched in astonishment as on the last line his voice trailed away to nothing, and his Guinness bottle fell limply to his side.

"Is he over?" said James, and half rose anxiously from his seat.

But Matthew showed no signs of falling, standing upright, staring at the entry to the tent as if he had been turned to stone. All John Julius had seen was a group of rich-looking Yankees coming in; the country was full of them now that the troubles were over, but on the racecourse the public tent wasn't where they usually did their drinking.

In the middle of them Matthew had seen Clancy. Later she was to tell him that she had dragged the others forcibly into every tent and hut on the racecourse in her attempt to find him, marked there on her card as the owner of the little mare called Clancy. Up on his table he stayed unmoving, looking over at her in her cream-colored dress and the saucy little brown hat with the shining hair cut short beneath it, long slender legs in pale stockings, and her own sweet gleaming smile, looking back at him over all their heads as if there were not another soul in the swarming, reeking tent.

Beside her some respectable matron held a handkerchief to her nose.

All round him his fellow revelers sensed at last that there was something strange, and fell into an uneasy quiet, only a few of the thicker souls clamoring for the fun to go on.

"Get on wid' it, Matt! Willya get on wid' it."

"Here, Matthew, have another bottle and get on wid' it."

"Willya hush," Matthew said, and didn't even look at them, and surprisingly they hushed, leaving him staring over the sea of confused and strangely silent faces, that would give him only a moment before they would lose interest and start the clamor up again; over the island of strange silence at Clancy in the middle of her well-dressed friends, who were as confused as John Julius and James, sensing some atmosphere they didn't understand.

Matthew saw none of them.

"Clancy," he said over all their heads, and by the door his grandfather sat up.

"Aha," he said.

"Clancy." Matthew's voice was hoarse with drink and excitement and shock, and he couldn't wait long enough even to get down before he asked his question. "Clancy," he asked from the tabletop above the wavering heads. "Clancy, darlin'. Did you ever get to marry anybody else?"

"Who else," she said, "would I marry." And was to tell him afterward also that he was the loveliest thing she had ever set her eyes on, up there on the table, so lost in the thick fumes of drink that she could hardly see him, waving his Guinness bottle and dancing on his hat.

"For God's sake, Clancy McPartland, who is that?" cried the stout lady with the handkerchief.

Clancy smiled her beautiful white smile over at where Matthew had leapt romantically down to come to her, bringing the table with him, and only saved from total disaster by the outstretched, loving arms of all his backers.

"That," said Clancy serenely, pushing forward through the crowd to gather him up, "is my fiancé. And I'm over twenty-one," she added as she reached him.

Chapter 24

In the spring following his meeting Clancy, Matthew wrote to his father, who had been waiting for just such a letter. When he and Clancy had been married in Tuam the previous autumn, Owen's beloved Bess had been mildly but anxiously ill, and he had felt unable to leave her. That visit would have been in order, but with curious insight, once that opportunity was past, Owen did not wish to go to Owenscourt until his son invited him.

"Won't you come now, Pop?" the letter said. "There's nothing to be nervous of anymore. The fighting's over and we're a country on our own at last. We'd sure like you to see now what we've done to Owenscourt."

"Will I go?" Owen asked Bess, the longing clear in his face.

Bess lifted her head from where she was delicately repotting some young cyclamens in what Owen still called the glasshouse. She had become so accustomed to flowers in Glendon House that she couldn't live without them. Her fine hair was now gleaming silver, under the sunlight through the glass. Owen thought she grew more fine and exquisite with every year she added.

"Why would you not?" she asked him.

"Because of leaving you."

"Don't be foolish, Owen. I'm perfectly well now and I can easily manage for a few weeks. Jolliff will look after me. If it makes you any happier, I'll go for a while to my sister in Salem."

"Do that." Owen seized on the idea, salving his tender conscience. Deep inside him he knew that he must go to Owenscourt now, or he would never go at all.

"But not for all the time," Bess added. "I'm much too happy here."

Owen understood her. That was why he wanted to go. He too had come to love almost too much the wooden house on the green slope above the sea, cool and fresh in the summer when through the open windows the lighthouse washed the rooms with pale light. In the winter snug and warm when the same winds tore at the windows and clashed the branches of the bare trees. In the calm and gentle companionship of Bess, it would be easy to slide here into unmoving contentment as he got older, and in the end, go nowhere.

"All right, then, I'll go," he said, trying to sound reluctant and to keep the small break of excitement from his voice. Bess smiled at him above her plants.

Once he had decided to go he could hardly bear the time taken in the preparations; every hour of the luxurious crossing no more than a bore to be put through; every marked stage of the journey down to Galway an eternity.

He only grew a little calm when at long last, in Galway City, he hired a doubtful Buick, and set out on the road to Oughterard and Owenscourt.

The grand gates had been painted. Black. With the points of them tipped with gold, and a bright-faced child to race out to open them for him, waving to him cheerfully where once she would have given a respectful bob. Owen was so choked with emotion, rebuking himself for a fool, that he could barely manage to start the motorcar again to move those last few steps from the road onto the estate.

The avenue, as he chugged slowly up it, was smooth and

free of weeds, the mossy banks neat on either side, the arching trees controlled. So far so good; he could have been driving up there in the carriage with his parents, his father alert to the smallest lack of care. He felt quite sick with pride and fulfillment. It had all come as he had longed for, and the boy was handling it well. His father could have come back himself and not faulted Matthew. Through the trees he could see the slope down to the lake, smooth and cropped and green. No doubt the agent's house at the end of the avenue would have been refurbished also. Who, he wondered, did the boy have as his agent now? Obviously old John Julius couldn't do it all. A good one, he hoped, since he was giving all his mind to these horses.

At the end of the avenue the agent's house was no longer there. Stupefied, Owen slammed on the brakes and heaved the Buick to a halt.

The stables had been enlarged to include all the yard and garden of the agent's house that had backed onto them. All had been demolished to encompass the much larger stableyard that now ran out to the bend in the avenue where it turned towards the house, bordered by a snow-white paling and an edging of bright flowers. The bigger extended stables gleamed with white paint sharp and smart against the red brick. Order and cleanliness were everywhere. A boy stood with a bucket above the well that was now inside the fence, and someone was whistling in the harness room. On the far side the sun picked lights from the varnish of a massive horsebox, drawn up along the fence, and the clock under the white cupola above the coach house was telling the right time for the first time since he could remember.

Dumbly he looked over toward the house. The stone had been cleaned to its pale original gray and all the paintwork was new, the front door glossy between the pillars. For a while he couldn't understand why he could see it all so clearly, and then a surge of pure rage clamped his hands to the wheel.

The windbreak elms were gone.

All except one, the last one on the far side of the house, the deprived rooks still circling as they had once circled over the whole green row. A cry of sheer deprivation escaped him. On the first steep little slope down to the park, a garden of some sort had been laid out, its intrusion blinding him to the excellent state of the smooth green sweep of grass down to the lake.

For a long time he sat there, earning the curious glances of the stableboy, coming and going from the well, trying to know whether he should rage or weep; trying to understand that it was all done and nothing now could undo it. Before God, he hadn't given Matthew Owenscourt for this.

Slowly he moved the motor forward, the whole neat, splendid place, apart from the one stableboy, apparently sleeping in the warm May sun. He glanced at the turning off to the farmyard, and wondered what in God's name destruction he would have encompassed there. When he walked up the three steps to the portico, there was still no one there, so he turned the big shining brass knob, and went in the front door.

The first hall mollified him until he realized that, short of tearing it all out, there was little the boy could have done to it. The same china seemed to be in the same presses on the walls, and the two fires smoldered as they had always done, even on the warm day. Grunting his first note of approval, he moved on.

The beautiful round hall with the staircase rising effortlessly round its curve had been a deep rich red, going warmly up through the colored light coming from the cupola at the top of the house. Now from where he stood in the first archway, it chilled him with a pale and almost colorless green. For a moment his face crumpled as if it had been once more taken from him, and he still a boy. Looking over at the arch through to the dining room, he could see that it was the same pale useless color, where there had once been a flocked wallpaper thick as velvet, of a good dark bottle green.

He never saw how clear and elegant all the pictures hung against the pale walls. How much bigger and lighter the hall seemed, the lovely staircase rising almost insubstantial, marked by the mahogany thread of its narrow handrail. Flowers massed against the delicate green, soft with their own color.

He saw none of it.

Nor did he ask himself what he would have said if Bess had wanted to decorate their own house in Barnegat with dark red and bottle green. He only saw that he had given Owenscourt to Matthew and the boy had ruined it.

Furiously he wheeled and went back out of the front door, nor did he stop his irritable marching until he had gone blindly down the full length of the park. From long-forgotten habit, when he reached the bridge beside Boru's grave, he sat down and stared back at the house, trembling, racked with sorrow and disappointment and resentment, and sheer uncomplicated anger.

It took him a long time, in the silence and the sun, with the fish jumping in the lake behind him, to see what he was looking at. A clean, handsome, freshly painted house, its equally well-kept stables stretching at its side behind a border of bright flowers. The slope down below the portico was a blaze of color; purple and white and pink and a clear bright blue, dark patched with small conifers and winter shrubs. The grass all the way down to the lake was smooth and perfect, never a thistle to be seen, and the pastures away to the left, with a dozen or more horses in them, looked in equally good condition. Even the bridge he sat on had been restored, the broken stones replaced, and the moss cleaned.

Slowly, slowly, his anger ebbed, and he began to see it for the beautifully managed estate it was. After a while, touched with shame, he began to realize something else, and sat there a long time incongruously, a middle-aged man in his immaculate suit, with his head down in his hands, the tears trickling between his fingers for all the things he didn't want, but had found it so impossible to let go.

The rumble of wheels made him lift his head, and he went from the last tears straight into a roar of laughter.

"Well, in the name of God, John Julius," he cried, "when are you expecting the baby? What is the like of you doing in that yoke?"

John Julius drew up the pony and looked down at him from the basket trap, and didn't bother with a greeting either.

"I might ask," he said, his eyes shrewd on the other man's face, "what you are doing, sitting alone down here, when you are expected up at the house as a guest."

Owen didn't try and pretend.

"I'm sitting here," he said, "having just managed to stop making a father and a mother of a fool of myself. Come and sit a moment."

Stiffly John Julius climbed backwards out of the trap and lowered himself beside Owen.

He nodded up at the house.

"It's a fine sight, isn't it," he said.

"It is indeed," Owen answered him. "It is indeed. And here was I as mad as a hornet with that, because it wasn't exactly as I left it."

There was a moment's silence and John Julius pulled out his pipe.

"You didn't want it exactly as you left it, Owen," he said. "You wanted to sit here and see your father coming over that fence on one of his white horses with Boru at his heels."

Owen had to pause, hearing it put into words, knowing that that was exactly what he had expected. And everything else as well.

"That's exactly true," he admitted. "I swear to you I was ready to accuse him of digging up Boru and throwing the bones in the lake."

The smoke from John Julius's lucifer rose straight into the still air; pungent.

"I wanted," went on Owen, with difficult and very recent honesty, "to give him Owenscourt so that I could get it all back. I wanted Matthew to realize all my dreams, and it never entered my head that he would have quite different dreams of his own."

"They'll be no worse," John Julius said. "Different, but no worse."

"I know that now. What a fool!"

John Julius slapped him on the knee.

"Come on up to the house," he said. "They'll be wondering where you are. The car there and you gone."

Together they climbed into the little trap, and trundled off up towards the house.

"Jesus Christ," said Owen. "I feel like my mother and Emmett."

From the heights of his pony he had always despised his brother in the basket trap.

"It suits me," the old man said. "My knees are too rheumaticky now for a horse, and it's an easy step up into it."

"It's in a very good state."

"The man never touched a thing in Owenscourt. I think he was afraid to. Everything in the coach house was still there. This had been sewn up again in sacking of course, when your father died. But all the others were covered, you know, even for the night, and when he locked the whole place against you, it all came to little harm. Although Matthew has no sense for anything except his motorcars."

"Motorcars?"

"Mad on them."

Owen remembered like a forgotten dream Jacques, and his own long-ago talent with the Renault, both mechanically and in driving it. A talent that had been submerged in all that happened afterwards.

"How interesting," he said.

"Well, at least he has the sense," John Julius said, "to keep them garaged in the stableyard and to go in and out the back so as not to be disturbing the horses."

"And who is the agent now, John Julius?"

John Julius gave him a look.

"I am."

"You can handle it all?"

He had to admit there seemed little wrong with the hale old man with his flat tweed cap over his white hair, a heavy jacket of the same tweed, and a tartan muffler in the neck of it.

" 'Tis only my knees," said John Julius, aware of his scrutiny.

"And where do you live, John Julius?"

He was thinking of the agent's house.

John Julius's voice was patient.

"In the house, Owen, where else. You forget I am the grandfather now. And to be a great-grandfather before the year is out."

Owen snorted with laughter.

"What a fool I am. Sorry, John Julius. And that's the greatest news!"

The old man smiled and eased the little trap to a stop.

" 'Tis well no one saw us," he said. "We must be a sight for sore eyes. I'll let you down here and put the trap away. You can walk on to the house."

This time Matthew and Clancy were both waiting for Owen on the portico, but before he went to them he took a flat parcel out of his car.

He laid it on the hall table, and when all the greetings and the first excitement were over he went back to get it; one of the centers of his visit. It had taken a long time to bring it safely here.

"I've brought you a picture," he said.

Carefully on the inlaid mahogany table that had been there as long as he could remember, he unwrapped the Chinese Masterpiece, reframed again in a fine frame of narrow gilt, as senseless and incongruous as it had ever been.

Matthew and Clancy looked at it in silence.

"It's Dublin Castle," said Matthew then helpfully.

"Is it?" said Clancy. "But it's China."

"What is it, Pop?" said Matthew in the end, and took Clancy's hand as if to reassure her that she didn't need to have it if she didn't want to.

"I believe it actually is part of the river over at Holly House," said Owen. He hardly knew himself how to describe it. "It used to hang at the bottom of the stairs in the Dublin house. Somewhere, at some time, our mother and father painted it together, and as long as they lived it was a joke between them. We never really understood, and nor did anybody else, but I know it was terribly important to them. It was"—he stumbled, trying to find words for everything that foolish picture had seemed to hold, even to him and Emmett as small children—"it was them. And—and it was their house. And that—that was good, you know."

Slowly Clancy picked it up; a little faded but the whole nonsensical thing still clear, with Dublin Castle down among the buffaloes on the Chinese river.

She smiled her beautiful shining smile.

"A sort of talisman," she said.

"Exactly."

She leaned over and kissed her father-in-law on the cheek and there were tears in her bright eyes, knowing how long it had been kept.

"Then," she said, "it will be exactly the same in this house."

She moved over and took a small picture from a hook at the bottom of the stairs, and hung the Chinese Masterpiece in its place, and Matthew could hardly bear to look at his father's face.

"Pop," he cried then. "There's another picture. Sure is marvelous but we don't know who it is. C'mon up."

Owen followed them up the curving stairs and onto the flooding sunlight of the first landing, and there against the pale-green wall, his mother walked on the endless sands in Greece, her branch of oranges in her hand and her fair hair tumbling round her young face.

"She's just gorgeous," cried Clancy. "But who is she?"

"We found her wrapped in blankets behind a wardrobe in Holly House."

"She's your grandmother, Matthew," said Owen when he could speak, and inconsequently across Matthew's mind flashed Mrs. McPartland's words about an Irish peasant.

"Jesus," he said then, and, "Gee," said Clancy, but the delight was the same on both their faces.

"We'll take her down," Clancy said, "and hang her above

the fireplace in the dining room. She'll be perfect there, and we'll just be so proud of her."

"There's something else," Owen said then. "Something that I really came for."

He led them again downstairs, looking at the familiar pattern of colored light on the hall floor that had been red Turkey carpet, but was now gleaming wood, scattered with pale rich rugs. Belatedly he had to begin to admit to Clancy's taste. He went ahead of them into the little room that had been his father's office.

"My den," said Matthew in half apology for the cluttered desk and the form and stud books ranked along the shelves.

Owen smiled at him and reached up to open the picture, fumbling a little for the spring behind it.

"It's as well you hadn't redone this room," he said.

"Hadn't time yet," Matthew said, and came closer as his father opened the door.

"Well, I'm goddarned," he said, but Owen was already feeling up inside the safe.

"There's money," he said then. "Nothing like as much as there should be, but it will be gold. I had the house sealed the moment I was twenty-one, and I hope my uncle thought I had forgotten, and that I caught him short."

Clancy stared at him, unaware of the whole strange tale, and Owen turned to his son.

"Give some of the money to Emmett, Son," he said. "For his Order. He won't want to take it, but he should have it. Aha!" He was feeling again in the safe. "This is what I wanted."

Carefully he took out a fine square inlaid box, and blew off the dust, and it opened as if it had been opened yesterday.

"My Uncle Hugh Charles," he said, and they didn't understand him, "was a strange man. There were some things that even he couldn't do.

"Come here, Clancy."

He turned the box to her, and as his father had long ago done for his mother, he began to take out the things inside it, smiling at her face. Opal and aquamarine and pale gold taking the gleam of the afternoon sun; amethysts and silver and the glorious collar of pearls. One by one he lifted out the things he had remembered his mother wearing all her life, and hung them round Clancy's neck and placed the rings on her fingers, his face fulfilled and loving. Even rich little Clancy gasped at the collar of pearls.

"There are two more pictures in Holly House," she said. "The lady is wearing this."

"My grandmother," Owen said.

"They're all so beautiful." Clancy didn't know what to pick up next and Matthew seemed speechless, looking at his father. "So simple. Such class. Oh, gee, so heavenly. Whose are they?"

"Yours," said Owen. "They were my mother's."

Clancy was hung like a Christmas tree now, as Celia had been when she and Matt and their love were young.

"Oh, Pop," she said. She cried. And flung her arms around his neck and kissed him.

"But, Pop." Matthew said then diffidently. "Pop, what about Bess?"

Owen shook his head.

"Not these, Matthew. These are for your wife. They would have been for your mother had we ever reached here, but we didn't. So they had to wait for you. And Clancy."

"Pop. How can we ever thank you."

Clancy was enchanted, and Owen watched her as she handled the lovely things with tenderness and appreciation. She had been right for Matthew after all.

"What about Holly House?" he said then suddenly.

They were putting it all back in the box.

"There's two fellows in there as wet as an October day," Matthew said. "No idea how even to get down and dig a ditch."

"Your cousins," said Owen wryly.

Matthew shrugged.

"They waste the land. We're building a small house for them down by the road. There's neither of them married nor ever likely to, if you ask me, and we'll be giving them all the land they feel they can handle. We'll restore Holly House then and let it in the winter for the hunting and the summer for the fishing. Restock the river. It has very good stables."

"It would have," said Owen dryly again.

"And very fine furniture," said Clancy.

"Did you ever," said Owen, and they didn't see the connection, "did you ever hear anything of Peggy D'Arcy?"

"Who's Peggy D'Arcy? What a grand name."

"And, Pop, who anyway are the two weeds in Holly House? They always call me Cousin Matthew. It makes me feel Midwestern."

"They'd be your second cousins," Owen said. "Sons of my Uncle Hugh Charles and his first wife, Alicocq."

"Alicocq!" Clancy laughed. "No one could be called Alicocq."

"No one except Aunt Alicocq," agreed Owen in a brief tribute to her uniqueness.

"I'll take these lovely things upstairs," Clancy said, and Matthew was beginning to heave out Hugh Charles's packages and bags of gold, and heaps of yellowing tallies.

Owen wandered over to the window, the rooks outside rioting in the remaining elm, and the light fading down above the lake.

Who was Peggy D'Arcy?

And who was Alicocq?

Who indeed were all of them who had been involved in this long complicated tale of Owenscourt and Holly House. He remembered clearly how his mother, in joke, used to refer to Gardiner Street and the Shops and Owenscourt as all his father's kingdoms. Well, Owenscourt was the last of the kingdoms and he had given it to Matthew, who was already talking of buying a new stable outside the Curragh and setting up a house in Dublin.

He felt at the end of it all deep satisfaction and content, and turned back to Matthew, who was staring stupefied at a heap of golden guineas.

"Like pirate's gold," he said.

"There won't be very much, I'm afraid, Son," he said. "When you add it all up."

"I have enough," said Matthew. "But thank you, Father. Thank you for it all."

Owen smiled again. He would stay with them a few weeks and see all that they had done. And then go and visit with Emmett.

After which he would go back to what was now all the kingdom that he wanted. And to Bess.